Anna Jacobs grew up in Lancashire and emigrated to Australia in 1973, but loves to return to England regularly to visit her family and soak up the history. She has two grown-up daughters and now lives with her husband in a spacious waterfront home. Often, as she writes, dolphins frolic outside the window of her study. Inside, the house is crammed with thousands of books.

Visit the author's website at
www.annajacobs.com

STAR OF THE NORTH

Marjorie is the pretty one of the Preston sisters. So pretty that when a performer at her sister's music room breaks her leg, Marjorie is asked to fill in as the assistant to the singer Denby Sinclair. This leads to their marriage and, for her, a new life as a performer. Being on stage fulfils Marjorie's dearest ambition, but also leads to heartbreak as old secrets are exposed and her career ruined. Alone and away from the North, she struggles to make a living for herself and her unborn child. When a kind man rescues her, their way leads back to her family in Hedderby, where she must face a rich man who wants her at any price. Then danger threatens all their lives.

ANNA JACOBS

◆

STAR OF
THE NORTH

CHARNWOOD
Leicester

First published in Great Britain in 2006 by
Hodder and Stoughton Limited
London

First Charnwood Edition
published 2007
by arrangement with
Hodder and Stoughton Limited
a division of Hodder Headline
London

The moral right of the author has been asserted

British Library CIP Data

Jacobs, Anna
    Star of the north.—Large print ed.—
    Charnwood library series
    1. Music-halls (Variety-theaters, cabarets, etc.)—
    Fiction 2. Lancashire (England)—Social
    conditions —19th century—Fiction
    3. Large type books
    I. Title
    823.9'14 [F]

    ISBN 978–1–84617–691–3

Published by
F. A. Thorpe (Publishing)
Anstey, Leicestershire

Set by Words & Graphics Ltd.
Anstey, Leicestershire
Printed and bound in Great Britain by
T. J. International Ltd., Padstow, Cornwall

This book is printed on acid-free paper

PRESTON FAMILY TREE

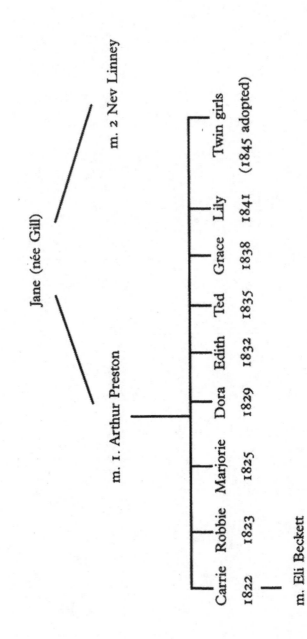

Jane (née Gill)

m. 1. Arthur Preston   m. 2 Nev Linney

Carrie	Robbie	Marjorie	Dora	Edith	Ted	Grace	Lily	Twin girls
1822	1823	1825	1829	1832	1835	1838	1841	(1845 adopted)

m. Eli Beckett

1

Marjorie was hurrying back into the mill from the necessary. Closing the outside door she stepped back into the warm, moist atmosphere that kept the cotton happy but was uncomfortable for the operatives in summer. She was wearing as little as was decent because of that, they all were.

When the overlooker stepped out of the store-room into the corridor and put one arm across to bar her way, her heart began to thump and she took a quick step backwards. They all knew what he was like.

'I could fine you for lingering,' he said.

'I'm not lingering. I'm on my way back to my spindles.'

'Then start moving.'

But she knew if she stepped forward he'd make free of her body before he let her pass and she couldn't bear the thought of him touching her again. He kept the girls he fancied working on the ground floor and often tried to fumble with their breasts. Some of them let him, knowing they'd not get fined or scolded if they did. 'I'll move if you step back and let me pass.'

He smiled and stayed where he was. Then Mr Forrett, the owner, came round the corner and she sagged against the wall in relief.

1

'Ah, there you are, Benting.' The owner looked from one to the other and his smile said he knew exactly what was going on.

Marjorie seized her opportunity and slid quickly sideways past the two men, hearing them laugh as she rounded the corner and waited for the carriage that pulled and twisted the yarn to move across and let her get into her station.

'Something wrong?' the girl next to her asked.

'Benting! He caught me coming in.'

Her companion pulled a sympathetic face. 'He's awful, isn't he?'

As they walked home Marjorie told her sister Dora what had happened. 'I don't know what to do about him. He's getting worse lately.'

'Slap his face for him. I will if he ever touches me.'

'He won't. You're too flat-chested. That's why he's got you working upstairs.'

'But I'd definitely slap him if he did.' Dora tossed her head.

Marjorie sighed. It would take a lot to drive her to that. She was too soft for her own good, she knew. She hated quarrels and upsets, just wanted to live her life in peace. And she could do that at home now, because they'd all moved in with her mother's second husband a few months ago and Nev had proved to be a kind man, who always made sure there was food on the table, didn't drink and didn't thump you for no reason.

She considered telling Nev what was happening, but couldn't see that doing any good, so she just tried to put it behind her once she left the mill. But she didn't sleep well, had nightmares about Benting sometimes.

The following morning she was nearly late and arrived at the mill breathless from running.

The overlooker was standing by the gate, watch in hand, checking the operatives in. He didn't say anything, but the way he watched her made a shiver of anxiety run down her spine.

She tried not to go to the necessary until the midday break when there would be other girls around, but in the end she was so uncomfortable she had to seek his permission to leave her place.

The look he gave her worried her sick, it was so triumphant. When she'd relieved herself, she had to brace herself to leave the necessary and go back inside.

He was waiting for her in the corridor again, put out his arm again to bar her way just as he had the day before, and smiled at her like a huge cat about to pounce on a helpless bird.

When she backed away from him he followed her swiftly, trapping her at the end before she could open the door. He waited a minute, looming over her, clearly enjoying her fear, then he reached out and grabbed her breast.

As she batted his hand away, he laughed. 'Behave yourself, Preston.'

'It's *you* who should behave yourself. Shame on you, Mr Benting. You've a wife and children at home.'

He scowled at her then and pressed his lower body against hers.

She felt disgust rise like sickness in her throat and suddenly found the courage to raise her knee sharply and catch him in the groin. There

3

was surprise as well as pain on his face. She shoved him aside before he could pull himself together and ran back into the steamy atmosphere of the main room.

He watched her for most of the hour that had to pass before the siren sounded for the midday break. And all afternoon long, she could feel his eyes following her.

As they walked outside, her sister Dora came up to her and whispered, 'Is it true?'

'Is what true?'

'That you kneed Mr Benting in his privates.'

'How do you know that?'

Dora chuckled. 'Betty was going to the necessary and saw what happened. She came running back up the stairs before he could turn and see her. She said you didn't even notice her.'

'He'd got me cornered and was touching me. Why won't he leave me alone?'

'Because you're pretty. He watches you more than he does the other lasses. Everyone knows that.'

When he came in again, the overlooker's expression was so black and furious that Marjorie's heart quailed inside her.

He walked across. 'Don't think you'll get away with skimping your work this afternoon, Preston!'

'I've never skimped my work, Mr Benting.'

'Only because I keep my eyes on you. And don't be so cheeky.'

A short time later he came by again and fined her twopence for 'insolent language'.

4

She stared at him in shock. 'I didn't even speak.'

'You were insolent earlier, though.'

'I was defending myself.'

He leaned towards her, 'And you told folk what'd happened. I take exception to that, Preston!'

'I didn't tell anyone. Someone saw us.'

'Liar!'

Half an hour later he told her he'd be docking her a further twopence for leaving waste on the floor. She was so angry now she couldn't hold the words back. 'That's not fair! Fluff blows all over the floor and you know it. You're just getting back at me for what happened.'

'*Not fair!*' His voice rose to a shout that could be heard above the clicking and whirring of the spindles, 'How dare you speak to me like that! You've cheeked me for the last time, Preston! You're sacked. I can find a dozen lasses who'll be glad of your job, lasses who won't answer me back like you do.'

She stared at him in shock. 'But — '

'You heard me! Pick up your things and leave the mill this minute.'

There were murmurs of disapproval all around, but he glared at the women under his control, daring them to side openly with Marjorie.

'And don't think we're paying you anything. You've been getting lazier by the week.'

'But I've nearly a week's money owing.'

He laughed in her face. 'We don't pay wages to folk we dismiss.'

Just then the mill owner came over to them, drawn by the shouting. 'What's the matter, Benting?'

She turned to Mr Forrett and answered before the overlooker could speak. 'He's just sacked me, that's what's the matter, sir, and I didn't do anything to deserve it.'

Mr Forrett looked down his nose at her. 'If Benting has sacked you, there must be a good reason.'

'But there wasn't!'

'Get out!' He jerked his head in the direction of the door.

'I'm owed nearly a week's wages.'

He too laughed at her. 'We don't pay money to sacked hands. Get out of my mill this minute and don't come back, or I'll call the police and have you thrown into jail for trespassing.'

She stood there for a minute, feeling so shocked she couldn't move or speak. Benting was smirking at her from beside the owner, so somehow she held back the tears and went to fetch her shawl and the cloth that had held her dinner from the bench at the side of the room, then walked out with her head held high. At the door she turned and stared across the big room with its heavy machinery moving slowly to and fro, but the other women were looking anywhere except in her direction and the two men had turned their backs. Benting was talking away, waving his arms about, making up to the owner as always. He was a good overlooker, that was the trouble, and under his rule, the machinery was kept in good working order, so Mr Forrett let him do as he pleased.

Why should they care that they'd taken her living away from her? They could always find someone else to take her place.

What was she going to do now? Just as important, what would her stepfather do when he found out she'd been sacked and had no money for him? Nev was very careful with money.

Once she was out of the mill she didn't try to hold back the tears, couldn't, so ran down to the river and found a place to weep where no one would see or hear her.

When she'd cried herself to a standstill she sat for a few minutes looking along the shallow, rushing water towards the bridge that had given the town its name — Hedderby Bridge, nestling in a long, narrow Pennine valley. She'd often wished she could follow the river right to the very end. She'd never seen the sea, had never seen anything but this one small town.

She wished men would have more respect for her, didn't like the body that had grown plump in embarrassing places now that she was getting enough to eat. If she was ugly perhaps they'd leave her alone.

She stood up. There was no putting it off any longer. She'd better go home and tell Nev and her mother what had happened.

★　★　★

Athol Stott pushed his manservant's arm away, hating how clumsily he moved his hand now. The accident had left him badly scarred, robbed him of one leg and turned his right hand into a useless claw. It had also robbed him of his independence. His gesture spilled the small glass of laudanum over the bedcovers. 'I told you not yet, fool!' he said in the slurred voice which was all he could manage from a face twisted into a gargoyle by the scars caused by the scalding steam. He still dreamed of the night the boiler had blown up, woke screaming with the memory of the pain.

'But sir, the doctor said to give it to you at — '

'I know exactly what the doctor said, but if I can manage without that damned stuff for a few minutes more, then I shall. And each day, I'll push back the time I take the dose. That stuff turns you into a mindless idiot.' He winced as he moved incautiously and jarred the stump of his leg, which was taking a long time to heal. 'Send my wife to me.'

He lay there staring round the bedroom which had become a prison to him. The past few months had passed in a blur of pain and the dreamy haze caused by the laudanum, but during the past week or two he felt to have started regaining some ground and he intended to take control of his life from now on.

It took longer than he'd expected for Maria to come upstairs. She stood at the end of the bed, staring at him. She rarely came closer nowadays.

'Terson says you're refusing to take your laudanum.'

'Yes.' He frowned at her. 'I delayed my last few doses and the pain wasn't too great to bear for a while. That fool of a doctor has been giving me too much and I intend to reduce the amount I'm taking. I want to see him at this time tomorrow. Tell him not to be late. I need to talk to him while my mind's clear.' He gestured towards the side of his body which had been worse affected. 'There's got to be something we can do about this. I won't spend the rest of my life lying in bed.'

'Dr Barlow said you'd improve slowly and you have. You must be patient, Athol. I know it's hard, but — '

He glared at her. 'Damned if I'll be patient! And don't talk to me like that, woman, as if I'm a child. You're still my wife, still owe me obedience, and if you don't do as I say I'll make you regret it, I promise you.' She looked at him steadily, didn't speak a word, but her eyes spoke her resentment for her. And something else, something that flickered into life and then vanished again.

'No one can perform miracles, Athol, not me, not the doctor.'

'Dr Barlow, tomorrow,' he repeated.

'I'll arrange it. Now let Terson give you the laudanum.'

He watched her leave the bedroom, then Terson came back in, looking wary. 'Three-quarters of the usual dose, please.'

'But sir — '

'Did you hear me?'

Frustrated beyond bearing, Athol deliberately spilled another dose of laudanum before he let his manservant tip the reddish liquid into his mouth, coloured by the wine they mixed the painkiller with. And it still tasted foul. At a lowered dose he didn't sink completely into the grey nothingness the drug had brought him at first. That had been the price he'd paid for relieving the unbearable pain.

He lay there trying to think but his thoughts had blurred again, even if not as badly. He'd consider his future plans later, when this damned stuff wore off.

★ ★ ★

As Maria left her husband she shuddered and let out a long sigh of frustration. She hesitated for a moment, then went along to her bedroom. Once there, she sat on the rocking chair by the window, closing her eyes and leaning her head back. There were noises coming from the servants working downstairs and she had household duties to attend to, but she ignored them and concentrated on regaining her composure.

Since the accident, each time she visited her husband the loathing she felt towards him seemed to deepen. She'd known for a long time that he was a truly evil man and she'd considered running away from him, would have done so if it hadn't been for her sons. She had cousins who would hide her and give her money to live on. Only — if she took his sons away from him, Athol would hunt her down, she was sure. And she loved Isaac and Benjamin so much, couldn't bear to leave them, let alone allow them to be brought up by a cruel man like their father. No child deserved that.

When the doctor had visited her a few days after Benjamin's birth, she'd wept hysterically and begged him to tell Athol it would endanger her life if she had any more children. And dear Dr Latimer had done that for her. Athol had declared himself satisfied with two sons and mocked her for being stiff and useless in bed, telling her she'd be no loss and he'd be happy to find other women who would enjoy his attentions. That hadn't upset her at all and knowing he wouldn't be sharing her bed again had been the main thing that enabled her to stay with him.

Sadly, Athol wouldn't allow Dr Latimer to attend his family any more, because the doctor and he had quarrelled over the way Athol treated the men who worked at the family's engineering works. So now they called in Dr Barlow, whom Maria disliked intensely and who was, she felt, far less modern in his ways than Dr Latimer.

After the accident she had hoped, heaven forgive her, that Athol would not recover from his horrendous injuries, but he had astonished everyone by clinging to life. Now, when he was not drowsy from laudanum, the light of evil seemed to burn even more malevolently than before in his eyes. So she'd done a wicked thing. She'd increased his dose and kept him in a twilight world, which had spared them his viciousness and allowed her to run the household as she wanted.

But if he'd realised he could manage with less

laudanum . . . She shuddered. What would her life be like if he recovered enough to leave his room and take charge of the household again?

As usual the rocking and a few quiet minutes alone soothed her and soon she was able to return to her daily tasks. Whatever it took, she would have to cope for as long as her children needed her. But once they were grown, she'd leave. Somehow.

★ ★ ★

Marjorie entered Linney's Lodging House by the side door and found Nev and her mother in the kitchen. Her heart sank. She'd hoped Raife would be there, because the kindly old man always seemed to make things easier between her and her stepfather.

'Eh, what are you doin' home at this time of day?' her mother exclaimed.

'I've been sacked. And it wasn't fair!' She couldn't help it, she burst into tears again.

Nev came to guide her to a chair. 'Sit down and tell us about it.'

So the story came out.

'Why didn't you tell me that overlooker was pestering you?' he asked.

She shrugged, feeling uncomfortable even to talk about it. 'He does it to all the lasses who work there. He doesn't usually settle on one person, but lately . . . well, it's been mostly me. And I haven't encouraged him, I haven't!'

'I'd have had a word with him if I'd known. What's the fellow's name again?'

'Benting. But it wouldn't have done any good because he's good with the machinery and can do no wrong in Mr Forrett's eyes. Anyway, the master touches the lasses sometimes as well.'

Nev leaned forward to put an arm round Marjorie's shoulders, the first time he had made any gesture of affection towards her. He pushed his handkerchief into her hand. 'Here. Wipe your eyes, love. It doesn't matter about the job. I was going to ask you to give it up anyway.'

She wiped her eyes and blew her nose for good measure. 'Why?'

He gestured to his wife. 'You know the doctor's told Jane to rest till she's had the baby, and she has been doing, but she gets lonely on her own, needs company. My father's busy with his music these days and anyway, it isn't a man's job to run a house, so I've decided I need someone to look after this place for me and keep an eye on Jane and the lodgers. And who better than Jane's own daughter? Do you think you could do that?'

She stared at him in surprise. It was the last thing she'd expected him to suggest. 'You mean, you're not angry with me about losing my job?'

'Not with you, it's *him* I'm angry with.' He gave her one of his quick, shy smiles. 'Will you do that for us, Marjorie love, look after the house and keep an eye on your mother till after the baby's born?'

She thought about what he'd said then looked at him doubtfully. 'I'm not all that good at housework and organising things. Our Carrie's the one for that. I know I'd make a lot of

13

mistakes.' And she didn't fancy being shut in the house most of the time, not seeing her friends, being with her mother who would expect lots of attention and fuss. The work at the mill was hard, but at least she had some fun with her friends there. They had singsongs sometimes at the dinner break or when they walked home. She loved that.

Nev frowned at her. 'You'll have me and my dad to help and advise you, and you know the rules for running a common lodging house after living here for a few months — the town council's rules *and* mine. I'm sure you'll be able to cope all right.'

'What about Mrs Terrill and the washing? Will she still be coming in?' Marjorie hated washing, the way it made your hands red and crinkly, the sheer hard work of lugging hot water to and from the boiler, heaving sodden clothes in and out. Nev might have a modern box mangle, but washing day for such a large family still left you exhausted.

It was his turn to screw up his face in thought. 'Yes, she'd better keep doing it. There's a lot of washing with all of you children, especially now that we've bought you enough clothes. You'll have enough on with the rest of the housework and cooking.'

Marjorie watched him give his wife a fond smile. He'd never complained about Jane bringing six of her ten children to live with him, you had to grant him that, and he'd proved a good stepfather. He looked at Marjorie expectantly and she could think of no way of refusing him. 'I could try.' But she knew how finicky Nev was about keeping his house nice and she wasn't sure she'd do it well enough to suit him. She did tend to go off into daydreams and her sisters were always teasing her about that. 'I'll do my very best, I promise you.'

'That's all anyone can do.' He patted her shoulders again and moved away.

She didn't mind him touching her, because it was a friendly gesture, so unlike that other man's touch. The thought of Benting's big dirty hands pawing at her breasts still made her shudder.

★ ★ ★

Terson asked to see Maria that evening.

'I wish to give notice, ma'am and felt I should speak to you first, since the master is not — well, not fully himself yet.'

She looked at him in dismay. 'Oh, no! *Please* don't leave us. I rely on you to look after my husband. I'll raise your wages and — '

He held up one hand to prevent her continuing. 'I'm sorry, ma'am. I'm not a nurse, wasn't hired for such duties, and since the accident Mr Stott has been impossible to please.'

She could sympathise with him. Athol's bad temper seemed to permeate the whole house and everyone who lived there was only too aware of the brooding presence on the first floor.

'I'll stay on until you've found someone to replace me, ma'am — if he'll let me,' Terson added. 'But I'd appreciate it if you'd find other help as quickly as you can.'

When he'd left the room, she stood there for a few minutes, dreading the scenes that would surely follow when she told her husband. She hoped desperately that she'd find someone reliable to take care of Athol, because she never wanted to touch him again.

After a while she decided to get it over with and went to tell him. His face turned dark red with fury and she thought for a minute that he'd have an apoplexy — wished he would. However, his colour gradually subsided and a calculating look replaced the anger in his eyes. 'We'll need to get someone else quickly, then. In fact, get two people in so that one of them can be available at night. If we hire two strong men, they can carry me out into the sun as the weather improves. If I keep to the back garden no one will be able to gawk at me.' He scowled round. 'I'll go mad if I have to stay in this damned bedroom much longer.'

'The doctor said you'd be better lying down. That leg still hasn't fully healed and you've been so restless lately you're irritating the stump again. You know how badly it reacted when they fitted you with that wooden leg. You should have taken things more easily.'

'Damn the doctor! It's my leg and my life. If I can't walk again, I'll have to be carried or pushed everywhere and I won't put up with that. I'm *not* spending the rest of my life shut up in here. I'll find a way to get free of it.'

He lay there for a minute with his eyes half-closed. She recognised that expression only too well and wondered what he was plotting now, feeling relieved when she heard the front door bell.

'That'd better be the damned doctor,' he said.

'I'd be grateful if you'd not use such coarse language in front of me, Athol.'

He let out a nasty, sneering laugh. 'I don't need your gratitude, so I'll continue speaking how I choose. Now make yourself useful, for once. Go and fetch the doctor up.'

She was relieved to get out of his room but stayed at the foot of the stairs while Dr Barlow was with her husband, in case she was needed.

When shouting erupted in the bedroom, she went up a few steps, hesitated and went back down again. Whatever was going on in there, she didn't want to be involved.

It seemed a long time till the doctor came downstairs, his colour heightened and an air of suppressed anger about him. 'Can you spare me a few minutes, Mrs Stott?'

'Yes, of course.'

In the small parlour she used now that she was on her own in the evenings, she gestured to a chair.

'Your husband wants me to perform a miracle so that he can walk again and use that twisted right hand. I told him that couldn't happen, but he wouldn't accept my opinion. What's more, I don't think it wise to reduce the dose of laudanum, which he did without consulting me. He's too restless and one part of the stump has begun suppurating again.'

'He hates taking laudanum, but when he takes less he becomes rather — difficult.'

Dr Barlow looked at her with sympathy in his eyes and after a minute added, 'He also tells me Terson is leaving.'

'Yes.'

'Pity. The man is meticulous in keeping Mr Stott clean and in carrying out my instructions.'

Upstairs, Athol looked at his manservant who was preparing his next dose of laudanum. 'If you want good references and a bonus when you leave, I need you to do something for me.'

Terson looked at him, head on one side. 'How much are you offering?'

Athol let out a crack of ragged laughter. 'Five guineas extra if you do as I ask and keep your mouth shut.'

'I'll be happy to help you, sir.'

2

Nev looked round the kitchen and sighed. Marjorie was doing her best, but even a couple of weeks had shown that she definitely didn't have a flair for running a household like theirs. Nor was she all that good a cook, because she forgot to stir things or take them out of the oven at the right time. He could do better himself, had learned to cook after his mother died, but he didn't intend to do it again, not with a wife and stepdaughters around. He looked across at his father and grimaced, spreading his hands helplessly.

Raife smiled in that gentle way he had. 'That lass hasn't it in her to organise a busy house.'

'No. Neither has my Jane.' He reckoned both Marjorie and her mother were born mainly to please men, with their softly rounded bodies, big blue eyes and obvious need to be looked after.

'Does it matter so much that the place is untidy? She does clean it thoroughly.'

Nev considered this and nodded. 'I'll give her that, Dad, but I like it to be tidy as well, at least some of the time, and it's never tidy at the moment. I make good money and I want to live nicely. Why can't she put things back in the right place afterwards? Is that so hard?' He shrugged, smiling wryly at his own foibles. 'I know I'm a fusspot, but that's how I am.'

'Are you sorry you married Jane?'

19

'No, I'm not.' He gave his father a slightly embarrassed smile. 'I like having a family, if you must know, and those lasses of hers are grand, so is young Ted.' He hesitated, then admitted what his father must have guessed, 'I was lonely before. I was glad when you came back to live with me and I was glad when the others did too.'

'Then you'll just have to put up with how Marjorie does the job.'

Nev looked thoughtful. 'Perhaps — or perhaps not. We'll see how things go. She looks after her mother well, at least. Jane's been much happier since Marjorie was around.'

'That's because she has someone to gossip with. What the two of them find to talk about all day, I don't know.'

Nev grinned. 'Jane's never short of something to say. She's on about the baby's name again.'

'I thought she was going to call it Peggy if it was a girl, and Frank if it was a boy.'

'That was last week. This week it's Sylvia and Joseph. Marjorie says she's always like this when she's expecting.'

'What do *you* want to call it?'

'Morgan if it's a boy, after Mother's family. And that's what it *will* be called. Only I'm not telling Jane that yet.'

'What if it's a girl?'

'It won't be.'

Raife hid a smile. As if you could decide what a baby was going to be. He'd never thought to see his son married. He'd left his wife and Nev many years ago, once she'd inherited some money, enough to live off, which had taken the responsibility for her off his shoulders. They'd quarrelled so much and stopped sharing a bed long before, so she hadn't been at all unhappy about his going. His older son had gone with him, but Nev had stayed with her. Well, she'd have made a fuss if he hadn't. It was from her that his son got his pernickety ways. She'd been a pain to live with, not wanting anything out of place, going mad if you walked any dirt in.

He'd only come back to Hedderby Bridge because after his other son died it was either throw himself on Nev's mercy or go into the poorhouse. Nev had a reputation in the town for being a miser and he was indeed very careful with money, but who could blame him? He and his mother had worked hard for their success with the lodging house. Raife might have grown to dislike his wife, but he could give credit where credit was due: she had been a hard worker all right.

Now, at nearly forty-seven Nev was awaiting the birth of his first child and fussing over his wife like a hen with one chick. The baby had come as a shock to him and to everyone in the family because Jane was forty-five, past the age of childbearing you'd have thought. She had ten living children by her first husband and Raife had heard her complain recently that ten was enough for anyone. How she'd cope with this new one, he didn't know. She didn't seem able to cope with anything practical, though she was a pleasant enough woman.

Oh, well, time would show all that.

Edmund Stott looked round the engineering works, proud of what he'd accomplished since the explosion a few months ago. It had been caused by misuse of the safety mechanisms on the old steam engine, thanks to his cousin's refusal to spend money on necessary improvements. But Athol's penny pinching had cost more in the long run and money had had to be spent to rebuild the back part of the works after the explosion, far more money than it would have taken merely to replace the old steam engine, because Athol hadn't been insured, another of his cost-saving tricks.

Edmund had stopped working here after his marriage. Athol had been furious that he'd married his mistress, but Edmund loved Faith, who was not only his beloved wife but the mother of their child, first of many he hoped. However, he'd come back to save the family business when Athol was incapacitated. And he was loving it. Without Athol's harsh approach to running the big workshop, there was a happy, busy feel to the place. He only wished it could continue this way.

He'd been surprised at how long it had taken his cousin to recover from the accident, surprised and relieved. But now Maria said Athol was reducing the amount of laudanum he was taking and starting to impose his wishes on the household again. It could be only a matter of time before he took an interest in the engineering works and then Edmund would have

22

to leave, because he and Athol were chalk and cheese.

On that thought he went out of his office to hurry the men up and close down the works for the day. He was longing to get back to the hamlet of Out Rawby, where his wife and little son were waiting for him.

★ ★ ★

Marjorie looked at the clock in the grocer's shop and decided to nip along to the Dragon to see her sister before she went home. She'd been served quickly today so would only be a few minutes late getting back and Mr Marker had promised that the errand boy would deliver her purchases within the hour.

She sighed as she walked along Market Street towards the Pride. She still wasn't used to being shut up in a house all day, with only her mother and old Raife to talk to, especially now when her mother could only talk about the baby and needed help even to go to the necessary. Marjorie tried to be patient but sometimes she felt like screaming with the frustration and boredom of her daily life.

She smiled as she approached the Pride. She loved the music room and went to see the show at least once a week, more if she could manage it. Pushing open the door of the pub next door, she waved to the women cleaning the big public room and went behind the counter to the doorway of the family's living area, calling 'Carrie! Are you there?'

23

Her eldest sister appeared from the scullery, smiling to see her. 'Hello, love. Come in. Have you time for a cup of tea?'

'No, thank you. I just had a few minutes to spare and thought I'd pop in.' As they sat down, she asked eagerly, 'Who's performing in the music room next week? I haven't seen any posters up yet.'

Carrie smiled. 'I don't know. Eli hasn't said. Are you coming to the show on Saturday?'

'You couldn't keep me away.' She sighed and began to fiddle with the edge of her sleeve.

'What's the matter, love? And don't pretend there isn't something wrong.'

Marjorie tried to hold back the tears but couldn't. 'Everything!'

Her sister put an arm round her. 'Tell me.'

'I don't like staying at home all the time. And,' she gulped, 'I'm not getting any better at running the house the way Nev wants it. He's so *fussy!*' She looked at Carrie in despair. 'I'll *never* be able to do things to his satisfaction, I know I won't. And anyway . . . ' she mopped at her eyes, ' . . . I hate it. There were bad things about working in the mill, but at least there were people to talk to. We girls could have a laugh together as we ate our lunch or sing as we walked home. Mam's driving me mad. She never stops talking, and it's all about the baby. I try to listen but it's getting harder and harder.'

'Oh, dear.'

'When you think how well we live now, how we have enough to eat every day and decent clothes to wear, I shouldn't complain. But

24

Carrie, I hate being shut up inside a house all the time.'

'That's what you'd do if you were married, stay at home and look after your house.'

'I know. I always wanted to get married but now I'm not so sure. Only what else is there for a woman to do? I'm getting on for twenty-one and haven't met any lad I really fancy spending the rest of my life with. You're so lucky with your Eli.' She sighed, caught sight of the clock on the mantelpiece and stood up. 'Oh, dear, I'm going to be late and Nev will get angry again. Does it show that I've been crying?'

'No. You look as pretty as ever.' Carrie straightened her sister's bonnet and gave her another hug. 'Just put up with it till Mam has the baby, because she really does need you. Then we'll think of something else for you to do.'

'But she'll need me even more afterwards to help her look after it. You know what she's like with babies.'

'We'll find someone else to help her, but at the moment she isn't well. I thought she was looking very tired and drawn when I came round the other day. She's too old to have another baby. It's draining all her strength.'

She watched her sister go, shaking her head fondly. Marjorie was a bit of a weak reed, but good-natured and so pretty Carrie was jealous sometimes. She not only had soft, womanly curves, but her cheeks were rosy and her hair a lovely shade, not quite auburn, but with red glints in the dark brown that most of the Preston family had inherited from their father.

25

Her sister would never satisfy Nev, who was an old fusspot, though a kind man. Carrie would have to think of something. She was usually good at sorting out problems.

* * *

When Marjorie got back, panting a little from hurrying, she found her mother lying on her bed groaning. 'What's wrong, Mam?'

'It's the babby. It's coming, an' it's nearly a month early.' She let out another groan then began to sob. 'It hurts an' it's not usually so bad.'

Marjorie heard the back door open and rushed out to find Raife in the kitchen. 'Can you go and fetch Dr Latimer? The baby's coming but there's something wrong. Mam's in terrible pain.'

The doctor didn't come for an hour, by which time Nev had got back and was sitting with his wife, who was screaming and twisting with pain. His presence seemed to comfort her more than anything and although men didn't usually stay with their wives at such times, she wouldn't let go of his hand.

When the door knocker sounded, Marjorie ran to open it. 'Oh, thank goodness you're here, Dr Latimer. Mam's having the baby early and she's really bad.'

He sent Nev out of the room and made a quick examination of Jane, then turned to Marjorie. 'Send for Granny Gates, then go and get my special bag from home. And if my wife's there, ask her to come and help as well. The baby's not sitting right.'

She looked at him in horror then ran to do his bidding. Nev said he'd go for Granny Gates. Raife looked at her. 'You can run quicker nor me, love. You go to the doctor's for that bag.'

So she started off through the streets, forgetting her shawl, forgetting everything in her worry for her mother, not even noticing the admiring glances of the men she passed in her headlong rush.

Carrie's friend Essie, who was housekeeper to the Latimers, opened the door. 'The doctor wants his special bag,' Marjorie panted. 'Mam's having a baby and something's wrong. And he wants Mrs Latimer to go and help him. He's sent for Granny Gates too.'

'Oh, dear! Mrs Latimer isn't here and I know for a fact that Granny Gates is helping someone else give birth. It's a first-timer, so she won't be able to leave.' Essie stood for a minute then said, 'I'd better come with you and see if there's anything I can do to help. Wait here. I won't be a minute.' She was back with the doctor's special bag almost immediately, then turned to fling her shawl round her shoulders and snatch up some clean cloths. 'Right, let's go.'

They got back to hear Jane screaming again, though she sounded weaker now to Marjorie. Nev was pacing up and down the kitchen. 'Granny Gates can't come,' he said. 'What are we going to do? Where's Mrs Latimer?'

'She's out so I've come to help the doctor.' Essie looked shrewdly at Marjorie's white face.

27

'You wait in the kitchen, love. Your mother won't want you to see her like that. Get plenty of water boiling. The doctor likes to keep everything clean.'

She went into the bedroom with the bag and bundle of cloths, to find Dr Latimer bending over the bed. 'Your wife isn't home, doctor. It's her morning for the mothers and babies clinic. And Granny Gates is busy with another woman, so I came to help you.'

He looked up. 'Thank you, Essie. The baby's been trying to come out feet first, but I think I've turned it.' He bent back over Jane. 'Next time, you need to push really hard, Mrs Linney. It'll go better, I promise you.'

But Jane didn't seem even to have the strength to answer him, let alone pushing hard, however he coaxed. He exchanged worried glances with Essie.

Another contraction seemed to do some of the work without much help from Jane.

'It's coming on nicely,' he encouraged and she made a bit more effort with the next contraction. 'Yes, well done.'

She spoke in a series of faint gasps. 'Is it — a boy? My Nev — did want — a boy.'

Just as the baby's feet came out, she went limp.

'She's fainted, doctor.'

Gerald Latimer thrust the baby into Essie's hands. 'Hold the baby for me.' He bent over Jane, feeling for her pulse and letting out an exclamation of shock.

Essie watched him, cradling the tiny squirming

28

infant in her arms, as always feeling her heart soften.

The doctor closed Jane's staring eyes and straightened up with a sad expression on his face. 'She's dead.'

'*Dead?* She can't be. She was just speaking to us.'

'Yes, but this sort of death can happen suddenly. I knew she wasn't strong and shouldn't have another child. I've been treating her with digitalis because her heart wasn't functioning properly. I think the heart just stopped working, as they do sometimes. She'll not have felt any pain.' He knew all about using digitalis because he had to take it himself. Physician, heal thyself, he thought wryly. Only he couldn't. Once the heart was worn out, that was it, whoever you were.

Essie had tears in her eyes as she looked at the dead woman, then the baby squirmed in her arms. 'Dear Lord, what are we going to do about the child?'

He came over and took the baby from her, laying it on the bed and attending to the umbilical cord, then looking down at it. 'For all she's arrived a little early, she's a healthy little thing. We'll have to see if we can find a wet nurse. It's the only hope.' He wrapped up the infant again and passed her to Essie. 'Can you clean her up?'

'Yes. And then I'll lay out the mother.'

'I'd better go and tell the husband.'

She watched him walk out, not envying him the task of informing Nev Linney of his wife's death. The two of them hadn't even been married a year.

In the kitchen Raife and Marjorie were sitting at the table and Nev was standing looking into the fire. He swung round as the doctor came in. 'Is Jane all right?'

Gerald sighed. 'No, I'm afraid not. Your wife had a weak heart, as I've told you, and the strain of giving birth was too much for her. I'm afraid she passed away just after the baby had been born.'

The three people in the room stared at him in shock and it was a moment or two before any of them spoke.

'She's dead?' Nev said, his voice little more than a whisper. 'My Jane's dead?'

Marjorie began to sob and as the sobs grew louder Raife gave her a little shake. 'Don't give way, lass. We're going to need you.' He left her to go to his son, who had tears streaming down his face, and put his arm round his shoulders.

Nev didn't seem to notice that he was crying, but spoke in a tight, harsh voice, 'Take me to see her, doctor. I need to see her to believe it.'

'We'll do that in a moment. It's not all bad news. You have a daughter, a healthy infant.'

'It's a wife I wanted, not a daughter!' He dashed away the tears with the back of one hand, but more followed.

Gerald shook his head sadly and led him into the parlour they'd been using as a bedroom so that Jane wouldn't have to face the stairs.

Only after seeing his wife lying so still and pale did Nev believe what had happened. He flung himself down by her, sobbing aloud. 'Jane, Jane, why did you leave me?'

Essie looked at the doctor, but he didn't seem to know what to do so she moved forward and laid one hand on Nev's shoulder.

He shook her off. 'Leave me alone.'

'You can't give way to your grief, Mr Linney. You have a daughter to care for.'

He turned then and glanced briefly at the infant in her arms. 'I don't want her.'

Her voice was sharp. 'Shame on you for saying that. She's only got you in the world now and if *you* don't care for her, who will?' She thrust the child into his arms, having seen before how this could work a miracle.

But he pushed the baby away. 'I don't *want* a baby. I want my Jane.'

They let him weep for a little longer then Dr Latimer intervened. 'We have to tend to your wife's body now, Nev. You wouldn't want her to be left like this. Essie's going to lay her out properly for you. What shall I do with the child?'

But Nev only stared dully at him.

'Shall I see if I can find you a wet nurse?'

Raife, who'd been listening from the hall, came. 'Give the child to me till you've finished in here. And yes, doctor, please find us a wet nurse. Doesn't matter what we have to pay. Find a good one. This'll be the only child he has and my only grandchild, so if no one else will, I'll make sure she's properly cared for.'

He took the baby and carried her into the kitchen, cradling her in his arms. Marjorie stared at him, making no attempt to take the baby, not

31

that he'd have let her. 'You'd better go and fetch Carrie.' The Prestons always turned to Carrie in a crisis.

She nodded and hurried out.

He was left alone with his granddaughter. The child had a look of both Jane and Nev, he thought. When they were born you could see the resemblance that would come later, then it faded until the child was older.

There was a knock on the front door and since there was no one else to answer it, Raife did so.

'There's been an accident at the mill,' gasped the girl standing there. 'They said the doctor was here. There's a lass injured.'

Raife went to tell Dr Latimer, then when he'd left, looked at Essie. 'Have you got everything you need?'

'Yes.'

'I want to help lay her out,' Nev said suddenly.

'Nay, son, there's no need for that. You leave it to Essie.'

Nev shook his head, his face taking on that stubborn look. 'I *want* to do it and I'm *going* to do it. It's the only thing I can do for my Jane now.'

Raife looked at Essie, pleading silently for understanding.

'There's no reason he shouldn't help,' she said, in her calm, firm voice. 'I helped lay out my sister and I was always glad of that, glad I could do that last thing for her.'

Nev looked at her gratefully, repeating, 'Do that last thing for her. Yes, that's what I want.'

Raife sat down near the fire, rocking the baby

gently, watching it fall asleep, so small and dependent. He shouldn't say 'it'. She was a girl, though she didn't even have a name because Nev had been so sure it'd be a boy and Jane had changed her mind almost daily about names.

★   ★   ★

Marjorie arrived back a short time later, accompanied by her sister and brother-in-law.

Eli looked at Raife. 'How's Nev taking it?'

'Badly. He's helping Essie lay her out. I'd wait in here a bit, let him come to terms with what's happened. Eh, poor Jane! Who'd have thought it?'

Still with her arm round her sister's waist, Carrie moved across to the baby, who looked so peaceful in her grandfather's arms that she didn't offer to take her from him. 'What can I do to help?'

'Nothing much till they've finished in there. The doctor's going to try to find us a wet nurse. Eh, I hope he can. They don't thrive on cow's milk.'

Eli looked from one to the other. 'Do you want me to find the others and tell them what's happened to their mother?'

Carrie frowned. 'Wouldn't it be better to wait till we've got a few things sorted out? There's not much they can do at the moment.'

'Nay, they have to know,' Raife said. 'And they'll want to be here.'

Eli set off, relieved to have a task to do that got him out of the house. He went to the mill for

Dora first, as it was closest. He'd go to the corner shop for Edith afterwards and finally to the school where Ted, Grace and Lily, the three youngest Prestons, were pupils.

At the mill the overlooker said immediately that Dora would be docked a day's pay if she left work early.

Eli looked at him in disgust and some of the operatives nearby, who'd been lip reading, stopped work briefly to scowl at the overlooker's back. Rumour said the mill was an unhappy place to work these days, and that this man was one of the causes. Eli could certainly sense the hostility.

A voice called, 'Shame!' and when Benting spun round to see who it was, another person called the same word from a different part of the floor.

'Where's Dora?' Eli asked.

A woman stepped forward. 'She's up on the first floor. I'll go and fetch her for you.' She hurried out and they stood waiting for her return.

'It's not good to interrupt a day's work,' the overlooker said. 'We have to keep up production.'

'It's not good for a woman to die. The lass needs to know.'

'It won't make any difference to her mother whether she leaves here now or later, will it? But it'll make a difference to us.'

Eli swung round and began to pace up and down, sickened by the man's callous attitude. This was the one who'd pestered Marjorie.

When Dora appeared she ran round the edge

of the room to him. 'What's wrong?'

'Let's get out of here, love, and I'll tell you.'

She burst into tears at the news and he put his arms round her, but couldn't let her go on weeping for long. 'We've got to tell the others. Will you go and fetch Edith from the shop? I'll get the young ones from the school.'

It was a subdued group who gathered in the kitchen of Linney's, the loudest sound being the thin wailing of the baby, who was now turning her head from side to side in a vain search for food.

Essie, having finished her sad task, took Carrie in first to see her mother. 'She looks peaceful, doesn't she? The doctor said she went so quickly she could have felt nothing.'

Carrie wiped away a tear. 'She does look peaceful. How terrible for Nev!'

'Shall I stay on here? I'm sure Mrs Latimer wouldn't mind.'

'No. I can manage now. Thank you for your help. You're always saving us Prestons.'

The two friends hugged one another then Essie set off home.

There she found Granny Gates waiting. 'I thought you were at a birth in Ledden Alley?'

'I was. The babby was too frail to live, died a few minutes after it were born. It were her first too, poor lass.'

'We've just had a mother die on us, Jane Linney,' Essie said sadly.

'Eh, never!'

'Do you think the lass who lost the baby would act as wet nurse for Mr Linney's little daughter? She'd get well paid.'

'Aye, I reckon she would. She's not got a husband, because he were killed, and she got upset when her mother said it was for the best that the babby died. I'll go round and ask her, if you like.'

'I'll come with you.'

3

Gwynna Jones lay on a stained straw mattress in the corner of the kitchen, her back turned to the world, weeping quietly and desperately. Her parents had let her have the baby in the privacy of their bedroom, but now they'd moved her back out here, where everyone could see how upset she was. Her mother might say it was for the best that an unwanted bastard had died, but Gwynna had held the tiny baby in her arms for a few precious minutes, watching her daughter struggle for breath and fail to find it. She couldn't believe that was for the best. She'd wanted the baby so much, because it was all she'd ever have of Patrick, who'd died in an accident at the mill before he even knew about the baby he'd fathered.

'You can stop that skriking! Tears do no one any good an' I'm sick of your sniffling,' her mother said abruptly. 'We all lose childer. You'll have others. Tomorrow you can go and ask for your job back at the mill. Here, get this down you.' She held out a bowl of pobbies, a rare treat, and the only kindness her mother had offered. But the smell of the hot milk and the sugar sprinkled over the pieces of bread in it turned Gwynna's stomach and she shook her head.

There was a knock on the door and she watched her mother put down the bowl and go to answer it. Granny Gates stood there with another woman. Gwynna didn't want to see Granny again, so turned her back.

'Did you forget summat?'

'No. We want to speak to your Gwynna.'

Essie stepped forward because she saw Mrs Jones frowning and shaking her head. 'It's about a job.' She saw the woman brighten and turn to look at the corner of the room, where a lass was lying with her back to the world.

'Gwynna, get up and speak to the lady.'

The girl didn't stir and Essie was sure she heard a sob.

'Let me talk to her.' She walked across and bent down, her heart going out to the tightly curled figure. 'Hello, lass. I'm right sorry you lost your baby.' She waited.

The girl rolled slowly over to look up at her. 'If you meant that, you're the only one as is sorry besides me.'

'Gwynna!'

Essie made a dismissive gesture with one hand, otherwise ignoring the interruption. 'There's a baby just been born further down the Lanes whose mother died having her. Would you come and act as wet nurse? The father can afford to pay you.'

'She'll do it!' Mrs Jones said quickly.

Gwynna sat up. 'Whose baby is it?'

'Nev Linney's.' She waited, hearing Granny shush the girl's mother.

'Is it a girl or boy?'

'A girl. She's very small because she was born a month early. You'd have to live in so you could tend the baby during the night.' She glanced round, taking in the mess on the table, the dirty floor. Nev definitely wouldn't want the baby to come here.

Gwynna cast a resentful glance at her mother. 'It'd suit me fine to live somewhere else.'

'But you'll pay her wages to us,' the mother put in quickly.

'Oh no, you won't.' The girl's voice was flat and emphatic, sounding stronger now. 'The money I earn will be mine or I'll not do it.'

'We've had the expense of keeping you while you've been expecting.'

'I worked as long as I could and you took all my wages, as well as pawning nearly everything I owned last week. That's all you're getting out of me.'

'We shan't take you in again if you don't give us some of that money.'

'I shan't ask you to take me in because I'll not land myself in trouble twice. If my Patrick had lived he'd have married me, so there's been no need for you to act as if I'm a whore. He was the only man I'd ever been with and well you know it.'

'Don't use such words in my house.'

'It's how you've treated me.' Gwynna turned to Essie. 'Can I come with you now?'

'The sooner the better. The baby needs you.'

The girl stood up, swaying dizzily so that Essie had to steady her for a moment. She straightened the clothes she was wearing, made a small bundle of her possessions and wrapped a ragged shawl round her shoulders. 'I'm ready.'

'Don't you have anything else you want to bring?'

'I told you. They pawned everything. *She* drinks as well as Dad.'

Outside she stopped to stare at the weak sunshine and draw in a shaky breath. 'I never even asked how much Mr Linney will pay me, but I don't care, just as long as I get away from *them*.'

Granny patted her arm. 'You leave it to Essie to arrange everything, love.' She turned and left them.

Slowly, leaning on Essie's arm, Gwynna walked down the hill towards Linney's, stopping to stare at the house then at herself. 'I've nowt but these rags to wear. What will they think of me?'

'They'll think you're a godsend. The baby was crying when I left. She won't live without you.' Essie knocked on the front door.

Nev opened it, his reddened, puffy eyes bearing instant witness to his grief.

'This is Gwynna Jones who's just lost her baby and has agreed to wet-nurse yours.'

He wrung the girl's hand, muttering, 'Thank God, thank God!' then stared down at it and back at Essie. 'She'll have to wash herself. I'm not having her touch my baby till she's clean.'

'She's not had a chance to get cleaned up,' Essie said gently. 'And her mother pawned her clothes.'

'I'll get Marjorie to lend her something to wear, though it'll be too long for her. You're sure she's not diseased?'

Essie clicked her tongue in annoyance. 'Stop talking as if she isn't here and can't understand you, Nev Linney. Give the lass a chance. She's young and healthy.'

He looked at her for a minute, then back at the girl. 'Sorry, love. I'm not — not myself today. Sorry about your loss, too.' His voice wobbled on the last words and his face crumpled for a moment like that of a child fighting back tears. 'Come through to the kitchen.'

Essie couldn't help it, she put an arm round him. 'Eh, lad, it's been a sad day for all of us. We'll get through it together, you'll see.'

He leaned against her for a minute then straightened himself and nodded. 'We've plenty of hot water. She can wash herself in the scullery.'

Gwynna followed them down a long hallway with soft carpet on the floor into the kitchen, which was the biggest one she'd ever seen and seemed to be full of people, all staring at her.

'This is Gwynna Jones. She's going to be the wet nurse,' Essie explained as she took the newcomer through into the scullery. 'I'll get — Oh, thank you, love.' Marjorie brought a bowl of warm water, set it down and laid a towel next to it before going back to the kitchen.

Essie was about to leave the poor girl in privacy when she saw Gwynna sag suddenly against the wall. 'Do you want me to stay and help you?'

'Please.' The word was little more than a sigh.

Just as they were finishing, there was a knock on the door and Marjorie peeped in again. 'I've

41

brought some clean clothes.'

'Come in and shut the door,' Essie said. 'We don't want everyone seeing in. Gwynna, this is Marjorie, who looks after the house here. It's her mother who's just died.'

The two young women nodded, staring, assessing each other.

'Dora let me have some of her clothes. She's not as tall as me, so they'll fit you better, but they'll still be too long, I think. We'll get you some things of your own tomorrow, Nev says.'

'Doesn't she mind me wearing them?' Gwynna saw that like Nev this lass had reddened eyes and it made her feel better to be among people who weren't brisk and happy. Maybe here they'd let her grieve in peace for her baby.

'No, she doesn't mind. We're all glad to find someone to help us.'

When she was dressed Gwynna turned to her companion. 'Can I see the baby now?'

'Yes.' Essie led the way back into the kitchen which was still full of people. 'Let her get through, you lot.'

They moved aside and to Gwynna's surprise, she saw that the baby was in the arms of a silver-haired old man, who was rocking her gently near the fire. Everyone had stopped talking to stare but she didn't care about them. It was the baby who mattered to her. She walked across the room and when the old man stood up and held the infant out to her, she took her gently, holding her close and staring down at the tiny face.

Even though she was small, this baby was rosy,

unlike hers, who had been born a blue-white colour. This one had been crying and there were still traces of tears on her reddened cheeks. Gwynna wiped one away with a fingertip then stroked the soft cheek with the back of the same finger. The baby moved its head, blindly searching for the breast. Without looking up, Gwynna asked, 'What's she called?'

'She hasn't got a name yet,' Raife told her. 'The mother wanted to call her Sylvia last I heard but my son isn't sure.'

'Sylvie is nicer,' Essie said. 'I read about a French lass called Sylvie once and I've always liked that name.'

Nev stepped forward, looking down at the baby and speaking in a husky voice, 'Sylvie. Yes, we'll call her Sylvie.' For a moment longer he stared at his daughter, then turned once more to Essie for guidance. 'What'll we do now?'

'We need a bedroom for Gwynna and the baby. She can't feed her here.'

'The crib's in our bedroom, but the baby can't go in there. We took Jane's body upstairs and she's lying there.' He was frowning, and seemed unable to make a decision.

'There are other bedrooms, aren't there?' Essie asked as the baby hiccuped and began to wail again.

When he didn't speak, Marjorie said in her soft, gentle voice, 'Gwynna can have one of the front bedrooms, can't she, Nev?'

'Yes. Yes, of course. Eh, I can't seem to think straight.'

'I'll show them where to go, then I'll fetch the

crib,' Marjorie said.

'No.' Nev shook his head. 'No, I'll fetch it. I need to see Sylvie feeding, need to know she'll be all right with Gwynna.'

Essie was about to protest that it wasn't fitting for him to see a strange lass put his daughter to the breast, then bit back the words. It came to her that he needed to see life, not death, needed to be with his baby daughter so that he could learn to love her. She put an arm round Gwynna and guided her towards the stairs, turning to smile over her shoulder at Nev. 'Come on, then. Let's get your daughter settled.'

As she went upstairs Gwynna glanced round in wonder. This was a palace compared to her parents' house. The bedroom she was shown into had stained polished floorboards with a carpet square in the middle. The bed was high with lots of covers — you'd never be cold in that. There was a chest of drawers, a wardrobe, two wooden chairs and a washstand. Such luxury! Was she really going to sleep here?

Nev appeared in the doorway, holding a crib.

Essie was also studying the room. 'She'll need a lower chair than those to sit on when she's feeding your Sylvie.'

'There's a low chair in our room. We put it there special.'

'I'll come and help you carry it back,' Essie prompted when he didn't move.

They lugged the well-upholstered chair along the landing and set it by the window.

Gwynna sat down, ignoring them, her eyes only on her charge. Lifting her top, she bared her breast and guided the baby gently towards it. After a moment's fumbling Sylvie began sucking greedily.

Tears began to rain down the young woman's cheeks and when Essie looked, Nev was weeping again as well. 'There now,' she said gently. 'You can see that your daughter's going to be all right. You won't lose them both.' She didn't understand why she was so sure that Sylvie would survive, but at that moment she was utterly certain of it. 'Now, my lad, let's leave Gwynna to feed her. Where are the baby clouts? We'll need to bring everything into this room. And we'll need to feed that lass well so that she makes plenty of good, rich milk for your Sylvie.'

He seemed grateful to have something to do, carrying out Essie's instructions meekly and finding the things he and Jane had prepared. Only once, as they went past the bedroom he and Jane had shared and he caught sight of the still figure on the bed, did he stop and seem uncertain what to do next.

Essie gave him a minute to gaze at his dead wife, then put her arm round him and said quietly, 'Let's go down and get Gwynna some food now. She'll be hungry and thirsty, I've no doubt. And I'll ask the doctor's wife to come round and see them both, to make sure everything's all right. She's good with new mothers and babies, Mrs Latimer is.'

'Yes, we'll get that lass some good food. You see Mrs Latimer.'

She thought he was still acting without

45

thinking, parroting her words back at her, but he stopped at the top of the stairs to look at her, really look.

'I'm grateful for your help today, Essie love, more grateful than I can say. I'm just a bit — well, lost at the moment, d'you see?'

'Anyone would be,' she agreed. 'It's been a sad day for you and for all Jane's family — and for that poor lass too.'

In the bedroom Gwynna fed the baby and the worst of her grief was eased just a little by the fact that she could help Sylvie survive. Without even thinking what she was doing, she murmured encouragements and endearments as the child sucked vigorously. She didn't forget her own baby, never that, but already she was feeling protective towards her new charge.

And she'd got away from her family, could perhaps make a new life for herself if she managed to save some money while she worked here.

*　*　*

Unlike her first husband, Jane Linney didn't suffer the shame of a pauper's funeral. Nev buried her in style two days later, with a proper hearse drawn by black horses and a grave in the churchyard, where a stonemason would later place a white marble headstone.

'I'll be buried alongside her when I go,' he said at frequent intervals. 'I'm not a young man myself.'

'You'll not be going for years, son,' his father

told him each time he said it. 'We're a long-lived family, us Linneys.'

But it was Essie who gave the widower's thoughts a new direction. 'Not you,' she countered when he made his statement to her for the third time. 'You can't die now and leave little Sylvie without anyone to protect her.'

'She's got brothers and sisters to do that.'

'They'll be having children of their own one day. Carrie's married already and the lads are taking a real interest in Marjorie. I've seen heads turn when she walks past in the street.'

He looked at her as if he didn't understand what she was saying, or didn't want to understand.

'Life goes on, Nev,' she said in a softer tone. 'I've lost all my family, but I'm still here.'

'I keep forgetting you're not part of *our* family,' he said, sounding surprised. 'What with you and Carrie being so close, and you taking such an interest in my Sylvie.'

'I like babies,' she admitted. 'I hope you don't mind me coming round.'

'I'm glad you do. Let alone it's a pleasure to see you and talk a bit of sense, it's always tidier after you've left.'

She chuckled. 'Poor Marjorie. She hasn't a tidy bone in her body, has she? Some people are like that.'

'I don't know what to do with her. It irks me her leaving things around as she does, but you can't deny she's a hard worker in her own way. Underneath the clutter the house is usually clean, and she dealt with the lodgers last night for me, did all right, too.'

'You'll just have to get used to a bit of untidiness. You couldn't manage without her now that Jane's gone.'

But he still said with a sigh, 'If only she'd learn to be tidy, though. It irks me to have things in a mess.'

★ ★ ★

When the family got back to the house after his mother's funeral, Robbie noticed the lass who was nursing his baby sister as soon as he walked into the kitchen. She had such a fierce look to her as she sat in one corner staring at them all and cradling the baby against her that he couldn't stop watching her. It was as if she felt it necessary to protect the infant from something, though from what he couldn't imagine. There were only family here today, apart from Essie.

He was sure he'd seen the lass before, not just in the street but to speak to, and couldn't think for a moment where. Then he remembered suddenly: she'd been Patrick's girl. The poor fellow had been dead for months now. Was it his baby she'd had? Robbie did a quick calculation and guessed it could have been. She'd been a lot prettier in those days, he remembered, but was thin now and angry-looking. Her hair, which he remembered as light brown and wavy, had been tied back with a ribbon, but was now scraped back into a knobbly bun at the nape of her neck. It didn't suit her. And she was wearing clothes that didn't quite fit, that looked as if she'd thrown them on anyhow.

He sighed and went to lean against the wall. He'd come along today because it was the right thing to do, but it had been a miserable sort of day, overcast with sudden showers and hardly a glimpse of the sun. Nev had reddened eyes and looked upset, and old Raife was watching his son carefully, as if worried about him.

After they'd had something to eat and drink, Nev stood up and clapped his hands to get their attention. Everyone turned to stare at him except Gwynna, who was rocking the baby and frowning into space as if her thoughts were miles away.

'I just wanted to tell you all,' Nev began, 'that I'd like you children to stay here with me. I'm your stepfather still, though your dear mother's been taken from us . . . ' He faltered for a moment, then took a deep breath and continued, 'And well, I want you to go on thinking of this as your home.'

'That's very generous of you, Nev.' Carrie spoke for everyone as usual.

They all nodded.

'And of course,' he added, 'we've Gwynna with us now looking after Sylvie for me and I hope she'll be happy here, too.'

Robbie could see first wariness when Gwynna heard her name, then surprise. Well, Nev was good at surprising people. He'd amazed them all after he married their mother by being an excellent provider and looking after them properly, as their own father never had. He'd even taken in Robbie when he lost his job at the engineering works, doing it without question or complaint. Robbie had changed his opinion of his stepfather then and had started to like him for his own sake.

'That's all, really,' Nev finished and sat down, trying to smile but failing.

Marjorie took him another cup of tea and gave his hand a quick squeeze. Essie cut him another piece of cake, but he only crumbled it between his fingers then set the plate down.

Robbie didn't stay long after that. He wanted to get back to the work he loved and forget about his mother being dead. She hadn't been much of a mother and he couldn't grieve deeply, didn't suppose the others would, either. They weren't heartless, but when Jane hadn't been occupied with the latest baby — and there had nearly always been a 'latest baby' — she'd given all her attention and all her affection too, it felt like, to her husbands, first his father and later Nev. The children had brought themselves up, really, or rather Carrie had done most of the rearing. It wasn't till recently that he'd realised how much Carrie had done for them all.

Once back at the engineering works he went to check what Mr Edmund wanted him to do and stopped in shock to see Mrs Stott in the office talking to her brother-in-law. She looked so worried he left them alone and waited till she left to speak to Mr Edmund.

★ ★ ★

Hal Kidd walked on to the stage of the music saloon in Manchester, tripped and went back to look at the spot where he'd tripped. He scratched his head, walked round the spot, then looked at the audience and spread his hands in bewilderment. As he stepped backwards a man walked briskly across the stage, not stumbling at the place where Hal had tripped, and going straight off at the other side.

Again Hal mimed bewilderment and went back to where he'd entered, strolling forward, whistling tunefully. He tripped again in exactly the same place and staggered across the stage before righting himself and running back to glare at the empty space. By now the audience was chuckling and calling out to him.

The new piece was going just as he'd planned, Hal thought, hiding a smile and carrying on with his act. By the time he finished his finale, a comic song, the big room seemed full of laughter and when he bowed the applause was loud and enthusiastic. He walked off, tripping one last time, surprising a final laugh out of them.

'You did well, lad,' the manager said. 'You couldn't come back next week, could you? We've got an unexpected vacancy — higher up the bill.'

'Thanks, but I'm booked elsewhere next week. If you write to the agency in London, I'm sure they'll fit me in here for another week later. I've enjoyed appearing here.' Well, he always enjoyed himself, loved making people laugh, couldn't imagine another life now.

As he reached the room where the men changed their clothes, his smile faded at the sight of the man standing in the corridor, arms folded, anger radiating from him.

'Father.'

'I want to talk to you, Harold.'

'When I've cleaned off the make-up and changed my clothes.'

'You look like a nancy boy with that stuff on your face.' He waited impatiently while Hal cleaned up and changed, then led the way out. 'Where can we go in this godless place?'

'We can talk in a coffee house down the road. It stays open late for the theatre trade.'

They found a table and Hal ordered a coffee, while his father declined to have anything.

'Is everything all right at home?'

'No, it isn't. Our Hilda's husband was killed last week.'

'I'm sorry to hear that. How — '

'It's left me short-handed in the shop, so I've come to give you one last chance to do your duty, give up this immoral life and work in the family business.'

Hal closed his eyes for a moment, knowing he could never do that and knowing that his father would erupt with rage when he refused, whatever his reasons. 'You know your sort of life wouldn't suit me, Dad. Besides, I'm starting to do well on the stage and — '

'I'm ashamed to see a son of mine playing the fool like you did tonight.'

'The audience loved it.'

'It wasn't their son acting like an idiot.' He breathed in deeply. 'But I'm prepared to forgive you and leave the shop to you, as I'd once planned, if you'll just come home and buckle down to some honest work.'

Which was as near a plea as his father could get, Hal knew. He hoped he'd hidden the shudder that ran through him at the mere thought of going back and working closely with a man who was a tyrant to anyone in his power. James Kidd didn't beat his wife and children, but he might as well have done, because he bullied them unremittingly. Only Hal had been different, his spirit unquenched whatever his father did to him. His sense of humour had got him into trouble time after time during his childhood, though his mother had tried to protect him when possible. But it hadn't always been possible and his father had clouted him as he'd never had to clout his three meek little daughters.

Hal had run away when he was fourteen to go on the stage, playing the fool and general dogsbody for another comedian at first, doing anything to gain experience.

When his father had found him, he'd refused to go back. Then his father had lost his temper and beaten him severely, breaking his nose. Hal caressed it, as he did sometimes. It was a reminder, that bump in his nose was, of what his father was like and it only made him more determined to go his own way. Besides, he could never give up the stage, never.

'Flora Netting is still unwed,' his father went on. 'Your mother says she won't look at another fellow, still wants you.'

Hal sighed. He liked Flora — well, he liked most people — but not in that way. He'd never met a lass he could fall in love with, and if he did, she'd probably not fancy him. He was of medium height only and had a very ordinary, if not ugly face, especially with that twisted nose. And though he was only twenty-eight, his light brown hair was thinning already. His face was perfect for a comedian, with its wide mouth and big, dark eyes, but not so good for attracting the lasses.

'Sorry, Dad. I'm doing well as a comedian and I love it.'

His father's great fist crashed down on the table. 'Then you're no son of mine and you need never come back home again.'

For a moment, Hal thought his father was going to let go of the rage which seemed to simmer in him all the time, but he didn't. He shoved the table away from him, spilling what was left of the coffee, and stood up, pushing his way out through the late-night crowds. Hal let out a sigh of relief as the door slammed· shut behind him and turned to apologise to the serving lass waiting to mop up the coffee.

As he left the place he dropped a threepenny bit in the hat sitting empty in front of the old man, calling out, 'Get yourself something to eat, Grandad!' He knew the money would probably be spent on booze, but still he wanted to make someone happy and take the nasty taste of his father's glaring face and cruel ultimatum away. He might not want to work in the family shop, but he did like to see his poor little downtrodden mother and sisters sometimes.

He walked slowly back to his lodgings, hands

in his pockets, enjoying the balmy night air. The stroll calmed him down a little, but though he was tired, it was a long time before he fell asleep.

It hurt the way his father despised what he did, when so many other people enjoyed it and thought Hal good at it.

★　★　★

'How are Faith and little Brice?' Maria Stott asked Edmund when she went to see him at the engineering works.

'They're both well. Faith would love you to go and visit her if you have time, but it's best if she doesn't come to see you any more, I think.'

Maria sighed. 'You're right. Only I daren't come to your house, either. Athol's increasingly alert and he wants to know where I'm going every time I leave the house. He'd be furious with me if I went to see Faith.'

'Damn him! Make no mistake about it, I'm doing this,' Edmund gestured round him, 'for you and the boys, not to help him.'

'I know. And I'm more grateful than I can say. When he asked me to come and look round so that I could tell him how things were here, I was glad of the opportunity to warn you.'

'You think he'll be taking over again here? Making more trouble?'

'My husband will make trouble as long as he breathes, but I don't see how he can ever work here again. His right hand is so twisted by the accident he can't use it and his face is

55

. . . grotesque.' She shuddered at the thought. 'He can't get on with the artificial leg, either, and his balance has been affected, so he needs help to move about. Unfortunately Terson is leaving us, so Athol is insisting on choosing the men who look after him from now on. He wants two and I think he's going to employ some of the men who used to work here, the ones you got rid of.'

Edmund looked at her in consternation. 'I'm glad you warned me. I thought he'd be bedbound for the rest of his life.' Had hoped for it, because Athol had caused him and others enough trouble, not to mention causing one man's death in the explosion. The magistrate might have called it an accident, but Edmund knew it had been a direct result of Athol's orders to override the safety mechanism on the steam engine. He had warned his cousin several times about the danger.

She avoided his eyes, her expression bleak. 'I thought it best to keep Athol calmed by increasing the dose of laudanum. He jars his stump, he's so restless, and it just won't heal properly. Well, he's always been difficult to deal with, as you well know. But he's refusing to take any laudanum in the daytime now, just at night to help him sleep.'

Edmund was surprised that she'd found the courage to trick her husband, but didn't blame her in the least. His cousin was the nastiest man he'd ever met, and if Athol took charge of the works again, then Edmund would leave and take Robbie Preston with him. 'What exactly does he want to know?'

'How the place is running now we've got the new steam engine installed. He's talking of coming here himself to check it after the men have gone home at night once he has his new menservants. And — he wants to talk to you, wants you to come to the house.'

Edmund drew in a deep breath. 'I hate going to see him.'

'I know. But I'd be grateful if you'd do it. If *you* don't run this place, what will we have to live off? Getting the new engine and repairing the burnt-out part of the works has taken most of our money. Please don't let him provoke you.'

'All right. I'll come for your sake. When does he want to see me?'

'Tomorrow, about eleven in the morning. But first, if you'll show me over the works, I'll try to understand enough to report back to him. You'll have to explain things to me. He never let me come here before.'

He led her round, introducing her to the smiling, busy men on lathes and other machinery. They were, he knew, finding their work more satisfying these days without Athol Stott breathing down their necks and were therefore producing more. She asked intelligent questions and nodded as Edmund explained what the men were doing. The huge flywheel of the steam engine seemed to fascinate her and she stood watching the cogs mesh together as they turned and turned with clumsy grace, carrying power to the other machines in the works, so that men could make smaller machines and parts for the railways that had spread across England in the course of the last ten years and changed everyone's life.

After the two of them had left the big shed, men turned to one another.

'Summat's up,' said one. 'He looks like she's brought him some bad news.'

'Aye. An' Mr Edmund were happy enough this morning.'

'Well, if *he's* coming back, I'm leaving,' a third said.

'Oh, yes?' the first one taunted. 'And where will you find another job in Hedderby? Not to mention another house for you and your six childer?'

'I'll go an' live in Manchester if I have to, or Bolton or Rochdale. I'm not working for *him* again. What if that boiler had exploded when we were all working here? There'd have been more than one of us killed when the walls at the end collapsed. He's a nasty devil that one is, as wicked as they come.'

★　★　★

Marjorie found life at Linney's a little easier with Gwynna in the house. Not that she grew close to the other lass, who wasn't prone to chatting and seemed interested only in two things: little Sylvie and eating. Her appetite made Marjorie remember how hungry she'd often been when her father was alive.

The two of them hadn't much in common. Like her sister Carrie, Marjorie didn't dote on babies. After helping rear so many younger brothers and sisters, she sometimes thought that if she never held another baby as long as she lived it wouldn't upset her. For that reason, she didn't encourage any of the fellows who had started trying to persuade her to walk out with them. She didn't want to settle down to a life of hard work and making do, not to mention having babies. What if she was like her mother and kept on and on having them? Eleven had been born alive to her mother, counting Sylvie. Eleven! And three others miscarried or stillborn. It made Marjorie shudder even to think of that. Her mother's body had been slack and shapeless. She looked down at her own trim body, pleased with it now. No, she wasn't going down that track, definitely not.

Only she didn't know which other track she could go down.

Whenever she could get out of the house, she went round to see Carrie at the Pride. The music room fascinated her and she often went there on a Friday or Saturday night because Eli let her in free. She'd sit in any corner where there was space, singing along with the rest of the audience, still humming the songs as she walked home with old Raife, who was the pianist there. Sometimes Dora or Edith came with her, but they preferred lantern shows or other attractions at the Methodist church, where they could meet lads. The new minister seemed to be trying to draw young folk into his fold.

What Marjorie dreamed of was going on the

stage, only her voice wasn't good enough. But you could still dream, couldn't you? Of course she didn't tell anyone about that, not even Carrie. They'd only laugh at her.

★ ★ ★

Maria got home and reported on conditions at the works to her husband. 'Shall I advertise for two menservants, Athol?'

'I don't think that'll be necessary. Terson has heard of a couple of men I know slightly who're seeking work, and he's promised he'll stay on for a week or two to train them.'

'Oh?'

'Tell him to bring them to see me tomorrow.'

'Who are they?'

'None of your business.'

She changed the subject quickly. 'Edmund's coming tomorrow, as you asked. Perhaps the men should come another day? You don't want to tire yourself out.'

'It's not likely my cousin will stay long. I want to get this settled.'

'Are you sure of these men? Shouldn't you get someone more skilled at nursing? I could — '

He glared at her. 'Leave Terson's replacement to me and get on with your housekeeping. Now that I'm better I'll take charge of my own affairs again.'

She left the bedroom and stood for a moment on the landing outside, eyes closed, hands clenched into fists. A great shudder racked her, but she didn't dare make any sound.

Did you go to hell for praying that someone would die?

Hell couldn't be much worse than life with Athol Stott.

4

A few weeks after Jane's death Eli came back from Manchester looking very pleased with himself. He went across to kiss his wife's cheek and nodded a greeting to Marjorie, who had just popped in. 'I've booked some really good acts for the coming weeks.'

'That's nice.' Carrie went on polishing the surface of the bar in the music room. She cared more about how the place looked than what happened on stage. She left that sort of thing to Eli and his cousin Joanna, who were the joint owners of the Dragon and the music room. Joanna's husband Bram had started off being interested in the Pride, but was more interested in his own singing these days. He'd started appearing at music saloons in Manchester some weeks, others he sang at the Pride. He kept trying to persuade Joanna to sing with him, because she had a beautiful voice, but she kept refusing, saying she couldn't face the thought of everyone staring at her.

Carrie agreed with her. She wouldn't like to go on the stage, either. She realised Eli was still talking and tried to give him her full attention.

'There's a fellow called Denby Sinclair — that's a silly sort of name, Denby, I bet it's only his stage name — anyway, he comes from down south and has a lovely tenor voice, they say. He works with a young woman, turning his songs into a sort of story, but he's the main one in the act, not her. She pretends to be hard to get till he sings to her, then in the end she dances with him. They say the ladies love him. And then there's a comedian, a fellow called Hal Kidd, billed as The Prince of Laughter. He's supposed to be very good but he's just starting out.' He grinned at his sister-in-law. 'So you'll have two young men to swoon after this week, young Marjorie.'

'I don't swoon over them! But I do enjoy coming here and I always hate the evening to end.'

Carrie shot a quick glance at her and wasn't surprised to see that soppy expression back on her sister's face. She was getting a bit concerned about the way Marjorie mooned around here, dropping in at every opportunity, even watching the performers rehearse if she could. Her sister was no more practical now than she had been as a girl, though she would be twenty-one in October. 'Isn't it time you got back to Linney's?'

Marjorie sighed and pushed herself to her feet. 'I suppose so. It just gets worse there, Carrie. It's all baby talk. None of us Prestons ever got fussed over like Sylvie is. I'm fed up of babies, the mess they make, the smell of them. Absolutely fed up!'

'Well, it's only to be expected that Nev will fuss, isn't it, her being his only child? And he can well afford it.'

Her sister shrugged and left for Linney's.

Carrie looked at her husband. 'She's not happy staying at home all day. I don't know what to do about her.'

63

Eli plonked a kiss on her cheek and sat down on the edge of the table. 'She's not your responsibility any more, love. She's old enough to look after herself.'

'She's still my sister whether we live together or not, and she's too dreamy to look after herself. Don't you miss your family?'

'Not at all. I've more than enough on my plate with my wife and the Pride.'

'Did you get any more music for Bram?'

'Yes. They had a few new songsheets in. He's never satisfied, that one.'

'He's very ambitious.'

'Not too ambitious, I hope. He's popular here in Hedderby and I don't know what we'd do without him. I doubt Joanna will ever leave to go on the road with him, so he'll have to stay in Lancashire, and where better to live than over the pub? Though with your cooking, he runs the risk of getting fat.' He laughed and ducked as she threw a cloth at him.

★   ★   ★

The following Thursday evening, Marjorie came along to the show, wearing a new dress and with her hair freshly washed and shining. There wasn't the same crowd as there would be on a Saturday, when they'd started doing two shows, one at six o'clock, the other at eight-thirty, but still there were plenty of people stealing an hour or two from the drudgery of the working week. There was even a group of gentry at one of the front tables. The county folk sometimes came

64

'slumming it', as she'd heard one tell another in a scornful voice, but that didn't stop them laughing at the jokes and joining in the singing with as much gusto as the common folk.

'Your sister gets prettier every time I see her,' Eli whispered in his wife's ear as he stood waiting to make his way to the Chairman's table, from where he'd introduce the acts and control the show. 'See how the young fellows are looking at her.'

'She doesn't even notice them. She's more interested in what's happening on stage. Hadn't you better start?' She watched fondly as he walked across the big room, looking to her as much a gentleman as those at the front table in his dark, well-tailored evening clothes. He sat down in the little alcove to the right of the stage and leaned back to smile at the audience, some of whom were already calling out greetings to him.

He waited for some latecomers to sit down, then hit the gong standing next to him on the table. Gradually the audience shushed one another till most had stopped talking.

Raife and his little group of musicians filed across the stage and took their places on the smaller, lower stage to the left. Raife played a few crashing chords on the piano, which silenced the few still speaking, then looked across at Eli, who boomed out in that loud voice he could summon up on these occasions, 'Good evening, ladies and gentlemen.'

They chorused a 'Good evening' back at him.

'Can we have a round of applause for our

orchestra, ladies and gentlemen?'

When the applause died down, the group of five played a short overture then Eli introduced the first act, a local brother and sister who sang together and were popular enough to appear here every few weeks. They were good fillers, but would never be more.

Marjorie sat in the back corner of the long, rather narrow room, which had once been the stables for a coaching inn. She kept out of the way of the men serving drinks to the audience in between acts, enjoying herself as usual, even though she was on her own tonight.

The new comedian, Hal Kidd, came on the stage, tripped over nothing and went back to stare at the spot. People began to laugh before he even spoke a word. Eli was right, she thought as she applauded loudly afterwards, Hal Kidd *was* good. It wasn't what he did that was comical, so much as the man himself. And he had quite a nice singing voice, too, for his comic song.

Then the new singer came on and she forgot everyone else. Denby Sinclair was fair-haired, very handsome and even dressed in ragged clothes, as he was now, his charm reached out to the audience. She watched entranced as he strolled across the stage to stop near the orchestra and sing a sad song about loving a girl from a distance, a girl who didn't even know he existed. She hadn't heard the song before, but it had a very catchy chorus and some of the audience clearly knew it because they joined in when he gestured an invitation to sing the chorus with him.

As a girl strolled on to the stage and pretended to be studying the gardens painted on the backdrop, he hissed at the audience in a stage whisper, 'That's her!' and began to sing a well-known love song, a tune which had toes tapping and women smiling. The girl showed no sign of hearing it or even of seeing him.

When he'd finished the girl began to walk across the stage as if leaving. A few of the audience called out, 'Don't go! Look at him!' She pretended not to hear them.

Marjorie watched entranced, wishing she were that lucky girl.

Suddenly the girl dropped her handkerchief and when Sinclair picked it up, he looked soulfully into her eyes, but she gave a quick nod of thanks, looking scornfully down at his ragged clothing.

As she turned to walk off the stage he began to sing again, this time a song no one had ever heard before, 'My Heart Is Yours'. He must have bought the song for his own use, as some performers did. It had a beautiful melody and a chorus that was easy to remember. This time the girl stopped and turned to stare at him. Gradually, he approached her again, taking her hand and leading her into a little dance in the middle of the tune, then finishing the song alone. Once she mis-stepped and he pulled her back into the rhythm of the dance, his smile rather fixed for a moment or two.

'Do you love me?' he asked after they had finished the little dance.

She nodded.

At that there was a roll of drums and he threw off his rags, now wearing a gentleman's evening clothes, which made him look even more handsome. The women in the audience sighed audibly, Marjorie with them. He began his final song, another one that was new to the audience, and the girl joined in, though only in a minor way.

Once he'd finished singing the audience applauded loudly, some standing up to clap and cheer, so that he came back and condescended to sing another verse and chorus, this time without the girl. As he bowed to another round of applause, he gestured towards the side of the stage and the girl came on briefly, bobbed a curtsey then vanished again.

When the evening ended, Marjorie helped with the clearing up as she waited to walk home with Raife.

Eli stopped next to her to ask, 'What do you think of this Denby Sinclair?'

'He's wonderful.'

'I got us a winner there, didn't I? Give him another year or two on stage and I won't be able to afford to hire him.'

She dreamed about Denby Sinclair that night, dreamed she was the one dancing with him.

★   ★   ★

Behind the stage in the crowded men's dressing room, Denby glared at Raife, who was putting on his outer garments. 'I gave you the music. Why didn't you follow it exactly? There should

68

have been a flourish before my encore.'

'I can't read music. And it seemed to me the audience was more interested in hearing you sing again than in listening to any flourishes.'

'I've planned every detail of this act and I want that flourish *exactly* where I put it.'

Raife shrugged. 'I'll come in tomorrow morning and we can go over it.'

'We'll do it tomorrow afternoon. I like to sleep in after a show.'

'All reet. Suit yoursen.' Raife walked out, grimacing at Eli, who fell in beside him.

'What's the matter?'

'That Sinclair fellow. He needs to learn a few manners, that one does.'

'The audience liked him.'

'They don't have to work with him. I can't abide uppity folk who look down their noses at you and forget their manners.'

'Never mind his manners, he'll bring folk in, which is the important thing. Word's getting round and the lasses are flocking in to see such a handsome fellow. See if we aren't sold out completely tomorrow night.'

Raife joined Marjorie. 'Ready to go home, lass?'

She sighed. 'I suppose so. I hate to leave all this.' She gestured round her.

He looked at her in concern. 'This is only a make-believe world, love. Never forget that.'

'It's better than my real world. I wish I could be in this one all the time, only I don't have a good enough voice.'

'You've a very pleasant voice, Marjorie love,

don't put yourself down.'

'But not good enough to go on the stage.'

'Eh, I didn't think you'd want to do that.'

'I'd like it more than anything. Only I'm not good enough. It's not fair. There's Joanna with a beautiful strong voice and she refuses to sing in public, while I long to and can't.'

He was shaken by her vehemence. 'You're better off where you are, believe me. There's a lot goes on behind the scenes that you don't see. It isn't all sweetness and light.'

She stopped to scowl at Linney's. 'Well, I'm not spending the rest of my life trapped in that house. Working in the mill was better than this. At least I had someone to talk to and have a bit of fun with. If it hadn't been for that overlooker, I'd still be there. It isn't fair. I hate him!'

Raife was too wise to argue with her but went to bed still worrying about her. She wasn't happy and he didn't like to see young folk fretting their lives away. He wondered whether to tell Nev about her wanting to sing in shows, then decided against it. Whether she liked it or not, at the moment Marjorie was dependent on his son's good will and he didn't think Nev would look kindly on an ambition to go on the stage.

Any road, it'd never happen. As she'd said, she didn't have a strong enough voice.

★   ★   ★

Robbie and Mr Edmund walked slowly home after work to the village of Out Rawby, where Robbie lived in his master's house. It still surprised him that the engineer could chat to him on equal terms, aye, and listen to his opinions, too. But tonight Mr Edmund had something on his mind, something that was making him frown and sigh. Greatly daring, Robbie asked, 'What's wrong?'

'My cousin Athol. He's getting better.'

'Oh. Is he coming back to run the works?'

'Perhaps. If he does, it won't be for a while yet, though. His leg hasn't healed properly and he's having trouble with the artificial leg, but he's starting to take an interest in the details of what we're doing and I'm afraid he'll want to return to the old ways.'

Robbie couldn't think what to say to that. He knew that if Mr Stott returned he'd be out on his ear, as he had been before. What he didn't know was whether Mr Edmund would stay on.

'I can't work his way,' Edmund said at last. He looked at the younger man striding along beside him. 'And I doubt you can, either. You've a real knack for machinery and should train properly as an engineer.'

Robbie could feel his cheeks growing hot at this compliment. 'If I'm doing all right, it's because of your help.'

'I could help some men till the cows came home and they'd not grasp things as quickly as you do.'

'You have to pay to do the real training though, don't you?' Robbie had been dying to ask this for a while now.

'Unless someone will take you on without paying.'

71

He stopped walking to look very solemnly at Robbie, whose heart began to beat faster in hope that this was leading up to something. There was silence for a moment or two and Robbie watched the long shadows cast by the late evening sunshine as he waited impatiently for his master to speak.

'It's about time we got things sorted out. I'm prepared to take you on and train you, which will take three years or so. I'll have to ask you not to get married during the training period, because you'll need to spend time at other engineering works, bigger ones than ours.'

'I'm not walking out with anyone, nor am I looking to.'

'Love seems to come searching for you, rather than you going out seeking it.'

'Well, I'll make sure it doesn't find me at home, then. I'll do anything to become a proper engineer, Mr Edmund, anything.'

'You'll need to work in the evenings first to improve your reading and writing, as well as learning to draw properly. It'll be a busy time.'

'There's nothing I'd like better.'

'We'll bear it in mind, then. Though I can't draw up the formal apprenticeship papers until things are settled with my cousin because I can't train you if I've no place for you to work.' He clapped his companion on the shoulder. 'Now let's get moving. Faith will be wondering what's happened to us.'

Robbie watched Mr Edmund smile fondly as they set off walking again, and knew he was thinking of Mrs Stott and his baby son. One day, perhaps, Robbie would want a wife and home of his own, but not before he could provide for them properly. He'd never forget his own childhood and how hungry he'd been sometimes, how poorly his father provided for them. And if there was the slightest chance of him training properly as an engineer, he wasn't going to spoil it by getting wed, or even getting a lass in trouble.

* * *

The following day, Edmund left the works in the charge of Sam Powking, an older man with a sensible head on him whom he was using as foreman for the time being. He really needed to hire an assistant engineer, but at the moment he was managing with Robbie's help, though that meant working longer hours. He walked up the hill to his cousin's house, feeling a faint sense of apprehension, not relishing the thought of the coming meeting.

Athol was propped up in bed and looked much better than the last time Edmund had seen him, though the twisted face that reminded him of a dog snarling would come as a dreadful shock to anyone who hadn't seen it before. When Terson ushered him into the bedroom he wasn't invited to sit down, which annoyed him. 'How are you feeling? Maria tells me you're getting better.'

'Damned slowly, though.'

Edmund took a chair and placed it near the foot of the bed, sitting astride it facing the invalid. When Athol didn't speak, he kept silent. He'd seen his cousin play this game too often to fall into the error of filling the silence with talk and giving away information.

In the end Athol broke the silence. 'I see you've just about drained my bank account.'

'It was that or close down the works, since you hadn't taken out insurance against fire or other mishaps. I've done that this time, by the way.'

'Well, you got your new engine in the end.'

'The engine belongs to you, actually. And it's a beauty, which will last you for many years to come and provide extra power if you should ever want to extend the works.'

'Hmm. I've been studying the accounts and I think we need to cut the men's wages to pay for the renovations more quickly.'

Trust Athol to think that way! 'If you do that, I'll leave. The men aren't generously paid now. If you cut their wages still further, they'll find it impossible to make ends meet.'

'Who cares about that? Most of them have children who can bring in an extra bob or two. Men seeking work are ten a penny. I want to see my money build up again in the bank. And anyway, I don't think you'll really leave.'

'Believe me, I will. And good, experienced men are not ten a penny. Some of your men do double the work a beginner would, and do it better, too.'

The two stared at one another, then Athol grunted. 'We'll leave it for now, but when I come back I intend to find ways to cut costs.'

So Edmund stated the obvious. 'As long as

you don't do that at the expense of safety, like last time.'

Athol's expression grew furious. 'If you'd stayed on at the works, the accident would never have happened.'

'*You* sent me away because I married Faith, actually. I didn't have the choice of staying on.' He saw Athol scowl and open his mouth, so held up one hand in a gesture to prevent him speaking. 'I'll just warn you once: if you say anything derogatory about my wife, I'll leave immediately and open up my own business.'

For a moment the two men stared at one another, then Athol pressed his lips together as if holding back further comments, so Edmund went on, trying to make sure his cousin accepted the facts, something he wasn't sure about. 'If I'd stayed on at the works I'd have closed down the engine and not used it, so it wouldn't have exploded. You'd have saved a lot of money that way, even with the expense of a new engine. It's no use employing an engineer if you don't listen to him.' He watched Athol suck in his breath as if in pain and fiddle with the bedcovers for a moment. In spite of what lay between them, he couldn't help feeling sorry for the wreck of a man his cousin had become, remembering the tall, arrogant figure which had stalked round the works before the accident.

'It seems we must work in harness for a time because of this.' Athol waved with his twisted hand at the space where his right leg should have been. 'But I want you to understand that I'm on the road to recovery now, so don't start feeling as if *you* own the works. You don't and you never will.'

'I don't want to. I'm already considering alternatives for my future. I'm only staying until you're well enough and have hired another engineer.'

'One last thing. I hear you've taken Preston back. I want that man sacked at once. He's already proved disloyal, and I didn't think even you would bring him back into *my* works.' Athol glared at his cousin.

Edmund forced back an angry rebuttal. No one could expect a man to hold back when his sister had been kidnapped and her life threatened, as Robbie's sister Carrie had been. Why no one had arrested his cousin Athol for that he would never understand, but rich men often got away with crimes that would have sent a poor man to the gallows. And no one had expected Athol to recover from his horrendous injuries.

With an effort, he spoke calmly. 'Without him I'd have to hire an assistant engineer. Robbie's good with machinery and comes much more cheaply than a trained engineer would. We save at least a pound a week by employing him.'

'You've always got an answer, haven't you?'

'It's the simple truth.'

'In that case we'll keep him on for the time being, but if he puts one foot out of line, he goes, whatever you say.' He stiffened, half-closed his eyes then wriggled as if in discomfort.

'Do you need some more laudanum for the pain? Shall I ring for Terson?'

Athol glanced at the clock. 'Not yet. I manage for a few minutes longer without that damned stuff each day. Too much of it clouds the brain. Besides, I've someone else to see after you.'

Edmund waited, trying to keep his face expressionless and pushing aside the unwanted feeling of pity for his cousin.

Athol sighed. 'You may as well leave now. I just wanted you to understand that I *am* coming back to take charge.'

'I've always understood it.' Which was a lie. Everyone had expected Athol to die of his injuries — and Edmund wouldn't have mourned his loss. Nor, he thought, would Maria have done. How must it feel to be tied for life to a husband like that? He and Faith felt extremely sorry for her.

And he *would* get his own works one day, which he would run in a fair and decent manner.

5

On the Friday of his first week's engagement in Hedderby, Denby Sinclair sat on the edge of his bed and stared round the tiny bedroom of the lodging he'd been found. What a godforsaken place this town was! How was he going to pass the time till this evening? Unfortunately, as he'd agreed to perform for two weeks at the Pride, it was cheaper to stay here in Hedderby than spend money going to and from Manchester each weekend.

He felt he'd moved beyond small places like this, but no other jobs had been on offer. One day he'd play only the biggest places, theatres as well as music saloons, and preferably those in or near London. But at least he was in work most of the time, unlike some performers, and recently one or two newspapers had called him 'a rising star' though it had taken a few years to get this far. In a few weeks' time he was going to play in London for several weeks and was looking forward to that, hoping it would lead to better things.

To make matters worse, in Hedderby they housed the unmarried men and women in different lodging houses, so he couldn't even console himself with Maud's soft, willing body. He'd take her for a walk in the countryside on Sunday if it was fine and find some private spot to lie with her and . . .

There was a knock on his bedroom door. 'Mr Sinclair?'

He pinned a smile to his face and opened it to see his landlady standing, looking anxious. 'Is something wrong, Mrs Carson?'

'I'm afraid so. I hate to be the bearer of bad news, but Elyssa, your young lady assistant, has had an accident and I'm afraid she's broken her leg.'

He stared at her in shock for a moment or two, then closed his eyes, afraid of letting his real feelings show. The stupid bitch! Maud might have a passable voice and be quite pretty, though in a coarse sort of way, but she was so clumsy he only dared give her the most simple movements on stage. Now she'd ruined everything. His latest act, which had proved very popular, depended on having a pretty young woman in it. All the stupid females in the audience pretended they were her, as some of them had written to tell him. 'How the h — how did that happen?'

'She tripped on a loose carpet runner and fell down the stairs, apparently. They've taken her to the infirmary.'

He forced himself to ask the proper questions to show his concern, 'Is it bad? How is she?'

'I'm afraid I don't know. Her landlady sent her daughter round to let us know, but the child knew no details.'

'I'll go and visit Mau — Elyssa later, but first I'll have to do something about my act. The show must go on, you know. However upset we feel, we performers never let anything stop us as long as we can stand upright.'

She nodded and turned away before he'd finished. He could see that she wasn't interested in what he had to say and she'd already proved to be impervious to his charm. He shouldn't have wasted the effort on a woman like her!

He put on his top hat and overcoat, picked up his case of song music, then made his way down the hill to the Pride. First things first. He needed to work out a new act with that stupid pianist. When he passed the pub next door he was tempted to go in for a beer, but knew it'd look bad if he was seen drinking during the daytime, so with a sigh of regret went past the open doors of the Dragon and entered the music room next to it.

The owners were standing at the back talking earnestly to one another. Eli Beckett turned at the sound of footsteps. 'Have you heard about Elyssa?' he asked at once.

Denby nodded and tried to look sad.

'Is there something you can do about your act?'

'Yes, of course. That's why I've come. Is that pianist around? I may have to change my songs.' He tapped his music case. 'It's surprising that you have a man who can't read music leading the orchestra here.'

'Raife is well liked in this town and you only have to sing a tune for him to follow it.'

'Mmm.' The fellow was probably the owner's uncle, Denby thought sourly. It was amazing the amateurs who sneaked into these small-town music rooms. He saw a girl standing nearby and automatically threw her a smile. She was pretty and was looking at him as if he were God. He enjoyed seeing that look in women's eyes, but this lass had *respectable* written all over her, so after another brief smile he turned his attention back to the matter in hand. 'I'll have to find another girl to assist me when I go back to Manchester, but in the meantime . . . I don't suppose you know of anyone in the town who could fill in for Elyssa? It isn't hard.'

They both frowned in thought then slowly shook their heads.

Joanna took it on herself to elaborate. 'There are one or two local women who sing at the Pride occasionally, but they're older and wouldn't suit your act at all.'

Marjorie couldn't help hearing this conversation. She'd been listening to Bram try out one of the new songs Eli had brought back from Manchester. When the idea of offering to take Elyssa's place popped into her mind, her heart started thumping in her chest. Could she? Dare she? Here might be a rare chance for a little excitement — if she was brave enough. She took a step forward then stopped. No, she couldn't do it. She wasn't a good enough singer.

But her movement had attracted the attention of Mr Sinclair and he was staring at her again, his eyes moving up and down her body, not in an impudent way but as if he was assessing her. When he raised one eyebrow questioningly she took another step forward, gathered all her courage together and said hesitantly. 'I could try to do it, if you like, Mr Sinclair. I'm not a very loud singer, but I can hold a tune and well, if it'll help you . . . ' She heard her voice wobble and stopped, feeling hot embarrassment colour her cheeks.

Eli and Joanna were staring at her in surprise but she didn't care about them. It was Denby Sinclair who needed someone, him she had to convince. He walked over to her and she waited breathlessly, wondering if he'd dismiss her offer out of hand. Instead he lifted her chin with one fingertip.

'You're pretty enough. Sing something for me.'

'What shall I sing?'

'Anything.'

So she sang the chorus the girl had sung on stage with him last night. As usual her voice sounded too soft and nervousness made her breathe in the wrong place.

'When did you learn that?' he demanded. 'I bought that song for myself. Have you heard someone else using it?'

'I learned it last night when I was watching the show. I really enjoyed your act, Mr Sinclair.'

He smiled. 'You're a quick learner then. Get up on the stage and sing that chorus again. Let's see how well your voice carries.'

She couldn't move for a minute and he stopped to wait for her. Then, as if he understood how nervous she was feeling, he moved closer and offered her his arm, which was kind of him. She took it gratefully and moved forward with him, sure that Queen Victoria herself couldn't have a more splendid escort.

On stage Bram was discussing the new song with Raife.

'I wonder if we could interrupt you for a moment or two?' Denby asked with one of his charming smiles. 'My regular assistant has broken her leg and this young lady wants to try out for the part.'

Bram stared at Marjorie with the same surprise as his wife Joanna had, but obligingly moved to one side.

Marjorie stepped on to the musicians' platform then up on to the stage itself. She'd stood here before when no one was around, imagining herself performing, but she'd never tried to sing.

From below her Mr Sinclair gave her another encouraging smile and that helped calm her pounding heart.

'Would you give her the chorus for 'My Heart Is Yours'?' he asked Raife, then turned back to her and said softly, 'I know you can do it.'

She listened carefully to the musical introduction, took a deep breath and came in at the right time with the chorus. When she'd finished she looked questioningly at Mr Sinclair, not even aware of the other people in the room.

'Do it again.' He walked halfway down the room then turned to face her.

She started singing, feeling a bit more confident this time because he hadn't laughed at her or told her she'd be no good.

He didn't say anything but walked right to the back and called, 'Again.'

The third time she tried to imagine she was singing to him alone and had to send her voice right down the room to him. When she'd

83

finished she waited anxiously as he came striding forward with that wonderful smile on his handsome face.

'What's your name?' He gave her a conspiratorial glance. 'Fancy me not asking you that before. I do apologise.'

'Marjorie Preston.'

'Can you act?'

'I don't know.'

He threw back his head and laughed. 'I hope you can, Miss Marjorie Preston, because if so, you've got yourself a new job.'

She had to press the flat of one hand against her chest because she felt as if her heart would jump right out of it. 'I'll do my very best, Mr Sinclair. I'll try so hard not to let you down.'

There was silence in the long narrow room, then Raife called out, 'You two had better go somewhere then and rehearse the moves. Bram here's got a new song to practise and Mr Kidd wants to try something out. If you come back in an hour or two, I'll stay on a bit longer and play for you. Marjorie love, don't forget you're going to need a pretty dress and you'd better let Nev know what you're doing.'

Denby looked at him, surprised by the tone of authority in his voice, then saw that the other people in the room were nodding. It seemed the old man had more status with the management than he'd realised. He was sorry now he'd been so sharp with him the previous day. 'Thanks, Mr — er . . . '

'Linney. As I told you yesterday.'

84

'Where can we rehearse?' Denby asked the new girl.

Marjorie stared at him blankly.

It was Eli who solved the problem. 'You can use the big room in the pub. There'll be hardly anyone in it at this time of the morning. I can't help you with the stage dress, though.'

'I'll borrow Elyssa's,' Denby said impatiently. '*She* won't be able to use it now, after all.'

★ ★ ★

To Denby's surprise the new girl picked up what he wanted her to do quickly, learned the rest of the song in a very short space of time and moved about gracefully as they practised the moves.

'You could be really good with some training,' he said idly, surprised by the glow of pleasure on her face. Clearly she was stage-struck. 'Have you ever wanted to go on the stage?'

'Oh, yes. But I didn't think I had a strong enough voice.'

'You have a charming voice and I don't want an assistant with a loud one because it's me who's the centre of the act. What I need is a woman who'll look pretty, sing in tune and play her part exactly the way I tell her. Which I think you'll do very nicely. And actually, for a soft voice yours carries quite well.'

After an hour's practice they left the Pride to walk along to the infirmary and ask Elyssa if they could borrow her stage costume. 'Poor girl,' Marjorie said in her soft voice. 'She'll be so upset.'

They found her lying in bed in an almost empty ward. She'd been weeping and her face was blotchy, her eyes were swollen. Because the new girl was there Denby forced himself to speak gently, asking Elyssa if he could send a message to her family seeking their help.

'They'll say I told you so,' she sobbed. 'You know they didn't want me to go on the stage in the first place. Can't *you* look after me?'

'You know I can't. It wouldn't be proper. And anyway, the show must go on. I'll be busy training Marjorie and then I'll have to move on. No, I'm afraid you need your family to look after you till your leg gets better, Maud, and I'm sure they won't refuse, given the circumstances.' He took out a little pocket book and scribbled down her parents' address. 'Now, Marjorie will need to borrow your costume.'

'I don't want *her* using it.'

'*Maud.*'

She looked at him pleadingly, but he wasn't having that. 'I'll pay you five shillings for the hire of the dress for the rest of the two weeks,' he said. 'And for the loan of the right sort of corset.'

'All right. But she'd better not dirty the things. They're in my room.' She scowled at Marjorie and snapped, 'It needs to be worn with the long stays.' Then her voice softened as she added, 'Denby, can I see you alone, please?'

'I'll go outside,' Marjorie said hastily.

Denby waited until she'd left then turned to the girl in the bed, not smiling now. 'Well?'

'I can come back once my leg's better, can't I?'

He looked at her then decided on the truth. 'No. I was going to find another girl anyway. You're pretty enough, but you don't move well on stage.'

She burst into loud sobs and a woman came in, scowling at him. 'She won't get well if you upset her like this.'

'I'd better leave then.'

'Denby, wait! Surely you can't — not after all we've been to one another . . . ' Her voice trailed away as she saw his cold expression.

'It's over, and not just because of the leg.' He turned and walked out.

★   ★   ★

On the way back Denby stopped to buy a piece of writing paper and paid the shopkeeper an extra halfpenny to borrow pen and ink. He scribbled a hasty note to Maud's family and folded the piece of paper carefully, so that the message was inside, then begged the loan of some sealing wax to secure it. After purchasing a penny stamp from the post office he put the letter in the post with a feeling that now he'd done his duty by the girl.

Outside he offered his arm to Marjorie, who took it, feeling flustered but proud to walk through the streets with him.

At the women's lodging house, a stern-faced woman at first refused to allow him inside, then grudgingly admitted him, standing by the bedroom door as he took Maud's dress from the hook where it was hanging and sorted through

87

her underwear. He clearly knew what he was looking for.

'Shocking!' the landlady muttered quite audibly. 'No better than she should be, that one.'

Denby ignored her and studied Marjorie carefully. 'Try these on. I think you're a little plumper than she is, but it may not matter.'

'She's not trying them on with you here,' the landlady said in scandalised tones. 'I run a respectable house here.'

So he went to pace up and down the entrance hall while the landlady stood guard outside the bedroom. When the door opened again he looked up and saw Marjorie standing on the landing, her hair loose about her shoulders and her figure shown to much better advantage in the costume than in her own nondescript garments. The audiences would love those soft curves. 'That looks good. Walk down the stairs.' He watched carefully, delighted by her innate grace. He just hoped she could retain that grace of movement on the stage. If so, with a little coaching she'd be much better in the role of his assistant.

If she could perform in front of an audience. That was the main thing to find out now.

'Poor Maud,' Marjorie said in her soft voice. 'I do feel sorry for her.'

He took her hand. 'Hang Maud.' He saw the shock in her eyes and added hastily, 'I have to think of the audience. We can't disappoint them. *You* are my Elyssa now — and theirs. Go back up and change into your normal clothes, then we'll try it out on the stage.' As she turned, he saw her feet more clearly. 'Wait! What about the shoes?'

'Maud's are too small for me, I'm afraid. I couldn't even get my foot into one.'

'Is there a pawnbroker's in town?'

'Yes.'

'We'll go and see if they have anything that fits.' He turned to the landlady. 'Is there someone who can deliver the costume to the Pride?'

'My son will do it for threepence.'

He felt in his pocket for the coin then waited for Marjorie to rejoin him, restored to good humour now. What a bit of luck finding a girl like her! And in Hedderby of all places! His instinct told him she'd be the perfect foil for him on stage, the same instinct that was never wrong about how he performed, though it had let him down a few times in other parts of his life.

★   ★   ★

When Marjorie and Sinclair had left, Raife sighed. He didn't like to think of her being mixed up with that fellow, but she'd looked so starry eyed when she stood on the stage and sang that Raife hadn't had the heart to spoil things for her. It was only for a few days, after all, and would be something she'd remember all her life.

'Can we try out my new piece, Mr Linney? Do you have time?'

He turned to smile at Hal Kidd, the comedian. 'Of course we can. I must say I enjoyed your act last night, son. You've a real gift for comedy.'

'Thank you.'

'Have you heard the news? Elyssa's broken her leg and they've taken her to the infirmary.'

'Poor lass!' Hal said automatically. He didn't much like Elyssa, who was rather spiteful, but he felt sorry for her, as he'd feel sorry for anyone who was dependent on Denby Sinclair. He didn't know when he'd taken such a dislike to anyone, but the singer had assumed an air of superiority, expecting the other performers to defer to him, and that had annoyed Hal. And yes, Sinclair had a very good voice and looked handsome and charming on stage, but off stage he didn't always bother with the charm and then his real nature was revealed.

Only last night he'd made Elyssa cry after the performance, claiming she'd messed up his act for no reason that Hal could tell. He'd treated Raife scornfully too at first, till he found out Raife was related to the owners. Everyone else liked the old man for himself and he was a very good musician whether he could read music or not. Once he knew his cues, Raife came in with the right sort of musical accompaniment at exactly the time Hal wanted, and he was as pleasant as you like to deal with.

'Sinclair will have to find hissen a new lass when he leaves here,' Raife said, 'else he'll have to change his act.'

'He's a good-looking fellow.'

'Aye, but handsome is as handsome does, I allus say!'

Hal looked quickly sideways. 'You don't like him either.'

'No. He's a bad 'un, I reckon. He'll probably go far, though. He looks good on the stage and women have allus been fools for good-looking chaps.'

Hal smiled and let the subject drop, continuing to explain his new comedy routine. 'What do you think?'

'Sounds good. Let's try it out,' Raife urged.

When they'd finished rehearsing, Hal walked back to his lodgings. He'd watched enviously from the side of the long music room as Sinclair poured out his charm and yet again a young woman fell for it. Hal had been nerving himself up to speak to that particular girl, because she'd popped in both days to watch the rehearsals and she had such a fresh, pretty face that he wanted to get to know her. But lasses didn't notice him when Sinclair was around. And why should they? He was probably shorter than her, too, because she was quite tall.

With a wry smile, he left his things in his bedroom and went out for a stroll in the sunshine. It was a nice little town with a pretty river running through it and of course the bridge it was named for. While he was standing on that bridge, he thought of a new bit for his act, about a lovelorn lad, which brought another wry smile to his face. That was him, wasn't it, a lovelorn lad who never got lasses interested in him? He couldn't see that changing now. He was twenty-eight after all, and never been kissed in

91

passion. Lasses liked him, but only as a brotherly figure.

★ ★ ★

When they got back to the Pride, complete with a pair of pretty shoes which Mr Sinclair had bought for her, Marjorie began to feel nervous again.

Denby squeezed her hand. 'Don't worry. You'll be good on stage, far better than Maud.'

'How can I be? I've never performed in public in my life before.'

'You were made for it. I can tell. You move gracefully, look pretty and your voice is sweet and tuneful. Maud had never been on the stage, either, when I first found her, but I taught her how to do it and turned her into my Elyssa. I can teach you too.'

'In just a few hours?' She didn't think that was possible. Carrie and Robbie were the clever ones of the family and Marjorie knew she wasn't nearly as quick on the uptake as they were.

'Well, you've seen the act so you know how it should be and we'll tell the audience how you've stepped in at the last minute to help me, so they'll be on your side, especially with you being a Hedderby girl. Audiences love that sort of thing.'

She didn't feel as sure as he did but was determined to do her best and not waste this chance for a bit of excitement.

When they went into the Dragon, Carrie came hurrying across to her sister. 'Nev came round to see if you were here. He was worried about you. You didn't let him know what you were doing, did you?'

'Oh, dear! I completely forgot.'

'Well, I think I've made it right with him, but don't forget to apologise for not telling him what's happened. He's coming to see you perform tonight and bringing Dora with him.'

Marjorie could feel her apprehension grow at the mere thought of that. 'I wish they wouldn't! It'll be far worse with them watching me.'

'Are you nervous, love?'

She nodded. 'But I'm not letting that stop me. Oh, Carrie, it's what I've always wanted to do.'

'Go on the stage?'

'Yes. You know how I love coming here.'

'This is only for a week or so, remember.'

'Yes. But it'll be something to think about afterwards, something special. I get so fed up of being shut up inside that house.' She saw Mr Sinclair looking at her and blushed. 'Sorry. I shouldn't be wasting time chatting when we need to practise on the stage.'

He smiled — he had such a lovely smile — and put one hand on her arm. 'I keep telling you, you'll do fine. Now, go and change into that pretty dress. It'll give you more confidence. And my name is Denby, not Mr Sinclair.'

She turned to her sister. 'Will you come and help me change, Carrie?'

'Of course. We'll go up to my bedroom.'

Marjorie was sure nothing would give her confidence, but found that the dress did help. It was so pretty, very full-skirted, made of pale blue tarlatan printed with little flowers in blue and lavender, and it had a deep frill round the bottom. She had a struggle to get into the stays but with Carrie's help she managed. They made her waist much smaller and pushed up her breasts, showing them off in a way that both embarrassed and thrilled her.

Carrie looked at her doubtfully. 'It's a bit . . . revealing. That neckline's far too low.'

'The ladies who sit at the front wear dresses just as low cut.' Marjorie twisted and turned in front of the mirror. 'I've never worn anything half as pretty. I wish I could always wear clothes like this.'

'Well, if it's what you want to do, I wish you well, love.'

'It *is* what I want.' Taking a deep breath, Marjorie walked out to rehearse and had the pleasure of seeing Mr Sinclair's — no, Denby's — eyes brighten at the sight of her in all her finery, with her hair properly pinned up. Only he came and pulled the pins out of her hair and spread it over her shoulders instead.

'You have lovely hair. Leave it loose.'

She could see Carrie frowning, but ignored that. 'Whatever you think best.'

* * *

Bram looked at his wife as they got the place ready for the first show of the evening, in which he'd be singing. 'How did Marjorie go in the rehearsal?'

'She did well — ' Joanna hesitated then added

94

reluctantly, ' — more than well. She floated through it with a smile on her face and even Raife admitted she's got talent.'

'It's a bit different when there's an audience watching. I hope she won't let that put her off.'

'I don't think she will. She's not like me.'

'One day I'll get you on that stage. It's a shame to keep a voice like yours hidden.'

She laughed. 'You'd have to drag me on by my hair. The mere thought of standing up there in front of so many people makes me shiver. I'm not confident like you, Bram. You have to accept that.'

In the little room behind the stage where the performers sat while they waited to go on, Marjorie could feel her nervousness increasing by the minute. She'd come in here early to avoid seeing Nev and to get away from her family, but the minute she stepped out on to that stage, they'd all be watching her.

Denby sat down beside her and laid his hand on hers. 'You did beautifully earlier when we were rehearsing. You only have to do the same thing and the audience will love you.'

'My family will be there this time, though.'

He smiled and raised her hand to his lips, kissing it, his eyes meeting hers. 'You'll notice only me. Come. It's time to go on. I can hear Mr Kidd finishing his act.' Still holding her hand in his, he led her out on to the stage.

★ ★ ★

Nev sat there dumbfounded. He couldn't believe it was their Marjorie up on the stage, she looked so pretty, moved so gracefully and sang beautifully. Like the rest of the audience, he applauded loudly. This was his stepdaughter, a Hedderby lass, singing and dancing up there like a young princess.

Beside him Dora was equally surprised and not a little jealous. She was a few seconds late in joining in the applause because she just couldn't believe it was her sister up there.

In another part of the audience Jack Benting scowled at the stage.

His neighbour nudged him. 'Aren't you clapping our Hedderby lass?'

'I were a bit dumbfounded like. She used to work at the mill, that one.' He looked the other way, not anxious to continue the conversation. It upset him to hear folk applauding *her* and he certainly wasn't joining in. But on his other side his own wife was clapping away just as loudly as the others, so he took a good long slurp of his beer. He hated this place. Before it opened he'd been able to spend his Fridays and Saturdays with his own kind, drinking beer without anyone counting how many glasses and talking of what they pleased, men's talk. Now his wife insisted on him bringing her here every week. It was a waste of money and spoiled his Fridays, but he didn't dare refuse because Melie could make his life miserably uncomfortable if he didn't do what she wanted.

★ ★ ★

After the show, Nev and Dora waited for Marjorie in the kitchen of the pub, and when she came in, everyone cheered and told her how good she'd been. Behind her Denby smiled and nodded, but was disappointed to find that her family had waited to walk her home. He'd intended to do that himself and to see if he could win a kiss from her as a preliminary to better things.

The stepfather came up to him. 'How much are you paying her?'

Nearby Eli hid a smile. He'd been about to check up on that little matter himself because he was quite sure Marjorie wouldn't have bothered to ask.

Denby kept a pleasant expression on his face only with difficulty. He had deliberately not talked about payment, hoping to get away with some token sum at the end of the performing week. He glanced sideways and saw the owner watching him. Better to give in gracefully. 'Thirty shillings,' he said, which was a little less than he'd paid Elyssa, but not much.

'Not enough,' Nev said at once. 'Two pounds or she doesn't go on tomorrow.'

Marjorie gasped and opened her mouth to protest, but Eli nudged her. 'Shh. Let Nev do this for you.'

'But I — '

'Sinclair is offering you less than he paid the other lass, and even with her he wasn't generous.'

'Oh.' She looked at the two men thoughtfully and wasn't surprised when Nev got Denby to

97

agree to pay her two pounds. It was the first time she'd earned anything like that amount and she wished she didn't have to give it to Nev.

'It's only fair that he pays you properly,' Eli went on, still in a low voice. 'Don't ever sell yourself short, lass. Considering it was your first time on stage, you were really good tonight, and will only get better.'

She was thrilled to get such praise from her brother-in-law. 'Do you truly think so?'

'Of course I do. I wouldn't lie to you nor would I let you make a fool of yourself in public. Besides, I've seen enough acts to know that you're a natural.'

'I still don't have a good enough voice, though.'

'Your voice isn't good enough for a solo singing act, I agree, but it's plenty good enough for you to appear with other people.'

She hadn't thought she was good enough for that, either. Later, when Denby had left town, she'd ask Eli how you found a job on stage as part of an act.

Nev beckoned and she went across to join him.

Carrie frowned at her husband. 'Why did you say that to her. This is only for the one week, surely?'

'Who knows what'll come of it? The other young woman won't be fit to go on stage again for a couple of months, so Sinclair will need someone. And your sister *is* good, far better than the original Elyssa.'

'Don't you go putting ideas into her head.'

'She's got them there already, love. *She* was the one who volunteered to help him out. No one was even looking at her, let alone suggesting her for the part.'

'But Eli, it'd not be decent to go off travelling around the countryside with a strange man.'

He shrugged. 'It's not your decision or mine whether she does that, Carrie love. It's up to Marjorie. She's old enough now to decide what she wants out of life.'

Which made Carrie worry even more about her next sister. She might not be responsible for looking after her brothers and sisters now, but they were still part of her and except for Robbie, she felt responsible for their welfare. She worried about Eli, too, sometimes. Her husband was very ambitious, was talking now about getting a proper theatre one day, when they'd only had the Pride open a few weeks. Where would it all end?

⋆   ⋆   ⋆

Back at Linney's, Gwynna sat in the kitchen, the baby asleep in a crib beside her. She loved this room, loved the warmth of it, the way people came and went, and not people who shouted at you or hit you. Friendly people. Little Sylvie was thriving and she was pleased about that. When Mr Linney didn't need her any more here, she was going to apply for a job as a nurse maid. Raife had told her about that sort of work and it sounded heavenly. She loved caring for little Sylvie and particularly enjoyed the company of Lily and Grace, the youngest of the Prestons.

Children were so direct and honest about what they felt.

The only person she wasn't quite easy with here at Linney's was Marjorie, who always had her head in the clouds. Gwynna couldn't believe how untidy she was. If this house had been hers, Gwynna would have had everything in its place and would have loved keeping it in apple-pie order.

There was a knock on the outside door that led to a hallway between the kitchen and the lodgers' area. Ted got up to answer it. 'There's a fellow wants a lodgings for the night.'

Dora was out with Nev at the music room and Edith wasn't back from the shop yet, so Gwynna stood up. 'I'll come. You keep an eye on Sylvie.'

The man at the door looked her up and down in a way she hated and she almost told him they were full, but she knew Nev would be angry if she lost him a customer. 'Threepence for the night, paid in advance,' she said curtly.

'Other places let you pay in the morning. How do I know you won't cheat me?'

'Because we've a good reputation in this town. Ask anyone. Pay in advance or you can't come in.'

He fumbled in his clothing and produced sixpence. 'Got any food?'

'Bread and dripping, penny a slice. Big cup of tea, penny.'

'I'll have two slices of bread and a cup of tea.'

As she took his money he looked at her avidly, as if he wanted to eat her as well as the food, and suddenly she felt nervous. 'I'll send Ted to show you the way. I've got a baby to feed. Ted! Ted, can you come out here, please?'

As soon as she mentioned the baby, the man stopped looking at her in that openly nasty way, thank goodness.

'I need your name for the record book,' she said. 'The police insist.'

'Wiv Blaydon.'

She nodded and stepped backwards as Ted came out of the kitchen to join her. 'Give this man a blanket and find him a place in the common room, then get him two pieces of bread and dripping and a cup of tea.' She was glad to get back into the kitchen, where Lily and Grace were lying on the rag rug looking at a book Raife had bought for them. When Ted came in to get the food, Gwynna said curtly, 'Lock that door after you've given that newcomer his bread and tea.'

He looked at her curiously.

'I don't trust him. I reckon he's what Nev would call a 'needy mizzler', the sort who'd sneak out without paying.'

'I can't see anyone getting away with that here. Nev keeps a careful eye on things.'

'I'll be glad when he gets back. And don't forget to go and get the tea cup back when he's had time to drink it.'

An hour later, after the younger children had gone to bed, she saw the handle of the door to the common lodgings area turn and held her breath. It turned back just as quietly when whoever it was discovered it was locked. 'Did you see that?' she asked Ted in a whisper.

101

He nodded. 'We've got a bad 'un there, I reckon. Wonder if the police are after him?' They got villains sometimes, who tried to pinch other folk's belongings, but Nev locked the lodgers in overnight and they didn't often get away with it. The police came regularly to check who was staying and they always complimented Nev on how well the place was run. He'd rearranged the house soon after he married Ted's mother and now the common lodgings area was completely separate and the door to it could be locked. They all preferred that because there were some strange people coming in for a night's shelter, people who looked as if they'd slit your throat for twopence.

Edith came home from the shop just then, full of tales of her customers, and things seemed to brighten up again in the kitchen. She was Ted's favourite sister, lively and clever, could add up anything in her head, and if she wasn't pretty like Marjorie, who cared? She made him laugh, cheered everyone up.

No need to be frightened, Gwynna told herself as she too settled down. There were enough of them here to be safe. Ted was nearly eleven, almost as tall as she was, and Edith might be wiry, but she was strong from lifting things in the shop.

Gwynna decided to tell Nev about the latecomer when he returned, though. There was something about the man that worried her. And why had he tried the kitchen door?

When Nev heard who the latecomer was, he scowled. 'If I'd been here that one wouldn't have got a bed. Remember that, everyone! Wiv Blaydon is not to be admitted again. And I'll tell him so myself in the morning.'

'What's he done?' Ted asked.

'He's a thief and maybe worse. Used to be a prize fighter, now finds easier ways to get his hands on money. He grew up here. I wouldn't trust him an inch. If you'd left that door unlocked he'd have stolen something.'

6

Terson brought two men into the house and led them upstairs to his master's bedchamber. As they stood at the foot of the bed, shifting their feet uncomfortably and holding shapeless felt hats in their hands, Athol studied them carefully. He knew Wiv Blaydon and Tait Arner from his days at the engineering works. Wiv had left to go and work in Manchester, but he'd brought the fellow into town especially to help teach Eli Beckett a lesson for daring to defy him. When his uncle died, Beckett had refused to sell him the land next to the pub and had built that damned music room on it instead. Sadly, Athol's plan hadn't worked because he'd underestimated Beckett's friendship with Bram Heegan, who had a network of Irish brutes ready to defy their betters.

Well, both those men would find out that Athol wasn't a spent force yet, not by any means.

The two men were ugly brutes. Wiv was an ageing prize-fighter, taller than common people usually were, with a battered face, while Tait was shorter but built like a tree trunk and just as gnarled. He had his feet planted wide now and was staring back openly. The fellow had been a labourer at Stott's, but Athol's cousin had dismissed him for skimping his work and fighting on the job. Now Tait harboured a grudge against Edmund and against most of the world as well, it seemed from the way he talked. Which suited Athol's purpose just fine.

He envied them their sturdy bodies so keenly that for a moment or two he couldn't speak, only choke back the rage that boiled inside him whenever he wasn't doped by laudanum.

'I've explained about the job, sir, and given these men some details about the services you'll need from them.'

Terson was speaking in that toneless voice he could summon up at will and which usually meant he disapproved of something. In this case, no doubt, the kind of men Athol had chosen to bring into his house as possible replacements for him. Well, let the fellow disapprove. He'd soon be gone. Athol didn't care about the niceties of life any longer because with a face like his, he could no longer go about in polite society. He didn't need a finicky valet now to look after his clothes, but men who could help him as he needed with various embarrassing aspects of personal care. He also wanted men who would do other jobs for him, who wouldn't balk at anything as long as he paid them well.

'Well?' he asked them. 'Think you can do it? You won't be put off by having to look after my body? Or by being asked to do other jobs for me?'

'I'm happy to do owt if I'm well paid, sir,' Wiv said. 'And we've all got bodies. I don't suppose yours is all that different to mine when it comes down to it.'

'Same goes for me — sir.'

Tait spoke more slowly with a broad

105

Lancashire accent. He hadn't stopped looking round since he'd come in, when he wasn't studying his new master, that was.

'I've had some bloody tight weeks since yon cousin sacked me,' Tait added suddenly.

'Never mind that,' Athol said. 'He's probably done you a favour because now you can work for me and earn far more money.' Tait didn't look convinced but he ignored that and went on, 'The first and most important thing about coming to work for me is that you do *exactly* what I want at all times. No drinking on the job, either. You save that for your night off. In fact, no doing *anything* without my say so. And not a word about what goes on in this room or this house to others. You'll be paid very well indeed for your silence, more money than you've ever earned in your life before, I dare say.'

They looked at him, then exchanged satisfied glances and nodded.

'What about your family, Tait? You've a wife and children, haven't you?'

'As long as I give them some money, they'll be no worry. I shan't miss them bloody kids allus making a racket an' quarrelling, that I shan't.'

'Let's see how we all feel after a week's trial, for which I'll pay you two guineas each, one in advance.'

They brightened and assured him of their pleasure at the prospect of serving him. He knew better. Their pleasure lay in the money to be gained. But he didn't mind that. At least men like these would bring no stupid moral scruples to the tasks he needed doing.

106

He caught Terson's eye. 'Ask Mrs Stott to join us.'

★ ★ ★

Maria stared at the two men in shock when Athol introduced them to her, looked at him quickly, saw the mockery in his face and summoned up her calm, obedient expression only with difficulty. But she was horrified by them and knew he'd noticed that, would be amused by it. And the shorter one seemed to have his cruel nature written on his face.

'They'll have to bathe regularly if they're to live in this house,' she said, 'and they'll need some new clothes.'

Now Athol's mockery was aimed at the men. 'You heard my lady wife. She has a sensitive nose. You'll wash regularly so as not to offend her — or me. Terson, see that they're bathed and decently clad before you start showing them what's needed.' As the men turned to leave, he added sharply, 'Another thing. You'll treat my wife with the greatest respect at all times, and my children too. Nor will you lay one finger on any of the maidservants in this house. That's how things are done in the homes of the gentry, so that's how you'll behave if you want to earn the best money you've ever seen in your lives.' He watched them consider this.

Wiv nodded first. To Athol, he seemed the more intelligent of the two, though Tait had a certain low cunning. 'Well, then, lady wife, perhaps you'll see about finding them a bedroom?'

'Certainly.' But something inside her shuddered to think of these two brutes — she could think of no other word to describe them — living in her house. And she knew her maidservants would be upset too.

'Leave me, then, Terson. I shan't need any help for the next half-hour, after which I'll need a piss and a dose of laudanum.'

Maria breathed in slowly and deeply, furious at the way Athol had started to use coarse language in front of her.

When the three men had left, he leaned back against his pillows with a sigh. 'Well, they didn't faint at the sight of me, at least.'

She couldn't resist asking, 'Can you not find decent men to serve you?'

'Tait and Wiv are decent enough for my needs. Finicky men like Terson find serving me distasteful. And I need someone strong enough to lift me easily. I shan't be staying in this bedroom for ever. Already I'm managing for longer each day without that damned laudanum. Soon I intend to be out and about.'

She inclined her head.

'Tomorrow I wish to see my sons.'

She frowned at him. 'You don't usually bother with them.' She saw anger rise in his face and added quickly, 'At what time?'

'In the morning, about ten. You'll bring them here and leave them with me. It's time they grew used to this new face of mine.'

When she left she held back her shudders till

she'd reached the safety of her own bedroom, then closed the door and leaned against it, feeling sick to her soul. He was mad, quite mad. She'd thought that for a while and was convinced of it now. He was planning something or he'd not have employed men like those. But she wasn't going to let him destroy her sons' lives. This time, whatever she had to do to stop him, she would.

She took a few minutes to compose herself then went to consult her housekeeper.

Mrs Ibster, who had already encountered the two new men, couldn't hide her dismay. 'I never thought to see people like that employed in a gentleman's household.'

Maria hesitated then decided to be frank. 'Nor I. But if you betray your feelings to my husband, he'll dismiss you and appoint someone of his own choosing. I need you here most desperately, Mrs Ibster. He's getting better at last and will soon be out and about again.' Her voice broke and she couldn't continue, only look pleadingly at the woman who'd been her housekeeper ever since she married and who knew many of the dark secrets of this unhappy household.

The two women looked at one another in silence then Mrs Ibster risked patting her employer's hand and Maria clutched hers for a moment, blinking rapidly to banish the tears this unspoken sympathy called up. 'Thank you.' It was a mere whisper.

'We'll manage,' Mrs Ibster said in her usual brisk tone. 'Them two can sleep in the west attic, which has its own stairs, so that the girls and I feel safe. And we'll have bolts put on the inside of all our doors as well, if you don't mind — your bedroom too, don't you think?' She was relieved when her mistress nodded agreement. 'It won't take much to furnish a bedroom for them. I doubt they're used to the niceties of life.'

'My husband wishes them to be clean, at least.'

'Thank the Lord for that.'

'I've no doubt they'll eat heartily. Where shall you serve their meals?'

Mrs Ibster thought for a moment. 'They'll have to eat with the rest of us servants. It'd look strange for them to eat anywhere else.'

'I'll have a word with Terson, see if he can teach them a few table manners before he leaves.'

★　★　★

When the housekeeper and Terson showed them up to the bedroom they'd share, both men grinned as they took in its comfort. Tait went to bounce on the bed and grunt his approval. Wiv looked at the housekeeper's body appraisingly, but at the sight of her frosty expression he abandoned any hope of getting her into bed. Perhaps the maids would be more accommodating. What his master didn't see wouldn't bother him.

Mrs Ibster looked at Terson and said with chilly politeness, 'Perhaps you could show them where the bath house is, then send them to the kitchen for hot water?'

He nodded. 'Certainly, Mrs Ibster.'

'They'll need some clean clothes.'

'We'll go out and buy some before they bathe. I'll need one of the maids to sit with Mr Stott while we're away, though. I'll give him his medicine before I leave, so he'll be drowsy.'

'I'll do it myself. But don't take too long, please. I'm a busy woman.' The girls she employed hated to go in that room, she knew, but so far at least the master had always treated her with politeness, even if he did have a mocking tone when he spoke to her.

When she'd gone, Tait looked at Terson. 'Tight-faced old besom she is.'

Terson had already taken their measure. 'Yes, but she's a good housekeeper, so treat her right and she'll see you comfortable. She's in charge of food and keeps a good table for the servants. Stay on her right side and you'll eat like kings.'

Wiv licked his lips, Tait nodded acceptance.

'Only thing is, she's a bit particular about table manners and anyway, if you're a gentleman's servants, you won't want to look ignorant in front of the other staff.'

'I know my manners when I bother,' Wiv said. 'I'll teach Tait for you.'

'You're sure?'

'Oh, yes. I can handle a knife and fork with the best of them. I was brung up proper, even if I didn't stay proper.'

'That'll be a great help to me. Now, let me see to the master, then we'll go out and buy you some clothes. When you get back you can have a

111

bath and change. If you're taken on permanently, you'll need to wash regularly and I expect he'll buy you some more clothes.'

'We'll be living a comfortable life here,' Wiv said with relish.

'You'll pay for it in other ways. He's not easy to serve.' Terson hesitated, then added, 'Never forget that he's in pain all the time. A lesser man would have given in to it. He's got courage, you have to grant him that. But the pain makes him sharp-tempered, then he lashes out, so watch your step.'

As he led the way downstairs, Terson could only be grateful that his time here was coming to an end. There was an atmosphere in the house since the accident that gave him the shivers sometimes. And it upset Mrs Stott too, he knew. He'd seen her more than once coming out of the master's bedroom and hurrying into her own room, looking upset.

★ ★ ★

Marjorie had never been as happy in her whole life. After the first night of performing she wasn't nervous because she found it easy enough to move around the stage with Denby, acting and singing. He gave her such confidence and spent time coaching her. She knew she was improving all the time. And Raife, dear Raife, was helping her to sing better, showing her how to manage her breathing and get the best out of her voice.

The other performers were just as friendly, especially the comic. What a dear, kind man Mr

Kidd was! He'd explained all sorts of things to her while she was waiting for Denby to arrive the other day. Why Denby didn't seem to like him, she couldn't understand.

After the two Saturday night shows, Denby asked her to go for a walk with him on the moors the next day because the weather promised to be fine.

'Oh dear, I'd really like to, but I don't think Nev will let me.'

'You're twenty-one, aren't you? Your own woman, surely?'

She smiled. 'Not quite twenty-one yet. Besides, I live with Nev and he's very good to us, so I don't want to upset him.' And she didn't want to risk being alone with Denby, who set her senses swimming he was so handsome. She had enough common sense to know what he wanted from her, but Gwynna's situation had emphasised how hard life could be for an unmarried woman expecting a baby so Marjorie didn't intend to get into the same sort of trouble, not for anything.

Anyway, Denby would be leaving Hedderby the following week and she would still be here. She didn't let herself forget that, didn't let herself dream of anything more permanent with a man like him. With a smile she took her leave.

Denby watched her go, admiring the light, fluid way she walked and held her body.

He went for a walk on his own on the Sunday, thinking seriously about what to do. He had to find a permanent replacement for Elyssa and dammit, Marjorie was perfect for the part. But he wasn't sure whether that family of hers, who guarded her so carefully, would let her go on tour with him. During the walk he decided to try to persuade this Nev to give permission for her to work as his assistant. Surely the man wouldn't quibble when he found she'd be earning good money? And once they were on the road together, Denby was sure he could charm her into his bed. He'd seen the way she looked at him. But even if he couldn't, she'd enhance his performance and that was more important than anything.

On the Sunday evening as they sat together waiting for their turn to go on stage, he said quietly, 'Would you consider doing this with me permanently?'

Marjorie stared at him, her blue eyes wide with surprise. 'You mean — become your assistant, leave here with you?'

He smiled and took her hand, 'Yes. I find it easier to obtain engagements if I have a young lady assisting me, and if I make my act into little stories. It's a bit of an improvement on straight singing and it goes down well.'

'I'd *love* to do it permanently. Oh, Denby, are you sure? Am I really good enough?'

It amazed him that she had any doubts. 'Haven't you heard the applause after we've done our act?'

'Yes, but I thought that was for you. I know what my voice is like — far too soft — and I haven't any experience apart from these few shows, and well, I didn't dare hope.'

'My dear girl!' He leaned across to kiss her

114

cheek. 'Of course you're good enough. And more than that, I love working with you. Haven't you realised that yet? You're as different to my previous Elyssa as chalk and cheese, though you'll have to keep the same name, because the bills will already have been printed for my next shows.'

She beamed at him. 'I like the name.'

'I thought it'd be best if I came and asked your stepfather's permission.' He waited for her to speak but she just sat there, brow furrowed. 'Well, is something wrong?'

She sighed. 'I'm not sure he'll let me do it.'

'We'll persuade him.'

'Let me speak to him first, please.'

'Very well. Whatever you wish.'

★ ★ ★

Hal had finished his act and was sitting in the corner waiting for the finale when they'd all go on stage and sing a final song together. Not all places did this, but Raife was keen on it and certainly the audience at the Pride seemed to love it, joining in lustily in the choruses of the simple, well-known song chosen. After that, the audience always moved on without prompting to what they regarded as their own song, 'Pride of Lancashire' a catchy tune that Raife had written specially for the music room.

Hal went into the wings to watch Sinclair's act because of *her*, mocking himself for doing so. The fellow had turned all of his undeniable charm on that poor lass and Hal felt sick to his guts to think of her falling in love with such a selfish sod. Sinclair had treated the other assistant scornfully, making her cry more than once that Hal had seen, so who knows what had happened behind closed doors? Once a bully, always a bully. And they all knew he'd been bedding the other one.

So far, however, Sinclair had been kind enough to Marjorie, and Hal would guess he hadn't managed to bed her because her family were keeping a close eye on her, with Raife always there to walk her home after the shows. He was glad of that. He might not be able to attract her himself, but he still admired her, wished he had a chance with her, enjoyed chatting to her. If her family let her go on tour with Sinclair, sadly, there was nothing Hal could do to prevent it. She *was* good on stage and that fellow knew it. He'd be a fool to lose someone like her.

With a sigh for his own foolishness, Hal continued to watch her. She was better with the timing tonight, seemed less nervous altogether. And the audience loved her, not just because she was a local lass, but because she was good on stage, with a hint of vulnerability in her pretty face that was very appealing.

★   ★   ★

Nev was worried. People he met in the street kept congratulating him on his stepdaughter's talent. Well, he'd seen for himself how pretty she looked on stage and how nicely she sang. But

116

who was he to judge? What did he know about artistes?

He took his father aside. 'How good is Marjorie? I didn't think she had a strong enough voice to go on stage.'

Raife looked at him shrewdly. 'Worried about her, are you?'

Nev nodded. He felt a bit embarrassed as he added, 'I've grown fond of them, all of them. I know they're not my children, but I *feel* like their father now, and well, they have no one else to look after their interests. So tell me how good she really is.'

'Very good indeed. You're right that she's not got a strong voice, but it's true and sweet, and it carries surprisingly well. But that's not what makes her good. It's how she is on the stage. She has a — a presence that comes across to the audience. She's graceful, people like to watch her and she likes to perform.'

'Oh, dear.'

Raife knew exactly what Nev meant by that. 'You'll not stop her doing it, lad, not if she's got the taste for it.'

'But it's not *respectable* for a young woman to go on the stage. Maybe it's all right for women who're married to actors, but if our Marjorie went off performing all over England with that fellow, I'd be worried sick about her.'

'I would too.'

'You would?' Nev looked at his father in surprise.

'Yes. I reckon Sinclair's ruthless under all that charm. He wasn't at all polite to me at first, not till he realised I've got some say at the Pride, then suddenly he couldn't have been nicer. But his sort don't fool me. They allus give themselves away.'

Both men were silent for a few moments, then Nev asked, 'Do you think he'll want her to go on performing with him?'

'Bound to. His act's twice as good with her in it.'

'Well, I can't let her go off on her own with him. It's going to upset her, I can see that, but I just can't in all conscience give my permission.'

'She's nearly twenty-one.'

'But not quite. There's another three months to go till her birthday. Till then, she has to do as I say. And by then he'll have found someone else for his act.'

'Unless she runs away with him.'

More silence, then Nev said, 'She won't do that. Not our Marjorie. She's too soft to stand up to anyone.'

Raife wasn't so sure about that. Even soft women found backbone when they fell in love and that girl looked at Sinclair as if he was the sun and moon rolled into one.

* * *

The next day Marjorie asked Nev if she could speak to him privately. Heart sinking he led the way into the parlour, gestured to a seat and waited.

'Denby's asked me to go with him and be a permanent part of his act. He says I'm good on

118

stage. Isn't that wonderful?'

Nev sighed and contemplated his hands for a minute, then looked up. 'No, it isn't. You *are* good on the stage, I'm not denying that, love, but it's not respectable for a young, unmarried lass to go off with a fellow like him.'

She stared at him open-mouthed, then as his words sank in, tears formed in her eyes. 'I thought you'd be glad for me. I'm earning good money, far more than I'd ever have made in the mill, and Denby says I'll earn more when we're better known.'

'It's not the money. It's not even the appearing on stage. It's — well, you're not wed to him and you'd be travelling all over the place together. It's not respectable. I'd be failing your mother if I let you go, and failing you, too.'

She began sobbing. 'You can't stop me!'

'I can. You're not twenty-one yet.'

Her sobs grew louder. 'I'll run away.'

'If you do, I'll never let you come back, so you'll be giving up your whole family as well as your good name. How would you feel if you never saw your sisters and brothers again?'

'I hate you!' She ran out of the room and up the stairs, still weeping loudly.

Heart heavy, Nev went back into the kitchen and saw Gwynna looking at him. 'She wants to go off with that fellow and become an actress. It's not decent, so I'm not letting her do it.'

'You're right. I've seen him walking down the street, acting like a cock on a dunghill. I'd not trust him as far as I could throw him.'

119

He stared at her in surprise. 'I thought you'd be on her side.'

'No, I'm on yours. I lost my good name once and people treated me badly, even though they knew I'd only been with one fellow and we were going to get wed if he hadn't died. It's worth everything, your good name is, and so I'll tell Marjorie if she asks me.'

'You do that, lass.'

There was the sound of the front door slamming shut. He ran along the hallway and flung it open to see Marjorie running down the street without even a shawl over her head. For a moment he contemplated running after her but knew he'd never catch her up.

'She'll have gone to see her sister,' Gwynna said from behind him. 'She and Carrie are very close.'

'Do you think so?'

'Yes.'

'Well, Carrie's a sensible lass. She'll tell her the same thing. Now, can I have a cuddle of little Sylvie?'

Gwynna passed over the baby and Nev settled his tiny daughter in his arms, murmuring to her in a low voice that the infant already seemed to recognise. Gwynna had never seen a fellow fuss over a baby like he did, but it was nice, made you wish . . . She let that thought go. No good daydreaming.

'You're looking after her well,' he said. 'I'll make sure we help you find another job when this is all over. We won't turn you out into the street.'

She could feel tears rise in her eyes. 'Thanks. I appreciate that.'

What she'd really have liked would be to stay here, to be part of this big, loving family, instead of an outsider. But she might as well wish for the moon. Still, it was good that she wouldn't just be turned out. Made her feel a lot safer. She'd never go back to her own family now, never.

★ ★ ★

Marjorie burst into the Dragon and rushed through to the kitchen to find Bram there poking up the fire. 'Where's Carrie? I need to see her.'

'She's gone to the shop. She'll be back in a minute.'

'Can I hide upstairs and will you tell Nev you've not seen me if he comes asking?'

He set the poker down hastily and gaped at her. 'What on earth's happened?'

So she told him.

He stood biting his lip, worrying whether to be honest with her, and came to the conclusion that he had to be. 'I'm afraid I agree with Nev.'

Her mouth dropped open and more tears rolled down her cheeks. 'I thought you'd understand. *You* go off and sing all over the place. Why shouldn't I do it too?'

'You know why, because you're a lass. I can take care of myself. You can't.'

Carrie came in just then and Marjorie poured out her tale yet again.

'Nev's right. It wouldn't be respectable. You're not thinking straight, Marjorie love. It's one

121

thing to appear here in Hedderby where we can keep an eye on you, see you're not insulted, but you'd be on your own if you went off singing all over the place and you know what people think of actresses.'

'I wouldn't be on my own, I'd be with Denby! *He* would look after me.'

'He's not a relative, you've only known him for a week and if you want my opinion, he'd be more concerned with his own career than with looking after you. And the way he looks at you, he'd be trying to get you into bed as soon as you were out of our sight.'

'I'm not that sort of lass.'

'We're all that sort of lass when we fancy a fellow.'

Anger replaced the tears and Marjorie stood there, hands on hips, eyes flashing. 'Well, I'm going to do it, whatever anyone says! You'll not stop me and neither will Nev.'

'Even if you can never come back here to see your family again? Nev never says anything he doesn't mean, you should know that by now.'

The anger vanished as quickly as it had risen and Marjorie backed away with more tears rolling down her cheeks. 'You're all against me.'

Bram moved to bar the doorway. 'Don't go out like that, lass.'

She shoved him aside and ran off through the streets again, heedless of who saw her. When she got to Denby's lodging house she hammered on the door and insisted on seeing him. The landlady refused to let her in and went to fetch him.

Denby, who had been half-expecting this, moved at once to put his arm round her. 'Stop crying, Marjorie, it won't do any good and you have to appear on stage again tonight. You won't look nice with swollen eyes, will you?'

She gulped and made a huge effort, managing to stop. 'I'm coming with you,' she repeated. 'I am! Whatever they say.'

'They're your family. They're only thinking of what's good for you.' He began to walk along the street with her, his mind furiously busy. He'd suspected they'd be like this, only he hesitated to do the only thing that'd convince them because it meant taking a risk. 'Let's leave it a day or so. I'll think of something to persuade them. Trust me.' He managed to coax her into a more optimistic mood and since for once they were alone, he also managed to kiss her and plant a few seeds. 'You're so beautiful, Marjorie love, so very beautiful. I think you've bewitched me.'

She went home thrilled that he thought her beautiful, smiling at the thought that she could bewitch a man like him. She was still unable to see how he'd persuade Nev to let her go and the trouble was, her stepfather had hit on the one thing she couldn't face, being cut off from her family. If she thought she'd never see them again, she didn't know what she'd do.

Perhaps Denby would find a way to persuade them. He had to, for both their sakes.

7

The Pride was closed on Monday and Tuesday nights, so Marjorie spent two days without seeing Denby. She missed the excitement of performing and felt down in the dumps as she did the housework.

When she tried to talk to Gwynna about how unfair it was of her stepfather to forbid her to go on the stage and how sad that her own sister didn't understand her feelings, the other girl said sharply, 'Don't expect any sympathy from me because I agree with them. You should be glad you've got a family that cares about keeping you safe. My mam and dad are drunkards and we never had enough to eat. I got beaten regularly, even when I was expecting, and it's no wonder my poor baby died. I don't think you have anything at all to complain about. I wouldn't want to stand on a stage and let men look at me like that. It's not decent.'

This was the longest speech Marjorie had ever heard from Gwynna, who usually kept her thoughts to herself and she stared at the other girl in shock before drawing herself up and snapping, 'It's perfectly decent, though I'm not surprised someone like you doesn't understand. And you're not the only one who didn't have enough to eat when you were younger. We often went hungry. What's more, I *wouldn't* be free with my favours. I'm not like that.'

'Ha! You think you wouldn't, but when you get started on kissing and such, especially with a fellow you're fond of, it's hard to stop sometimes. But you'll go your own way and learn by your mistakes, as we all do. I don't know why I bother arguing.' Gwynna swung round, picked up the baby and walked out without a backward glance.

Marjorie carried on with the housework, conscious that Nev was likely to pop in and out and that Raife was playing the piano in the parlour. She wished she could be alone to think. After half an hour she decided to go out to the shops for the day's food and finish tidying the kitchen later.

As she came out of Marker's grocery she nearly bumped into Denby. She stopped dead, not knowing what to say. Was he waiting for her?

Without a word, he took the basket from her and offered his other arm, not speaking until they were away from the shop. 'Have you a few minutes to talk?'

'Yes, of course.'

'Let's walk by the river, then.'

'All right.' Serve them right if she was late back. They could wait for their dinner. They could wait for ever for all she cared!

They strolled down to the river, where Denby led her across to a fallen tree, set the basket of shopping down and pretended to dust a seat for her. Smiling, she fluttered her skirts and sat on it, happy when he settled beside her. Her heart was beating faster now, as it always did when he was near. He took her hand and she made no objection, waiting for him to speak.

'I think you and I were meant to meet, meant to perform together,' he began.

She looked at him eagerly. 'Have you thought of a way to convince them?'

He raised her hand to his lips. 'Yes, but I shall first need to convince *you*.'

'I don't understand.'

He still had tight hold of her hand and was looking at her with a slight smile. 'It's happened very quickly, but I've fallen in love with you, Marjorie, and I wondered if you could possibly care about me?'

She didn't know what to say. She hadn't dared let herself think of him in those terms. His gaze seemed so penetrating all of a sudden that she looked down, still not speaking, her thoughts a tangle of hope and longings.

'Because if you do care for me, I think we should get married.'

Her heart did a great leap in her chest and she looked quickly up again. Now he was smiling tenderly at her. 'Do you really mean that?'

'Of course I do, my darling. I wouldn't say it otherwise.'

'I love you too, but I hadn't dared let myself hope,' she confessed. 'I didn't see how a man like you *could* think of me in that way.'

He laughed softly. 'Foolish Marjorie. Haven't you seen yourself in the mirror, seen how pretty you are?' When she didn't speak, he prompted, 'So your answer is . . . ?'

'My answer is yes. I will marry you, Denby.'

'Then you've just made me the happiest man on earth.'

She could see nothing wrong with this hackneyed phrase. She felt filled with joy that bubbled through her body like the water rippling over the stones nearby. When he took her in his arms, she went willingly. At his kiss, she nearly swooned with delight.

He was breathing deeply as he put her to arm's length. 'Will your stepfather be at home?'

'Yes. He's there now.'

'Then I shall go at once and ask his permission to marry you. They'll see no problem in letting you come with me if we're married, I'm sure. I can't provide you with a fixed home, not yet, my darling, but we shall be together and that's what counts.'

She cared for nothing but to be with him and when he pulled her up and started walking back she was lost in a dream of delights to come. She only remembered the basket as they were about to cross Market Street, so that they had to go back for it.

'See what you do to me,' he said in a low and throbbing voice.

'You do it to me, too.'

Denby was very satisfied with her reaction to his proposal and even more so with her reaction to his kiss. She'd be good in bed, he was sure. And if he had the teaching of her, as he suspected he would, then he'd make sure she grew enthusiastic about making love. In fact, her presence would make his life so much easier as they travelled round the country, not only on stage, but off it as well.

When they got to Linney's he put one hand on his heart and smiled at her. 'I'm nervous. Feel how my heart's pounding.'

'How can you be nervous, a man like you?'

'Because this is so important to me.'

She sighed blissfully and closed her eyes for a moment, then led the way round the side.

★ ★ ★

Nev stared at Denby in astonishment. 'You want to marry her!'

'Is there anything wrong with that?'

'But you hardly know one another!'

'We were attracted to one another from the very first day. Marjorie's a lovely girl and I'm a lucky fellow to have won her affection.' He watched carefully as he trotted out all the hackneyed phrases lovers used and saw that Linney still didn't believe him. Well, it was Marjorie who needed to be convinced and *she* believed every word he said. He waited, well aware that you could say too much.

'I don't believe in folk rushing into marriage, especially when they're near strangers,' Nev said at last.

'I'm very certain about my feelings — and about Marjorie's. And I'd love to take more time to court her, if only to convince you and the rest of her family that I'll make her happy, but I have no choice. I must leave next week and travel to Leeds. From there I go to London. There's no way I can stay.'

Nev shook his head. 'I still think you should wait. Come back later. See if the feelings are still there.'

Marjorie, who had been listening outside, pushed the door open and walked in. 'Well, I don't want to wait and why should we? I love Denby and I love being on the stage. I'd never settle into my old life again after this past few days, *never!*'

Nev chewed the corner of his lip, trying to think how to persuade her to be sensible. 'I'll talk to your sister and my father, but I'm afraid the answer isn't likely to be yes, Mr Sinclair.'

'If you don't give me permission to marry, I'll definitely run away,' Marjorie said, taking Denby's arm. 'I'm not giving up this chance just because *you* like to take things slowly. I'm leaving after Sunday's performance, with or without your permission.'

Denby let her speak, watching in amused admiration as anger lent colour to her cheeks and made her eyes flash. His eyes met the older man's and he allowed himself a quick smile of triumph. 'My fiancée has made her choice, Mr Linney. And I think we won't wait for you, but will go and see her sister right away.'

When he'd heard the front door close behind them, Raife went into the parlour where his son was sitting slumped in dejection. 'You'll not change her mind, lad.'

'But the man's an actor, Dad. He doesn't mean a word of it, just wants her for an assistant.'

'He wouldn't have to marry her for that. And

she's good on stage, you can't deny that.'

'But none of us like him.'

Raife hesitated, then said quietly, 'I've tried to. I've bitten my tongue a few times when she was talking about him. If you want my frank opinion, I think he's a selfish opportunist. But they go together really well on the stage, you've seen how they are. They spin magic and take folk out of themselves for a few minutes. In real life — well, I reckon she's making a hard bed for herself but you only learn that sort of thing through experience. A lass that age isn't practical, not when she's in love. If you don't let Marjorie marry him now, she'll marry him in three months' time — *if* he's still willing to marry her. Better to give in and stay friends with her, don't you think? Then if she's ever in trouble, she'll come back to us for help.'

But Nev wasn't ready to admit defeat yet. 'Perhaps her sister will persuade her to wait.'

'I doubt it.'

★　★　★

Carrie gaped to see her sister storm into the kitchen of the Dragon hand in hand with Denby Sinclair, looking flushed and upset. Setting down the bowl in which she was mixing some drop scones, she asked, 'What's wrong?'

Marjorie burst into tears and Denby moved quickly to put his arm round her. 'I've asked your sister to marry me and she's accepted, but your stepfather won't give his permission. We're hoping you can help us change his mind.'

130

'*Marry!* But you hardly know one another!'

'I love him,' Marjorie said, her voice muffled by his chest, 'and I'm going with him whether we're married or not. I am, I am!' More sobbing made her next words completely incomprehensible.

Carrie watched Denby pat her back and murmur softly to her. He was good looking, had been kind to her sister and yet — somehow she still couldn't take to him. But she prided herself on being realistic and a moment's thought made her understand that she could do nothing to stop this. Her sister always had had a stubborn streak. All the Prestons did.

Eli came in just then, stopping short in the doorway and looking at her questioningly. She held her hand out to him and he went to stand beside her. 'Marjorie and Mr Sinclair are to be married.'

As she glanced back at the other two, she saw a distinct look of triumph in Denby's eyes and for a moment their gazes locked, then he bent once more over Marjorie, trying in vain to stop her weeping.

Carrie moved forward. 'She'll only cry more if you're too sympathetic, Mr Sinclair.' She shook her sister and said crisply, 'That's more than enough. You're supposed to be happy.'

Marjorie gulped to a stop and stared at her from tear-drenched eyes. 'You'll support us? Tell Nev to let us get married?'

Carrie nodded. 'Yes, of course I will.' She held out her hand to Denby. 'I wish you every happiness, Mr Sinclair. I'll also tell you to your

131

face that I don't know you well enough to have confidence in you, but if you ever hurt my sister in any way, you'll have me to answer to.'

He bowed his head. 'Thank you. And please, I'm Denby to you now.'

'Denby, then.'

Eli moved forward, holding out his hand. 'Let me offer my best wishes too.'

★ ★ ★

Carrie's meeting with Nev was quite short. 'You'll never persuade her to wait. And we've no proof that he's not to be trusted.'

He looked at her shrewdly. 'You don't like him, either?'

'No. I can't work out why, though. But it's Marjorie's life, her choice.'

'I feel responsible for her, for your dear mother's sake.'

She moved forward and took him by surprise, kissing him on the cheek. 'You've been a wonderful stepfather to us, but you can't do the impossible.' She hid her amusement as the kiss made him blush scarlet. None of them had realised when he married their mother that the shrewd businessman with a reputation for making every farthing do the work of a halfpenny was actually shy. Nev was still unfolding towards them in some ways, still learning to show his affection. That he missed her mother she had no doubt and she'd seen for herself how much he loved his baby daughter.

He sighed. 'I'll give my permission, then.'

Carrie hugged him again. 'We'll all worry about Marjorie when she leaves. She's too gentle for her own good sometimes and will let him rule her, I'm sure. But at least if anything goes wrong, she'll know where to come for help.'

★ ★ ★

Marjorie and Denby Sinclair were married on the Saturday afternoon by special licence. All her family were in attendance, dressed in their best. And if the parson was disapproving, the atmosphere a little stiff, she cared nothing for that. All her dreams had come true. She was to marry a handsome man, travel round the country, perform on the stage and live an exciting life.

What more could any girl want?

As they spoke their final vows, the mill siren sounded. By the time they came out of the church, the street was full of workers hurrying home after their shorter Saturday. A group of girls stopped at the sight of her and one exclaimed, 'Marjorie Preston! I saw you on the stage last night. You were wonderful.'

'What are you doing?' another asked, looking curiously from her to Denby.

'I've just got married,' Marjorie said proudly. 'My name's not Preston any more but Sinclair.' She smiled at her husband, who put his arm round her shoulders and nodded to the group of eager lasses.

Jack Benting had been walking past as she spoke, and he stopped short to glare at her, then look at her husband. 'You'll be sorry you've took *her* on. She's a lazy bitch, allus teasing the fellows.'

There was a gasp of dismay from most of the people there.

Benting smiled triumphantly at Marjorie then looked at Denby. 'You'll not be the first with her. She's had a dozen lads behind the mill and — '

Sinclair's fist stopped his next words and sent him sprawling on the ground.

Eli stepped quickly forward to stand by his side as Benting heaved himself to his feet. For a minute it hung in the balance whether he would continue the fight, then he spat on the ground at Marjorie's feet. 'You're not worth it.'

The girls clustered round her, making soothing sounds, telling her not to let it upset her and turning to assure Denby that the overlooker had been lying. He moved them gently aside and offered his wife his arm. 'Thank you, but I'd never believe anything like that about her, never.' He meant it too. He could nearly always tell a virgin from an experienced girl.

One of them sighed audibly and looked at him with a dreamy expression on her face.

He gave Marjorie a little tug. 'We have to be going now.' He looked at the girls. 'Thank you for your kind words. We hope to see you at the Pride tonight.'

They moved on, but Benting had cast a shadow over the small celebration at Linney's, and Marjorie ate hardly anything.

'Well, he stuck up for her. You have to give him that,' Eli said to Carrie.

'That Benting should be taken out and hanged,' she muttered. 'What a nasty thing to do! I want our Dora out of that mill as soon as possible. What if he starts picking on her next? She's growing fast, getting a good little figure now that she's eating properly.'

★　★　★

Word had spread about the marriage and at the Pride that evening, the audience was in a particularly festive mood. When Denby came on stage, everyone stood up and cheered. Voices called, 'Congratulations!' They insisted on Marjorie joining her new husband on stage so that they could cheer both of them before they would let the act continue.

Similar scenes were played out at the second house that night and when the show ended, Marjorie was flushed with happiness again.

Only as they went upstairs to the front bedroom at Linney's, where they were to spend their wedding night, did she lose her happy look and become apprehensive.

'What's the matter, my love?' he asked, looking forward to this part of the evening.

'I don't want to disappoint you. Oh, Denby, you didn't believe what that horrible man said, did you?'

'No, not for a minute.'

He pulled her into his arms and kissed her until she was breathless, then said in a throaty voice, 'Now, wife, let me pleasure you.'

It was hard to wait but he took his time, not

135

out of love but because he was experienced enough to know that how he treated her tonight would set the tone for their future together. He wasn't surprised to find her still a virgin, but managed to rouse her to passion and didn't forget to withdraw at the crucial moment, because he wanted no damned brats spoiling things for them.

Marjorie was a valuable find, malleable and trusting, the perfect foil for him on stage, useful off it — together they would go far, he was sure of it. And he'd make sure nothing from his past rose up to spoil that. Well, his immediate family didn't leave the village where they lived and he rarely went back there, so why should it?

8

Wiv lifted his new master off the commode while Tait cleaned him up, amused by the way Athol Stott became rigid with anger every time this had to occur. He didn't mind doing this and he didn't think Tait did either. In fact, it was the easiest job he'd ever had. But the gentry liked to relieve themselves in private, it seemed. Well, he couldn't see Mr Stott ever managing completely for himself again, the way his right hand was twisted into a useless claw and the stump of his right leg sore and inflamed. Even without much laudanum, he was too dizzy most of the time to stand on the one leg he had left.

If Wiv played his cards right, he was set for life here.

By the time they'd got their master clean and dressed, he was lying with his eyes closed, a fine sweat on his brow. Wiv took the towel and wiped the sweat off.

Athol opened his eyes and glared, slapping his manservant's hand away with his good hand. 'How many times do I have to tell you to use a clean handkerchief for that?'

'Sorry.'

'Sorry, *sir!*'

Wiv suppressed a sigh and repeated the 'Sir'. He looked at the man lying on the bed, realising from the rigid set of his face that the pain had set in again, but knowing now not to offer the laudanum before it was asked for. 'Can I do anything else for you, *sir?*'

'You can go for a stroll this afternoon at letting out time. Go past the works and watch the men come out. If you recognise anyone, get into conversation.'

Wiv frowned.

'Well, what's the matter?'

'I'll do whatever you say, of course, but I think Tait here would be best for that, sir. He grew up round here and he knows a lot of people. I only spent a short time at the works.'

Athol shot a sour look at his other henchman, who had proved much clumsier than Wiv and who had jarred his stump badly that morning. 'I suppose so. You hear that, Tait?'

'Yes, sir.'

Wiv cleared his throat to gain his master's attention.

'Well?'

'I was just wondering if you'd decided whether to take us on permanently, sir. Only I'll need to fetch the rest of my stuff from my old room, if that's so.' He held his breath, trying to work out whether he'd upset Mr Stott or not.

'Leave us!' Athol said curtly to Tait, who threw a suspicious glance at Wiv before obeying this order. Only when the door was fully closed did Athol say, 'I'll keep *you* on, Wiv, but I'm not sure about Tait. He's clumsy and stupid with it.'

Wiv nodded. He'd come to that conclusion himself. 'If I could presume, sir?'

'Yes?'

'I have a brother, Renny. He's very strong and

as gentle as a lamb. I did wonder if maybe he could come here and help?'

'He sounds like a simpleton.'

'No, sir, just a bit different from other folk. He's always finding sick creatures to care for, yet never gets bitten or scratched. He's like a — a man-nurse.'

Athol let out a short mocking laugh. 'I suppose that's what I am now, a sick creature to be nursed.' After a moment's thought, he shrugged. 'Why not? He can't be worse than Tait. I presume you have to go into Manchester to sort our your affairs? Right then, bring your brother back with you. I'll try him out, but that's all I'm promising.'

Wiv turned to leave.

'One moment.'

'Yes, sir?'

'I've been wondering . . . you really don't mind doing these — distasteful tasks for me, do you?'

'No, sir.'

'I find that hard to comprehend.'

Wiv couldn't help smiling. 'I've let myself be battered and bashed to earn money when I was prize fighting. I've robbed and bashed others, too, which is risky. This,' he waved one hand, 'is the most comfortable life I've ever lived, with good food, soft bed . . . a man doesn't need much more at my age. As for looking after you, well, that part doesn't worry me at all.' He glanced at his master, whose face was unreadable and decided he'd said enough.

'Thank you. How much time do you need to

sort your affairs out?'

'If I can leave on the six o'clock train to Manchester this evening, I'll be back tomorrow afternoon — only I'll need some money to pay off a few people.'

'Tell my wife to give you both the two guineas I promised. Will that be enough?'

Wiv hesitated.

'All right, how much more do you need?'

'Five guineas in all, sir.'

'Very well, tell her five guineas. Now, leave me alone for half an hour unless I ring.'

When Wiv had left, Athol breathed in deeply and had to concentrate fiercely to avoid tears trickling down his cheeks. No one would ever understand how much he loathed his infirmity, his dependence on others — or the utter relief of finding a man who truly didn't mind tending to his needs.

★　★　★

On the Tuesday afternoon Essie smiled as she got ready to go to Linney's. She always looked forward to seeing little Sylvie and cuddling her, and her visits gave Gwynna some time off to go for a walk and generally relax. And then there was Nev. He seemed lost and sad without Jane, but Essie could usually manage to cheer him up.

Suddenly there was an anguished cry from the parlour and Essie spun round, running towards the hallway even as she heard the sobbing start. She stopped dead in the doorway at the sight of her master lying on the floor with her mistress kneeling by him, weeping. It was obvious he was dead. She'd seen that look too many times to mistake it. For a moment longer she stood there, shocked by the suddenness of his passing. He'd seemed a bit tired lately, but not ill, had asked her only that morning to bake him his favourite cake.

Pulling herself together she went to kneel beside Mrs Latimer, putting an arm round her as she wept. After a minute or two Essie said gently, 'Come and sit on a chair, Mrs Latimer dear. There's nothing more you can do for him now.'

The other woman allowed herself to be led across the room, seeming bewildered, very unlike her normal capable self.

Best to talk about it, Essie decided. It never did any good to lock things away inside you. 'What happened?'

'Gerald was talking to me and all of a sudden he stopped, clapped one hand to his chest and groaned, then crumpled to the ground. He didn't say a word, he just — fell. And when I knelt beside him, I could see he was dead.'

Mrs Latimer was starting to regain control of herself so Essie waited, giving the other woman the time she needed to start coming to terms with what had happened. She felt tears trickle down her own cheeks. He'd been the best of masters — the very best — and a wonderful friend to the poor of Hedderby. He'd be sorely missed by everyone who knew him, but most of all by this woman, who had been as much friend as wife, the two of them so close that one often finished a sentence the other had begun.

'We'll have to send for Dr Barlow,' Mrs Latimer said eventually. 'Could you do that, please, Essie? I'll be all right now.'

'Yes, of course.' Wiping away her tears, Essie went outside and stopped a passing lad, offering him a penny to run and ask Dr Barlow to see Dr Latimer, urgently. He brightened at the thought of earning a coin for such a simple task, took it from her and was off the minute she stopped speaking.

Feeling slow and heavy with grief she went back into the house. It had happened, the thing she'd dreaded for some time now. When your employers got older, you had to think of your own future and she'd figured out a while ago that if anything happened to the doctor, who was much older than his wife, Mrs Latimer would go and live with her widowed sister because she'd be penniless. Her mistress had talked of putting some money aside for the future, but neither she nor the doctor could keep coins in their purses when someone needed help, so Essie doubted there would be enough left to support the doctor's widow.

And there would be no place for Essie with her mistress's sister. Mrs Petherby had a comfortable home and a housekeeper who had been with her for many years — and had for a long time been trying to get her sister to hire someone instead of Essie, saying she needed a more respectful housekeeper. Mrs Petherby had also kept telling Mrs Latimer to persuade her husband to build up a wealthier clientele and refuse to attend poorer patients who couldn't afford to pay him. As if the doctor would ever have turned down a request for help! As if Mrs Latimer cared about money, as long as she had food on the table and people to help.

There seemed little doubt that Essie would have to find another job now. She sighed at the thought. It wouldn't be easy in Hedderby, where there weren't a lot of gentry needing servants. Only — if she left town she'd never see the baby or the rest of the Prestons again, and they were as near to family as she had now.

It was a hard world, it was indeed, and you could never trust life to be kind to you. She would go to the same agency in Manchester as last time, she decided. If it was still there. It had been fifteen years since she'd needed to find a job and it was a daunting prospect at her age.

But she'd never find employers as kind as the Latimers, not if she searched for a hundred years.

★   ★   ★

When Essie didn't appear on the Tuesday afternoon, which was one of her regular days for visiting Linney's and playing with little Sylvie, Nev kept looking at the clock and saw Gwynna doing the same. 'She's never been late before.'

'No. She comes round here at two, regular as clockwork. I hope she's all right.'

He paced up and down a bit then, as the clock fingers nudged half-past two, said gruffly, 'I think I'll go and see if she's all right.' He grabbed his overcoat and hat, then hurried out into the cold

143

wind that was scouring the pavements and whirling dead leaves into corners.

At the doctor's house he knocked on the kitchen door and when Essie opened it, he saw at once that she'd been crying. Without thinking he put his arms round her. 'What's wrong, love?'

She rested her head on his shoulder, explaining in a muffled voice.

He was horrified. 'Dr Latimer dead! Eh, he wasn't that old. And how will the town manage without him?'

'I don't know. And for me there's something else: I'll have to find a new job, probably in another town because I'd know if there were any places going in Hedderby. I'll not be able to see little Sylvie . . . or Carrie . . . or any of you.'

He held her more closely, letting her weep on his shoulder. He didn't want her to go, hated the thought of it.

After a minute or two, she pulled back and blew her nose on a soggy, crumpled handkerchief. 'I should be ashamed of myself, being so selfish when Mrs Latimer's lost so much more than I have. Come in, Nev love. I'd really welcome a bit of company at the moment.'

So he sat in the kitchen, accepted a cup of tea and a scone, but for once didn't even taste what he was eating. He kept thinking of Essie leaving, and that upset him. She'd become a good friend to the whole family and he really valued her help and advice. 'Are you sure there are no jobs here?'

'Fairly sure. I know most of the families who employ housekeepers like me. And even if I did get another job in Hedderby, they'd not let me come and go as I have done here, so I'd hardly see anything of you and the girls.' Fresh tears trickled down her cheeks. 'When you've no family left, friends become more important to you.'

The parlour door opened, footsteps sounded in the hall then the front door opened. They heard Dr Barlow offer the widow his condolences in his booming voice and clump off down the path. There was the sound of lighter footsteps inside the house, but they didn't come towards the kitchen and another door closed quietly.

'She's gone back into the parlour to be with him.' Essie pushed herself to her feet. 'I'd better see if I can do anything for her. She shouldn't be alone just now.'

'Shall I stay for a bit, in case you need help with anything?'

'Yes please, Nev. I'm not myself this afternoon and that's a fact.'

He studied the kitchen as he waited. There was a clock ticking loudly on the mantelpiece, something covered with a cloth on the table and a row of shining pans. Marjorie had never managed to get this bright, clean look to the kitchen at home, nor had Jane. His mother had, though, and he was reminded of it now, missed it all over again. He lifted the edge of the cloth and found a newly baked cake sitting waiting to be cut and eaten. It smelled wonderful, rich with fruit and something else, a spicy sort of smell. He sighed. You only got cakes like that when they were home baked. He had to buy his from the baker's now and they never tasted as good.

It was then that the idea came to him. *He* could offer Essie a job as housekeeper. He could easily afford it and he couldn't think of anything nicer than having his home set to rights again. She'd be good company too.

When she came back, there was fresh moisture on her eyelashes. 'I wonder if you'd call in at the undertaker's on your way home, Nev, and ask him to come round. And could you post this letter to Mrs Latimer's sister?'

Accepting this as dismissal he pushed himself to his feet, hesitated, but didn't say anything about the housekeeping job just then. He'd discuss it with his father and see what Raife thought. It didn't do to rush into things. He'd rushed into marriage with Jane, his childhood sweetheart, and she'd been a disappointment to him everywhere but in bed, kind-hearted and loving, but so untidy — and not very clever. Essie was a clever, sensible woman, though. He didn't know why he was hesitating, really.

★　★　★

Marjorie had never even been to Manchester before, let alone leaving Lancashire completely and going into Yorkshire. She felt very apprehensive as she and Denby got on the train, but during the first short journey from Hedderby she calmed down a bit as she stared out of the window, exclaiming at seeing so many houses. Those on the outskirts of the city had gardens, but those closer to the centre were often built in

146

terraces with small yards behind them. And there were mills and workshops too, all sorts of bigger buildings, some tumbledown, some new.

Victoria Station in Manchester left her almost speechless. 'It's like a palace,' she whispered, 'so big and grand.'

As the train belonging to the Manchester and Leeds Railway pulled out of the station, Denby watched her lazily. He was glad to be on the move again because he'd felt Hedderby to be a bit below him. He wasn't sure about his engagement in Leeds, either. The best music rooms were in London and the second best in Lancashire as far as he was concerned, but two weeks in Leeds was better than two weeks living on his savings.

After a while Marjorie turned to him and smiled. 'I'm so glad you bought the stage costume for me to keep. I love wearing it. It makes me feel like a princess.'

He pulled a face at the thought of the tawdry costume. 'I'll buy you a better one soon.'

'Can you afford it?'

'I'll have to. And I'll buy some better day clothes for you, too. When we get to London we both have to look smart if we want to make a success of ourselves. Still, I shan't have to pay you wages now, so that'll more than cover the cost of your clothes.'

She frowned. Carrie had told her to insist on being given some money every week so that she wasn't totally dependent on him. She knew why Carrie had told her that — because none of her family really trusted him — but her sister had also told her how much he got paid for singing and that information had made all the difference. With so much money coming in, he could easily afford to give his wife a few shillings every week. And she was tired of handing over all she earned to someone else, as she'd had to with Nev.

It was best to start off as you meant to continue, but she had to nerve herself up to make her stand. 'I'd like to be given something every week, Denby. Not as much as in Hedderby, but something, so that I don't have to ask you for every penny.'

'What? You can't mean it!'

'I do.'

'Who put you up to that? Was it your sister or that damned stepfather of yours?'

Her heart began to thump nervously and her voice wobbled, but his sarcastic tone annoyed her and stiffened her backbone. 'It was my own idea. You get well paid for the act, so you can easily afford to give me something.' Why was he so careful with money? He was nearly as clutch-fisted as Nev.

'Wives usually work *with* their husbands and the money they earn goes into the family purse,' he said in slow, careful tones, as if explaining things to an idiot.

'I shall be in strange towns and I'll want to feel secure. Besides, a woman has things to buy.'

He grunted and scowled at her. 'How much were you thinking of?'

'Ten shillings a week.'

His scowl relaxed just a little and she guessed

148

he'd been expecting her to ask for more, so she added quickly, 'more when we get better paid for the act, but ten shillings to start off with.'

'I'll give you five shillings a week.'

She shook her head. 'Ten is fair.'

He breathed in deeply. 'If I give you ten, you'll have to buy your own clothes.'

'Not for the stage. They're too expensive. And not if you want me to dress very fine.'

For a moment it was touch and go, then a smile slowly crept across his face. 'I've been working with stupid girls for so long I'd forgotten that clever ones are different. All right, madam wife. Ten shillings a week pin money it is.'

She felt almost sick with relief. She was learning, she thought, learning all sorts of things, including how to stand up for herself. Denby didn't know that it was fear driving her in this, fear of being alone in a strange city with empty pockets. She didn't know why that thought upset her so much, but it did.

A cloud of dark smoke on the horizon signalled their approach to Leeds. Like Manchester it seemed huge to Marjorie as the train rumbled past street after street. The railway station hadn't long been built and was very large, full of busy people: porters with trolleys, a boy selling pies out of a big basket, a group of young ladies chattering and laughing as they walked along two by two under the stern eye of an older woman.

Denby frowned at her. 'Don't gape round like that. You look like a country bumpkin.'

149

She tried not to stare but it was hard when there were so many new things to see as they followed the porter wheeling their luggage.

A cab took them to their lodging house where a severe-faced woman greeted them, looking suspiciously at Marjorie as if she didn't believe they were married. They had a room with a double bed, washstand, wardrobe and chest of drawers, plus a small table with two hard wooden chairs tucked under it. This left hardly enough room to move. She busied herself unpacking their clothes and hanging things up so that the creases could drop out.

'My shirt needs ironing before the show tomorrow,' he pointed out. 'If you ask the landlady she'll let you borrow an iron. They're used to that in these places.'

She didn't say anything, but she felt annoyed that he hadn't asked her, just told her. Clearly he expected her to wait on him from now on. It was what all wives did, but she couldn't help it, she didn't like domestic chores and had hoped to escape from them. Which was silly of her. How could you ever avoid the need to look after yourself and your clothes?

When she'd finished unpacking, he stood up. 'Let's go and look at the music saloon before you start on the ironing. I've not played there before and I want to be sure it's as big as my booking agent told me.'

They asked directions and decided to make their way there on foot. 'Fresh air is good for the vocal chords,' Denby said, breathing deeply.

To Marjorie the air tasted sooty not fresh.

They crossed one corner of an open space called Woodhouse Moor, as the landlady had said they would when giving directions. Marjorie would have liked to stroll across the grass for a while but Denby hurried her on, going downhill now towards the city centre. He seemed irritated by her desire to slow down and look at things as they reached Briggate, where the music saloon was situated, but she couldn't help it because it was the busiest street she'd ever seen. They passed shops and businesses all jumbled together: a hat maker, a chemist, a printer and a confectioner, while opposite was a brush maker, a newspaper office and a saddler. Further on a bank, a cabinet and clock case maker, an auctioneer's then an ironmonger. Beggars pleaded for money, errand boys pushed past them and a fine lady turned up her nose at the world as she stepped from her carriage into a draper's shop.

'You'll find out that all big northern towns are the same — shops, people, lots of traffic.' He yanked her back. 'Look where you're stepping. You don't want to arrive smelling of horse dirt.'

At the pub where the music saloon was held, he stopped to scowl. 'From what my agent said, I'd expected it to be bigger than this.' He stopped outside to look at a poster, his scowl vanishing when he saw his name near the top of the bill in big letters. 'At least they've given me decent billing. One day I'll be the top name on these posters, you'll see.'

'*We'll* be at the top,' she corrected, pointing to the small print under his name, 'with Elyssa'.

151

She felt a perverse need to assert herself. Even after a few days of marriage, she was feeling disappointed at the way Denby thought only of himself and treated her like a servant. All he cared about was going on stage and the money this brought in. His loving talk had vanished completely once they were married. And he spoke so scornfully of children that she wondered what would happen if she fell for a baby. He'd said she wouldn't and had explained how to prevent that by withdrawing from her at the crucial moment when they made love. She just hoped he was right. She'd hate to be like her mother and have child after child. And you couldn't take babies and children on the road with you, so she'd be the one left at home to look after them. She'd hate that.

She wanted to keep appearing on the stage, something she loved doing, and Denby was the key to that, so even if he hadn't proved as wonderful as she'd expected, he was giving her what she wanted most in the world.

The manager was standing at the entrance to the saloon and seemed gratified to see them a day early. 'You'll want to rehearse, Mr Sinclair. I've got our pianist coming in tomorrow morning, sharp at eight.'

'Can I walk the stage, practise our movements?' Denby asked. 'We're recently married and my wife has only just started appearing with me, so we need to practise a little more than usual.'

'It's not a big stage, lad. You'd better not take big steps or you'll be walking off the edge of it.' He laughed heartily at his own pleasantry as he led them forward, past rows of hard wooden chairs all facing the narrower end of the room.

Denby scowled at the stage. 'What about behind stage? What amenities do you have?'

'A room for the performers to sit in and wait — unless you'd prefer to sit out here and watch the show.'

'Show me.'

The shabby room made Denby's scowl deepen. 'We'll have to change into our costumes at the lodgings and hire a cab to bring us here,' he told Marjorie.

She nodded. It wasn't nearly as comfortable here as at the Pride.

They rehearsed carefully in the empty room with only the manager to watch them, singing their songs without a pianist. Marjorie moved about as Denby had taught her. This stage was smaller than the one at the Pride, with a painted scene as backdrop which looked dirty and whose paint was cracked and peeling at the edges. As always when she was actually performing, Marjorie lost her nervousness and felt as if she were in another world, even now when they were only rehearsing.

'You move well, Mrs Sinclair,' the manager said, his eyes lingering on her breasts. 'Very nice little act.'

'You're getting better,' Denby admitted.

'Thank you. Um, I was thinking of the part where I reject you.' She paused, wondering if he'd mind her making a suggestion. 'Could I

153

maybe peep at you once or twice, and you pretend not to notice?'

He frowned and half-closed his eyes, as if seeing the scene, then nodded. 'We'll try it.' A little later he said, 'Yes, that works fine. Don't forget to do it tomorrow.'

By this time the afternoon was moving towards evening, so they strolled slowly back to their lodgings, stopping for a meal of roast beef and potatoes at an eating house on the way.

'Don't forget about my shirt.' Denby lay down for a rest and Marjorie went downstairs to borrow an iron. Nothing was perfect in this world, not even the life of a performer — or marriage to Denby Sinclair.

★　★　★

The following evening Marjorie felt a little nervous about going on stage in a strange place. When Denby realised that, he put his arm round her and gave her a quick hug. 'You'll be fine, darling, just fine. Trust me.'

She tried to smile at him, grateful for his support. Luckily they heard the Chairman introducing them just then, so she followed Denby forward on to the stage, sweeping a curtsey to the audience and winking at them. Her nerves vanished as soon as she started moving. She knew what to do and did it, loving this magical world they seemed to create around them.

Afterwards the audience applauded loudly but when Denby gave a solo encore, some people

154

called out, 'Where's the lass? Fetch your lass back, too.'

He beckoned to her, saying in a low voice, 'Come and curtsey again.'

As they were making their way out of the saloon to buy something to eat before the second house, the manager stopped them. 'You should find a song where your wife can join in for the encore,' he told Denby, jerking his head towards Marjorie. 'The audience like her. I thought they would when I saw you two rehearsing. Don't disappoint them.'

Denby was very quiet as they ate some cake and drank rather strong tea, so Marjorie said nothing. 'Well, clearly we need to find something to sing for an encore,' he said at last. 'What else do you know or shall I teach you a new song?'

She named one song after the other and he frowned, then at last settled on, 'When I go walking with my lass'.

'We'll need to rehearse it. Drink up.' He whisked her back to the saloon, but this time to the yard at the back.

She thought it romantic to stand under the stars and sing together, but he frowned when she said that. 'Just concentrate on getting the damned song right! And make sure you parade up and down with me gracefully. We'll practise it properly before tomorrow. I just hope it works all right tonight. If they want an encore, that is. Now, we'd better get back inside. Don't let me down.'

During the interval he went to see the leader of the band and arranged for their new song to be added if an encore was needed.

Marjorie sat quietly till it was time to go on stage. The nerves that had gripped her before the first performance were nothing to how she felt now, because for some reason Denby seemed angry with her and she had worked out why. It was because the audience had called for her as well, and he liked to be the only star in the sky where the stage was concerned. But she couldn't help it if the audience wanted to see her as well as him for the encore.

Star performers. Nowadays people were using that phrase to describe performers who got to be well known on the stage. She liked the word. Her husband would be a big star one day, she was sure, he was so good on stage. And she'd be performing alongside him, a lesser star. That thought made her feel happy.

When the audience shouted for more and Denby moved to the centre of the stage, holding out one hand to her, she came forward feeling proud and happy, and they sang together beautifully, as usual. She'd been afraid she'd mess up the new song, but she didn't.

The manager was waiting for them as they came off, smiling. 'That was quick.'

Denby smiled back. 'We'll rehearse it tomorrow, work out some better moves. My wife learns quickly.'

The other man smiled at Marjorie. 'Not much need for rehearsing. You move very well on stage, Mrs Sinclair, if I may say so.'

She was surprised to receive a compliment on her own behalf and went to bed with it still echoing in her ears.

To her surprise Denby wanted to make love, even though it was late and she was exhausted. She didn't enjoy it nearly as much as usual and wished he'd just let her go to sleep. But it was a wife's duty to answer her husband's needs, she supposed, so she pretended to enjoy it. She hadn't realised they would do this every single night, though.

She hadn't really thought about anything but appearing on the stage when she rushed into marriage. She smiled into the darkness. Well, she'd achieved that dream, hadn't she? Half a loaf was better than no bread.

★ ★ ★

Robbie noticed Tait Arner lingering outside the engineering works, talking to some of his old friends, and stopped to watch. He'd heard that Tait was now looking after Athol Stott and had wondered about that. A strange choice to employ a rough fellow like that. And what was Tait doing hanging around the works? Was it his master's idea? Was Stott well enough to plot mischief again? Or was it Tait's own idea to come here?

Still frowning Robbie went to look for his master and found him in the engine room, talking to the stoker, laughing at something the man had said. He smiled with them, thinking how nice it was that Mr Edmund always had a kind word for everyone, even though he wouldn't allow any slipshod work. Now that they'd got rid of the main trouble-makers, no one took

157

advantage of Mr Edmund's kind nature, because he knew exactly what he was doing — and exactly what everyone else should be doing too. And his disappointment if something wasn't done well was just as hard to bear as another man's harsh reprimands.

Once the boiler was damped down for the night and the works quiet, they locked the place up and left it in the care of the night watchman. As they walked back to the village of Out Rawby Robbie told his master what he'd seen.

'Perhaps he was just seeing his old friends.'

'I doubt it. Tait's not left Hedderby, only stopped working for Stott's, so he can see his friends at the pub any time. There must be some reason for him to come to the works, and I worry about what that may be.'

'You think my cousin may be up to something?'

'Yes, sir.'

'Maria says he hates anyone to see how he looks now or how helpless he is, so I suppose if he wants to know something, he has to use other men's eyes. Make sure Tait doesn't come inside, though, Robbie.'

'I will.'

'I feel sorry for Athol, you know. I never thought I would, but I do. We're lucky we didn't get injured in that explosion.'

'Yes, sir.'

But Robbie didn't feel sorry for Athol Stott. How could you feel sympathy for a man who'd kidnapped and threatened his sister Carrie, a man who'd made his employees' lives a misery, underpaid them and put them all in danger by continuing to use a steam engine that was unsafe.

And he felt quite sure Stott was plotting something. A man like that wouldn't just lie there and leave things to others because Athol Stott didn't trust anyone. Mr Edmund, on the other hand, was too trusting.

Robbie wasn't. And he intended to keep his eyes open from now on.

9

On the day after Dr Latimer's death the house knocker was never still. Poor women banged the crêpe-clad door knocker timidly to offer their sympathy to Mrs Latimer in hushed voices, saying how much they'd miss the doctor. Essie and the daily maid answered the door so many times they couldn't get on with their work. And the mistress, usually busy all day long, spent most of her time sitting in the parlour where the coffin stood on trestles, staring at the fire or staring at the box in which her husband's remains lay. She seemed lost without him.

Towards teatime the knocker sounded again, an imperious rat-a-tat this time. With a sigh Essie pulled the pan from the hottest part of the hob and went to answer it. She found her mistress's sister standing there, with her personal maid behind her.

'Mrs Petherby. Do come in.' She knew better than to offer any conversation, because Mrs Petherby liked servants to know their place and the last time she'd visited had told her sister roundly that she was too lax with her housekeeper.

Essie went to knock on the door of the parlour and when there was no answer, peeped in it to see her mistress lying asleep on the couch. She turned to tell Mrs Petherby, adding in a whisper, 'She's so tired maybe we should let her sleep,

160

ma'am? Shall I show you up to the spare bedroom?'

'I know my own way upstairs and you no doubt have work to get on with. The house looks downright untidy today and I'm sure you haven't dusted that hallstand.'

She looked round with such a sour expression that Essie had to bite her tongue not to protest that the maid had been running to and from the door all day instead of getting on with her work. Mrs Petherby wasn't the sort to accept any excuses. 'Would you like a tea tray sent up, ma'am?'

'Yes, please.'

Essie made the tea, set out the tray with one of the best embroidered cloths and sent the maid upstairs with it. She'd rather keep out of Mrs Petherby's way as much as she could.

Later that afternoon Bet came hurrying into the kitchen. '*She's* come down and Mrs Latimer's woken up — well, I think *she* went into the parlour and woke the mistress on purpose. She's talking away at her like she always does, and the mistress is letting her, not answering. I peeped through the crack in the door. Eh, the missus looks so sad, it fair breaks my heart to see her.'

Essie didn't say anything but she wondered whether the two women were talking about Mrs Latimer's future. It seemed a little premature with Mrs Petherby having only just arrived, but this visitor wasn't the sort to be tactful.

Essie prepared dinner and served it herself, feeling outraged to see Mrs Petherby sitting at the head of the table in the master's place. Her mistress didn't eat enough to feed a sparrow and when she tried to coax her, Mrs Petherby told her to mind her own business and leave her betters to mind theirs. Even that didn't prompt the mistress to say anything.

After dinner Essie was summoned to the parlour.

'Please sit down,' Mrs Latimer said. 'You'll no doubt be wondering what's going to happen to you now.'

'Yes, ma'am.' Essie looked in puzzlement at her mistress, who was speaking in a dull voice very unlike her usual one.

'After the funeral I shall be giving up this house and going to live with Amelia, as you've probably guessed.'

Essie nodded.

'Unfortunately I shall have no further need for your services. I shall miss you greatly.'

'I'll miss you, too, Mrs Latimer dear.'

'I'll give you excellent references, of course, and I'm sure you'll easily find another job.' Her voice faltered for a moment then she took a deep breath and continued, 'I'll give you a full quarter's wages when you leave. I'm sure Gerald would have wanted that. You've been the best of housekeepers to us both.'

She couldn't continue, but bent her head and began to weep. Mrs Petherby nodded dismissal to Essie, adding with a sour look, 'I hope you appreciate my sister's generosity. She has so little money of her own now that it's particularly kind of her to think of you in this way. But then she always was too kind for her own good.'

Mrs Latimer looked up. 'Amelia, please. Essie's been a real treasure and I don't want her going short if she doesn't find a job straight away.'

With a sniff, her sister sat back.

Essie left feeling angry at this. But then she often did feel angry when Mrs Petherby and her uppity maid visited. They both seemed to look down their noses at the whole world. How Mrs Latimer could even consider living with a woman like that, Essie didn't know. It was asking for trouble.

She sat down by the kitchen fire with a tired sigh. The washing-up was finished. Bet, who was only a daily maid, had gone back to her own home and Essie's feet were aching. Usually she found some knitting or sewing to occupy herself with, but tonight she was content to sit and watch the flames.

A few minutes later there was a knock on the outer kitchen door and she opened it to find Nev standing there, twisting his hat round in his hands and looking nervous.

'Can I have a word with you, please? It's important.'

'Yes, of course, Nev love. Come in. I'd welcome a bit of company tonight. It's been a long, hard day. Would you like a cup of tea and a slice of my fruit cake?'

'Yes, please.' He brightened and sat down.

She told him what had happened, finishing sadly, 'I do so hate looking for a new job. You never quite know what you're getting into.' She summoned up a half-smile. 'Well, that's enough about my troubles. What can I do for you? I hope little Sylvie is all right?'

'Yes, she's fine. What I came about was — ' he began.

The door to the kitchen opened suddenly and Mrs Petherby stood there. 'I thought I heard voices!' she said in an outraged tone. 'How dare you entertain a man in here! And giving him your mistress's cake, too. I call that stealing.'

Nev stood up, open-mouthed in shock at the way the old lady was speaking to Essie. 'She's done nothing wrong,' he protested. 'She's upset about the doctor too, you know.'

'Don't speak to me like that, my good man. Kindly leave the premises at once.' Mrs Petherby turned back to Essie, ignoring Nev's very existence. 'My sister's in bed and has taken a sleeping draught, as you know. Since she isn't here to look after her own interests, I must do it for her and I take great exception to your taking advantage like this.'

'I'm not taking advantage!'

'Don't you *dare* answer me back!'

Nev, who had been moving towards the door, turned round and marched back to stand beside his friend. 'Leave her alone!'

'I'm doing nothing wrong, as my mistress would be the first to tell you,' Essie repeated. 'She's aware that my friends come to visit me sometimes.'

'If you don't even know it's wrong to entertain a *man* at this hour of the night — and in a house of mourning too — then the situation is even worse than I'd thought. I kept my lips closed when you were acting so familiarly with my poor dear sister, but this is too much. She's always been too weak with her staff. Well, I'm not. You're dismissed. You can pack your bag and get out of the house this very minute!'

Essie gaped at her, then sat down suddenly on legs that had gone shaky.

It was left to Nev to say, 'I never heard anything as ridiculous. Anyway, you can't dismiss her. You're not her employer.'

'I think you'll find that my sister will be guided by me in this as she will be guided in everything else from now on. And if you don't leave the house within the hour,' she pointed one forefinger at Essie, 'I'll call in the police to throw you out!'

She folded her arms and stood there in a pose of triumphant power.

★ ★ ★

Carrie was feeling sad, wondering where her sister was and what she was doing. Once the pub had closed, Eli put his arm round her. 'Penny for them.'

'I was worrying about Marjorie.'

'She'll be all right. Sinclair's doing well on the stage, so they'll not starve.'

'But will she be happy?'

He shook his head fondly. 'No one can guarantee happiness.'

'And there's something else. Why hasn't she written to us? She said she would do as soon

165

as she got to Leeds.'

'She'll have been busy. You can't look after your brothers and sisters all their lives, love.'

'I can't help it. I was more their mother than Mam was. She was always too busy having babies to care about the rest of us, even the little ones.' She hesitated. 'And talking of babies, Eli . . . ' She hesitated, not knowing how to tell him.

'You're expecting.'

She nodded.

He took her in his arms, cradled her face in his hands and kissed first one cheek then the other. 'That's wonderful news. I had been wondering.'

'I wasn't sure how you'd react.'

'Did you think I'd throw a fit?' He chuckled. 'It takes two to make a baby, you know. Besides . . . '

'What?'

'I feel differently about *our* baby. Don't you?'

She nodded. 'I feel protective about it already, but Eli — ' she hesitated then finished off in a rush, ' — what if I'm like Mam, having one baby after the other? Eleven of us, there'd be if she hadn't sold the twins. I love you as a wife should, Eli, but I don't want that many children.' The mere thought of it filled her with panic.

'Then we shan't have them. There are ways to limit the numbers, not foolproof, but ways that help.'

'Are you sure?'

'Of course I am, silly.' He turned her round to lean back into his embrace and they stood together staring into the dying fire. Then she shivered and he pushed her gently away. 'You go up to bed now, love. I'll finish down here.'

She went as far as the foot of the stairs, then turned. 'You're *sure* you don't mind, Eli?'

'Of course not.'

As she went up, inevitably her thoughts went to the two babies her mother had sold for adoption the previous year, just before she married Nev, twin girls they'd been and although Carrie had been horrified when her mother produced twins, she'd grown to love those two and had wept when they were taken away without warning. She'd never been able to understand how her mother could sell them, even if they had gone to good homes, and she had even more difficulty coming to terms with the idea of it now that she was carrying a child of her own. For a minute she cradled her belly with one hand. 'You'll be loved,' she told the child. 'You'll always be loved and looked after properly. You'll never go hungry or be beaten as we were.'

Then she undressed quickly and slipped into bed, snuggling down into the feather mattress as she waited for Eli to join her.

★ ★ ★

It was the flimsiest excuse for dismissal Essie had ever heard of, but she didn't dare cross Mrs Petherby because she was quite sure the woman would indeed send for the police, and anyway, her mistress needed her sister's help. 'I don't have anywhere to go,' she faltered. 'Can I not stay until morning? I'll leave first thing.'

167

'No, you can't! I shouldn't sleep a wink for worrying about what you were getting up to.'

Nev put his arm round Essie. 'You can come home with me, love. We've always got a spare bed for a friend.'

'Aaah!' With another triumphant look at Essie, she said in ringing tones. 'Not only a thief but immoral.'

'There's nothing immoral about offering a bed to a friend,' Nev said indignantly. 'What *is* immoral is what you're doing: throwing a decent woman out into the street at this hour of the night.'

'I'm doing it because she's taken advantage of my sister — and will probably do the same to you if you're fool enough to take up with her. I shall spread the word in this town that she isn't to be trusted and she'll find it impossible to obtain another post here.'

Essie stared at her in shock, unable to speak or move. Why was Mrs Petherby doing this to her? If she did spread such lies, it would indeed be impossible to find another position nearby. And if she had to leave without a character reference, how could she explain the last few years to a prospective employer?

Nev decided then that the scraggy old biddy was mad as a hatter and the answer to the situation came to him in a blinding flash. Taking a deep breath he said loudly, 'She'll have no need to find another job because she'll be marrying me. And if you dare to go round telling lies about my future wife — who will be staying with me and my stepdaughters, by the way, not just me — I shall consult my lawyer and take the appropriate legal action.' The word came to him suddenly. 'Defamation, I think they call it. Or is it slander?'

Mrs Petherby's eyes bulged and she opened and shut her mouth a few times, then sucked in a deep breath and snapped, 'Get out of this house at once, fellow, or I *will* call the police!' She then turned back to Essie and said in the chilliest of tones. 'Go and start your packing. I shall come and supervise what you're doing to make certain you take nothing that's not yours.'

Essie ignored her, looking at Nev in amazement.

He smiled at her. 'I mean it, love. I don't know why I haven't thought of it before. It's the perfect solution to all our problems, including little Sylvie, who's going to need a mother. Now, go and pack. I'll wait here and help you carry your things.'

She didn't know what to say, but even if he had only proposed to her for Mrs Petherby's benefit, his words gave her heart so she raised her head and said, 'I shall need Nev to come up to the attic and help bring down my big trunk, ma'am. Otherwise I'll not be able to pack my things.'

Mrs Petherby looked from one to the other, then said, 'He may do that, but he's not setting one foot inside your bedroom.'

'Nor are you,' Essie threw back at her. 'My personal possessions are private and I'm not having anyone going through them.'

'I shall definitely send for the police then.'

'Do! I'll get them to bear witness that I've been wrongfully accused.' Essie turned to Nev. 'If you'll come up to the attic with me, love, I'll make a start. Then, if you wouldn't mind, we'll need a handcart for my things. I've more than the two of us can carry after all these years working here.'

As they passed her mistress's room, there was no sound from it and she felt deeply saddened to think of leaving like this, without even a farewell. What would Mrs Latimer say in the morning when she found out what had happened? More to the point, what lies would she be told about her former housekeeper?

But as she laid her things in the big trunk whose lid had been covered in the dust of years, Essie's thoughts kept coming back to what Nev had said. Surely he didn't really mean it?

★　★　★

In a bedroom in the Dragon, Eli's cousin Joanna was quarrelling with her husband Bram about the only subject that ever came between them — her refusal to join him on the stage. He'd just arrived back from a singing engagement in Manchester and was too restless to sleep, especially with the news he'd brought back.

'I've been offered some work in London,' he said abruptly as she got into bed.

She paused, not blowing out the lamp yet because there was a sharp edge to his voice that was unusual for him. 'And shall you take it?'

'I'd be a fool not to. It's very well paid.'

'Oh.'

'I don't want to work away from you, though. I want us to perform together, travel together, you know I do. Joanna, love, couldn't you just try it once?'

'I'm *not* going on the stage and singing in public.'

'How can you waste such a beautiful voice? We could make a lot of money, see the rest of the country. Isn't it important to you that we're together?'

'I've told you till I'm blue in the face that I'd be terrified of getting up on a stage and singing for folk. I mean it, Bram, and no amount of coaxing is going to change that. I just — I can't do it.'

'How do you know? You've never even tried.'

'And I'm never going to try, either.' She was pleating the edge of the sheet, avoiding his eyes. 'I go cold inside at the mere thought of it. Please Bram, stop pestering me about it. I'll never change my mind.'

He slid beneath the covers and turned his back on her.

She got into bed with tears in her eyes, but she wasn't going to plead for a cuddle.

* * *

Ted came back to the doctor's house with Nev, pushing the little cart he'd made for the twins, which the family now used for all sorts of things. They knocked on the back door and a

171

starchy-faced woman answered it.

'You're to wait outside till *that woman* is ready to bring the trunk down,' she said, starting to shut the door in their faces.

Nev put his hand out to stop her. 'We'll wait inside. It's coming on to rain.'

'My mistress will be angry.' She backed away from them and scurried out of the room.

'Let her be,' Nev called after her. 'I'm angry too.'

'It's a big house, isn't it?' Ted said wonderingly.

'Shh, lad. I want to listen.' Nev tiptoed across to the open door that led into the front part of the house and stood there.

In the distance a door opened and he heard Essie's voice saying, 'I'm ready now if someone will tell Nev to come and help me.'

'Tell him yourself!'

'No. I'm not taking my eye off my things.'

Nev pushed the door open and shouted, 'Shall I come up now, love?'

'Yes, please.' The tone was distinctly relieved.

He went past the two sour-faced old women standing on the first-floor landing then up a second set of stairs to the attics, then called down to Ted to come and help him carry the trunk.

Ted ran up the stairs, eager to see as much of the house as he could.

'Such doings in a gentleman's household,' said the ugly old lady as he passed her. 'I'd not allow scruffy folk like this in *my* house.'

There was such a banging and clattering that

no one heard the front bedroom door open. As Nev and Ted began to carry the trunk down, Mrs Latimer came out on to the landing and asked in a bewildered tone, 'What's happening?' She looked at the trunk and back at her housekeeper. 'Essie, where are you going?'

She was clutching the banister rail and looked to be half-asleep. Nev stopped to say, 'Your sister has dismissed Essie, Mrs Latimer, turned her out.'

Some of the sleepiness vanished and Lydia took a step forward. 'Is this true, Amelia?'

'I found her in the kitchen with this follower of hers, making free with your food, and she was insolent when I reproved her. Of course I dismissed her!'

Lydia swallowed hard and leaned against the wall. 'I think I'm in the middle of a nightmare.'

Essie stood at the foot of the attic stairs. 'I feel a bit that way myself, Mrs Latimer, but it's all too real.'

They looked at one another for a moment, then without speaking hugged.

'Sister, stop this unseemly familiarity at once!' Amelia said loudly.

Lydia rubbed her forehead. 'I can't think clearly, Essie.'

'Will you be all right?'

'Mmm.'

'You won't . . . listen to any lies about what happened tonight? I've done nothing wrong.'

'I know you haven't. I'll come and see you tomorrow.' She rubbed her forehead again. 'I've got such a headache. Where will you be?'

'At Linney's.' Essie hesitated, then added, 'Nev's asked me to marry him.'

Lydia's face lit up. 'That's wonderful! You already love those children.' She turned to Nev. 'I wish you both well. The happiest years of my life were spent with my late husband.'

'Thank you, Mrs Latimer.'

Ted, standing quietly behind everyone else, watching with great interest, frowned as the thin woman in black next to the old biddy stepped quietly forward and slipped something into Essie's pocket, then stepped back and nudged her mistress, who nodded approval.

He didn't like that at all and moved closer, wondering what that woman had put in Essie's pocket and why? Worried, he pretended to stumble and clutched Essie for a moment as if to regain his balance. 'Sorry.'

Essie patted him absent-mindedly. 'That's all right, love.'

Amelia stepped forward. 'Before she goes, you'd better check that she hasn't taken anything.'

Lydia stared at her. 'Taken? You mean — stolen? Essie would never steal from me, never!'

'I fear she's already done that, ma'am,' Mrs Petherby's maid said. 'I watched her myself go into your bedroom when she was supposed to be packing. If you search her, I'm sure you'll find she's been stealing.' She darted forward and grabbed Essie's arm, crying, 'Don't let her get away!'

'She'd never do that,' Lydia said firmly.

'Don't listen to that old hag's lies,' Nev said. 'Let's get out of here, love.'

'You're not going anywhere till we've checked what my maid says,' Mrs Petherby stated, barring the top of the stairs.

Essie said proudly, 'They can search all they like and they'll not find anything. I've never stolen anything in my whole life.'

'Search her, Jane.'

Since it was clear that Essie's pinafore pocket was empty, the maid fumbled through the slit in her skirt for her pocket. Her smug expression faded as she found nothing. 'But I did see her take something,' she insisted.

'That you didn't!' Essie said. 'I don't know why you're making this up.'

Lydia took her sister's arm and pulled her to one side. 'Let them pass, Amelia. Look after her, Mr Linney. She's a treasure.'

'I shall.' He glared at Mrs Petherby, then turned to the other woman. 'If you ever need somewhere to stay in Hedderby, Mrs Latimer, there'll always be room for you at our house.'

'Thank you. I'm sorry, but I have to go back to bed. My mind's so fuzzy I can't think straight. What did you put in that sleeping draught, Amelia? It must have been far too strong.' She stopped again, shaking her head as if to clear it. 'I'll come and visit you before I leave Hedderby, Essie, to say goodbye properly and pay you what's owed.'

Essie nodded, tears welling in her eyes, then picked up the lumpy bundles of personal possessions, most of them wrapped anyhow, the bigger things in a quilt, others wrapped in her old cloak.

'Where did you get that quilt from?' Mrs Petherby demanded. 'You're not stealing my sister's bedding.'

'I made this quilt myself from scraps of material,' Essie said quietly, pointing. 'This was to have been my sister's wedding dress, this belonged to my mother.' Her voice broke on the last word.

'Amelia, stop this at once!'

'Some people just won't be helped — and when they run out of money because of their foolishness, their family has to come to the rescue.'

The two sisters glared at one another.

Nev tugged at Essie's arm and in silence they carried her things outside and loaded them on the handcart.

She stopped in the kitchen to pick up a pot off the mantelpiece. 'I keep a few coins in here.'

He glanced sideways once or twice, but didn't say anything because she looked pale and desperately upset.

As they were walking down the street with Nev pushing the handcart, she asked him suddenly, 'Why do you think that maid seemed so sure she'd find stolen property in my pocket?'

It was Ted who answered. 'Because she put a ring there herself. I saw her do it and took it out again when I bumped into you. I dropped it on the table in the hall as we were leaving.'

Rain or no rain, Nev stopped pushing to beam at him in the moonlight. 'You're a clever lad, young Ted, and no mistake.'

Essie gave him a smacking big kiss on the cheek. 'Thank you, Ted.'

He wriggled uncomfortably but let her cuddle him for a moment and even gave her a quick hug back.

'Well, let's get moving again,' Nev said briskly. 'There's rain trickling down my neck and I'm cold.'

At Linney's they found everyone sitting in the kitchen enjoying what had become a nightly ritual of hot milk and honey. Room was made for the three soaked people to stand next to the fire and so many questions were fired at them that none got answered properly.

Nev didn't even get as far as explaining that Essie was going to marry him because the girls soon swept her off to change her clothes, then Dora came back to fill one of the earthenware hotwater bottles for her bed.

'Poor Essie's that tired and upset,' she said. 'I'll take her up a cup of milk and then we'll leave her to sleep.'

So Nev said nothing. He'd tell them he was getting married the next day after he'd had a word with Essie. Surely she wouldn't change her mind?

10

In late November Denby and Marjorie travelled down to London to begin a four-week engagement playing at two places each night: first a music saloon then a variety theatre. They had a few days before they started so Denby took Marjorie out to buy some new clothes.

'You seem to know your way around London,' she said.

'I've appeared here before. Oh, and by the way, I have relatives who live in the country near London. I'll have to visit them before very long. My uncle Bill's very old and he's promised he'll leave everything he owns to me, so I can't neglect him.'

'Who are they? Do you think they'll like me?' She felt nervous of meeting any of his family. From the casual remarks he'd let drop she guessed he came from a much better background than she did and was terrified his relations would look down their noses at her.

'They're bound to like you, darling girl, but I want to go and see them on my own the first time, if you don't mind. They don't even know I'm married and my uncle Bill is very old, so I need to break the news gently. I don't know if he's up to seeing strangers because he was quite ill last year. You can come next time, perhaps.'

Surely he didn't intend to leave her alone in

London? She looked at his face and realised that he did. 'Oh.'

His voice grew a little sharper. 'I'll only be away overnight. You'll be perfectly all right in the lodgings. You and Mrs Brook seem to be getting on well.'

'Please take me with you, Denby.'

'It wouldn't be wise.'

'Then come back earlier. Don't stay away overnight.'

'I can't avoid it. The village isn't on a railway line, so unless I want to walk five miles in the dark, I'll have to sleep there.'

'Oh.'

He didn't even try to hide his irritation. 'Stop saying 'oh' like that. You sound stupid and childish.'

She gazed at him reproachfully, but he went to stare out of the window of their bedroom. Why didn't he want her to meet his relatives? Was he so ashamed of her?

After a minute or two he turned round, dropped a casual kiss on her forehead and pulled her close. She leaned against him with a sigh. She loved the rare occasions when he showed her affection during the daytime. Mostly, he only kissed her when they were making love. His breath was warm against her ear and she gave an involuntary shiver, cuddling closer to him. But his next words made her pull away again.

'There are bound to be times when we're apart, Marjorie, for business or other reasons, but I'll always make sure you're all right.'

She didn't dare make any further protests

179

because she didn't know what was normal and what wasn't for southerners, who sometimes seemed like a different breed of folk, or for performers either, though she was learning about that gradually.

He held her at arm's length and smiled again. 'After all, I could hardly manage without you now, could I? Both on stage and in my bed.'

She felt better at once, didn't know why she'd been so upset. Of course she'd be all right for one night.

★　★　★

Athol waited impatiently for Wiv to return. He had already come to rely on the man and must make sure he kept him happy here — which for Wiv seemed to mean paying and feeding him well. The housekeeper had told Maria that the man ate as if he'd been starved for years. And perhaps he had.

It was nearly two o'clock in the afternoon when there was a knock on his bedroom door and Wiv poked his head inside to say, 'I'm back, sir.'

'About time, too. Come in.'

As he opened the door, Athol could see someone standing behind him. 'Is that your brother?'

'Yes, sir.'

'Well, don't let all the warm air out, bring him in quickly!'

He came in, followed by a large man with a face as unlined and serene as a child's beneath dark hair that was threaded with grey. The newcomer was taller than Wiv and seemed to have enormous hands and feet. He came over to the bed without being asked, studying Athol openly.

'Does he have to stare at me as if I'm a raree at a sideshow?' Athol snapped, hating the clear-eyed scrutiny.

'This is my brother Renny, sir.'

Athol glanced sideways at Wiv, puzzled at how nervous he sounded. 'I'd already guessed that.'

'You're in pain, Mr Stott,' Renny said, 'inside and out.' He reached out for the cloth that was kept by the side of the bed and wiped Athol's forehead. 'I'll need to buy some herbs. They'll be better for you than that stuff.' He flicked one finger scornfully at the bottle of laudanum which stood on a small table nearby, together with a small glass and a carafe of water.

Without asking, he pulled down the covers and checked the inflamed stump of the amputated leg. His hands were so gentle that the protest died before Athol could utter it.

'If you don't start walking on that soon, you'll not be able to use it at all.'

'I know that, damn you, but it gets sore!'

'Show me the fitting they made for the artificial leg.'

Wiv ignored his master's glare and darted over to the dressing room to bring out the artificial leg the doctor had sent for, with its straps.

Renny took it in his hands, looked at the man on the bed and shook his head. 'This is no good. I'll make you a better one, softer leather, more padding and different strapping.'

Athol looked at Wiv. 'Can he do that?'

'If he says so.'

'Then get him whatever he needs.'

Without asking permission Renny sat down and took the invalid's hand.

The sick man stared at him, emotions chasing across his face: resentment, shame, anger, then an attempt at calmness that would have fooled no one.

'You won't get better properly, sir, till you let go of the hatred inside you.'

Athol shook off his hand, because it had tingled in his and made a shiver run up his spine. 'What's inside me is my own business.'

Renny studied him then said quietly, 'Your life touches so many other people's, it's not just your business.' He turned to Wiv. 'I'm glad you brought me. I'll try my best to help. We should all try to help one another. If I can do something for him, it may be to your good, too.'

Wiv rolled his eyes then looked pleadingly at his master. 'He speaks strangely sometimes but he really is good with sick creatures.'

'*Sick creatures!*' Athol spat at them. 'Don't ever call me that again.' As that large gentle hand rested for a moment on his shoulder, the pain seemed to ease a little. 'However, I will try his services for a week, the same as I did with you, because Tait is a clumsy fool. But he can stay on here as well because there are a few other jobs he can do for me in the town.'

Wiv let out a sigh of relief. He knew Renny was sometimes a bit strange in his ways and there were folk who feared him because of that, but he also knew what his brother could do — something his master would gradually discover. Though sometimes healing people the way Renny did was . . . well, a little frightening.

*   *   *

Maria met Renny that same evening, because he'd asked to meet everyone in the house. When the housekeeper told her that he wanted to see her, she sighed. She was quite sure she'd detest him as she detested the other two men Athol had chosen — just as she detested *him*.

She said she'd see Renny in the small parlour because it was the place in which she felt happiest of all. Now that she didn't have to sit with her husband in the evenings, she felt freer than she had for years and loved having her own room with the freedom to arrange it as she pleased, to embroider or not, as she chose, or simply to sit there and enjoy the peace and silence. The children enjoyed coming here too and usually spent time with her during the afternoon.

The housekeeper showed him in. 'This is Renny Blaydon, ma'am.'

The way Mrs Ibster said that surprised Maria, because there was a warmth to her voice that was noticeably lacking when she spoke about Wiv or Tait.

He stood in the doorway, studying the room then openly studying Maria, and for the life of her she couldn't say a word, or even move. Then

183

he smiled at her, a singularly sweet smile, a smile that surprised her. 'I'm very pleased to meet you, ma'am.' He moved forward unasked to look at her embroidery. 'That's beautiful. A spirit flower.'

She watched as he touched one of her embroidered pansies with his fingertip, surprised at how clean his hand was, how soft and pink the skin.

He studied her face. 'He's made you unhappy. I'm sorry. He's unhappy too, and angry. I'll try to help him, but I don't know if I can.'

She should have been offended at the familiarity with which he addressed her, but she wasn't.

'You have children,' he said. 'May I meet them, ma'am? I won't hurt them, I promise you.'

She found herself ringing the bell and asking for the boys to be brought down. They stood in the doorway, not sure what she wanted at this time of day, apprehensive, as they so often were in this unhappy house. 'Boys, I want you to meet Mr Blaydon, who's going to help look after your father.'

'Call me Renny,' he corrected. 'I don't like to use my father's name. He was an unkind man.'

Isaac, who was now seven, studied the large man carefully. 'You don't look like the other men who look after Father.'

Renny grimaced. 'I don't look like anyone much.' He gestured to himself. 'Too large and soft, that's me. But animals like me. And I like them. Do you have any pets?'

'We wanted a puppy, but Father said no,'

184

Benjamin confided. 'And Mrs Ibster says if we play with the kitchen cat and feed it, it won't keep the mice down.'

'Boys should have a dog to care for,' Renny said, 'as long as they look after it properly.' He looked earnestly at Maria. 'Children can learn a lot from animals. Would you mind if I try to change your husband's mind, then find your sons a puppy?'

'I wouldn't mind at all, though I'm not sure if it's wise. Athol doesn't like dogs and they don't seem to like him.'

'I'll be careful. You have to choose your pet animals with great care, if you're to love them and they you.'

She had a sudden strange fancy that his smile was bringing sunshine into the room, making it seem brighter. 'We'll only get a dog if my husband agrees. I won't have one if it's to be hurt or thrown out after a few weeks.'

'I'll make sure it's not hurt.' He looked at the boys, frowning a little. 'Isaac is the most like his father. You've done well with him, but we'll need to make sure he doesn't turn, like sour milk.'

The boys seemed at ease with the large man and indeed Maria felt comfortable with him too. But she was sure he wouldn't last long. If Athol didn't get rid of him, he'd no doubt leave of his own accord. Her husband had a way of making people unhappy.

'I'd better go back to the master now,' Renny said, taking a step towards the door. 'There's a lot to be done.'

He went out of the room without waiting for

her to dismiss him, moving so quietly he left no sounds behind him, only a sense of peace.

'I like him,' Benjamin said.

'I *think* I like him,' Isaac said. 'But I don't like him calling me sour milk.'

She laughed then. 'He only meant if life treated you badly, you might become sour, like milk does. I'll try to make sure life doesn't treat you badly, my darling boy.' She kissed him, smiling as he wriggled out of her grasp. 'Go back up to the schoolroom now and get on with your lessons.'

When they'd gone she sat for a while, her hands still, feeling unusually calm and rested, she didn't know why.

* * *

In the morning Essie woke with a start, unable for a moment or two to work out where she was. Then it all came back to her. She was at Linney's, her dear master was dead and she'd been dismissed. She couldn't hold back a soft, sad sound, but there was no one to hear so it didn't matter if she shed a few tears.

She didn't weep for long because she had to think about Nev's proposal, work out if he'd meant it. She pulled herself up into a sitting position, intending to get out of bed, but leaned back against the pillows instead. He couldn't have meant it . . . could he? No, he was just being kind, protecting her against *that woman* because she was his friend. She was a plump, middle-aged woman, not the sort to attract a

186

man and . . . she sighed. She wished she was pretty, wished she had a pretty face and body to attract him with, because there was nothing she'd like better than to marry him.

With a sigh she got up, sitting on the edge of the bed, shivering a little as she studied her surroundings. The room was quite large and well furnished. The bed was comfortable and although she'd not expected to sleep, she had, and slept well too. It must be late because it was fully light outside.

She had to face Nev some time. It might as well be now. Squaring her shoulders she stood up and began to get ready for the day.

Downstairs, Raife watched Nev see everyone off to work and then, uncharacteristically, sit down and stare at his hands, looking up anxiously towards the stairs every minute or two. He didn't even check that Sylvie was warmly wrapped when Gwynna took her out for a walk.

Raife glanced at the clock. 'Shall I see the last of the lodgers out?'

'What? Oh, yes. Thanks, Dad.'

Raife went into the big room and rang a bell. 'Five minutes to be out of here,' he called.

'Can't we stay a bit longer today?' one woman pleaded. 'It's bitter cold outside.'

'You know the rules. Room to be clear by nine.' He unlocked the outer door again, as he'd unlocked it several times that morning already to let people out. If they didn't lock it, half the blankets would be gone by morning. 'Give me your blankets as you leave.'

One by one they grumbled their way out.

These were the last, the most feeble or the most feckless. He felt for them, he really did, but you couldn't take the burdens of the world on your shoulders. There were enough problems in the family. Not a word had they heard from Marjorie since she'd left with that fellow she'd married. Not a single word! He'd never have believed she could be so thoughtless, so downright unkind. They were all worried about her because they didn't even know where she was staying in London, or where she was singing.

When the room was clear he folded the blankets, put them in a pile and went back into the kitchen to find his son still sitting in the same place. He sat down beside him. 'What's the matter, lad?'

Nev looked at him, pressed his lips together then opened them to suck in a little air before sighing it out again. 'It's Essie. I asked her to marry me yesterday when we were at the doctor's, only after we got back there wasn't time to talk. The girls whisked her upstairs before I could think. Now she's late coming down and I'm worried that she's changed her mind and is avoiding me.'

'Do you want her to change her mind?'

'No, of course not. It'd all fit together so neatly, us marrying, and anyway,' he blushed, 'I like Essie. She's a fine woman.'

'You liked Jane too, and rushed into marriage with her.'

'Essie's not like Jane.'

Even as he spoke there was the sound of a

188

door closing upstairs and footsteps coming down the stairs.

Raife moved towards the side door. 'I'll leave you to speak to Essie in private. I'll be sweeping out the lodgers' room.' He paused to add, 'Don't take all day about your talk. It's cold out there.' But he wasn't sure his son had even heard him.

Nev stood up as Essie came into the kitchen. 'Good morning, love. Did you sleep well?'

She blushed at the mere sight of him, couldn't stop herself. 'Yes. I can't think how I came to sleep so late, though. I never usually do that.'

'You had a hard time yesterday. You were exhausted. I'll get you a cup of tea, shall I?'

'I can — '

But he was already taking the teapot from the side of the kitchen range, where it stood keeping warm for the next person to use it. 'The kettle's not long boiled. Sit yourself down, lass.'

So she took a place at the table, wishing she had something to do with her hands, wishing he'd look at her. Should she say something? No. Best wait and let him speak.

When he came to put the teapot on the table their eyes met and held, so that he stood there holding the big brown teapot until it burnt his hand and he set it down with a yelp.

'You've hurt yourself. Let me see.' She was up and round the table at once, taking hold of his hand and tutting over the patch of reddened skin. 'Why didn't you use a cloth to hold it?'

'I wasn't thinking straight.' He grabbed her hand and held on to it tightly. 'Essie love, if you've changed your mind, if you don't want to

189

marry me, tell me now and put me out of my misery. I've been awake since the knocker-up did his rounds, worrying that you wouldn't want me.'

'I wouldn't want *you?*' She could hear her voice wobble. 'I was worrying that you didn't really mean what you said or had changed your mind.'

He closed his eyes for a minute in sheer relief, but he didn't let go of her and she didn't try to pull away. Then he opened his eyes and said simply, 'I do want to marry you, Essie love. I really do.'

'Why?' She had to know, couldn't agree to anything unless she was sure about why he was doing this.

'Because it makes sense on so many counts. I need a woman here.' He waved one hand around, but his eyes never left her face. 'I've a baby to bring up, children to look after — and I regard Jane's children as a sacred trust, I really do — not to mention I've this business to run and one or two other things to attend to as well. But Essie, it can't just be any woman I marry. It's got to be *you.* You and me, we get on so well, we're *right* together.'

'Your wife's only been dead for six months.'

'Aye, I know. There's some would say I'm fickle, but life has to go on. And well, I was fond of Jane, always have been ever since I was a lad, but she was that feckless! I hadn't thought about that. She couldn't manage a house to save her life and money ran through her fingers like melted butter. And it was no use scolding her, she was just like a child, couldn't understand why I was angry. This time when I marry I want more, I want a woman who'll work alongside me, as well as sleep alongside me.' He broke off to stare at her in consternation. 'Essie . . . Essie lass, don't cry. I didn't mean to upset you. I won't say a word more, I promise, not if you've changed your mind, and — '

'Come here, you great lummox and give me a kiss,' she said in a husky voice. 'I've been sitting up there worrying you didn't want *me*, that any woman would do.'

He took her in his arms and held her close. They were much of a height, and his girth made it hard for them to kiss easily. But they were both smiling as they leaned forward and sealed their bargain in the usual way.

'Can I come in now? You seem to have sorted out your differences.'

They turned to see Raife standing in the doorway.

Nev kept hold of Essie's hand. 'Aye, Dad. And you can be the first to congratulate us. Essie's going to marry me. What do you think of that, eh?'

The kindly old man beamed at them both. 'I think it's the best news I've heard for a long time. You're well suited to each other.' He advanced on Essie and planted a smacking great kiss on each of her cheeks in turn. 'Welcome to the family, lass.'

Upon which she both cried and laughed at the same time.

11

The following day there was a message that Bet was ill and couldn't come to work. Lydia made breakfast for her sister and herself, leaving the uppity maid to clear up the kitchen, something the woman clearly didn't feel to be her job at all. Lydia went to join her sister in the small dining room and tried to force some food down, but soon pushed her plate away.

Amelia looked at her disapprovingly. 'You'll do no one any good by refusing to eat, though this is not the sort of breakfast I would set before guests.'

'If you hadn't dismissed my cook yesterday, you'd have nothing to complain about.' She took a deep breath and said quickly, before she lost courage, 'I'm going round to see Essie this morning. I owe her money and — '

'One does not pay wages to servants one has dismissed for unsatisfactory conduct.'

'I never found Essie's conduct unsatisfactory and *I* didn't dismiss her.'

Amelia put down her knife and fork. 'Because you always were weak. Well, let me make it clear now that in my house there will be no indulging of servants. They are there to serve us, not to chat or sit around, and I certainly don't allow mine to have followers.'

Lydia stared at her, remembering all too clearly how her older sister — no, *half*-sister, it always helped to remember that — and their mother had dominated her childhood, both being cut from the same cloth, and how wonderful it had been to marry Gerald and leave them. She didn't know how she was going to cope with being dependent on Amelia, who would no doubt bully her again. Only — dear Gerald had left her so little money. She simply couldn't live on what would be left.

She spent the morning, at her sister's insistence, going through her possessions and being told which could be taken with her to her new home and which should be sold or given away.

And all the time guilt was eating at her. How could she have let Amelia treat Essie like that? She'd been half-stupefied because of the sleeping draught, but even so, she shouldn't have let her sister send her housekeeper away. In the end she could bear it no longer. 'I'm going round to see Essie now,' she repeated. 'I need to make sure she's all right.'

'I forbid it. You're not thinking clearly. She'll take advantage. That sort of person always does.'

Lydia thrust herself to her feet and left the room, snatching up her everyday mantle as she went through the hall. Amelia tried to prevent her from opening the front door, but though her sister was much bigger than she was, anger lent Lydia the strength to push her way outside and she didn't even try to listen to the words that were shouted after her.

By the time she knocked on the front door of Linney's, she had calmed down a little. What she'd done was foolish, given her circumstances, and she would no doubt be made to regret her defiance of the one who now held the purse strings. But she couldn't, she simply couldn't leave without speaking to Essie, not after all the years they'd lived and worked together.

Nev opened the front door, smiling when he saw her. 'Do come in, Mrs Latimer. I expect it's Essie you want to see.' He showed her into the parlour and she paced up and down, unable to sit.

A minute later the door was opened and Essie hurried in. Without hesitation she went to hug her former mistress. 'I knew you wouldn't leave without saying goodbye. I told Nev so.'

'I'm so sorry for what my sister did.'

'It doesn't matter.' Essie blushed. 'Actually, it brought me and Nev together, so it worked out for the best.'

'You're still going to marry him, then?'

'Yes. We settled it all this morning. I'll have a family again. I can't tell you how happy that makes me.'

Lydia fumbled in her pocket for her purse. 'You must let me give you the wages you're owed at least.'

'No thank you, Mrs Latimer. My Nev's very comfortably off and I have some savings of my own. You need the money more than I do now.'

Lydia hesitated, then put the purse back into her pocket and sighed. 'It doesn't seem fair.'

'Do you *have to* go and live with your sister?'

'What else can I do?'

'Perhaps ... ' Essie looked at the other

woman, then finished her sentence, ' . . . you could earn your own living instead? You're younger than me, still have plenty of energy.'

'What could I do?'

'All sorts of things. Become a nurse — you know you're good with sick people. Or — I know! You could run a boarding house. The Pride needs somewhere for the show people and there isn't really anywhere suitable. There are a couple of people offering rooms, but Carrie says Eli isn't happy with the standard they provide, nor are the performers.'

Lydia stared at her open-mouthed, then burst into tears.

When she had calmed down, Essie said, 'I'm sorry. I didn't mean to make you cry.'

'You didn't. It was my own stupidity that upset me. Just because I've lost Gerald doesn't mean I've lost my wits, does it? Only I've been acting as if I have no mind or abilities of my own.' She stood frowning, staring into space, then shook her head and smiled at Essie. 'I'm not sure about running a boarding house, but I may have another idea.'

'What are you going to do?'

'Advertise for another doctor and keep my husband's practice going. Surely there must be some young fellow looking to start up?' Her expression turned deeply sad as she added, 'I'll bury Gerald then take my time about deciding what to do. I'm not completely penniless.'

'How will you deal with your sister?'

'The same way she deals with me. Bluntly. She'll scold me dreadfully but in the end she'll leave me to my fate, prophesying disaster all the way and warning me not to turn to her if things go wrong. Though I do think she'd take me in if I was destitute. For all her sharp words, she has a strong sense of family. Our mother brought us up like that.'

When Essie had seen her former mistress out, Nev came to join her. 'Is everything all right?'

'Yes, love. We've sorted it all out. Or rather I nudged her into sorting her life out for herself.' She gave him a wry smile. 'I warn you, I'm a very managing sort of woman, given half the chance.'

'I'm looking forward to you taking charge here. How soon shall we be wed?'

'As soon as you like,' Essie said recklessly, reassured by the beaming smile he gave her in response to that statement.

★ ★ ★

Denby kissed Marjorie goodbye, ignoring the tears tracking down her face. He'd rather have stayed with her, but he hadn't seen his family for a long time and wanted to check that they were all right. As he sat on the train, he tapped the fingers of his left hand impatiently on his thigh, unable to settle to reading the newspaper he'd bought. Then he remembered the letter Marjorie had given him to post to her family.

Pulling it out of his pocket, he broke the sealing wax and unfolded the piece of paper, reading it scornfully. Same old drivel. Why people bothered to write to one another when they'd nothing to say, he didn't know. The family's letters to Marjorie had been just as dull, not worth the reading. With a laugh, he tore the missive into little pieces, as he'd torn up all the ones she'd given him to post — and the ones that had come to Leeds for her. They couldn't write to her now because they didn't know where to find her as he'd carefully refrained from telling them where he would be playing in London.

Life was a lot easier without families interfering. He'd learned that the hard way. Opening the train window he flung out the tiny pieces of paper and watched them fly off into the fields.

When he got to Upper Saxton he stood for a minute outside the small station, staring round. Some might praise the charms of country life, but he'd never stopped being thankful he'd escaped from this damned village.

He called first at the inn to book a room for that night and leave his luggage. The landlady's face lit up at the sight of him and when he murmured in a low voice, 'Later?' Clemmy nodded, with a slow smile that promised much.

Once outside he gritted his teeth and did what he'd come here for — went to visit his wife and children. No one answered his knock, so he opened the cottage door and went inside, scowling at the low ceilings and untidiness. Confident that Alice would be home because she rarely went out, he made his way out into the back garden and sure enough, she was working in the vegetable garden at the far end of the long

197

plot on which the cottage stood.

He waited until she looked up, then sauntered towards her. 'I thought it was about time I came to visit the children.'

She heaved herself painfully to her feet. 'As long as you've brought some money with you.'

'Of course I have. I've never once let you go without, never broken our agreement.'

'No, I'll grant you that. But it's because you're scared of my brothers, not because you care about me or your sons.' She looked him up and down, grimacing as if she didn't like what she saw. 'You're not expecting to stay here, I hope? I like my bed to myself.'

'No, of course not. I've booked a room at the inn.'

Her lip curled scornfully. 'Clemmy always was a soft touch.'

'Clemmy Royner is a warm-hearted woman, unlike you.'

'She's a fool where men are concerned.'

He didn't pursue that. It'd only lead to their usual arguments. Alice didn't really care who he slept with and would have fought tooth and nail if he'd tried to climb into her bed again. 'All right if I come and visit the boys after they get home from school? You *are* still sending them to school, aren't you?' He'd insisted on that.

'Of course I am. I suppose you can come round to see them. Your visits disturb them for days, though, so try not to excite them too much this time.'

'I'll take them out for a walk.'

'You'll see them here, where I can keep an eye

198

on you and hear what you're telling them.' She scowled at him.

He scowled right back. Nothing had changed. They couldn't spend five minutes in one another's company without getting into an argument. 'I'll go and visit my uncle Bill then.'

'That's the real reason you keep coming back here,' she taunted. 'You hope to inherit the farm one day. Well, don't be so sure of yourself. He knows you'll only sell it.'

Denby grabbed her arm as she turned away. 'What do you mean by that?'

'I mean your uncle's not as stupid as you like to think. And you let go of me this minute, or I'll set the dog on you.'

He stepped back, repulsed as always by her size. She was the fattest woman he'd ever seen, had started to put on weight soon after their marriage and had now grown huge enough to appear in a sideshow at a fair. 'I don't know why I bother with you.'

'You don't need to as long as you keep sending my money. And if you start making a fortune, don't forget to increase what you send. You're dressing pretty fine these days.' Her eyes raked up and down him, not in an admiring but an assessing way.

'That's all show, to impress people. With what I pay you, I have to watch my money very carefully. I'll be back later.' He turned and left her, walking a mile along the lane to the farm where his uncle Bill lived, cursing the mud, nearly losing his hat a couple of times, the wind was so strong. As he walked, Alice's words echoed in his ears, but reason told him he was uncle Bill's only living relative, so who else could the old man leave the farm to? Still, it didn't hurt to keep the old man on his side and make sure of his inheritance.

He knocked on the door, knowing the dragon of a housekeeper would take exception to his walking straight into the house, though he'd done that often enough when he lived nearby.

She answered it and stood there, saying nothing as she too looked him up and down. Then she held the door open. 'You'd better come in, I suppose.'

'Is my uncle around?'

'He's out in the fields at this time of day, what did you expect? That he'd be sitting by the fire? You should know him better than that.'

'Out doing what? It's not the time of year for field work.'

'He likes to walk his land. Knows every plant and bush, he does. Good farmer, your uncle.'

'Where is he today?'

'East field.'

So with a grimace at the prospect of more mud, he tramped through the copse and along the path that led to the east field, where he found his uncle leaning on a gate, so lost in thought he didn't even see his nephew coming.

Denby raised his voice, because the old man was nearly eighty and rather deaf. 'Hello, Uncle Bill.'

The old man turned round to stare at him. 'You're back then, are you?'

'Yes. I always come to visit you as soon as I get

to London, don't I?'

'Mmm.'

'How are you keeping?'

'As well as can be expected at my age.'

'You look as hale and hearty as ever.' More's the pity, Denby thought.

'Ah, well. Us Dallows usually do. Long lived, we are, even if we don't produce a tribe of children. I doubt you'll make old bones, though, because you take after your father, not your mother.' He turned and began to walk towards the house. 'I suppose you'll want a cup of tea and something to eat.'

'That'd be nice.'

When they were seated, his uncle said, 'Well, aren't you going to tell me all about that act of yours?'

'Of course.'

'You can give me a song or two as well after we've eaten. I was a good singer myself when I was young.'

Denby nodded. This was a ritual with them. Alice didn't understand that his uncle was proud of what he did, liked to hear him sing, had even come up to London a time or two to watch him perform. His wife wasn't proud of him. Never had been. Said it wasn't a man's life prancing around on the stage. He'd not have married her if he hadn't got her with child. And if he'd known sooner what was in the wind he'd have run away from Upper Saxton before her brothers caught him and forced him to wed her. Worst day of his life, that had been. Worst two years of his life as well, living with her and working on

201

the farm. In the end he'd borrowed money from his uncle and escaped, leaving her with enough to manage on, promising to send more. And he'd kept that promise. But as she said, only because her damned brothers were the sort of men who'd come hunting for him if he didn't.

When he left the farm he strolled back to the cottage, feeling rather smug about the world. He'd done what he'd mainly come for: visited his uncle and kept the old man happy. Now he'd see his sons, who were fine little fellows though very tiring after an hour or so, then pay off his wife, earning himself another few weeks' freedom from her.

Once he'd done his duty, he'd enjoy a pleasant evening drinking in the inn — and an even pleasanter night with Clemmy, who was more fun in bed than any woman he'd ever known, and a lot more inventive, too.

★ ★ ★

On the Saturday after Renny's arrival in Hedderby, Tait went to the Pride with his wife and two couples they'd known for years. Just showed what the world was coming to, when a man's wife dragged him out of an evening. Women should stay at home where they belonged, but try telling that to Sheila. The show was excellent and he enjoyed himself, amazed that his employer would pay for him to attend. Which reminded him to look round and memorise every detail of the big room, as he'd been instructed.

When Bram Heegan appeared on the stage and began to sing, Tait scowled. He hated that Irish bugger and one day he intended to thump the hell out of him. Bram had interfered in Tait's life a couple of times and if he hadn't had so many friends that he rarely walked home alone at night, he'd have got his come-uppance before now.

Tait's companions were nodding their heads in time to the music and the men were downing beers as quickly as they could get hold of them. He nursed his beers carefully, having been ordered by his master to drink no more than three.

'What's up with you, lad? Lost your thirst, have you?' one mocked.

'*He* don't like us getting drunk.'

'*He* isn't here now.'

Sheila elbowed the man nearest her. 'Don't you tempt him into wasting more of his money on beer. Besides, I don't want him losing this job.'

Both men ignored her and grimaced at Tait.

'Mr Stott has ways of finding things out, even though he's stuck in bed most of the time,' Tait told them, shivering involuntarily. He scowled down at the amber fluid in the pot, then looked at his friend and neighbour. 'Would *you* like to cross him?'

'Hell, no!'

'How's work going?'

'Better than before. Mr Edmund knows what he's doing. He doesn't stand any nonsense, but he's fair enough. As long as it's safe to leave what you're doing, you can go and have a piss any time you need one now. And if you work late, he slips you an extra bob. Can't complain about that, can you?'

'No. I suppose not. He'd no call to sack me, though.'

'Ah, stop complaining, you stupid sod,' one of them said good-naturedly. 'It was your own fault. You should have worked harder when you had the chance instead of causing trouble. But you've landed on your feet now, haven't you?'

Tait wasn't so sure about that, but the comedian came on just then. It was Hal Kidd, back for a return visit 'by popular demand' the posters said and only a few weeks after his first appearance. In spite of what he considered his grievances, Tait couldn't help laughing, the fellow was so funny.

Before he knew it, the evening was over and he was walking back to the house where he worked, leaving his wife to walk home with their neighbours. He looked at his new home and shivered. Damn big place it was for such a small family, and he'd only seen a few of the rooms. The missus probably had a room just to fart in! He slouched into the kitchen and found Mrs Ibster there chatting with Renny. That brought a scowl back to his face. Renny Blaydon was going to take his job at this rate, unless he did something about it. Only what could he do without upsetting his master?

'Was the show good?' Mrs Ibster asked.

'Yes. Bloody good.'

'Mind your language in my kitchen!'

Only the thought of her cakes and scones made him take a deep breath and say, 'Sorry.'

He went up to bed, not looking forward to reporting about the Pride to his master the next morning.

★　★　★

At the Pride Hal was invited by the owners to come and have a cup of milk and honey with them after the performance. He accepted with pleasure because they were a nice bunch, not half as toffee-nosed as some.

Carrie passed round the steaming cups.

'I haven't had this for years.' He sipped appreciatively. 'Mmm. Nice and sweet.'

'The show went well,' Eli said. 'Your new act is even better than your old one. How many sketches do you have in your repertoire now?'

Hal smiled. 'Quite a few. I have to keep a notebook to remind me which sketches I've done in which theatres.'

'Do you enjoy the travelling life?' Bram asked.

'Mostly I do. I think I'd go mad stuck in the same old job day in day out, like my brothers are. But it can get a bit chilly in winter, not only travelling but some of the lodgings are stingy with the coal.'

'You haven't seen my sister and her husband anywhere on your travels, have you?' Carrie asked.

'No, sorry. Though I think I'm on the same programme as them in London in two weeks' time. How's she doing? Is she enjoying life as a singer?'

'We don't know. She hasn't written to us.'

'Eh, never! You must be that worried.'

'I'd be grateful if you'd ask her to write when you see them. Tell her we're all disappointed in her neglect of her family, and upset too. Just a couple of lines, if she's busy.'

'I'll do that, I promise.'

The talk turned back to the Pride. They were having some minstrels performing the following week, chaps who blacked up their faces and sang songs made popular by slaves in America. Eli was hoping the group, which was quite well known, would bring the crowds in.

'They're very popular,' Hal agreed. 'You can't go wrong with a minstrels act. I've heard even that the Queen and Prince Albert enjoy them.'

As he walked back to his lodgings he felt pleasantly tired. He could never go to bed straight after a performance because he was too wound up to settle easily to sleep. The milk and honey seemed to have helped tonight, though. An image of Marjorie came into his mind, so pretty, so good-natured. He was surprised she hadn't written to her family. She didn't seem like the sort of lass to neglect those she loved.

Perhaps Sinclair hadn't let her write. Hal wouldn't put anything past that one after the unkind way he'd treated the other lass who'd performed with him.

12

For Dr Latimer's funeral the church was crammed with mourners, most of them poor people who had not been invited, but had come to pay their respects.

Amelia sat beside Lydia at the front of the church and twisted round to look at the crowded pews. 'People like that shouldn't be allowed at a gentleman's funeral.'

Lydia's eyes were bright with tears but she smiled through them, proud of the turnout. 'They've come because they loved him, because he cared for them.'

'They should have waited outside.'

'He wouldn't have wanted that.'

When the service was over and the coffin had been lowered into the grave, Lydia stood for a moment then stiffened her spine and walked from the churchyard to the waiting carriage. Voices murmured their regrets as she passed, faces showed genuine grief for his passing and that gave her the courage to do what she must.

When they got home, she took off her bonnet and black veil with a sigh of relief. To her sister's horror, she hadn't invited anyone to come round to the house after the funeral because she hadn't lived the sort of social life that demanded this. She was glad. Hard enough to face life without Gerald by her side, without having to maintain a calmness she didn't feel.

'We can leave the day after tomorrow,' Amelia announced as they sat and waited for a tea tray to be brought in.

Lydia took a deep breath and said it. 'I've decided not to come and live with you after all, though I'm truly grateful for the offer of a home.'

'Not come to me? But you must. You've no way of living now you're a widow.'

'I think I have. I must try, at least.'

'Try to do what?'

'I shall advertise for another doctor to take over the practice, a younger man, perhaps, and act as his assistant and nurse, as I did with Gerald.'

Amelia's face turned dark red with anger. 'I forbid it!'

'You can't stop me.'

Amelia spent a full half-hour trying to persuade her sister to change her mind, then heaved herself to her feet. 'I wash my hands of you, Lydia Latimer. You always were a fool but since I believe it's grief which has turned your head, I shall not take further steps until you've come to terms with your widowhood. But I shall leave today. When you come to your senses, my offer of a home is still open — as long as you apologise and promise never to go against my advice again.'

Lydia stood up, unable to believe that her sister had given in so easily. Amelia was usually much more tenacious when she thought something should be done. Was it possible she hadn't wanted to share her home with anyone? 'Thank you, dear. I thought you'd disown me,

208

which just goes to show that you still care about me.'

'Caring is one thing, encouraging you in this foolishness is quite another.' Amelia moved towards the door.

When her sister and maid had been driven off to the station, Lydia sent Bet home then went to sit in the parlour, feeling the silence closing her in like a heavy curtain between herself and reality. Bet would be back tomorrow, but for today she wanted the house to herself, needed it.

She wept a little for Gerald then resolutely wiped her eyes. All the weeping in the world wouldn't bring him back again. She couldn't settle to anything, fidgeting round the parlour, then going to stand in the kitchen and wonder what she'd come there for. What she really needed was a good long walk, but it would shock people if she went out. Maybe if she left very early the following morning, perhaps she could stride out across the tops and clear her head of this dull, heavy feeling.

★   ★   ★

Denby arrived back in London early the next afternoon, to Marjorie's relief. She hadn't really thought he'd desert her, but she'd felt unsafe without him in this bewildering city. She'd gone for a walk the previous afternoon, but had been nervous all the time in case she couldn't find her way back to the lodging house.

'Did you miss me?' he asked, kissing her hard and nibbling her ear.

'Of course I did.' She waited for him to say he'd missed her too, but he didn't. 'How's your uncle?'

'Not well at all. He sends his best wishes, though. Hopes we'll be happy, all that sort of thing.'

'Can I come with you next time?'

'It'll be a while before I visit him again. His housekeeper will let me know if he needs me, or if anything goes wrong.'

'Oh.'

He forced a smile, wishing she wasn't so clinging. It was hard to stay affable all the time, but if he got angry with her, she went to pieces and that made her perform badly. When she was cheerful, she seemed to radiate happiness and that rubbed off on the audiences. Several people had commented on how she enhanced his act. Which reminded him.

'We'd better get you a new stage costume,' he said abruptly. 'That one of yours is a bit shabby for London. No time like the present. Get your bonnet and coat, and you'd better wear a scarf. It's damned cold outside.'

'I haven't got a scarf. I forgot to bring one from home.'

He suppressed a sigh. 'Then I'll have to buy you one.' She'd forgotten several things when she packed, or had lost them on their travels.

He took her to a theatrical costumier who had second-hand clothes for sale as well as being able to make new stage clothing like the outfits he wore. There was a trick to looking like a tramp and then suddenly tearing off the outer clothes

210

and appearing smartly dressed. And of course that sort of clothing cost money. To his relief they were lucky enough to find a dress which suited her perfectly at a reasonable price. She was a bit concerned about the low neckline, but he persuaded her that it'd look just right on stage. Indeed, it looked so good on her that he could hardly keep his hands off her till they got back to the lodgings. Her body was a lot younger and firmer than Clemmy's.

She was worth all the risks he was taking. Definitely. Things were going to go even better for him now he had her, he just knew it.

★   ★   ★

'Well?' Athol demanded. 'Tell me *exactly* what that damned music room looks like now.'

So Tait tried to describe the Pride, stumbling and moulding the air with his hands as he struggled to find words to convey the scene to his master.

'So the place was full?'

'Yes, sir. Not a seat left empty.'

'And Beckett was the Chairman?'

'Yes, sir. Good, he is. Got a really loud voice and makes you laugh.'

'Well, he's not going to make people laugh at my expense for much longer.'

'Excuse me, sir?' Tait couldn't understand what his master was on about, but when he didn't get an answer, he didn't dare ask again, just exchanged glances with Wiv and stood waiting to do what he was told.

Athol made a rasping noise in his throat and stared at them. 'That'll do for now. You can go again next Saturday, Tait, only next time you're to hang around outside till all the lights are out and see if it's possible to break in.'

'Break in, sir?' Tait looked at him in panic. 'I'm not much good at that sort of thing. I'm too clumsy.'

'I don't want you to actually break in, you fool, just find out how easy it would be to do it if you wanted to.'

'Oh. But it'll be dark, sir.'

'There will be a moon.'

'If it's not cloudy.'

'Stop making objections. Just do it.'

There was a knock on the door and Renny came in, carrying the artificial leg, its smoothly jointed wood cradled in his arms. 'I need to try this on you now, sir. I think you'll find the harness fits better.'

Tait let out a sigh of relief at the interruption. Now that arrogant bugger could get angry at someone else.

Athol scowled, but let them strap him into the harness that kept the leg in place. 'Well, stand me up.'

'Not yet, sir,' Renny said. 'Just sit on the edge of the bed. There are a few things I need to check. Besides, you'll do better getting used to it without putting weight on it at first. Just wear it for a short time the first few days.'

'I want to stand up now.'

Wiv reached out to help him, but Renny put out one hand to prevent him. 'No, sir. It'll chafe you unless you take this very gradually indeed.'

'I'm the master, not you, so do as you're damned well told.'

The room seemed to go very still. Wiv and Tait looked down at their feet.

Renny moved a step backwards and spoke in a chilly voice. 'I won't let my work be spoiled. If you want to learn to walk again, you'll need to do it my way or I'll leave and go to someone who'll listen to me. I *know* what I'm talking about, have helped people before.'

The silence seemed to throb with Athol's anger, but with something else too, something that stood against the anger, that changed the whole feeling of the room.

The man lying on the bed locked gazes with his new servant, who looked calmly back at him, and it was Athol who lowered his eyes first. Even then the silence went on for a long time before Renny broke it.

'Now, just sit there for a few minutes, then we'll stand you up gently for a minute or two.'

Athol didn't answer, but he did let Renny finish fitting the harness. As the man worked, he gazed down at the contraption with utter loathing and muttered, 'Damned thing!'

'It'll be hidden by your clothing, sir,' Renny said. 'You'll limp, but eventually you'll walk by yourself, wherever you want to go. Worth going carefully at first, don't you think, to get around again?'

When he laid one hand on his master's arm, Athol didn't knock it away, just sighed and closed his eyes. 'Damn you all!' he muttered. But he made no further protests.

After the artificial leg had been removed, he sat leaning against the pillows and grumbled, 'I don't know why I put up with you.'

Renny smiled. 'Because I can help you better than anyone else can.'

The noise surprised Tait and Wiv, because they hadn't heard it before — their master was laughing.

When he stopped he leaned back against the pillow, looking faintly surprised, staring at Renny as if he'd suddenly grown a tail.

'There's something else I need to talk to you about, sir,' Renny said.

'What the hell else do you want?' But his tone was resigned, not angry.

'To talk about your sons.'

'What about them? They're not causing trouble, are they? I won't have them running wild.'

'They're not causing any trouble, sir. But they should be doing at that age. I don't think they get any chance to run. If they don't run and play they won't grow up with strong bodies.'

'They've a governess to take care of them. It's not up to you to worry.'

'Miss Cavett is terrified of them disturbing you, so she keeps them quiet. Too quiet.' Renny let silence work for him again, allowing his master to think about what he'd said.

'She's a fool.'

'No, sir, she's not. Just a timid lady, who's doing what she thinks you want. We can easily solve the problem by giving your sons a dog.

214

They can play with it round the back of the house and take it for walks. It'll give them exercise without disturbing you.'

'I don't like animals in the house. They only get petted and spoiled.'

'I don't like them being spoiled either, sir. Animals must be properly controlled and their owners must show they're in charge. It'll do your sons good to be responsible for a puppy. Lads need to learn responsibility as well as get plenty of exercise.'

Athol scowled at him. 'You always have an answer, don't you?'

Renny gave him one of those long, wide-eyed looks and said gently, 'They need a dog, sir, if they're not to grow up into weaklings.'

'Oh, very well, but they'd better keep it away from me! And it'd better be kept clean.'

Later that night when he and his brother were getting ready for bed, leaving Tait on night duty in the dressing room next to their master's bedroom, Wiv said to Renny, 'How the hell do you do it?'

'Do what?'

'Make *him* do what you want.'

'Same as I would with any wild animal. Mind over matter, tone of voice. They don't understand words, but they understand power.'

Wiv looked at him and shook his head. 'I'm no wiser. Nor I don't understand what you're trying to do.'

His brother laughed softly then got into the bed they now shared, with Tait sleeping on a narrow bed to one side. 'I'm attempting the impossible with Mr Stott, trying to tame him, like you do with any wild animal.'

He was asleep almost as soon as he lay down, but it took Wiv a while to follow his example. He was wondering if he'd done the right thing bringing his brother here. Renny stirred up trouble sometimes without meaning to, simply by insisting on doing things his own way. A couple of times Wiv had thought Mr Stott would erupt, he'd become so angry with Renny. And his brother would never change what he was doing when he considered himself to be in the right. That had got him into trouble many a time, even during his childhood. So there were bound to be more confrontations.

Well, Wiv decided in the end, he'd just make the most of this comfortable life while he had it, and pray that it'd continue. No need to tell Renny about some of the instructions he'd received from Mr Stott and some of the things his master had threatened to do to the folk at the Pride when he was half delirious.

Though with his brother, you didn't always need to tell him things. He seemed to know some things by instinct. What would Renny do if he found out Mr Stott was seriously planning vengeance on those who'd once gone against his wishes, those whom he blamed for his present crippled state?

Wiv hoped desperately that Renny wouldn't try to stop him.

★　★　★

Maria watched with regret as Renny got her husband upright and allowed him to walk to the door and back, if you could call that lurching gait walking. She wasn't sure she wanted Athol up and about again, interfering in her life, though he paid her little attention these days because his main focus was on himself and whatever those men of his were doing at his behest.

He looked better than he had since the accident, and she put that down to this Renny, who was . . . strange. But somehow she had no fear of the man, nor did her sons. Which continued to surprise her.

Athol moved along, his face set in grim lines of determination and also pain. But he made no complaint. You had to grant that he was brave. She hated the twisted claw of a hand, which bumped slightly against his chest as he moved because the arm was permanently bent, too.

'That's enough for now, sir.'

Athol turned to scowl at the man whose soft voice directed his actions these days. 'I can do more!'

'Yes, I know you can. But your leg can't.'

With a groan of frustration Athol returned to the bed. Before he would let Renny touch him, he turned to his wife.

'You're doing well, better than anyone could ever have expected,' she said, seeing he expected some comment from her. 'I'm glad for you.' And in a way, she was, because she knew what torment his incapacity had been for a man who had always been strong and active. But she wasn't glad for herself. She hated the thought of him starting to come downstairs, sitting with her, taking over her life again. He stared at her and she hoped she'd kept her expression calm, not shown her real feelings.

'You can leave us now, Maria.'

She bowed her head and moved towards the door.

When she'd gone Athol turned towards Renny. 'I suppose you want to take the leg off now?'

'Yes, sir. We must.'

'Damned well do it, then!'

He allowed them to remove the harness and settle him in the bed, drank another of Renny's herbal potions and lay back with a sigh. It had hurt to move, but he wouldn't let himself give in to that, was determined to master the pain. Through half-closed eyes he watched Renny set the room to rights, moving surely and even gracefully for a big man.

He hated Renny Blaydon! Hated him for his strength, both physical and mental, and the power over his master that gave the fellow. The potions Renny made controlled his pain and didn't leave Athol half as drowsy but one day, he promised himself, the man would regret ordering his master around. It made no difference that the orders were helping Athol's recovery. He loathed anyone telling him what to do, always had.

But he would continue following those softly voiced instructions for the moment, because he was making far more progress doing things Renny's way than he had when following Dr

Barlow's instructions.

Once he had recovered his mobility, though, Renny Blaydon would find out who was master here. And certain others would find out he was still a man to be reckoned with — however long it took.

★　★　★

The next day Renny went for a walk, as he did every day, but this time he brought back a puppy, a lop-eared creature whose large feet promised a big animal when it was fully grown.

Mrs Ibster met him at the door. 'That thing isn't coming into my clean house, Mr Blaydon.'

'Not until he's washed. But he's hungry and desperately needs some food. Could you . . . '

She waved one hand to the kitchen maid. 'Get it some scraps and then get it a tub and some hot water. *Outside.*'

'Thank you,' Renny said in his usual tranquil tones, then looked down. 'Come.'

The puppy looked up at him trustingly and tottered along at the end of the piece of rope tied round her neck. Once she raised her head and barked at a cloth flapping on the line, shrill little cries that floated up to the schoolroom. And not all the governess's threats could stop the two little boys from rushing to the window and gazing down joyfully into the back garden.

'He's done it, he's brought a puppy back!' Isaac exclaimed.

Benjamin didn't waste any more time but made for the door and the two of them raced

219

down the two flights of stairs as quickly as they could, followed by Miss Cavett calling to them to come back this minute.

Isaac got to the puppy first, but when Renny held up one hand, he paused, his eyes on the little creature who was gulping down the food the maid had brought out. The maid too was watching, smiling a little.

'She needs some water, Isaac,' Renny prompted.

'I'll get you a bowl, Master Isaac,' the maid offered.

The lad trotted off with her, proud to do this service for the little animal.

Benjamin edged closer, thumb in his mouth.

'She's frightened,' Renny said quietly. 'Don't shout or move too suddenly. She doesn't know who you are.'

Isaac, who had returned while he was speaking, stopped and looked at him questioningly.

'Move forward slowly and put the bowl down in front of her, then step back.'

When the boy got close, the puppy cringed away, as if expecting to be hit.

'She's been ill-treated, needs love and tender care. Can you two look after her, can you be kind to her even if she bites you or messes on the floor?'

Two heads nodded, two pairs of eyes never left the puppy.

'What's she called?' Isaac ventured.

'Whatever you think suits her.'

'Migs?'

'Good name.'

An hour later, bathed and dosed with yet another of Renny's herbal mixtures, the puppy was carried inside by Renny, too sleepy now to be afraid.

'She's not afraid of you,' Benjamin said. 'Even when you touch her.'

Renny smiled down at him. 'She knows I'll not hurt her.'

'How does she know?'

'Because in here,' he tapped his chest, 'I don't want to hurt her.'

Isaac frowned. 'My father says it's good to have people afraid of you, then they do what you want.'

'People do what I want without being afraid of me. That makes everyone happier.'

A frown creased the lad's face, but he didn't say anything.

The governess, who had followed her charges down and hovered at the edge of the group, looked at Renny in dismay, but his eyes dared her to contradict him and she only muttered to herself as they walked up the stairs. Since *that man* had the master's permission to introduce this animal into the house she contented herself by speaking sharply whenever she had to say anything to Renny, keeping her distance from the little creature and ordering the maid to bring some bedding for it up to the schoolroom at once.

When Renny returned to his master, Athol said, 'I heard the barking. I presume you've brought a dog back.'

'Yes, sir. The boys are looking after her now. She's been ill-treated, but she's a clever animal and will repay their love.'

'How can you possibly know that?'

Renny shrugged. 'Sometimes I just know things that others don't.'

'And what do you *know* about me?'

'That I can help you — but only if you'll let me.'

For a moment their eyes met and Athol was the first to lower his lids and break the contact, but not before Renny had seen the vicious, feral expression in the depths of his eyes.

The battle for Athol Stott's soul might already be lost, and Renny was aware now that there was only the faintest chance of saving him, but the battle for those two boys' souls was one he would pursue to the death, if need be.

13

Essie was to be married on the Thursday, two days after the good doctor's funeral, because Nev didn't want to wait. That day she woke up in an uncharacteristic flutter, suddenly terrified of what she was doing. Marrying for the first time at her age! People must be laughing at her. She'd been sewing furiously to finish a new dress she had originally intended for church on Sundays. She went to throw back the curtains and then was drawn to the dress, which was hanging on the wardrobe door so as not to crush the full skirt. Was it too full for a woman her age? Too frivolous? No use worrying about that now.

There was a knock and Dora peeped in. 'Do you want me to bring you up a cup of tea?'

'I can come down and get it.'

'No, I'll get it for you. We're going to spoil you this morning, remember. And don't forget that I'm doing your hair.'

When the girl who would soon be her stepdaughter had gone, Essie blinked furiously. Far from resenting her marriage, the whole family seemed to have taken her to its heart, and even Robbie, who at twenty-two was independent and lived with his employer, was going to take time off work to come to the wedding. Only there wouldn't be a beautiful bride at the centre of all the fuss, simply a plump, middle-aged woman whose hair was more grey than brown

223

now, and whose face was starting to sag and show age lines. 'I wish . . . ' But she let the words she had been going to utter drift away. What was the use wishing for the impossible?

In another bedroom Nev was just as nervous. It had been easier the first time he'd married. He and Jane had just done the deed without all this fuss. Today the children had told him to stay in bed and have a lazy start to the day, but he wasn't used to lying around doing nothing. He opened the wardrobe and stroked the fine worsted of his dark grey frock coat, the first one he had ever possessed. Would people laugh at him for dressing like a gentleman? Well, let them. It was for Essie he was dressing so finely. He went to the window for the umpteenth time, to make sure the fine clear day he had hoped for wasn't changing.

It was a great relief when it was time to get ready and join the others.

In the kitchen he looked at his stepchildren, his heart swelling with pride. They were a credit to him, a fine bunch of young people, properly dressed now, properly fed, too, and surrounded by the older girls and Essie. He walked across to her and took her hands. 'You look really nice.'

'Thank you.' She blushed.

That blush touched him and he smiled as he let go of her hands and offered his arm. 'Shall we go?' The hand she laid on his forearm was trembling, so he patted it and smiled at her, forgetting the others. 'Nervous?'

She nodded.

'So am I. But I'm happy too.'

She searched his face anxiously as if unsure whether he meant it. 'Are you sure?'

'Very sure.'

Her smile was glorious. 'That's all right then.'

There were ten of them walking to the church, all dressed in their best clothes. Gwynna was with them because Nev wanted little Sylvie to be there at his wedding and anyway, it had been unthinkable to leave Gwynna at home on her own on such a happy day.

At the church they found Robbie, Eli and Carrie waiting for them. No one mentioned Marjorie, but they were all missing her and thinking about her today. They hadn't even been able to let her know about the wedding. Knowing how upset Carrie was about the absence of her next sister, Eli had debated going down to London to seek Marjorie out, but even if he did, she could hardly absent herself from a performance there to come back for a wedding here, so he left it. It was a shame, though, a great shame that she was the only member of the family not here.

To Essie's great delight, Mrs Latimer was also waiting for them at the church, hovering behind the others. The two women hugged one another convulsively, then Raife offered his arm to the doctor's wife and they all went inside.

As she stood at the front Essie suddenly lost her fear. The ceremony was brief and she made her responses in a firm voice. When Nev kissed her cheek she stared at him in wonderment as she realised she was now his wife. Years ago she had given up hope of getting married and now she was Mrs Neville Linney, with stepchildren and best of all a baby to raise. Never mind that she'd never bear a child of her own. She could still be a mother to this group of lively young people, and to this bonny infant.

And a wife to this plump, beaming man, who was holding her hand rather too tightly and sweating a little, in spite of the coolness of the day.

After they'd signed the register, the whole group walked along Market Street to the Dragon, laughing and talking now, the solemnity finished with. Carrie had a splendid meal waiting for them, the platters covered by dampened cloths to keep the food fresh. Bram and Joanna joined them briefly to drink the newly-weds' health.

Only as they were walking back to the lodging house together did Nev and Essie get a chance to speak privately.

'You're very quiet,' he said.

'Quietly happy,' she replied firmly, seeing the smile bloom on his face again.

'So am I,' he confessed. And he stopped walking to kiss her cheek right there in the street. 'I'm very fond of you, Essie lass. I think we'll do all right.'

Which brought tears of joy to her eyes.

★　★　★

Lydia thought about her problem and in the end wrote to her husband's old friend in London. Chandler Grey was a very well-known doctor, involved in training the new sort of young doctors at St Guy's Hospital. She explained her situation and her idea of offering her husband's practice to a young fellow who perhaps couldn't afford to buy into an established practice. He could lodge in her home as well, all in return for a weekly payment. And she could help him, as she'd helped her husband. She was a good nurse, if she said so herself.

Chandler wrote back to express sorrow at his friend's death, praised her idea and suggested she consider one of his former students, a talented man, older than most of his students, who had struggled even to find the fees for his training because of his family's opposition to his chosen career. In fact, Chandler had been going to ask his old friend to take Christy Pipperday into his practice, because he knew Gerald needed help.

In spite of Christy's lack of experience, which only time would cure, Chandler assured Lydia that he was a good doctor. He'd have liked to become a surgeon, but couldn't afford the fees, so he'd been working in a couple of dispensaries in London, where he'd gained valuable experience while attending to the needs of the poor. However the poor fellow had been ill recently so needed to get out of the slums of London and live a more regular life. Lodging with her would be the very thing, because Christy tended to forget meals and neglect his personal needs.

She wrote back at once suggesting Chandler's protégé come to see her.

Two days later there was a knock on the door

and she opened it to see a young man standing there, top hat in his hand, portmanteau at his feet.

'I'm Christy Pipperday, ma'am. Dr Grey said you wanted to meet me, to consider . . . You are Mrs Latimer, aren't you? I'd expected someone older.'

She blinked, then blinked again as she took in his appearance, unable to speak for a moment or two. He was so very tall, must have been at least six foot three or four. He had crinkly gingerish hair that needed taming and grey-green eyes, the latter magnified by the lenses of his round spectacles. He was thin and pale, and his clothes were rather shabby, his cravat awry as if he'd tugged at it. 'Yes, I am Mrs Latimer. Do come in, Dr Pipperday.'

'Thank you, ma'am.'

His voice was deep and cultured, the voice of the upper classes, yet his smile as she closed the door behind him was boyish and open. She gestured down the hall. 'Would you mind if we sat in the kitchen? I haven't lit a fire anywhere else today. My housekeeper has just left me to marry and I've only a daily maid, Bet, who's gone out to buy some food.'

'I like kitchens. Shall I leave my bag here in the hall?'

'Yes.' She led the way to the rear of the house and gestured to a seat at the scrubbed wooden table, going across to push the kettle on to the hottest part of the hob. 'I've just been making some oatcakes. Would you like one?'

He smiled. 'I'd love one. I was too excited to

buy any food and came here straight from the station.' He hesitated, then said in a rush, an anxious expression replacing the smile, 'I wonder, ma'am, if we could discuss the position straight away. If I'm not suitable I'd rather know at once, you see. I couldn't bear to get my hopes up in vain. What sort of man do you want?'

She swallowed a sigh. The sort of man she wanted was her husband and she'd wept for Gerald every morning that she'd woken up alone in the big bed. It was an effort to talk normally and she spoke slowly, thinking aloud. She should have worked out exactly what she wanted when she dashed off the letter to Chandler, but she hadn't, she who'd once prided herself on being well-organised. 'I want a man who'll treat the poor kindly and not charge them if they can't afford to pay, someone who cares about helping people more than about earning money — and who'll let me work with him, as I worked with my husband. Gerald — ' she had to pause for a moment after saying his name, ' — always said it was a pity I couldn't become a doctor too. I'm a good nurse, though, particularly with mothers and young children.'

'I promise you I'm not hungry for money.' He gestured down at himself with a wry smile. 'Perhaps that's obvious to you. My father disowned me for not going into the Army, as younger sons always do in our family. But I wanted to help people not kill them.'

She began to ask him questions about how he would treat various medical conditions, the sort of questions most ladies wouldn't even have understood. He betrayed some surprise at first but answered her carefully, pausing every now and then to consider a reply. After a while he looked at her in awe. 'I think you know as much as I do about medical matters.'

She shrugged. 'I know a fair amount because I helped my husband. I loved the work, don't want to give it up now. If I were a man, I'd be a doctor.'

'I'd wondered about some of the conditions attached to your offer but I can see the reason for them now. I can promise you that if you let me come here, I'll not waste your skills.'

'Well, we could try it for a month, if you like. You'll only get poorer patients during that time, till people start to trust you, so you won't make much money, but I have a spare bedroom. You should bring in enough to buy food for us both with a little over, though. They're very proud and hate to take charity, so most will try to pay you something, even if it's only a penny. You'd have to help with the living expenses, I'm afraid, because I'm somewhat short of money. My husband never saved any, you see. He said he couldn't let money sit idly in the bank while children were starving for lack of food.'

'And you didn't object to that?'

'No. He was a wonderful doctor and the poor of our town have been through some hard times in the last few years with trade being slack.'

'I wish I'd met him.'

She studied him, finding him very young and earnest. Well, that was good because she couldn't bear cynical men. 'I wish you had, too.'

'I'd be very honoured if you'll allow me to try to fill his shoes, Mrs Latimer, and if you'll not be too hard on me at first.'

She nodded. 'Then you'd better go back for the rest of your things.'

He opened his mouth, shut it, then confessed with a blush, 'They're at the station. I brought them with me in case you agreed to let me stay. Dr Grey seemed quite certain I'd suit and I didn't want to waste a minute. Anyway, I was between jobs. It's one of my faults, I'm afraid, impulsiveness.'

'Mine too.' She held out her hand and he shook it, still very grave and solemn. She remembered his wide smile, wondered if she'd ever smile so freely again.

★   ★   ★

When her husband went out for a walk Marjorie sat and wrote yet another letter to her family. She wept as she put pen to paper. Why hadn't they replied to her? Was something wrong? Were they angry with her? If only they weren't so far away, she'd go back and confront them, ask them.

Denby came home before she'd finished, scolded her in tender tones and consigned the letter to the fire. 'If they don't want to write back, you're not going to beg them. In fact, I forbid you to write any more letters.' He took her in his arms as she wept, patting her shoulders and keeping his irritation under control. 'Now, dry your eyes. I've been thinking about a new act. We'll need to rehearse it and I want to find a new song and buy it exclusively, but it must be a really good one to make my name with, and if it does, that'll bring in extra money from the sale of the sheet music.'

He kept her distracted and busy for the rest of the day, taking her to the two music saloons where they were to perform. Both were far grander than the one in Leeds. 'Lancashire and London,' he said, smug in his superior knowledge. 'They're the places for people like us. Nowhere else in the country has nearly as many music rooms, or such good ones. But in London they're more — sophisticated, more like proper theatres. They're starting to call them variety theatres or music halls.'

Two days later they started work, hiring a cab to rush from the music saloon to the variety theatre every evening. The latter was so grand, with a large stage and a balcony for the better class of person that Marjorie was awed by it at first and forgot her worries about her family because she was so busy. Denby found a song, 'My Dear Delight' and made them rehearse it and then work on another of the story-like sketches he seemed able to design with ease.

To her delight, Hal Kidd was appearing at the smaller place with them and she kept looking out for him, hoping he'd be able to tell her how her family was. But when she suggested to Denby that they linger to chat to him after his act, her husband scowled at her. 'That scrubby little fellow. Certainly not! I'm amazed he can even get an engagement in a place like this.'

232

'The audience like him.'

'More fools them.' He whisked her off to the next show.

* * *

Hal saw Marjorie long before she saw him and watched her performance from the rear of the big room where the audience sat, because there weren't any wings at this place for people to stand and watch. It was simply a matter of going out on to the stage through a curtained doorway. But it was a very popular place, for all its limitations, with a full house every evening, and his agent assured him that it was a good place to start in London. The bigger music saloons and variety theatres kept an eye on the new acts here and at one or two other popular places.

He was hoping to have a word with Marjorie — well, he'd promised Carrie and Eli that he'd find her and ask why she hadn't written to them. But he'd have wanted to speak to her anyway to see how she was for himself. He still dreamed about her, which showed how foolish he was.

As he watched her on stage he could see at once how much she'd improved since Hedderby. Beautiful she was now and so graceful. But Sinclair still hogged the act, using her only as background to his performance. She deserved better than that. The audience loved her, though, and called out for Elyssa when they shouted for an encore. Sinclair allowed her to sing with him, but again, the song was chosen to show off his voice not hers. And the sod had a good voice, you had to grant him that. But he didn't need to swamp hers like that.

Afterwards, Hal watched them come out of the big changing room with its curtained alcoves, arguing about something. Then Sinclair saw him, scowled in his direction and hustled her out, physically forcing her through the door. Hal could see the disappointment on her face, the way she twisted her head to glance back at him. Strange, that. Why was the fellow preventing her from speaking to him?

Because of the timing of their acts and the fact that they were both playing at two places each night, it was three days before they met by accident in the corridor and he made sure he barred the way out this time.

'Mrs Sinclair,' he said formally, 'I've been wanting to see you and — '

'We're in a bit of a hurry, I'm afraid,' Sinclair put in.

'Oh, we can spare a minute or two, surely, Denby?' she protested.

There was an awkward moment as her husband scowled at her, then he shrugged. 'All right. But just a minute.'

'I've got messages for you from your family,' Hal said.

'She doesn't want to hear them,' Sinclair said at once.

Her mouth dropped open in surprise. 'I *do* want to hear them! Denby, there has to be a reason why they haven't written and I need to know it. There's nothing wrong, is there, Mr Kidd? They're not ill or anything?'

'Of course not, except that they're worried about you because you haven't written.'

'Haven't written? Of course I have. I've written to them every week. But I haven't heard a single word back.'

'They say the same about you. They wrote every week to Leeds and you didn't reply, but they don't know where to write to in London.'

She stared at him in shock then said softly, 'I can't believe it. What can have happened to all those letters?'

'I don't know. Um — I hope you don't mind, but I wrote to them at the beginning of this week to say I'd seen you and you were well. I've been trying to catch you all week to pass on their message.'

'Well, now you've done it perhaps we can get on with our business,' Denby said, putting his arm round his wife's waist and trying to move her along.

'Just a minute, Denby.'

Hal watched her pull away again and stayed where he was, blocking the way so the fellow couldn't push her outside.

'How are they all, Mr Kidd?'

'They're well. Carrie's expecting, but I suppose you knew that already.'

'No, I didn't. Is she happy about it?'

'Delighted.'

'I'm glad for her, then. Oh, I do wish I could see her. I miss them all so much, but I miss Carrie most of all.'

Denby sighed audibly and pulled out his pocket watch. 'Marjorie.'

She ignored him. 'And the others? Did you see any of my brothers and sisters?'

'Not really. They were too busy working, though young Ted popped into the Pride once after school. I've some more news for you, some sad, some happy. Dr Latimer has died.'

Tears filled her eyes. 'Oh, no. Whatever will people do without him?'

'And Nev has married Essie.'

She gaped at him, then a smile replaced the sadness on her face. 'How wonderful! Oh, I must write and wish them happy.' The smile faded. 'But if my other letters didn't get through, this one might not, either.'

'I could send one for you with mine.'

Denby judged it time to intervene. 'Thank you for the news, Mr Kidd, but we really do have to go now.' This time he moved forward so purposefully that Hall was forced to step back. Indeed, Sinclair bumped him back so hard, he cracked his elbow on the wall and was pleased to see that it'd hurt him. Serve him right for interfering in what didn't concern him! He grasped Marjorie's arm firmly and literally forced her away before she could protest.

'Why did you pull me away?' she asked as he hustled her out of the saloon. 'We're not in that much of a hurry.'

'Because I don't like that fellow.'

'Mr Kidd? But he's a lovely man.'

'I think you'll have to allow me to judge that. I've more experience of the world than you and I don't trust his type.'

She was very quiet on the way home from

their second engagement and when they got to their room, turned to Denby and asked bluntly, 'Did you post my letters?'

He stared at her in surprise. Not as gullible as he'd thought. Well, it must be obvious to anyone with half a brain that the letters couldn't all have gone astray. 'No, I didn't.'

'What about my family's letters to me?'

'I destroyed them.'

There was silence in the room, then she asked in a voice that wobbled, 'Why, Denby?'

'Because I didn't want anything coming between you and the act. Because you needed to settle down into your new life. And I'm not sorry for what I did, either.'

She sat down suddenly on the bed as if her legs wouldn't hold her. 'Oh, Denby, that was cruel of you.'

'Sometimes you have to be cruel to be kind.'

'No, you don't. You don't *ever* need to be cruel. I shall find it hard to forgive you for this.'

'I'm your husband, so I do what I consider best for you and for us both. And I still don't want you to write to them. Now, let's forget all that and go to bed.'

He began to kiss her and when she tried to pull away, he laughed. This time he wasn't gentle in bed. This time he hurt her and she didn't enjoy making love.

When it was over he fell asleep almost immediately. But she didn't. She lay awake for a long time, upset with him. She knew he was selfish — it hadn't taken her long to realise that — but she'd put up with it because he'd treated her kindly in his own way. But this wasn't kindness, wasn't even reasonable. She still found it hard to believe he'd tried to cut her off from her family, couldn't understand why he'd thought it necessary. But he underestimated her love for them if he thought he could come between them. Nothing would ever stop her loving her family, nothing.

She'd write to them on Sunday while he was out taking his usual constitutional, a long letter giving all her news. Thank goodness she had her own money. She wouldn't even have to ask him for a stamp. And this time she'd post the letter herself.

A few days later she waited for him to give her the ten shillings she received every week, but he didn't. Finally she asked him for her money.

'I'm a bit short this week, I'm afraid.'

'I can't see why.'

'Well, I just am.'

She drew herself up, guessing this was retaliation for speaking to Hal and getting upset about her family. If she didn't make a stand now, he'd continue to bully and cheat her, and without money she'd be at his mercy. 'If you don't pay me, I won't perform.'

'You're my wife. You'll do as you're told.'

The anger which rose in her at his response was so unusual that for a minute she could only stand there, feeling hot resentment flow through her, surprised by its force. He must have thought she'd given in because he started to turn away. She grabbed his arm and pulled him round.

'I mean it, Denby. If you don't pay me I won't go on stage with you.'

'You don't mean that.'

'I do.'

'We'll see how you feel on Tuesday.'

When the time came for them to get ready to go to the music saloon two days later she did nothing, sitting near the window of their room, continuing to mend her everyday stockings.

'Time to get ready, dear,' he said.

She gave him a long, level look. He'd been very kind and affectionate for the past day or two, but that didn't change what he'd done to her, and he still hadn't given her any money. 'I'm not going anywhere. I told you I wouldn't when you didn't pay me last week.'

He stepped forward so hastily she thought he was going to hit her, but he didn't. Instead he came to an abrupt halt close to her and said, 'Get ready this minute!' He stood over her, arms folded, clearly expecting her to obey him. But she didn't give in. It would be too terrifying to be on her own in these strange places without any money in her pocket. She was trying to save up, in spite of needing new clothes and stockings, and had a little set aside. It made her feel safer. But she wasn't going to dip into that now.

She stabbed the darning needle in again to hide the fact that her hand was trembling. She heard him mutter an oath, saw him fumble in his pocket and felt the coins hit her lap. One fell on the floor. She put down her sewing and picked it up. 'Thank you.'

He said nothing to her all the way to the theatre.

It was her worst performance ever, she was so upset. And she didn't even care.

When they got back to their lodgings he took her in his arms, gently this time. 'I'm sorry, Marjorie. I'm afraid I'm jealous of your family. I've never seen a family so close and loving, never known such a thing. I wanted you for myself.'

She sighed as she put her arms round him. 'I'll forgive you this time, Denby, but don't come between me and my family again. They mean too much to me.'

He made love to her when they went to bed, bringing her to a wonderful release, then muttering, 'Damn!' and pulling away from her suddenly.

'What's the matter?'

'I was a little late pulling out of you. It probably won't make any difference. I still managed to spill most of my seed elsewhere.'

She lay there for a minute then got up to wash. By the time she slid into bed again he was asleep. He always did fall asleep quickly afterwards.

Again she lay awake, staring blindly into the darkness.

She might have forgiven him, but she couldn't forget what he'd done. Wouldn't trust him again, not in the same way as she had before.

Wished she hadn't rushed into marriage.

No, she didn't wish that. If she hadn't, she'd still be housekeeping for Nev. Or working in some other boring job. And she loved being on stage, absolutely loved it.

You had to take the rough with the smooth in life, she told herself. No one was perfect, not Denby, not herself. But that thought didn't bring her any easing of her unhappiness. She had made an uncomfortable bed for herself and must now lie on it.

14

When the letter from her sister arrived, Carrie prised off the sealing wax with shaking hands. As she read it, tears brimmed in her eyes. 'Oh, thank goodness! Thank goodness!' She stood for a moment with it clutched against her chest, then went rushing into the music room to find Eli, calling, 'Marjorie's all right. She's written!'

He took her in his arms, laughing and trying to calm her down so that he could find out what had happened. But when he read the letter, he grew grave. 'She says Denby destroyed the letters because he wanted her to settle in more easily.'

'I don't like the sound of that, Eli love.'

'Neither do I. Why should writing to her family stop her settling in?'

They were both silent.

'Why doesn't he want her to contact us?' she asked. 'It doesn't make sense.'

'Well, we've heard from her now. Let's hope she gets our reply.' He gave his wife a wry smile. 'And don't tell me you're not going to write back to her immediately.'

'Well, yes. I thought I would. Oh, I'm so relieved.'

'Can I get back to work now?' Once the door to the house had banged shut, he sighed and pulled his pocket watch out. He didn't want to worry her, not when she was so happy, but he was more than a little concerned about the star

242

of their new bill. Jamieson Mair was an older man, very popular in the north, but no longer appearing in the south, the agent had said, for family reasons. Eli had heard that he had an excellent voice, but hadn't had a chance to see him perform yet. He was late coming to the music room for rehearsal, very late, which didn't bode well.

In fact, Mair didn't turn up until the afternoon was nearly over and he looked distinctly the worse for wear, bleary-eyed with rumpled clothes.

'Are you not well?' Eli asked, hoping his suspicions about the real cause of the other man's condition were wrong.

Mair drew himself up. 'Of course I'm well. Just had a bad headache this morning. I'll be all right tonight. Now, let's go through the songs.' He walked past Eli and handed some music to Raife, who explained he didn't read music, just needed to hear the songs once and find out exactly how the singer wanted accompanying, then he'd be able to play them.

Mair scowled and opened his mouth, caught Eli's cold gaze and turned away from Raife, moving slowly up on to the stage, where he turned and sang his songs.

He had a good voice, but his appearance wasn't prepossessing and he put the minimum effort into embellishing his act, standing perfectly still and singing as if bored by it. Eli, watching from the back of the long room, could only hope that he'd do better tonight.

However as the show progressed that evening

there was no sign of Mair coming to get ready for his turn and Eli began to feel seriously worried. As Chairman he couldn't leave his place, so as the first half of the show drew to a close, he sent Bram round to the lodging house to find out where Mair was.

His friend returned looking grave and caught Eli before he went back to his post at the table near the stage. 'Mair's been drinking and has passed out. I can't rouse him. There's no way he'll be able to perform. What's more, Mrs Lodder says he must leave first thing tomorrow. He was sick on the floor in his bedroom last night and she's most put out about it.'

'Oh, hell, what are we going to do about the show?'

Joanna was going past just then making sure the waiters were doing their job properly, and stopped at the sight of their expressions. 'Trouble?'

They explained.

Eli looked at his cousin, turned sideways and saw Bram looking at her thoughtfully as well. 'Couldn't you try singing on stage, Joanna love? We're absolutely desperate for a new act tonight. Bram will be there with you. Surely this once . . . '

She shook her head, shuddering visibly. 'No! I keep telling you both: I can't face the thought of appearing in public, just can't face it.' She walked away.

Bram looked at his wife's rigid back thoughtfully, then turned to Eli. 'Leave it to me. She'll appear on the stage tonight if I have to drag her on. Make sure she's near you when it comes time to announce us. Beckon her over, use any excuse. I need to have a quick word with Raife about the music.'

'You can't force her to sing.'

'If I'm right, it's just nerves and once she gets over that, she'll enjoy it. She loves singing, and a voice like that shouldn't be hidden. If I'm wrong this'll prove it, and I'll stop nagging her.'

If he was wrong, it'd not only be embarrassing because half of Hedderby would be watching, but it'd cause an almighty row between them. He hated the thought of that because he loved his wife dearly. But he wanted to pursue a career as an entertainer, which meant travelling round the country, and he wanted to do it with her.

★ ★ ★

When it was almost time for the final act of the second half, Eli beckoned Joanna across. Since this wasn't unusual if he wanted a message passed or another drink fetching, she went to stand by his side.

Bram slipped out of the doorway into the house, dressed for the stage, and joined them before she noticed him.

'I'm sorry, love,' he said with a grin, taking a firm grip on her arm. 'But you're going on stage tonight.'

She turned as if to flee but he was far stronger than her. 'Bram, please. You know I'm afraid of that.'

'Darling, I wouldn't do this if I didn't know how beautiful your voice is. It's a dreadful waste for you not to share it with the world. Try it once, at least, for me.' As Eli banged with his gavel, Bram began to pull her towards the stage. She struggled desperately, forgetting where they were, forgetting about the onlookers, her eyes flashing with anger now.

Eli stood up and said in his loud, booming public voice, 'Ladies and gentlemen, Mr Mair has been taken ill, but don't worry, we have a surprise for you to replace him. Our own Bram Heegan will be appearing with his wife Joanna. It's her first time on stage and she is, as you can see, a trifle nervous, so he's coaxing her.'

The audience watched as Bram dragged Joanna on to the stage, with her fighting every inch of the way, threatening now to murder him if he didn't let her go. Thinking this was part of the act, they were soon laughing and applauding, calling out to two people most of them knew by sight, at least.

Once on the stage Joanna froze, staring in terror at the audience.

They only laughed the harder and began calling out more encouragements to her.

Bram watched her carefully. If she got too upset, he'd let her go, but he was staking a lot on her coping with this. She was a brave woman in so many ways. 'You *can* do it,' he whispered.

Her voice came out choked. 'I can't. Bram, I just — I can't!'

He forgot the audience completely as he gave her a quick kiss, didn't even hear the cheers and whistles as he gazed into her eyes and pleaded, 'Just try it. Sing with me, for me.'

Raife crashed out a few chords on the piano, then played the introduction to one of the songs they'd sung together many a time at Linney's during the sing-songs Nev loved so much.

While this was going on, Bram said in a pleading undertone, 'We were desperate for an act to fill in for Mair tonight, love, but I've already sung solo and doing it again wouldn't be enough to satisfy them. And you have a beautiful voice, you know you do. Can't you play along with me now, let me pretend to coax you?'

She looked at the audience, clapped one hand to her throat and shuddered, taking a step away from her husband.

He didn't know if her fear was real or not, still didn't know whether she would sing with him — or what he'd do if she didn't.

The musical introduction finished and she didn't even try to sing, but he could see how she swallowed hard and stared from him to the audience.

People cheered her on again, calling out to her by name.

And then it happened. Something changed in her and Bram saw her straighten her spine as her eyes turned towards Eli, who was nodding encouragement from the Chairman's table.

'Ready, love?'

'I'll — try.'

He nodded to Raife, who played the introduction again. Bram began singing and the music she loved so much added its own

247

persuasions, he was sure. She joined in with him, softly at first, breathing badly from nerves, then suddenly beginning to sing properly, letting her glorious voice soar out as it had never done in public before.

The audience quietened, listening raptly.

When they finished that song, Bram put his arm round her waist. 'I'm so proud of you, darling.' Then he spoke loudly, for the audience's sake. 'Shall we persuade her to sing another song with me?'

The audience instantly began to call out again, enjoying themselves hugely.

'Another song?' Bram begged.

She made great play of shaking her head. He went down on one knee and asked her again. She pretended to consider it. He stood up, took her hand and pulled her to the front of the stage, then began what they regarded as their special song, 'The Last Rose of Summer'. She joined in more confidently this time and as usual, their voices melded perfectly. They knew it so well that the harmonies were second nature. There was complete silence as the beautiful melody soared through the room. Even the waiters had stopped moving to listen.

When the song ended, the silence continued for a few moments more before the audience burst into applause, calling, whistling and cheering.

'I did it,' she whispered, looking at Bram in a dazed way.

'You did it beautifully. They loved it. Curtsey to them.'

She did as he asked, muttering, 'I can't believe I'm up here.'

'You'll sing that new song with me now?' he whispered as they finished acknowledging the applause.

She nodded.

When they got back to the kitchen afterwards, she sat down suddenly on a chair, trembling in every limb, and Bram knelt beside her. 'Will you forgive me, my darling?'

'I don't know.' Her teeth were chattering and he hurried out to the bar of the pub to get her a glass of brandy.

Carrie was sitting holding her hand when he got back. 'Here, sip this.'

Joanna took the glass from him, drank a mouthful without looking at what it was, then choked.

'You were wonderful,' Carrie told her when she'd recovered. 'The two of you together are very special, you know. You've both got good voices on your own, but together, well . . .'

When they went up to their bedroom, Joanna slapped Bram across the face. 'That's for what you put me through tonight.'

He looked at her in dismay. Surely she wasn't going to deny their talent?

She took a deep breath and stared at him. 'I'm sorry to say that . . . you were right. I can do it, can't I? The audience did love our singing.'

He pulled her into his arms, shuddering with relief, his cheek stinging from the blow. 'You were perfect. I was proud of you.' He held her at arm's length and smiled at her, exaggerating his

Irish accent. 'Will we do it together then, my darlin'? Go out and conquer England?'

'Yes.'

He danced her round the room, laughing and soon she was laughing with him.

⋆ ⋆ ⋆

By the time Christy Pipperday got up the next morning, Lydia had her plans in place. 'We need to let people know you're here. We'll put an advertisement in the *Hedderby Post*, and I'll go shopping today because Mr Marker at the grocery store will spread the word for us. I'll call in at a few other places too.'

'What can I do?'

She took a deep breath and said it. 'You can take charge of my husband's consulting room and go through his things, make sure everything you need is there.'

His voice was gentle. 'It'll be painful for you to see me in there.'

'Yes.'

'I'll respect his things, I promise.'

She forced a half-smile and nodded, then as he turned to go, said in a more normal voice, 'Not till after you've had breakfast.'

He wrinkled his brow in puzzlement. 'It feels quite late.'

'It is late. You slept a long time. You must have been very tired.'

'Yes, I was.'

There was a sound from the front of the house and he turned round sharply.

'That's my maid. She's cleaning out the parlour. She always sings hymns when she does that. We'll sit in there in the evenings. Now, what do you usually eat in the morning?'

'Anything.'

This smile was more normal. 'Then I'll cook you some ham and eggs, with bread and butter, and maybe some of my gooseberry conserve to finish with.'

'That sounds a feast. Much too expensive. A piece of bread and butter will do me.'

'No. You'll eat properly. You're too thin and Dr Grey said you'd been ill.'

He leaned back in his chair and offered her a lovely sunrise of a smile that lit up his whole face. 'You sound just like my old nurse.'

'I'm old enough to be your mother.'

'Not quite. You're what? Forty?'

'Forty-two.'

'I'm thirty. So you're not old enough to be my mother.'

She was surprised. 'You don't look that old.'

'No. People often tell me that. I was late starting my training because of the quarrels with my father, you see. My family don't speak to me now. They think I've let them down by becoming a doctor.'

'That's sad. I'd never do that to a child of mine. I always wished Gerald and I'd had children, but it wasn't to be.'

When she set the loaded plate in front of him, he tucked in with all the enthusiasm of a schoolboy, eating everything and wiping up the grease with his bread. She nudged the dish of

251

gooseberry conserve towards him and he hesitated.

'It feels greedy to eat more.'

'You'll need to build up your strength for when you start working.'

So he ate another slice of bread with the butter and conserve on it, talking intermittently about the dispensary he'd worked in before he fell ill.

Bet came into the room, stopped and stared at Christy whom she hadn't met yet. Lydia introduced them and the maid said with the frankness of the ordinary people in the town, 'I've never seen anyone as tall as you, Doctor. You'll have to be careful or you'll bang your head on doorways when you go out to see patients. Some of the houses in the Lanes have low doors that you step down through, low ceilings too.'

'I'm always banging my head,' he admitted cheerfully, then pushed his chair back and looked at Lydia. 'Will you come with me to show me round your husband's room? I shall feel like a burglar otherwise.'

So she took a deep breath and went with him. And it was easier than she'd expected, though still hard to see someone other than Gerald there.

When the door was closed behind them, she said what she'd rehearsed during a wakeful night, 'Would you mind if we said you were a distant cousin of Gerald's? Only, people might think it not quite the thing for me to share my house with a stranger.'

He looked at her solemnly, head on one side

as he thought this over. 'I don't mind at all, especially if it'll make things easier for you.'

She'd been holding her breath, worried that he'd take offence at this. 'Then you'll call me Cousin Lydia from now on, if you please.'

'Cousin Lydia,' he repeated with a smile. 'And I'm Cousin Christy.'

She needn't have worried about him taking umbrage at her small deception, she thought as she left him to it and went about her household duties. He seemed a very nice person. She hoped he'd prove a good doctor, too. The poorer people in the Lanes certainly needed help. Dr Barlow refused to attend them unless they paid him, but some couldn't even put bread on the table every day, let alone find the sixpence Barlow charged. And yet, these were often the ones who needed help most.

'I didn't know he was your cousin,' Bet said later that morning.

'Oh, didn't I mention it before? Sorry. Though he's Gerald's cousin, actually, not first cousin, but a more distant relationship. Gerald was going to ask him to come and work with us once he'd finished his training.'

'And now he'll be company for you. That's nice.' Bet got on with her work, curiosity satisfied.

★　★　★

Denby came home smiling broadly from a visit to the agency which obtained his engagements. He scooped Marjorie up into his arms and

253

swung her round in a circle. 'We've done it!'

'Done what?'

'Taken the next step up. We have an engagement at the Apollo for two weeks, appearing twice nightly, and also once nightly at Casey's Room just a few streets away. But it's the Apollo that counts. It'll mean more money, though we'll still only be third on the bill.' For a moment his smile slipped, then a look of utter determination made his face look different for a moment. 'One day, Marjorie, we'll be top of the bill.'

'Will we be getting more money at the Apollo?' She saw his expression suddenly turn wary.

'Why?'

'Because I need more. Ten shillings isn't enough when you don't pay for things. I have extra expenses here in London, and I need some new shoes.'

'How much more?'

'I want fifteen shillings a week.'

He glared at her. 'Do you think of nothing but getting money out of me? I can't believe how much you're costing me.'

She blinked in shock then something rose in her, something hot and angry which she had only felt in her old life in Hedderby when the overlooker was pestering her. 'I'm also bringing you in more money. Everyone says I'm good on stage, better than your old Elyssa was, and you know your act wouldn't be the same without me.'

'Only because I've taught you well. If it wasn't

254

for me, you'd still be mopping floors for your stepfather.'

The quarrel that followed brought the landlady up to hammer on their door and complain about the noise.

As Denby shut the door on her they stared at one another in silence, then he said in a tight voice, 'Twelve shillings and that's my last word.'

'Twelve shillings and you buy all my shoes for me.' She hated it when they quarrelled, and they'd had several short, sharp disagreements lately, but he was being unfair — and mean.

'Very well.' He picked up his hat and went towards the door.

'Where are you going?'

'Out. A man needs a bit of peace and quiet sometimes.'

She stared in shock as the door banged shut behind him, then sat down with a thump in the nearest chair. He was changing, getting sharper with her, looking at her sometimes as if he hated her.

Why? She couldn't understand it.

And because of that she was changing too. She was learning to stand up for herself since for the first time in her life she hadn't got Carrie or her family to do it for her. Tears gathered in her eyes and spilled down her cheeks and she brushed them away impatiently. What good did weeping do? It wouldn't change Denby's nature or make him respect her more. Stiffening her spine, she put on her outdoor things and went for a walk. She'd make it a long walk, too. Let him be the one to come home to an empty room, for a change. He never told her where he went. Well, two could play at that game.

Only it wasn't a game, it was her bright new life that was crumbling round her.

She saw a small public garden with benches and went towards it automatically, moving away from the street and looking for a seat where she wouldn't be disturbed. But the only bench she found was occupied. As she was turning away, the man looked up and they stared at one another in surprise.

Hal jumped to his feet. 'Marjorie! Mrs Sinclair, I mean. How do you do?' He looked beyond her as if expecting to see Denby.

'My husband's not with me.' She hesitated, then asked, 'Mr Kidd, could you spare a few minutes to tell me all the news from Hedderby, any tiny detail. I do miss my family.'

He nodded. 'Of course. It'll be my pleasure.' He gestured to the bench beside him. 'Won't you take a seat?'

She listened happily as he talked of Carrie and Eli, old Raife, the show he'd been in, anything and everything. Only when she began to shiver did she realise how cold it was. 'I think I'd better get back. I have to get ready for the show tonight.'

'Of course. May I escort you home?'

She hesitated, then shook her head. Denby would be furious if he found out she'd been talking to Hal and there was enough bad feeling between them without adding to it. 'I wonder — could we not mention that we met today? My husband hates me to talk about my family. I

256

— don't want to upset him.'

His voice was so gentle it wrapped itself round her like a warm shawl. 'Of course. Whatever you wish. But I did enjoy your company. And if I can ever be of service to you, please don't hesitate to ask.'

'Thank you. You're very kind.' He was a lovely man, she thought as she walked back, one of the kindest she'd ever met. He might not be good-looking like Denby, but the audiences loved him. He'd make a good friend and she didn't intend to let Denby prevent that friendship from developing.

When she got back, Denby still wasn't there, but a letter was waiting for her from Carrie. She tore it open and read it standing by the window in the last of the daylight, then read it again with a sigh and a tear. She pressed it to her cheek, kissed it, then put it away among her underclothing. She'd reply to it when she was on her own. No need to upset Denby again.

Where on earth was he? It was getting late.

★　★　★

Athol stood by the window, watching his sons playing with the dog. Renny was right, damn him! The two boys were running around and looking strong and healthy, which was what he wanted for them. The longing to be able to run again was like an ache, no, a pain. He dreamed about it sometimes, then woke to realise what he had become. The more fool he! He had to accept what his life was now.

He scowled down at the artificial leg. At least he was able to stand up and walk more easily round the room now. Renny was right about taking things slowly, but he'd said they'd soon be able to go downstairs. Athol would have to be carried down at first, but would be able to walk about once he got there. He'd make sure the staff kept out of the way when he was being carried, though. He wasn't having the maids gawping at that sight.

He turned impatiently and nearly overbalanced.

'You *must* learn to move slowly,' Renny said quietly from near the door.

'I know that, but I forget sometimes.'

'You're getting better at walking, though. Why don't you try to walk along the landing and back a few times today? Start building up your muscles again.'

Athol lifted his head, eagerness rising in him and spilling out into a smile, however hard he tried to conceal it. 'Yes. Go and tell the staff to keep away.'

'Is that necessary?'

'It is till I'm more secure in my walking.'

'Very well.' Renny left the room.

Wiv, standing quietly on the other side of the bed, stared fixedly at his feet.

Athol had a sudden desperate longing to hurry out of the door, to be *anywhere* but in this prison of a bedroom, but even as the urge to surprise Renny made him take a step forward he regained control over himself and stopped again. *Slowly and carefully.* With Renny's help he was going to do what that fool of a doctor said was impossible, walk again — and like a man, not a badly made puppet.

There was the sound of footsteps running lightly up the stairs and Renny came in, smiling as if he'd just been talking to someone and laughing with them. *No one laughs with me,* Athol thought suddenly. He pushed that thought aside hurriedly, not sure he wanted to dwell on it. Some people laughed easily. He never had, even as a child. It didn't matter. What mattered was having power over others, being master of your family, household and business. Making sure other people were afraid to cross you. That was what really mattered. 'Shall we go?'

'Yes, sir. But slowly.' Renny went to stand by the door, turning to watch his master move clumsily out on to the landing.

Athol paused for a moment in the doorway then made his way slowly to the far end, trying to walk like a normal person. He stood there near the head of the stairs, enjoying the light streaming through the tall, stained-glass window in the stairwell and throwing jewel colours across the walls, across him. It was wonderful not to be in his bedroom, wonderful — God help him! — to do something as simple as stand upright again.

He walked up and down several times, trying to hide the fact that it was hurting him.

'Shall we go back now, sir?' Renny prompted.

Athol started and stared at him. The fellow seemed able to read his mind and the damned stump was aching furiously. He nodded, biting

259

back a groan as he moved reluctantly back towards his prison, halting in the doorway for one last look over the banisters into the hall below. He'd be down there, and before too long. Then he'd make his mark on his household again.

15

Marjorie and Denby worked hard on their act in preparation for the new engagement and for a time their marriage seemed to go more smoothly. If they weren't rehearsing every twist and turn, she'd sew or mend, keeping her stage costume perfect, her husband's clothes in order and making herself some new underwear, humming as she worked.

Denby vanished sometimes in the afternoon, saying he felt like a brisk walk not a dawdling one with her, though since he came back smelling strongly of tobacco smoke, she didn't think he'd been outdoors much. But she said nothing. She'd come to terms with the fact that her hero had feet of clay, that he left everything about their daily lives to her and complained if she didn't do his washing and ironing exactly as he wanted. Well, she'd more or less come to terms with it. She did get angry at him sometimes.

To her dismay, she was finding life in London very tiring. The air never seemed as fresh as it had in Hedderby and she'd started taking an afternoon rest, something she'd never needed before. Perhaps it was the late hours they kept and the busy evenings that were causing this.

She received two more letters from Carrie and wrote back each time. She didn't return to the park where she'd met Hal, however, because it seemed disloyal to her husband to meet another man, however innocently. Hal was working elsewhere now, but she heard his name mentioned a couple of times as a 'coming fellow', one to watch out for, and that pleased her.

'Can we afford to get better lodgings than these?' she asked when they were booked for another engagement in one of the better music theatres.

'What's wrong with them?' He stared round as if he'd never seen the place before.

'Mrs Bowker is very disobliging about the washing and ironing, and I'm finding it difficult to keep up with things. Maybe that's why I'm feeling so tired.'

'You've no stamina! And coddling yourself, sitting around all day won't help.'

She looked at him indignantly. 'I have plenty of stamina! I worked long hours in the mill without feeling this tired.'

'Well, you'd better get used to a different way of life now. My agent is trying to fit a third theatre in, at least for one performance a night.'

Her heart sank. 'But Denby, I told you I didn't want to do that when you mentioned it before. I'm feeling too tired. Can we not just — '

'We need to make as much money as we can, get something behind us.'

'Well, if we move to some new lodgings, life will be easier and that should help.'

'No! I've stayed with Mrs Bowker a few times

262

and always find her obliging.' He scowled at Marjorie and was very grumpy for the rest of the day.

The following afternoon he came back from his walk beaming and brandishing a newspaper. 'Look! There's an article in *The Era* on us. See what it says about my singing.' He thrust the specialist paper into her hands.

She read with increasing excitement. 'It says nice things about me too. Look. 'Sinclair's wife enhances the act with her graceful movements and lovely face.' Oh, Denby, what a nice thing to say!'

'Yes. Well, I wouldn't have chosen you if you hadn't been pretty.'

He was in a good mood for the next few days and even conceded that maybe they'd look for new lodgings if they got more engagements in and around London.

When they went to the theatre that same night there was a letter waiting for him. He glanced at the address and stiffened.

She looked at him in concern. 'Are you all right, Denby?'

'Yes. Yes, I'm fine.' He shoved the letter into his pocket.

'Aren't you going to open that?'

'No. It's from my uncle. I'll open it later.'

'But he may be ill and — '

'*Later, I said!*' He gave her a push towards the room where they waited to do their act. 'For the moment we have a busy evening's work and I can't afford to be distracted.'

She said nothing but felt annoyed by his

secretive ways where his family was concerned. It was as if he was ashamed of her.

When they got back to their lodgings, he opened the letter and read it by the light of the single candle they'd lit on their way upstairs from the lamp Mrs Bowker left burning low in the hall to guide them upstairs.

In the bedroom Marjorie started to get undressed, yawning. If he wanted to make love tonight, she'd tell him no. She felt as if her limbs were made of lead and knew that fatigue had made her less graceful tonight.

'Damn her to hell!' Denby muttered, screwing up the letter, then unfolding it and reading it again.

'Is your uncle all right?'

'What? Yes. I mean, no. Not all right.'

'Who are you angry at? You said 'Damn her to hell!' just now.'

He stared at her as if she were speaking a foreign language, then thrust the letter into his pocket. 'I'm angry at my uncle's housekeeper. I'll have to go and see him on Monday, just a quick visit. I'll be back early on Tuesday.'

She waited for him to say it but he didn't. 'Shouldn't I go with you? Isn't it about time I met him?'

'Not at present.'

'But if he's your only surviving relative . . . '

'Look, if you must know, he doesn't want to meet you. He's a bit of a recluse. The rest of the world doesn't live in each other's pockets like your family does, you know.'

She didn't protest, because it'd be no use.

264

Denby went his own sweet way whatever she said or did.

When he'd gone on the Monday, not bothering to kiss her goodbye, she wept a little then decided to go out to the shops. She needed some lace to edge her new petticoat and a walk would do her good. Besides, it didn't mend the situation to sit and mope.

But even a long walk to and from the shops didn't take away the dreadful thought that had crept into her mind a while back and kept returning.

She shouldn't have rushed into marriage with him, hadn't known what he was really like, had made a dreadful mistake.

The longer they were married, the more Denby took her for granted and the more scornfully he spoke to her. Carrie and Eli weren't like that, neither were Bram and Joanna. It wasn't a good way to be and it hurt her.

What if relations between her and Denby grew worse? How would she stand that? Only . . . what could she do about it? Once you were married, you were trapped, just had to put up with how things turned out.

⋆ ⋆ ⋆

Christy went with Lydia to the mother and baby clinic. He seemed even taller when standing next to the undernourished women with their tiny babies, but he made a joke of that. Indeed, his manner with the women was perfect, caring and friendly, not at all condescending. And the babies seemed happy to be handled by him, looking up at him with toothless smiles if they weren't ill or stopping crying as if his arms were a haven. He was, she decided after watching him carefully, rather similar in manner to Gerald, a very caring man.

'Have you taken over all Dr Latimer's duties, Dr Pipperday?' asked one of the women who helped out at the clinic.

'Yes. Though as people aren't used to me yet I've not got as many calls on my time as I'd like.'

'I may come to consult you myself.' She blushed and lowered her eyes. 'I'm in an interesting condition, only I lost a baby last year and my husband is rather worried this time. He does so want a son.'

'Most men do. I'd be happy to examine you and hope you'll allow Mrs Latimer to assist me. She has a great deal of experience in women's matters and I intend to make full use of that. I've delivered a lot of babies and find it highly satisfying to bring a new life into the world.'

'It's almost as if you were Dr Latimer's son, isn't it? And so nice for Lydia to have someone here.'

The woman asked that with a smile, but he could see the wariness and curiosity behind it. He'd met that before in the dispensaries in London, a steely determination to make sure no moral lapse was being committed by those involved in charity work. And if that moral boundary was crossed, it wasn't condoned and the woman was driven away. He didn't want Lydia treated like that. 'I'm a distant cousin of

Dr Latimer, actually. I was going to come and work with him soon, but sadly he died before I could join him.'

'There! I knew it'd be something like that. Mrs Latimer wouldn't take a stranger to live in her house.'

His eyes met Lydia's across the room and he saw her blush. He wished he really were a relative. She was so much nicer than his own family. It still hurt that even his mother, to whom he'd felt close, had made no attempt to contact him, had allowed his father to cast him out in such a cruel way.

Well, that was water under the bridge now. He was making a new life for himself and, he hoped, would make new friends too in Hedderby. And as Dr Grey had foretold, he was feeling a lot better living a regular life in the fresh air of a town so close to the moors. Even the smoke from the mill chimneys was blown away most days.

★   ★   ★

The following day Tait came round to ask Dr Pipperday to go and visit Mr Stott. 'Ten o'clock today, the master said.'

Lydia, who'd been listening in the hall, stepped forward. 'Doesn't Mr Stott deal with Dr Barlow? It wouldn't be proper for Dr Pipperday to visit another doctor's patient.'

Tait shuffled his feet. 'I don't know about that. Ten o'clock, he said.' He tipped his hat to Mrs Latimer and clumped off down the path.

Christy turned to his mentor. 'What do you suggest I do?'

'Send a message to Dr Barlow, explaining what has happened and saying if Mr Stott is his patient, you'll refuse to visit him.'

The note, delivered by an urchin who'd been instructed to wait for an answer, received a prompt response, scrawled at the bottom of the page.

'You're welcome to take over with Stott. Not the easiest of patients.'

Christy showed it to Lydia.

'Oh, dear.' She bit her lip for a moment, then said, 'I'd better tell you how Mr Stott came by his injuries.'

When she'd finished explaining, Christy was silent for a moment or two then shrugged. 'He sounds a dreadful man but he's still entitled to my help.'

'He is dreadful. And vindictive if he feels himself the injured party, whatever the truth of the situation. What's more, a poor man would have been hanged for what he did. I don't like the thought of you becoming his doctor.'

Christy walked across town to the Stotts' residence, pleased to be greeted by one or two people en route, which made him feel less of a stranger here. At the large house he was shown into a parlour where a woman was waiting for him. He hesitated in the doorway.

She moved forward to greet him. 'I'm Mrs Stott. My husband sent for you, but before you leave I'd also like you to check my younger son, who's not well.'

'Should I not see the child immediately?'

Her expression tightened. 'No. My husband wishes to see you. Best to attend him first.'

'Is he ill?'

'He has his own reasons for summoning you. I'll show you up to his room.' She led the way back into the hall without further ado.

As he followed her, Christy frowned. Mrs Stott was very tense and had an unhappy look to her. Well, if half of what Mrs Latimer had told him was true, she had reason to be unhappy. He looked round at the richly furnished house. In spite of the wealth of possessions on display, there was an uneasy feel to this place. He had sensed it as soon as he entered.

She knocked on a door. 'The doctor is here.'

A man opened the door, a man with an open face and childlike eyes of a clear pale blue. 'Please come in, Dr Pipperday.'

'This is Renny, one of my husband's attendants.'

Christy nodded to the man and went into the bedroom.

Although he'd been prepared for the mutilations Mr Stott had suffered, and indeed, had seen horrific injuries of all kinds, Christy wasn't prepared for the way Mr Stott's injuries seemed to give him an evil look, as if he'd just crept out of hell. The flesh of one side of his face was puckered and twisted with dreadful lesions and the hand on that side was a useless claw. He was sitting in a wheeled chair by the window, watching the newcomer's reaction to him.

'You'll have to come over here, Dr Pipperday,

269

since I can't easily come to you.'

Christy walked across to the window, not hiding the fact that he was studying the other man in his turn.

'My wife wants you to see our son, but I'm having no doctor in the house unless I approve of him.'

'I was uncertain from your message whether it was you I'd come to see or not.'

'There's nothing more that doctors can do for me, apparently.'

Christy opened his mouth, then shut it again.

'What did you nearly say?' Athol snapped. 'Don't hide anything from me.'

'I can't be sure about that, never having examined you.' He stepped forward and gestured to the hand that was lying useless on Stott's lap. 'May I?'

'Why not?'

Christy picked up the hand, studied it and laid it down again. 'It might be possible to loosen the scars a little so that you were able to move that hand. Nothing will restore it to full use, I agree, but I've seen cases in London where some improvement has been possible.'

Stott's voice was suddenly harsh. 'Don't offer me such prospects unless you can make good on your promises.'

Christy picked up the hand again. 'I can't guarantee anything, Mr Stott, except that I wouldn't be making it worse. But I do feel some improvements may be possible, though the operation would be painful for you.'

Athol let out a crack of bitter laughter. 'Life is

painful for me, Dr Pipperday, every move I make.' He gestured to his manservant. 'Renny is as much nurse as servant, and has proved more useful to me than Barlow. What do you think, Renny? Might we trust this doctor?'

Renny surprised Christy by stepping forward and studying him more openly. 'How would you improve the hand?'

Christy picked up the hand again, pointing to the two areas where he would cut the scars and sew the flesh together differently.

They both stared down at it till Athol jerked it away.

'I think it wouldn't hurt to try, sir,' Renny said softly. 'You have little to lose.'

'Arrange it with Renny then.' Athol looked at the doctor. 'Better go and see my son now. Make sure he's all right, since I'm not likely to get other sons.'

'I can offer no guarantees for you or your family, no doctor can. Money can't buy life or health. But I can guarantee to do my best. I should inform you that I contacted Dr Barlow before coming here because you and your family were his patients, and I didn't wish to trespass, but he is happy for me to deal with you.'

'You can't be any worse than that old fool.' Athol made a dismissive gesture.

'I'll find out what's needed, sir,' Renny said and followed the young doctor out. 'Can I ask when you want to deal with my master's hand and what will be needed?'

Christy looked at him, thinking that Stott was a strange sort of master for a man with an open, guileless countenance like this one. 'If you'd come round to my house this afternoon, I'll explain in detail, show you the equipment. Find out from your master when *he* wants me to treat his hand. Any afternoon will suit me.'

Renny nodded then indicated a flight of stairs. 'The boys sleep up here, sir. Benjamin has a slight fever. I don't think it's serious but it's lingered for two days, so Mrs Stott is a little anxious.' He led the way and knocked on a door.

Mrs Stott opened it and Christy went inside. The boy wasn't seriously ill, and would, he felt, recover on his own. 'Make sure he takes plenty of fluids — boiled water would be best. In fact, all drinking water should be boiled unless you're absolutely sure of its provenance.'

'I'll tell my housekeeper,' Mrs Stott promised.

She walked to the front door with him herself and he told her what he'd proposed for her husband's hand. She shuddered. 'He'll be able to move it more easily?'

'Yes. I feel I can effect an improvement.'

She looked at him and said in a low voice, 'With a man like that, the less he's able to move, the better. He's dangerous, Dr Pipperday, make no mistake about that.'

He stared at her in astonishment.

She opened the front door as if she had not just said something outrageous. 'Thank you for coming so promptly.'

He walked home with his head in a whirl. He didn't like his new patient, but every injured person deserved his best service. What had Stott done to his wife to make her hate him so much?

272

Denby spent the journey fulminating over his damned bitch of a wife. How dared Alice demand more money? Did she think he had no expenses? She'd managed on what he sent for years, so what was different now?

It was the first question he asked her when he arrived in Upper Saxton. 'Why the hell do you need more money?'

'Because the boys are growing fast and need new clothes, because I'm tired of scrimping while you dress so finely and live an easy life.'

'Easy life! I play two music saloons, I'll have you know. That's four appearances a night. Hard going by any standards. If you push me like this I'll have to fit in another performance and that might strain my voice.'

'Poor thing!' she mocked.

So he hit her. She drove a man to violence, Alice did. Why couldn't she be more like Marjorie, who had a gentle voice and didn't nag?

Alice hit him back with the nearest object, which happened to be an ugly figurine he'd always hated. It broke on his head and for a moment he was too stunned to move. Then he felt something trickling down his temple and raised his hand to touch it. 'You've cut me, you bitch! How do you think that'll look on stage?'

She was behind the kitchen table now, a carving knife in her hand, looking so vicious it made him shiver.

'I don't care how you look on stage, Dennis.

My only concern is that you give me more money.'

'Denby! I keep telling you, I'm not Dennis any more.'

'You'll always be Dennis to me. More money.'

'Two shillings more a week, then, and that's it.'

'Five.'

'I can't *afford* five. Three.'

She sighed. 'I'm too soft with you. Three then. But don't forget to make up my money next time or I'll come chasing after you to London. And I'll have five shillings from you now to get your older son a pair of new boots.'

He dragged the money out of his pocket and flung it on the floor, then stormed out.

Puffing, she bent to pick it up, grabbing the table leg as the room spun round her. Lately she'd been getting a few of these dizzy attacks. Her brothers said she worked too hard. But she couldn't abide to sit still. She looked down at herself. She was hugely puffy now and couldn't understand why. She ate no more than the next person.

Sighing she sank down on her favourite chair and sat staring blindly out of the window. Dennis had looked so handsome and elegant today it had reminded her of when she was sixteen. She'd loved him desperately enough to give herself to him, but that had soon faded because he was a selfish pig and hadn't even wanted to marry her to give his child a name. She frowned. Now she came to think of it, he'd been wearing a new frock coat and his top hat had looked glossy and unmarked. Anger rose in her, overwhelming the brief nostalgia. He was telling lies about how he was going on! Suddenly she was quite sure of that. He must have more money to spare than the grudging amount he allowed her, which wouldn't have been enough to keep her and her sons in food as well as pay the rent if she wasn't so good at growing vegetables, and didn't earn a bit here and there helping out.

She'd go and see Dennis's uncle Bill and ask if she could start borrowing that fancy newspaper he had sent down specially from London, the one that told about the theatre and those who worked in it. What was it called? *The Era?* Yes, that was it. It was about time she took an interest in Dennis's career.

Denby walked along to his uncle's but found that the old man was away, staying with a friend in London, the housekeeper said. That worried him as he trudged back to the village. If the old man came to the show or saw reports about Denby appearing with his 'wife' there'd be trouble. Dammit! Why couldn't the old fellow stay put? It was risky, travelling at his age.

★　★　★

That Tuesday morning Marjorie got up later than usual because she was feeling queasy. Suddenly she had to run to the washbasin and vomit, after which she collapsed on the end of the bed and huddled there with her arms clasped round her middle, not noticing the chill of the

275

unheated room until she started shivering violently.

She knew what was wrong, of course she did. She'd seen it so often in her own mother. First you missed your monthly, then you started being sick in the mornings, then you started growing fatter.

She didn't want a child and she knew Denby didn't, either. It would interfere with their performing and he'd be furious. How had it happened? Then she remembered making love once when he'd not managed to withdraw in time. It must be that. His fault, but he'd blame her, she was sure. It was the sort of thing he did, blame others.

For a moment she was tempted to get on a train and run back to her sister Carrie. She half stood up then sank down again. She was sure her sister would help her, but it would be too humiliating to admit that her family was right and she'd been foolish to marry so hastily. And though Carrie or Nev would take her in, she'd be doing housework again, going mad from boredom.

Only — what was she going to do?

She crawled back into bed and pulled the covers round her, shivering violently. She didn't cry because she was beyond tears. She began calculating on her fingers. The baby would be born in August. She felt her stomach, which was as flat as ever. She hated the creature growing in there, absolutely hated it, because it would spoil her whole life. She'd never wanted children and still didn't.

276

Sometimes women got rid of unwanted children, but she'd known a girl in the mill who did that and who died in agony because of it. She shuddered. She didn't want to risk dying like that.

How long before the baby began to show? Two, three months perhaps? All women were different. Some didn't show until they were several months along. Maybe she could hide it from Denby for a while until she could work out what to do? She knew he'd be furious, knew he'd want the baby even less than she did, had to be prepared for his anger when she told him.

And in the meantime she'd save her money carefully, just in case . . . She didn't allow herself to think what the 'just in case' might mean.

She was late getting up and when she went down, found that the landlady had cleared away the breakfast things. 'I'd like some food, please,' she said firmly.

'Breakfast stops at nine.'

'You served Mr Phipps the other day at nearly ten o'clock. Why could he be served and not me?' She knew why, of course. Because Mr Phipps was a personable man of middle years who flattered the landlady and paid her extra to do his washing. 'We've paid for our meals and I insist you provide them. You're already making extra profit today from my husband's absence.'

There was a silence filled only by the stertorous breathing of the other woman, then she shrugged and said, 'Very well. But I'm not cooking anything.'

'Bread and cheese will be fine, thank you. And a pot of tea.'

It was the tea she enjoyed most. It seemed to revive her. They weren't supposed to cook in their bedroom, but she had a little kettle and made them pots of tea every day. She seemed to crave it at the moment. Its warmth and its familiar taste in her mouth were a great comfort.

After breakfast she went to lie on the bed and rest, but kept thinking she heard Denby's footsteps on the stairs, so couldn't settle. With a sigh she went down to pay for another scuttle of coal and built up the fire, then sat by it sewing, or rather staring into the distance with the needle poised over the material.

★　★　★

'Well?' Athol asked sharply.

Tait wriggled uncomfortably. 'You couldn't easily break into the Pride. He's had shutters made and they're locked in place once they've cleared up and shut the place down. There's nothing worth stealing in the music room anyway because he keeps the takings in the Dragon, though I couldn't find out where.'

'I don't want to steal his takings.'

Tait was tempted to ask what his master did want then, but stopped himself. If there was one thing he had learned here, it was not to ask questions. 'The only place you might get in is round the back. They lock the yard gate, but they have to go outside to the necessary, so the door's just on the latch.'

'I see. You may go now. I'll take a short nap. But stay within reach of the bell.' Athol lay back on the piled pillows and sighed. His stump hurt more than he admitted to Renny when he did his daily exercise, but not enough to stop him. He tried to hide the extent of the pain, but wasn't sure he'd succeeded.

He wanted to see the Pride. It was all right picturing it from advertisements in the newspapers, but the building had been finished after his accident — the accident that was Eli Beckett's fault — and he hadn't seen the place himself.

When he woke from an uneasy nap, he asked for Renny. 'Is there any reason I couldn't go out in the carriage? With the leg strapped on, of course.'

Renny pursed his lips and stood thinking.

'I know I would have to be carried out, but I'm sick to death of this house. I could go for drives, surely, even stop in the town centre and watch the world go by?'

'Why not? We'd have to be careful how we had you sitting, don't want to jar that stump. I know it's been hurting you, so don't pretend it hasn't.'

'We'll go out tomorrow, then. But I want some sort of gauze curtains on the inside of the carriage windows, so that I can see out but people can't see me. I'm not having them gawping at this.' He gestured impatiently to the burnt side of his face, the raw red gargoyle that sickened him every time he saw it in a mirror, then looked at his hand. He'd put off having the doctor operate on it, he didn't know why. Perhaps because it might slow down his progress. Perhaps because he already had as much pain as he could tolerate.

'Shouldn't be hard to do,' Renny said 'I'll ask Mrs Stott. She's good at sewing.'

'I'll ask her myself. Tell her I want to see her — now.'

Maria stared at him in surprise when Athol told her what he wanted. 'You're well enough to go out?'

'Only if they carry me to the carriage, Renny says. That man takes too much upon himself. He is, after all, only a servant.'

'He seems to know what he's doing. You've been getting steadily better since he came here.'

'That's the only reason I put up with his insolence. Never mind him, what about the carriage windows?'

'I'll go and measure them. I could buy some gauze and — '

He thumped on the bed. 'I want it doing for tomorrow.'

'I doubt we'll be able to. I can do the curtains by tomorrow, with Mrs Ibster's help, but I need something to hang them on.'

'Send round to Mearham and tell him what we need, tell him to do it today if he values my custom.'

'Very well.' She sighed as she walked down the stairs. Athol was getting back to his old form again, making demands, tossing orders at her, not caring whose life he disrupted.

On an impulse she walked round to Mearham's, feeling like some fresh air as she always did after visiting her husband. Being with

Athol made her feel dirty, afraid of being corrupted by his evil. She'd ask the coachbuilder for help and if he couldn't do the job today, then her husband would just have to accept that.

She found Mr Mearham in the yard at the side of his business and when she stopped by the wrought iron fence that barred the front of it, he came across to speak to her.

'Did you want something, Mrs Stott? Do come in.' He opened the small gate.

When she explained what Athol wanted, he smiled. 'That's easily done. If you could send your carriage round here, I'll have it back to you by mid-morning tomorrow.'

'Thank you. My husband is unreasonable, but he's been confined to his room for a long time, so you can't blame him for being a trifle impatient.'

'He's getting better then?'

She sighed and realised from the expression in his eyes that she'd betrayed exactly how she felt. 'Yes. Slowly, though.'

As she turned to walk back towards the town centre, Mearham watched her sympathetically. Poor woman! It must be hell being married to that sod. If he'd not been rich, Stott would have been arrested and charged for what he'd done. But of course everyone had thought then that he was going to die. Only he'd survived and dammit, the fellow was rich, could buy any services he wanted, could take revenge on any tradesman foolish enough to cross him.

No tradesman in the town wanted his custom. But even now, no one dared refuse it.

Denby returned and Marjorie could see at once that he wasn't in the best of moods. 'How's your uncle?'

'What? Oh, fine. It was a false alarm. Have you ironed my shirt for tonight?'

She wrinkled her brow, then shook her head.

'Well, what *have* you been doing?'

'Resting. I keep telling you, I get tired.'

'You're lazy, that's all. Go and get that shirt ironed. You know I like to start the week in a clean shirt.'

With a sigh Marjorie put down her sewing and went to find the landlady. Denby hadn't spoken kindly, let alone asking what she had been doing. He hadn't kissed her, either.

She stood stock-still on the stairs as she realised: *she hadn't wanted him to kiss her!*

The show went well that night, however. On stage they still seemed able to recapture something of the old magic. There was a larger audience than was usual on a Tuesday and the applause for Denby Sinclair and Elyssa was thunderous. And being Tuesday, there was only one performance in each place, to her relief.

As they were making their way out to find a cab after the last show, an old man stepped forward from the crowd at the stage door, leaning heavily on a stick.

'Dear God!' Denby breathed and turned to Marjorie. 'You take the cab home. I'll join you later.'

'But — ' He had already turned his back to

her and was hugging the old man, then guiding him out towards the street. She hesitated, then did as he'd asked her and took the cab home alone.

★ ★ ★

Denby looked over his shoulder and breathed a sigh of relief as Marjorie turned towards the side door where cabs waited for the artistes. She'd be all right with their cab driver, a very reliable man whom they used every day. He turned back to the old man. 'Uncle Bill! What are you doing in town? You're looking well, I must say.'

'Feeling well, too. Came to talk to you, lad.'

'Let's go and get something to eat and drink, then. I suppose you dined earlier, but I can't eat much just before a performance, so I'm hungry now.' It was a lie. He ate a good meal at lunchtime and a piece of cake or something similar when he got home after performing was usually enough for him. But he knew the old man would enjoy a drink and it would perhaps mellow him.

Once they were seated Bill didn't waste time coming to the point. 'I read in *The Era* about your new act — about your new wife, too.'

Denby forced a laugh. 'Oh, we just say that because it sounds better. Audiences like to think we're a pair of real love-birds.'

'And are you?'

After a moment's hesitation, Denby said, 'Well, I'm bedding her, but she knows the score.'

'She doesn't look like a loose woman. Got a pretty face.'

'Very pretty. Good on stage, too.'

Bill took a sup of beer, wiped the froth from his mouth with the back of one hand and shrugged. 'Just as long as Alice doesn't find out. She won't take kindly to you pretending to have another wife.'

'She won't care as long as I keep sending her the money.'

Bill looked at him. 'She will, you know. She's got her pride, like anyone else. You'd better take care what you're doing, nephew.'

'I will.'

After a moment's silence and another slow mouthful of beer, Bill changed the subject and began to talk about his visit to London. It was over an hour before Denby could end the evening, and see the old man back to his friend's house.

When he went to join Marjorie he was smiling, but she was sitting up in bed looking angry. 'Well, that was a turn-up for the books. A friend of my uncle's.'

'Why didn't you introduce me?'

'Because he doesn't like women. Wanted us to go out and have a drink together. And I didn't like to offend him.'

'You're ashamed of me.' Her eyes filled with tears.

'Don't be silly.'

'You are. I've never met your family or any acquaintances even. You're ashamed of me.'

'I'm too tired for all this.' He threw off his

clothes, got into bed and turned his back on her. Soon he was breathing evenly and slowly.

She lay awake for a long time, tired as she was. What he'd done tonight had hurt her deeply. What he was going to say when he found out she was carrying his child filled her with dread. In fact, her new happiness was crumbling round her day by day.

Where would this all end?

16

Three mornings later Marjorie slipped hastily out of bed. But she couldn't hold back the nausea until she got to the necessary out at the back of the house. When she turned round, Denby was sitting bolt upright in the bed, staring at her in horror.

'You're expecting!'

'I think so.'

'How the hell did that happen?'

'You forgot to withdraw one night.'

'I don't remember that.'

She stared at him in shock. 'Well, I do!'

'We'll have to get rid of it. I'll find out where to go.'

'No.' Of that one thing she was certain. She wasn't risking her life with some dirty old woman like the one in Hedderby and anyway, it was a baby.

His voice was nearly a shout. 'What do you mean, no?'

'I'm not killing our child.'

He was out of bed in a flash, shaking her hard. 'You'll do as you're told!'

'No! Let go of me! Let go!' She stuck her elbow in his middle and he grunted in pain before stepping back and glaring at her. She didn't let him say it again, but repeated, 'I won't do it, Denby.'

'Do you want to destroy all we're building up together?'

'No, of course I don't. And I certainly don't want a baby. But now it's there I'll not kill it. Anyway, it won't affect me for months. We could even do a new act around my condition. People like babies and we're married, after all. It's only to be expected we'd have children.'

His lip curled. 'I'm not going to be known on stage as a fatherly figure!'

'Then we'll hire a girl to work with you for a few months till I can come back with you.'

'And what will we do with the brat? Take it on tour with us?'

'Some people do.'

'Well, I'm not one of them.'

During the next few days he tried in every way he knew to persuade her to get rid of the baby. And at times she wavered till she thought of what that would involve. If she could have snapped her fingers and done it, maybe she would have. But she couldn't.

One day when she was feeling particularly tired, Denby came home with a packet from a herbalist.

'I've got some tonic here to pick you up. I'll just boil some water to mix it with.'

'Let me see that.'

'I'll do it. You're tired.'

She looked at him. He had that bright, happy air to him that he wore on stage. He was up to mischief, she was suddenly sure of it. She rolled quickly off the bed and snatched the packet from him before he could stop her, opening it to smell the contents. With a shudder, she cast them on the fire, where they burned quickly with an acrid smell.

'Why did you do that?'

'My mother tried that stuff once. It didn't make her lose the baby but it made her ill for weeks. The baby died soon after it was born, though.'

Their eyes met and he was the first to lower his. 'Don't be silly. It was just a tonic.'

'You're telling me lies because you think I'm stupid.' She could hear how flat her voice was, couldn't help it.

'Of course I don't.'

'You do. Well, I'm not clever like our Carrie is, but I'm not stupid, either. And I'm *not* going to risk my life by murdering our child.'

'No, but you'll murder my career, won't you?'

'We can manage.'

'No, we can't! Do you think I'm made of money?'

'You earn enough to keep me for a month or two while I have the child. I'm not greedy, won't ask for much.'

'I don't earn enough to keep you and pay someone else to perform with me!'

'Of course you do. I know how much Carrie and Eli pay their performers and you earn more than that now we're in London.'

He stared at her for a moment as if he hated her. 'Well, I have other expenses.'

'What other expenses?'

'I send money to Uncle Bill. The farm isn't doing as well as it used to.'

'You never told me that before.'

'I didn't think you needed to know.'

'We'll manage somehow.'

But the look in his eyes frightened her. She hadn't thought he *could* look at her like that. As if he meant her harm. And why hadn't he told her about the money?

What else hadn't he told her about?

⋆　⋆　⋆

Athol sat in the chair by the window of his bedroom staring out at the rain beating against the window panes. He looked down at his injured hand and tried to use it, failing even to straighten the cover over his lap. Could it be made to function better? If so, he was being a coward, he admitted that to himself at least. Didn't want to face any more severe pain. The memory of the explosion and the scalding steam still gave him nightmares from which he woke screaming hoarsely.

He preferred Renny to attend him when that happened, because the man radiated calmness and knew better than to offer him useless words. Tait just stood and shuffled his feet and kept asking if there was anything he could get his master.

The bedroom door opened and Athol looked up. It was as if thinking about Renny had summoned him. The dog had followed him and was hesitating in the doorway.

'Get that thing out of here!' Athol snapped and at the mere sound of his voice the stupid creature turned and fled.

Renny shut the door and came across to him.

'No need to shout at her. She'd have gone if I'd told her.' He studied his master. 'I had a feeling you needed me.'

A shiver ran through Athol as he stared back. It was uncanny how the fellow seemed to read his mind at times. 'I *was* thinking about you,' he admitted. He hesitated then stared down at his hand. 'And about this.'

'Time for the operation.' Renny's voice was flat with certainty.

'I suppose so. I'm not looking forward to being sliced open, though.'

'I can help you a little, but I can't stop all the pain.'

'How can you help me?'

'I can mesmerise you, if you'll allow me. It'll make the pain seem more distant, less severe.'

'I thought that mesmerism stuff was a hoax.'

'No. Though there are some people who don't respond to it.'

'I'm not usually a coward.'

'Whatever your faults, you're definitely not a coward.'

The compliment, impudent as it was, pleased Athol. 'Send round to that new doctor. Tell him to come and do his worst. Tomorrow, if possible. I'd rather get it over with.'

★　★　★

Christy was surprised by the summons. 'I thought he'd decided not to attempt to improve things,' he told Lydia when he rejoined her after speaking to Renny.

'I wish you hadn't suggested it. The more things that man can do, the more he'll be able to hurt other people.'

'You judge him very harshly.'

'With reason. I've helped a couple of the girls he'd ravished. Neither had been willing. Both had been badly mauled around by him. At least the accident has stopped that sort of thing happening.' After a moment's silence, she added, 'Don't ask me to come and help you. I won't touch him.'

'His manservant seems very capable.'

'Renny? He's a strange one. Can charm animals, apparently. No one's said anything bad about him, but people are wary of him.'

'People are always wary of those who are different. How much shall I charge him for this operation?'

She gave a wry smile. 'As much as you can.'

He smiled back. 'Five guineas?'

'Why not?'

* * *

The operation was to be performed in the patient's bedroom. Maria and Renny prepared the bed, raising the place where Athol would lie with a folded feather mattress and covering it with a clean linen sheet and towels. He sat brooding by the window, watching them.

When the door knocker sounded, he gripped the chair arm more tightly with his good hand but said nothing.

Christy came into the bedroom and glanced

around, nodding approval. He had brought a board covered by a clean cloth, which he laid on the bed. He took off his coat and rolled up his sleeves.

'No blood-stained operating coat?' Athol mocked.

'Definitely not. There is a school of thought which prefers everything to be kept as clean as possible. I subscribe to that. So if you can fetch us some hot water, Renny, I'll wash my hands and you can wash the patient's arm and hand.'

Renny did as he'd been asked, then he and Tait helped Athol hop across to the bed and lie down.

'If you can leave me with my master for a few moments,' Renny said, 'I'll try and see whether I can mesmerise him.'

They filed out and he approached the bed, speaking quietly about everyday matters.

Athol was about to order him to stop gossiping and get on with it when his eyes were caught by a small chain with a piece of faceted glass dangling from it. It caught the light and he had trouble looking away from it . . .

When Renny let the doctor in, Athol was lying quietly, his expression calmer than usual.

Christy examined the hand again, then took out his scalpel and, working quickly, cut the worst of the lesions. Renny and Tait had been instructed to hold their master's arm, and did so, but although it twitched and the man in the bed grunted, he didn't thrash around or struggle.

Working quickly, as he'd been trained in order to minimise pain, Christy cut out some scar tissue and sewed the flesh together again, mopping away blood with clean rags that Lydia had boiled for him. 'He's not to use the hand and no one else but me is to touch it or pull the bandages off.'

Athol blinked at him. 'It's over?'

'Yes.' Christy looked sideways at Renny. 'I was sceptical about your claims, but it seems you can help in these cases. May I call on you if I have other patients facing the scalpel?'

'Yes.'

'As long as I don't need him,' Athol put in.

'You of all people should be willing to help others in the same position as yourself.'

'Why should I care about others?'

'Because it's a sign of humanity.'

Athol merely turned up his lip. 'Bring me a brandy, Tait.'

'No!' Christy looked down at the man on the bed. 'It inflames the blood. No spirituous liquors for a few days.'

For a moment Athol glared at him, then shrugged. 'How much do we owe you, doctor?'

'Five guineas.'

'Ask my wife to pay you on the way out.'

Christy nodded. 'I'll call in every day to check the wound.'

As he walked down the stairs he shook his head. They had warned him how callous Stott was. He hadn't expected to see the evil lurking in the man's eyes, a light Christy had only seen before in the eyes of madmen. He'd never refuse to deal with any patient, but he wished suddenly that he didn't have to attend this man.

Carrie helped Joanna pack her bags. Her two cousins by marriage were going on their first tour, playing at music rooms in the north of England so that they could get used to performing together before they went further afield.

Joanna looked at her as they put the last garments into the travelling bags. 'I wish I wasn't doing this.'

'Don't be silly! When you and Bram start singing on stage, you love it. Even I didn't realise how strong your voice is because you've always held back before, haven't you?'

'Yes. And I do like it once we start singing, but before . . . Oh, Carrie, I feel dreadful each time, sick in my stomach, can't eat. Surely, if I was meant to be a performer, I'd feel happy about going on stage. Marjorie loves it, I've seen her face.'

'I know. But we're all different, and Bram — well, he needs more than just staying in Hedderby, you know he does. He's a restless sort of man.'

Joanna nodded. 'That's why I'm doing it. For Bram. I like running the Dragon and the Pride, wanted to keep doing it.' She sighed and began to fiddle with the folds of her skirt.

'Eli and I will look after things for you, you know we will.'

'Yes.' She looked up. 'Nothing is perfect, is it? Not even marriage to the man you love.'

After they'd left Carrie went to find Eli, who was
watching the rehearsals with the new performers
for this week. She linked her arm in his and
stood there until the two young women on the
stage had finished their singing and dancing.
They were billed as 'The Seaton Sisters' but
she'd guess they weren't related at all. Their
voices were pleasant and in their shorter stage
skirts, they'd give the young men in the audience
a treat, but they didn't move nearly as gracefully
as her sister Marjorie.

After the rehearsal had finished Eli turned and
put his arm round her. 'Bram and Joanna got off
all right, then?'

'Yes. They'll be well on their way to
Manchester by now.'

'You're going to miss her, aren't you?'

She nodded, one hand resting on her belly,
something she couldn't help doing, though he
teased her about it, because it seemed to bring
her nearer to her child.

'You and I will have to spend more time
together then, love. I can't have you pining.'

She knew he meant well, but she also knew he
wouldn't be spending any more time with her
than he did now. He always found a dozen things
to occupy himself with and lately he'd been
going over plans for a proper music and variety
theatre with two layers of balconies to replace
the long, single-storey music room they now had
at one side of the pub. As if they could afford
that yet, though the Pride was very profitable.

Besides, once he'd got the theatre sorted out he'd want something else. She knew her Eli. It was a good thing she wasn't a clinging type of wife, a good thing she had plenty to keep her busy.

When she went back into the pub itself, he didn't even notice that she'd left because he'd opened the newspaper and spread it out on one of the tables to read. She walked slowly round the big room at the pub, pleased with how clean it looked. Bonnie was just finishing cleaning and was putting the chairs straight again, her round face absorbed in what she was doing, her tongue sticking out at one side of her mouth. Bram's auntie might be slow in understanding but she had such a lovely, sunny nature and did her work so carefully that she made an ideal employee for a simple job like cleaning.

Carrie stopped next to her. 'I'm going to miss Bram and Joanna.'

'Me, too. He makes me laugh. And he stops people shouting at me in the street. He's paying a lad to walk me home now, but Mick's late sometimes.'

Carrie sighed. Why folk should want to pick on people like Bonnie, she couldn't understand. There were a lot worse things than being slow-witted.

An hour later Mick still hadn't turned up so Carrie offered to walk Bonnie home herself. She didn't know where Eli had disappeared to, but she'd welcome some fresh air. She tried to get out for a walk every fine day because the air inside the pub soon became blue with pipe smoke.

As they strolled up the lanes to the house where Bonnie lived with her sister and brother-in-law, a man walked down the street towards them, a man Carrie recognised. Tait Arner, servant to Mr Stott now.

'Let's cross to the other side,' she said to Bonnie.

But Tait crossed to the other side as well, grinning as if he knew something they didn't. When they got up to him, he put out his arm to bar their way.

'Move out of the way, please,' Carrie said sharply.

'Just wanted to pass the time of day with you,' he said. He leaned forward and stared at Bonnie. 'Haven't got Bram here any more to look after you, have you, idiot? Better watch out for yourself. There's folk as hold a grudge against that Irish bugger an' all who belong to him.'

Bonnie let out a whimper and clutched Carrie's arm.

Then a voice called, 'Hoy!' and Mick came running down the narrow street, not as big as his uncle Bram yet, but a strapping lad nonetheless.

With a nasty sneering smile, Tait tipped his hat to the two women and carried on down the hill.

Mick stopped beside them. 'Sorry, Bonnie. I forgot the time.' He looked after Tait and frowned. 'What did that fellow want with you?'

'Warning us that now Bram's gone we might not be safe.' Just wait till she told Eli what had happened. He'd be furious and would do something about it, she was sure.

'You'd better keep an eye on the time in future, Mick.' Carrie was still worried about the encounter with Tait, worried for herself *and* for Bonnie. By the time they got to Bram's parents' house, she'd reached a decision. 'I'll come in with you, if I may, Bonnie. And Mick, please wait for me. I'll give you threepence to walk back with me.'

He looked surprised, then grinned. 'Allus ready to earn a few pence.'

Inside she explained what had happened, then suggested Bonnie live in at the pub.

Bram's mother pursed her lips then nodded. 'It may be for the best. It's not that we need my sister's money, Bram makes sure of that, but she does enjoy her work.'

Bonnie nodded vigorously. 'I like to keep the Dragon clean.'

'And would you like to live there all the time?' Carrie asked gently.

'Yes.' She gave Carrie a big beaming smile. 'Then I could listen to the music every night.'

'I'll arrange a bedroom for you then.' She looked at Bram's mother. 'I'll send my brother Ted round for her things tonight.'

'Oh, we'll bring them down. I'll want to see where she's sleeping. And I'll want to visit her regularly.'

'Of course.'

Carrie smiled as she walked away with Mick striding along beside her. They kept an eye out for each other, the Heegans. Then the smile faded as she suddenly realised there was only one reason why Tait would accost them in the street like that: his master. Surely Stott wasn't going to start causing trouble again? But why else would Tait have accosted them?

She'd tell Eli what had happened and beg him to employ a night watchman again at the Pride. He said that wasn't necessary with the new shutters, but she didn't agree.

★   ★   ★

Hal saw the poster as he was travelling across London in a cab and turned his head as the horse clopped past, pressing against the smeary window to read which place it was advertising. Melling's, a nice little saloon theatre where he'd played himself a couple of weeks previously. He'd asked his agent not to book him in the same show as Sinclair, not having to pretend the antipathy he felt towards the man. But his request was mainly because being close to Marjorie upset him, especially as she seemed to have lost the starry-eyed look which she'd worn when she first got married. She wasn't happy with Sinclair, he knew that deep down. Only he hadn't the right to do anything about it.

She and her husband both ought to be pleased with life because Sinclair was doing well, would soon be top of the bills in the smaller London music saloons and variety theatres. Marjorie made a good foil for him on stage. Hal sighed. She was lovely but no lovelier than a dozen other young women he'd met in the various venues he'd played, so what was there about her that

299

made her haunt his dreams? A gentleness, perhaps? Many of the women who performed grew coarse-natured and cynical. Marjorie hadn't and he hoped she never would.

It seemed as if fate meant it to happen a couple of days later, when the axle on the cab in which Hal was travelling from his first to his second show, broke not far from Melling's. He wasn't hurt beyond a bruise or two and was relieved when he got out to see that the poor horse was all right.

'Sorry, Mr Kidd,' his cabbie said. 'I'll have it mended for tomorrow, but we'll have to find you another cab for tonight.'

Hal looked round. It was raining and he had an hour to spare between shows. Melling's was only a couple of hundred yards away, so he took shelter inside the theatre. He knew its owner-manager and by great good luck arrived there just as Marjorie came on stage.

John Melling grinned at him as they stood together at the back, talking in whispers. 'Still carrying a torch for her, are you?'

Hal looked at him in dismay. 'Is it so obvious?'

'To me it is. I haven't heard anyone else say anything. But when your agent told me you didn't want to appear in the same show as Sinclair, it seemed to confirm my suspicions.'

Hal was glad the rear of the big room hid his flush of embarrassment. 'I'd be grateful if you'd keep it to yourself. It's hopeless anyway.'

'She'd have done better with a chap like you, both on and off stage. He's a selfish sod, Sinclair, hogs the stage and doesn't allow her to put herself forward too much. He's not liked in the business, however good a singer he is, and only bothers to be nice to you if he thinks it might do him good.'

Hal sighed and they both fell silent to watch Marjorie glide across the stage. She was as good as ever, but to anyone who knew her it was obvious that she was tired.

Someone touched his arm and the doorman said, 'I've found you another cab, Mr Kidd.'

'Thanks, Fred.' Hal slipped the man a tanner tip, took a last look at Marjorie and went outside.

The manager followed him out into the foyer and stood next to the doorman watching the cab clop away. 'He's a nice fellow, Kidd.'

'Yes. Always a pleasant word, even for the cleaners.' Fred's gaze went towards the theatre door, from which came the sound of Sinclair's voice singing. 'Unlike some.'

'Well, the audiences love him.'

'The audiences don't know him, though, do they?'

Melling spread his hands and gave a slight shrug. You didn't have to like the performers and there were a few he'd not trust an inch. As long as they made money for him and were civil to his face, he could tolerate them.

★   ★   ★

Gwynna was out walking, taking advantage of a fine, mild day. She pushed little Sylvie in the brand new basket chair on wheels and went for a good long walk, turning back reluctantly. Sometimes she wished she could walk off into the hills and never come back. She'd always wanted to go up there, but had never managed to get very far on Sunday walks. It always seemed as if the best of the hills were still out of reach.

Halfway home she met Robbie Preston.

He smiled and fell in beside her. 'I was just going to call in and see Nev. I'll push this for you if you like.'

She let him take the handle and walked back beside him, finding it a relief to be able to stride out freely.

He smiled down at the rosy little face in the pushcart. 'She looks well, my littlest sister.'

'She is. Never ails except when she's teething and then she gets a bit fussy. But it's all over in a day or two and she's back to her sweet-natured self.' She sighed.

'Something wrong?'

'I was hired as a wet nurse. They don't need me any more now, so I shall have to start looking for another job.'

'I hope you get one in Hedderby. You feel like part of the family now.'

'Another sister?' She couldn't help the sharpness in her voice. She didn't want to be his sister, anything but.

He was silent then began to speak, avoiding her eyes as he did so. 'No, you don't seem like a sister, Gwynna, but I can't afford to take up with any lass at the moment. Mr Edmund is going to train me as an engineer without my paying him a premium, and the only condition is that I don't marry during that time. I'll have to go and work with engineers in other parts of the north, you see.'

'And how long will you be doing that for?'

'Three or four years.'

She summoned up a smile, well, she hoped her face smiled. Inside it felt stiff with anguish, because he had noticed her, only he'd rejected her. 'I wish you well. You'll be set for life if you're a trained engineer.'

'Yes. And it's what I want to do more than anything. I love machines, love working with them, designing and making them. I just seem to *understand* them, somehow. Mr Edmund's let me help with all sorts of things for the past year or two, and now what I want most in the world is going to happen. He's going to put me formally in tutelage.'

'What's that?'

'It means I'll be his pupil till I'm trained. I'll be legally tied to him for a few years. I'm — sorry.'

She didn't ask what he was sorry for. She knew. Something inside her, some bright and hopeful seed of happiness that bloomed whenever Robbie Preston came round to Linney's, faded and winked out of existence. But out of sheer pride she held herself tightly together around the emptiness, not wanting to betray the desolation she felt.

When she got back she saw to Sylvie's needs and left Robbie coaxing something to eat out of Essie. Once the baby was asleep Gwynna went looking for Nev and found him in the back room, staring thoughtfully around.

'Have you a minute to spare?'

He turned with a smile, the sort of smile that only lit his face inside his own home, for he was still a guarded and careful man with outsiders. 'Yes, of course, love. Is something wrong?'

'Not wrong exactly but, as you know, Sylvie is fully weaned now and I think it's time I looked for another job.' She saw the disappointment on his face. 'I want to make something of myself, become a proper nursery maid with a rich family. Essie's told me about it and I'm sure I can do it.'

'You could have stayed here. You feel like part of our family now.'

'But I'm not. And like I said, I want to make something of myself. Will you and Essie help me look for a job, give me references? I've saved up enough to buy myself some better clothes. I want a job with the gentry, you see.'

'Yes. Yes, of course I will. Eh, there's no holding you youngsters back today. This modern age is all rush, rush, rush. I blame the railways. They go so fast they make people think that's the way life should be. But there, I dare say you think I'm old-fashioned.' He patted her shoulder. 'Of course we'll help you. But look, lass, whatever you do, wherever you go, there's always a bed under my roof for you. As far as I'm concerned, you're as near family as makes no difference. If you want to be, that is?' He looked at her questioningly.

For answer, she flung herself into his arms and

gave him a big hug. 'I do, I do!' Then burst into tears.

'Nay, what's wrong?'

'You're all so kind to me. I've never known that before.'

He laughed. 'Well, is it a reason to cry?'

She wiped away the tears and summoned up a smile.

Not until she was in bed that night did Gwynna allow herself to weep for what couldn't be. And even then she didn't let herself cry for long, because if she got up with swollen eyes, they'd notice and ask why.

Well, at least Robbie liked her enough to explain, at least he'd noticed her. That was something to hold on to.

17

Athol's hand healed quickly, and although it was still twisted, he did have better use of it now, could hold a book or clutch a walking stick. But he would never have any control over the finer movements, Dr Pipperday said.

'Five guineas well spent,' Athol said. 'We'll keep that doctor. He knows far more than Barlow.'

Maria gradually realised that her husband was planning something. She could tell it by the way his eyes glittered and lost focus as he stared into the distance, and by the nasty half-smile that sometimes appeared on his face for no reason. She didn't dare say anything, of course, but she felt her stomach lurch at the thought of him causing more trouble in the town.

Now that he had some use of his right hand, he could hold a crutch, which made a big difference, so he was working hard at walking. He would have practised for longer each day if Renny had let him, but Renny said he'd cause sores on the stump.

In other circumstances, she'd have liked the strange manservant, but she didn't dare let herself warm to a man who served Athol. But the boys had no such reservations and thought Renny wonderful, spending as much time with him as they could, learning how to train the puppy, which had thrived since eating regularly and was growing almost visibly. The creature was going to be very big when it stopped growing, she decided, but she had no fear of it and all the maids were openly fond of Migs. But the dog reserved her greatest loyalty for the boys.

Isaac had calmed down a lot and she wondered whether he was growing up, or whether that was Renny's influence. Perhaps it was just because he could now run and shout every day, so was using up his energy and not bursting with frustration.

One day she found Athol sitting by the window in the library, watching his sons at play.

'They'll grow up big and strong,' he said. 'Real men.'

'They're certainly better for getting regular exercise,' she admitted. 'Renny was right about that.'

'Yes, damn him. He's right about a lot of things. But not everything.'

They watched in silence for a little longer, then he said, 'I don't like dogs and they don't like me. Make sure that one doesn't come anywhere near me or I won't be answerable.'

She didn't tell him that the dog shivered and crept past his room as if afraid of what lay inside. If he went out to join the boys, as happened occasionally, they became quieter and much more careful about what they said and did, while the dog went under the bushes and lay there in a watchful position.

She wished she could hide away too, but increasingly Athol was summoning her to spend time with him, though he mostly talked at her or questioned her about events in the town, or ordered her to fetch and carry for him. It would never have occurred to him to ask about her life and interests.

★ ★ ★

The next three weeks were difficult for Marjorie. Denby hardly touched her in bed, which both surprised and worried her. He normally wanted sex every night but now it was a couple of times a week and he took no care whatsoever to satisfy her needs, which she resented, knowing how happy he could make her if he wanted.

One night she couldn't face his touch and tried to stop him, but he forced her, behaving so roughly that he left her weeping and bruised. He didn't try to comfort her, let alone apologise.

It was then that she began to wonder if she could bear to stay with him. Only, she was married to him. Only last week she'd read in the papers how a husband had taken his children forcibly from his wife when she left his roof, how the law supported his right to do this. She reckoned Denby was capable of doing this, if only to spite her.

She wished she could have worked on stage with him without getting married, but she'd been besotted, ready to believe him a perfect lover. And he wasn't, just a good actor.

He looked her up and down one day, eyes screwed up, mouth set in a bitter line. 'You've started to put weight on.'

'Not much.'

'I can notice the difference and it's not flattering. You'd better eat less. We want you to stay thin for as long as possible.'

'I need to eat to keep up my strength.'

'Then get some damned corsets and lace yourself up. I'm not performing with a woman whose belly bulges.'

She could feel tears welling in her eyes at this unkindness and began tidying the room, determined not to break down in front of him. The only time he was at all civil to her now was at the theatre and she knew why — so that she wouldn't get upset and perform badly. Well, she was upset all the time, if truth be told, and knew her performances weren't as good as they had been.

When they got off the stage that night after their last performance they walked along to the greenroom to pick up their things. Suddenly two burly men stepped from a side corridor. Before she could speak, one of them grabbed hold of her arm and dragged her to the side while the other one moved up to stand close to Denby.

'Didn't expect to see us again, *Denby*, did you?' he mocked. 'Or perhaps I should call you by your proper name — Dennis?'

Denby spun round and tried to run away, but a third man stepped out to block the way they'd come.

'Oh, no, you don't!' the man who seemed to be the spokesman snapped. 'And if it weren't for the fact that you need that pretty face of yours to earn money for my sister, I'd give myself the pleasure of rearranging it. I'm sure the ladies wouldn't fancy you half as much with a broken nose.'

Marjorie couldn't keep quiet a minute longer. 'Denby, what's happening? Who are these men?'

The one holding her shook her hard. 'Shut up, you, and you'll not get hurt. He's probably lied to you as well as to everyone else. Now, have you got any things to pick up here?'

She nodded.

'Then you and I will fetch them while my brothers take Dennis out to the cab. Don't try to get help or I'm afraid I'll have to knock you out — and they'll hurt Dennis if we don't join them soon.'

For the first time she truly understood why women died to save their children. Instinctively she put her hand protectively in front of her belly and nodded.

But he saw the gesture. 'Hell, you're expecting! I've seen women do that before. You are, you're expecting *his* child, aren't you?'

She nodded, surprised to see sympathy on his face for a moment or two.

'You poor bitch. It's not your fault. He can charm the birds off the trees when he wants to, that one. But however sorry for you I am, I meant what I said. Don't try to call for help or I'll thump you.'

'I won't.'

She led the way into the greenroom, nodding to other performers who were getting ready to leave. No one seemed to find anything unusual in the fact that she'd brought someone with her, especially when her captor called her 'Sis'.

310

He picked up the bag she indicated and took her arm as they walked out, not letting go of it until he'd shoved her into a cab waiting in the shadows to one side of the main entrance. There was no sign of their usual cab or its driver.

'We'll go somewhere quiet and have a little talk,' one of the men said, after which no one spoke as the vehicle rolled through the streets.

She watched Denby, saw his eyes flicker from one man to the other, saw the fear in them.

What was he afraid of? And was he really called Dennis? The name seemed to diminish him, for some reason. She'd always disliked it.

★　★　★

Nev called Essie into the bigger of the two common lodging rooms after the previous night's customers had left. 'I've been thinking about something.'

'What, love?'

'Getting rid of this and turning it into a lodgings house for the artistes who come to play at the Pride.'

She frowned and stared round. 'Will they bring in as much money as the lodgers do?'

'Probably. Though I've got other things bringing in money, little businesses I've financed or bought over the years.'

'Have you? You never said.'

He shrugged. 'Doesn't pay to tell everyone your secrets, does it? And anyway, I'm telling you now, aren't I, trusting you?'

She didn't let herself smile. She was gradually

coming to know this man she'd married, just as he was coming to know her. She'd soon had the house running like clockwork and he'd commented a few times on how much he appreciated the order and tidiness, not to mention the meals. Her days were busy but wonderfully satisfying and as for little Sylvie, the child was thriving.

'What exactly were you thinking of doing, Nev?'

'Changing this into six separate rooms. I thought I'd get Carrie to come over and look at it. She's got an eye for things like that.'

'It's always nice to see her.' She cast a final look round and turned back towards the kitchen door, then stopped and said, 'I'd be glad to get rid of those nightly lodgers, if truth be told. It's hard to keep our part of the house smelling sweet with *them* coming in here every night.'

Soon afterwards a letter was delivered with Gwynna's name written on the back. Essie fingered the stamp on the outside of the folded piece of paper. Such a simple little thing that stamp, such a big difference to ordinary people when they could send a letter for only a penny. Not that she'd ever used one because she'd had no one to write to — until now. She smiled at that thought, delighted that Gwynna hadn't forgotten them. And if Robbie went to work away from Hedderby from time to time, as he said he'd have to, she'd write to him, too.

She prised off the sealing wax and unfolded the piece of paper, smoothing it out carefully. Someone must have written it for Gwynna, she thought fondly, because the poor lass couldn't read or write. She was working for the Hungerfords who were a wealthy family living in the country near Manchester. The mistress and head nurse had interviewed Gwynna and had employed her because the children had taken to her. The words of the letter weren't the sort Gwynna would normally use, but it said she was settling in nicely, that little Peter, her special charge, was a lovely child and that the head nurse was teaching her a lot. She would have a week's holiday at the end of the year and would come back to see them all then if that was all right.

Nev came into the kitchen and she passed the letter to him. 'It's wonderful having family, isn't it?' she said huskily.

He put the letter down at once and came to give her a hug. 'Aye, lass, it is.' He smoothed her hair back, flushed a little and added, 'And it's good having a wife like you, too.'

Which made more tears of joy come into her eyes. She became very brisk for the next few minutes till she'd pulled herself together.

★ ★ ★

Marjorie sat in the dark cab as it rumbled through the streets. The floor was covered in straw, which felt prickly through her flimsy stage shoes, and there was a stale smell to the vehicle as well as a sweaty smell coming from the three men who'd abducted them. She was so sensitive to smells at the moment the cab made her want to be sick.

What did they want? And why had they called Denby by another name? She opened her mouth to demand to know what this was all about, but they passed a brightly lit pub at that moment and the light showed clearly the brutal, lumpy face of the one who seemed to be the leader. She shivered and the question died unspoken.

The cab turned off the main roads down ill-lit side streets and came to a halt in front of another pub, a shabby sort of place this one, with a sign creaking outside and a few dim lights showing inside.

The man who'd escorted Marjorie out of the theatre helped her out of the vehicle with rough efficiency, making sure she didn't fall but also making sure she didn't get away.

She was taken into the pub, her head protected by his hand as they stepped through the low doorway into a room two steps below street level. The room smelled of stale smoke and unwashed bodies. Several men were still drinking in one corner. She thought of calling out to them for help, but they didn't even look up as she and Denby were hurried through the place and urged up some narrow stairs. A sputtering wall lamp at the top showed a narrow corridor, and they were taken to a room at the far end.

Inside there were three lamps burning and Marjorie blinked as the brightness hurt her eyes. It was a minute before she was able to make out the person waiting for them: a hugely fat woman sitting on a settle by the fire. The door was shut behind her with a thump that made her jump in shock.

Denby cursed at the sight of the woman and there was no doubt he knew her.

'Well, Dennis? Aren't you going to give your wife a little kiss?' the stranger taunted.

Marjorie couldn't hold back a gasp of shock, which drew the woman's attention to her.

After a moment's study of her face, she said 'You didn't know he was already married, did you?'

At the sight of the triumph on the woman's face, Marjorie kept back her tears out of sheer pride. 'No, I didn't and I don't believe you. Denby wouldn't — he *couldn't* . . . ' She turned towards him and couldn't finish the rest of the sentence because his expression showed clearly that he was guilty. She swayed as the realisation that she wasn't married sank in.

'She's expecting,' the man next to her said, catching hold of her arm. 'Better let her sit down, eh, Alice?'

The woman's face went cold and chill. 'She can stand.' She turned to Denby.

'What are you doing this for?' he demanded. 'I've kept my part of the bargain, haven't I? Sent you and the boys money every week and — '

He already had children! Sick anger coursed through Marjorie. No wonder he hadn't wanted her to have another one. No wonder he'd been shorter of money than she'd expected.

The woman smiled at Marjorie. 'Our sons fair dote on their daddy when he visits them, don't they, Dennis my love? But as soon as they're old enough to understand, I'll tell them what you're really like. See how they welcome you then.'

315

'You didn't answer my question, Alice,' he repeated. 'What are you doing this for? I need to earn money and she — ' he gestured to Marjorie, ' — makes that easier.'

'I'm doing it because you've set yourself up with another wife and *I won't have that!* I don't mind you having other women, but *I'm* your wife. She isn't.'

'How did you find out about her?'

'It was in that newspaper Uncle Bill takes, *The Era*. I got some of his old copies while he was away and saw your name in one. 'Denby Sinclair and his lovely young wife,' it said. Doing well, aren't you, Dennis lad? But you're *my* husband and don't you *ever* forget it!' She nodded to the three men and two of them grabbed hold of Denby. The third punched him in the stomach so quickly it must have been planned.

Denby gave a strangled scream and tried to fold up, to avoid the fist that slammed into him again, but they held him upright.

'Hurt you, did it?' the man taunted. 'Oh, dear. This one will hurt even more.'

Marjorie closed her eyes as they continued to beat him, not daring to try to intervene, not even wanting to. She felt sick to the soul at how she had been cheated.

He groaned and cried out, begging them to stop.

'That'll do,' Alice said at last.

As the men let go of him Denby crumpled to the floor and lay there weeping.

Her brothers looked down at him. 'He deserves more, treating you like that, Alice,' one

316

of them grumbled. 'You should have let me batter his pretty face.'

Denby moaned and covered his head with his arms.

'We have to make sure he can appear on stage tomorrow or he won't earn the money me and the lads need,' Alice said, in the tone of one who had had to repeat this several times.

'Well, I'm not going on stage with him again,' Marjorie said suddenly. 'I don't even want to go *near* him.'

Alice smiled. 'You're definitely not going on stage with him. You can stay here with me tonight while Marty here goes back to the lodgings and gets your things. Then you'll stay with me in the country till Dennis finds himself another partner. I'm not having him persuading you to go back to him. Oh, don't look so frightened. We're not going to hurt you or what's in your belly. I feel sorry for you, actually, but I intend to look after my own.' She turned towards her husband. 'If you pretend to marry anyone else, I *will* let Marty have his way with your face.'

Denby shrank back. 'I won't, I promise I won't. But Alice, Marjorie's good. I need her. Marrying her was just a trick to get her away from her family.'

'You're not having her. Anyway, she won't be able to do that sort of work for much longer, the condition she's in, so it's no big loss. You should have been more careful.' She jerked her head and two of her brothers picked Denby up. 'You'll be let go home tomorrow. In the meantime, a night on the floor won't hurt you.'

317

Only after he'd been dragged out did Marjorie realise he hadn't even looked at her, let alone apologised.

'He's a nasty sort,' Alice said conversationally. 'You'll be better off without him. Now, let's get to bed. I'm tired. Travelling doesn't agree with me.' She looked at Marjorie again. 'You'll have to sleep with me and my brothers will be sleeping next door. Don't even try to get away. I'm a very light sleeper.'

'Where would I go?'

To Marjorie's amazement Alice was soon asleep, snoring a little on the other side of the big bed. But she couldn't get to sleep. She lay there in the darkness letting the tears she'd been too proud to shed before roll down her cheeks, not bothering to wipe them away.

She wasn't married! That thought kept beating at her like a bell tolling for a funeral. *She wasn't married to Denby.* But she was expecting his baby.

What was she going to do now? Alice said they were taking her back to the country till Denby — no, Dennis — had found a new stage partner. After that, what? She wouldn't be able to appear on stage for much longer because of the baby, and anyway she couldn't do an act on her own.

As dawn turned the darkness grey, she came to one conclusion. She couldn't bear to go back to her family, just couldn't bear it. Call it pride or shame, she didn't know which, but she had to manage on her own. Where she would live, how she would earn money to feed herself and the child when it was born, she didn't know, but she'd find a way.

Her thoughts were tangled and fragmented and no solution had come to her when she at last fell asleep.

★ ★ ★

Marjorie's things were brought down from London and she checked them carefully, letting out a cry of anguish. 'Someone's stolen my money! All of it!' She turned accusingly as Alice came to stand at the bedroom door. 'Your brothers have stolen my money.'

'How much was it?'

'Five pounds and a few shillings.'

'It'll be Dennis who took it. My brothers aren't thieves, even if they are a bit rough.'

'He wouldn't do that to me. It *must* have been one of them.'

Alice grabbed the front of her bodice with one meaty hand and shook her like a terrier shakes a rat. 'No Lutter has ever stolen, nor ever will.'

Somehow Marjorie believed her. 'Sorry. I was upset. But how will I manage when I leave here? Surely your brothers can ask him for my money back?'

Alice sighed. 'I'm too soft, that's my trouble. All right. When I send them up to London to check what he's doing, I'll tell them to get your money back for you.'

'Thank you. That's very kind of you.'

The smile on her companion's face was anything but kind. 'No, it isn't. I shall enjoy annoying him. He deserves all he gets, that one.'

She hesitated then said abruptly, 'I was taken in just like you were, but my family made him marry me, while yours tried to stop it. I'm sure you wish they'd succeeded now.'

Marjorie considered this, then shook her head. 'No, I don't, in spite of everything. Because if I hadn't married him — or thought I'd married him — I'd not have had the last few months on the stage. And I've loved that. I miss it so much.'

'Rather you than me. I'd hate to parade up and down in front of strangers. I like my own cottage and my privacy.' She eyed Marjorie thoughtfully. 'Are you going to try to get away? Shall I need to keep you locked up?'

'No. I've nowhere to go.'

'Well, you're only staying here until things are settled with Dennis. I don't want to watch your belly swelling with my husband's child.'

But in spite of her sometimes harsh words, Alice was kind enough to her guest, feeding her well, finding things for her to do, to 'pay for her keep' as she phrased it. When Marjorie fainted while bending over weeding, her hostess decided she could do some sewing instead and gave her the family's mending to do, then bought some material and asked her to make a petticoat.

The following week one of Alice's brothers came to see her. They spoke privately in the little parlour at the front of the cottage, then he left. Alice came and tossed some money into Marjorie's lap. 'My brothers went up to London to see Dennis. They got your money. Though it's not going to last long, is it?'

'No. But it's something at least to tide me over

when I have the baby.' Marjorie fiddled with the coins, piling them up, like with like. 'I wish now I'd been more careful, but I'm not good with money.'

'You'll have to be with a child to support. And you'll need to get a job until that,' Alice pointed at her belly, which was still almost flat, 'is born.'

'I know.' She sighed.

Alice went back to her cooking, shaking her head. Impossible to dislike Marjorie Preston, however much you wanted to, but she was a butterfly sort of person and lovely enough to make a woman who was fat and had soon lost any youthful prettiness she'd once had jealous. Marjorie was kind, too, playing with the boys and telling them little stories. In fact, a perfect guest if you didn't mind the untidiness in her room and the way she sometimes forgot jobs when part-way through them — and the fact that she was carrying your husband's child.

But though Alice hadn't seen her cry, Marjorie's eyes were sometimes swollen and reddened, and she was sick every morning when she got up, though she'd tried to hide that at first until Alice told her briskly not to be so stupid.

Christmas came and went, Alice and the boys celebrated it with their family, leaving Marjorie alone in the cottage. She didn't weep, had mostly stopped weeping now because it didn't do any good. You could cry all you liked but you still woke up next morning to find nothing had changed.

★ ★ ★

321

It wasn't always possible to avoid being on the same bill as Sinclair, so when Hal's agent apologised for bringing them together for the following week's engagement, he shrugged and accepted it. He'd no doubt Sinclair would keep him away from Marjorie, but it'd be nice to see her again at least. She'd been looking so worn last time. It was a surprise that Sinclair was performing in that particular music saloon, though. Surely he was beyond that now, into the bigger places, which were just beginning to offer Hal employment as well?

He saw the fellow come backstage before Sinclair saw him. There was only a small room full of hard wooden chairs, with one mirror and rickety table where they could check their appearance. Hal sat frozen in shock for a moment or two because Sinclair was accompanied by a different girl! He couldn't go up to the man and ask what had happened to Marjorie, though he wanted to. And when he did catch Sinclair's eye, the other looked straight through him, as if they'd never met.

Hal went to watch them perform. The new girl wasn't a patch on Marjorie, but the audience still loved Sinclair, cheering and whistling when his act was over. Although he kept a smile on his face while he was on stage, Hal heard him berating his new Elyssa as they came off and saw that she was nearly in tears. Well, she had made one or two wrong turns and had come in late on one of the choruses. But she had a pleasant enough voice and was clearly trying her hardest.

After the show he got into conversation with

322

the manager. 'How come Sinclair has a new girl? I thought his wife was his partner.'

'His agent says she never was his wife, they only pretended, and now she's run off and left him, so he wants to break in the new girl in front of smaller audiences, which is a bit of luck for us.'

'What happened to the wife?'

'I've got no idea.' He called across to the man who worked behind the scenes, 'Not that piece, you fool!' And before Hal could say anything else, he was gone.

The following morning Hal got up early. He went to see his agent, who also happened to be Sinclair's agent, but he too had no information about what had happened to Marjorie. The only interest he showed was in how well the new girl was doing.

'She'd do better if Sinclair wasn't so sharp with her,' Hal said. 'Look, if you hear anything about Marjorie, let me know, will you?'

'Fancy her, do you?'

'I liked her, just want to check that she's all right. Sinclair may have left her in the lurch.'

The agent only shrugged.

★   ★   ★

Just after the new year began Alice said abruptly, 'You can leave tomorrow. Denby's got a new assistant. Just one thing . . . if I hear you've been anywhere near him, I'll send my brothers after you.'

'Do you think I'm stupid enough to go back to

him after what he's done to me?' Marjorie didn't even want to see him, hated him for what he'd done to her.

'You might not intend to but he can be very persuasive when he wants something. He turns on charm as easily as that.' She clicked her fingers, hesitated then asked, 'Where will you go?'

Marjorie had had enough time to work that out, though she wasn't sure it'd do any good. 'To the last theatre we played at. Mr Melling seemed a really kind man. Maybe he'll be able to help me find a job.' She wasn't sure, though, because his wife wasn't nearly as kindly as he was. 'Denby will have moved elsewhere by now.' It was her turn to hesitate. 'Who has he found for his act?'

Alice gave a sneering smile. 'Some young female called Elyssa. He always calls them Elyssa. I'm told she's not as good as you, though.'

'I hate him.'

'I doubt that.'

Marjorie looked at her. 'It's true. I was starting to dislike him even before you came to London and told me you were his wife, because he's selfish and lazy. He wanted me to get rid of the baby, even though I told him how dangerous that could be for a woman.'

'Why did you stay with him then if you'd started to dislike him?'

'Because I thought we were married and I'd promised 'for better for worse', and because I loved appearing on stage, absolutely loved it. I

324

miss it every single day.' She sighed. 'I'll pack my things, but I don't know how I'm going to get them to the station. That trunk's heavy.'

'My youngest brother will take you in the cart when he goes to market.'

Marjorie nodded then looked sideways. 'And thank you for being kind to me while I've been here.'

Alice shrugged. 'You helped out with the work. If you hadn't, it'd have been a different story.' Her expression softened just a little. 'And it's a nice petticoat you made me, the prettiest I've ever had.'

She made up for that moment of weakness by being very abrupt with Marjorie for the rest of her stay.

★　★　★

When the train arrived in London, Marjorie sat for a minute not wanting to get out. She felt more alone and afraid than she ever had in her life before. She'd always had her family nearby, especially Carrie, and then after her marriage, Denby had taken charge. Never before had she had to do everything for herself. Taking a deep, shaky breath, she got out of the compartment and signalled for a porter, relieved when one came hurrying over.

She went to the theatre first, taking a cab because she couldn't possibly carry her trunk. She checked the poster outside to make sure Denby — she could never think of him as Dennis — wasn't still playing there, heaving a sigh of relief when it was a new programme.

When she didn't give him a tip, the cabbie drove off without helping her and she didn't realise it till too late. She dragged the trunk towards the theatre a pace or two at a time, because she didn't dare leave her other bits and pieces lying around on the pavement and had to keep pulling them along too. Although the place wasn't open yet, the doorman recognised her and let her in, calling Mr Melling through to the foyer to speak to her.

The owner stared at her in surprise. 'Your husband said you'd rushed off to nurse your dying mother. Surely you know he's moved on from here?'

She took a deep breath and said baldly, 'He's not my husband. He pretended to marry me, but he had a wife already. When I found out I left him.'

John gaped at her, opened and shut his mouth, but couldn't decide what to say.

'I wondered — if you needed anyone for the chorus or for playing odd parts on stage.'

'Sinclair said you were expecting and that you'd probably not be back in London till after the baby was born. Was that a lie too?'

'Only partly. I am expecting his child but it's early days yet.' She eyed him warily, wondering if he'd turn her out, then saw the sympathy in his eyes and felt a little heartened. 'I'll have to make my own way in the world now and I won't show for a while, that's why I wondered . . . ' She didn't finish her sentence, because he was already shaking his head.

'I'm sorry, but we don't need any more girls for the chorus.'

'Well, then, I'm s-sorry to have troubled you. I wonder if you'd let me leave my things here while I try to find a job and somewhere to live?' Fear made her voice wobble as she stood up.

'Wait.' He couldn't bear to see her so white and unhappy.

She turned back to him.

'I can offer you a job, but it's only cleaning. One of the women who comes in daily has been taken ill and isn't likely to return.' His wife would be furious that he'd offered the job to Marjorie, but that was too bad.

'*Cleaning?*'

He nodded. 'Yes. Bit of a come-down but it's all there is. Do you have anywhere to live?'

She shook her head, still trying to come to terms with the idea of becoming a cleaner.

'I can let you have a room at the back of the theatre. It's hardly bigger than a cupboard, but it's got a little fireplace and with only you, it should be enough.'

'How much?' she managed to whisper, trying to be practical.

'How much what?'

'How much is the rent?'

'Nothing, but you'll have to clean the place out. It's been used for storage and the mice have got in, but the stuff that's left there can go down in the cellars or be thrown away.'

'I see.' Something else occurred to her, something that made fear skitter through her. 'Would I be alone in the theatre at night?' She didn't like the thought of that at all.

He shook his head. 'Heavens, no! My family and I sleep at the back upstairs and the night watchman and his wife have a room near yours. I find it much safer to have people living on the premises.'

She forced herself to be practical. 'How much do you pay your cleaners?'

'Ten shillings a week.'

It was so little to live on, but the free room made the difference. She'd spent most of her life trying to make one penny do the work of three, so she knew that she could manage on that — just. 'Very well. I'll take it.'

'If you can sew, you might make a bit more from time to time doing alterations and repairs. There are sometimes rush jobs to be done on the costumes.'

'I can sew. And I'll do anything respectable to earn money. Thank you.'

When she was alone in the tiny room, before she even thought of cleaning it out, she sat on the rickety bed which just had a rope frame across the base and a very dirty straw mattress on top of that. She crossed her arms over her body to hold her fear in and her shame, well beyond tears now. She'd gone from performing on the stage in pretty clothes, being admired and living comfortably, to being a dirty cleaning lady. Her hands would become red, as Carrie's had when she was cleaning the Dragon, and her back would ache when she grew bigger, as her mother's had. Life would be — difficult, horrible.

She hated Denby Sinclair even more for reducing her to this. She looked down at her belly, still almost flat, but which had a child growing inside it. She wasn't sure she could ever love *his* child, but she still couldn't kill it. A black beetle ran across the floor, clearly at home here. She lifted her foot and stamped on it, shuddering. There were mice too, she could smell their droppings. She'd have to get some traps.

★   ★   ★

John went up to his family's quarters on the third floor of the theatre. 'I've just hired a cleaner, Tilly,' he said cheerfully.

She spun round. 'What? You know I like to hire my own cleaners.'

'Um, well, this one was a special case.'

She sighed. 'Not another of your charitable acts?'

'Yes. She's expecting and hasn't got a husband. But it won't affect her work.'

'I'll make sure it doesn't. Who is she?'

'Sinclair's former Elyssa.'

Tilly gaped at him. 'The one who was living in sin with him? How could you? I'm not having a fallen woman living here.'

'She's not a fallen woman. He actually married her. She didn't know about the other wife and now she's with child. The police could probably arrest him for bigamy.'

'So she says!'

'I believe her. And Tilly — you're not to sack

her. If we can't help one another in this world, it's a poor look-out.'

'Hah! You help enough people for five other men.' She sighed. 'All right. But I do intend to make sure she cleans the place properly.'

'Naturally, but go a bit easy on her at first. For me?'

The following morning, when Tilly saw how pretty the young woman was, she felt angry — and jealous. She always was jealous of the pretty ones, though so far her John hadn't given her cause. But that didn't mean he might not be tempted, so she always kept an eye on the succession of pretty young women who passed through their small theatre. However, even she could see how unhappy this one was. 'What's your real name?' she demanded.

'Marjorie Preston.'

'Well, Marjorie, I'm prepared to believe that you were tricked by Denby Sinclair — he's a smooth-talking devil and I didn't take to him myself — but let me make it plain that if I find you committing any immoral acts on these premises, you'll be out on your ear. Is that clear?'

'Yes.'

'Yes, ma'am.'

'Sorry. Yes, ma'am.'

'Have you ever cleaned a theatre before?'

'No — ma'am.'

'Then we'll start as we mean to go on.' She proceeded to stand over Marjorie for the whole of the first day's work and when it was over, escorted her back to the tiny room and saw that it was cleaned out to her satisfaction as well.

330

Only when Mrs Melling had left could Marjorie sink down on the bed and give in to her exhaustion. Fear had somehow lent her the energy to do the work, but it had been a long, hard day, starting at six in the morning and finishing around four.

She had no clock, so didn't know what time it was when she pulled herself to her feet and looked round. She needed food and coal. It was a freezing cold day and the sky was heavy with rain. Outside she found a coal heap and wondered if she'd be allowed to borrow a bucket of coal. Only she had no bucket.

The watchman's wife found her standing there, shivering violently. 'They said a new one had started,' was her greeting. 'But they didn't say you were stupid enough to stand out here and freeze to death. I'm Sal Renkin.'

'Marjorie Preston. Do you think they'd let me borrow a bucket of coal?'

'Borrow? No. But they'll let you have enough coal to heat your room for a shilling a week, as long as you're not greedy. A bucket a day, Mrs Melling allows you for that. Go and ask her.'

'I haven't a bucket.'

'You haven't the sense you were born with, either. Come on. I'll take you to ask her then I'll take you out and introduce you to the shopkeepers so that you can buy what you need.'

Marjorie was shivering so violently by the time they knocked on the door of the Mellings' flat above the theatre that even Tilly was worried. 'Find her a bucket in the cellar, Mrs Renkin. There are some with holes in down there which'll do fine for coal. It'll be a shilling a week out of your wages,' she added to Marjorie, receiving only a nod in reply.

Later that night, Marjorie sat and ate a hot potato she'd bought from a street vendor and then, feeling suddenly hungry, a piece of plain bread. It reminded her of her childhood, when they'd thought themselves lucky to have anything to eat.

The next morning Mr Renkin, a taciturn man with only one arm, knocked her up as he went off duty.

Mrs Melling came down, saw her and said, 'Well, at least you're up in time.'

Mr Melling didn't come down till later, but he smiled at her as he passed through.

When she went back to her room, Marjorie disturbed a big mouse that was gnawing on her loaf, and screamed at the sight of it.

Mrs Renkin came running from just round the corner, saw what was wrong and looked at her in amazement. 'You weren't stupid enough to leave food uncovered. How did you manage till now? Have people always looked after you? My word, young woman, I feel sorry for that baby of yours, I do indeed. You'll probably drop it on its head. Have you any money at all?'

'A little.'

'Right, then. We'll get you properly sorted out.' In spite of her harsh words, she took Marjorie out and with rough kindness helped her buy a tin pantry box to keep her food in and a bigger one to keep her other bits and pieces in. 'It's no use the missus getting in the rat catcher. The little devils come back within hours. And our cat's so fat on the mice it catches, it lets half of them play round it.'

When she was alone, Marjorie lit a candle from the fire and sat down on the bed, which was her only form of seating. She could hear the music coming from the theatre, and if she went outside her room, she'd see the bright lights and happy people. But she didn't move, because all she wanted was to hide away from the world.

★　★　★

Hal kept his eyes open wherever he played, enquiring discreetly for Marjorie, claiming he had something of hers to return. Not that anyone believed him. But he ignored their knowing looks, or nudges and winks.

He perused all the theatrical posters, hoping to see her name, then realised that Marjorie Preston was too commonplace a name to use. Even if she'd joined another act, or set up solo, she'd no doubt call herself something more romantic sounding. He took to popping into other variety theatres and music saloons when he had time between shows, using his regular cabbie and spending quite a bit extra on his search.

But it was all in vain.

In the end he had to give up because he simply couldn't think of anything else to do. But he never stopped hoping. Or dreaming about her. She was the girl he wanted. If he couldn't have her, he'd have no other.

In other ways life was kind to him. People

enjoyed his act, he was good at thinking of new comedy sketches, so that he had a good variety to offer, and he was near the top of the bill in most of the places he played now, bigger places too.

It should have been very satisfying. But it wasn't enough, not for him. He wanted Marjorie beside him. Even a comic fellow like him could dream, couldn't he?

18

In early February, Athol Stott came down with
the influenza, as did many of the citizens of
Hedderby. Maria made sure her husband was
carefully nursed but kept away from him on the
pretence of avoiding catching the influenza
herself. It was a relief to have him confined to his
room again, but to her regret he recovered
gradually, though it took several weeks.

Better for everyone if he hadn't recovered, she
thought angrily. She'd prayed that he wouldn't,
but as usual her prayers hadn't been answered.
She didn't feel at all guilty about wishing him
dead because she not only hated him, he was
turning the house into a place of fear again as he
grew stronger.

Renny stopped her on the stairs one day and
said bluntly, 'You're not looking well, Mrs Stott.'

'I don't think I'm coming down with the
influenza.'

'No. But you're worrying. And your thoughts
are weighing you down.'

The way he looked at her made her shiver
suddenly. It was as if he could see into her soul,
see that she wanted her husband to die.

'What must happen will happen,' he said. 'But
you *will* find happiness again one day, of that I'm
certain.'

'I don't know what you mean.'

He smiled, one of his sweet smiles. 'I won't let

him hurt you or the children.'

She stopped pretending then. 'You can't stop him. As long as he's alive, he'll go on hurting people.'

'It's for God to dispose, not me and not you.'

'Let me pass, please.'

He moved aside, but his eyes caught hers and for a minute or two they stood staring at one another, then he smiled again and walked away.

She couldn't stop thinking about the strange encounter. Renny Blaydon was definitely not like other people and what he'd said puzzled her. How could he possibly believe a woman married to Athol Stott had any hope of happiness?

★ ★ ★

Marjorie debated selling the stage costume, but couldn't bear to. She was managing on her meagre wages and even saving a little, because she didn't have much appetite and anyway, there was sometimes sewing and mending to do for the performers, which brought in extra money. She had changed quite a lot and now watched every farthing she spent, terrified of being destitute after the baby was born.

Sunday was the hardest day of her working week, clearing up after the Saturday crowds. On Mondays, her day off because no theatrical performances were allowed on Sundays in this part of London, she sometimes allowed herself the treat of pulling her costume out and holding it against her. She'd remember her time on the stage, hum the tunes she'd sung and sway in time to the music. But as she put it away, she'd look at her red hands with the skin shrivelled by constant immersion in water and sigh.

Mr Melling let her read his old copies of *The Era* and sometimes she would see articles about how well Denby was doing. Then she'd weep out of sheer desperation as she looked down at her swelling belly. He didn't come to Melling's again and she suspected her employer had deliberately not booked him. Hal hadn't played here again, either. Not that she wanted him to see her like this, she definitely didn't.

One day in February she saw on the poster for the coming week *Bram and Joanna Heegan* and stared at it in consternation. It had to be them. But Joanna had been terrified of going on the stage and had always refused even to try it, so what had made her change her mind?

Marjorie was cleaning as usual early on the Monday, scrubbing away when she heard a voice she recognised behind her. The brush stilled in her hand. Bram. She turned her head away as she listened to what he was saying.

' 'Tis a nice little music saloon you have here, Mr Melling.'

'Thank you. You're early, Mr Heegan.'

'I like to know where we'll be singing and I never did need much sleep. I'll bring my wife along later to rehearse on your stage.' He walked down the side of the room, coming very close to Marjorie. She bent right over, making sure her face didn't show and holding her breath as he strode past. She scrubbed the same patch of floor over and over again and not till he'd left did she straighten up, rubbing her aching back with one hand.

Mr Melling came back and stopped beside her. 'Are you all right, Marjorie?'

She tried to smile at him because he was always kind to her but she failed.

'What's wrong?'

'I know Bram and Joanna. They're friends of my sister. If they see me, they'll tell her where I am.'

He stopped and turned a chair round, sitting astride it, his hands resting on the wooden crosspiece of its back. 'Don't you think it's about time you yourself told them where you are? You're doing work that's beneath you and you sit in that cupboard of a room all alone night after night. It's no life for a young woman with your talent.'

She shook her head, tears starting in her eyes. 'I can't bear to tell them. I'll make sure they don't recognise me but I beg you not to give me away.'

He sighed. 'You really need your family at a time like this.'

'They know I'm all right.' She stared down at the mucky water for a moment, then told him the truth, 'I've sent two letters, but I got people to post them in other towns. I didn't give them any addresses to write to, said we were moving on all the time. But at least they'll know I'm all right.'

'But surely they'll see in the newspapers that Sinclair isn't moving about? He's been in London for weeks now. And what are you going

338

to do after the baby arrives?'

Terror flooded through her at the thought of being solely responsible for another life, as it always did. 'I can keep working here, can't I? You won't sack me?'

His wife had already stated categorically that the girl must go once she'd had the baby, but he couldn't throw Marjorie out. 'Yes, you can keep working, but the baby will grow up and will need more than you can give it here.'

She nodded, feeling miserable as well as relieved. 'I know, but I can't seem to think beyond having it, I just can't. My brain seems . . . not to be working properly. *Please* can we let things continue like this for the time being? Once I've recovered, I'll work out what to do.'

'Very well. You do a good job with the cleaning,' even his wife admitted that, 'but you're worth more than work like this.'

She looked at him very solemnly. 'I sometimes think this is my punishment for being stupid.'

He grimaced and stood up, setting the chair back in line with the others. 'All right. We'll tick along for a bit as we are, see how we go.'

She watched him walk away, skimped on the cleaning for once and was out of the big room before Bram and Joanna returned to rehearse.

For the rest of that week she was on tenterhooks in case she bumped into them, but she didn't, though she heard them singing at night from her room, such beautiful, powerful voices. Once she went and stood in the corridor, peering through the door when it opened so that she could see them. They hadn't changed and the mere sound of their singing took her back to the Pride, brought tears to her eyes.

And then the programme changed and they were gone.

She was surprised at how bad that felt. Several times she had nearly given in to the urge to talk to them, even go back to Hedderby. But it was too humiliating to admit how Denby had cheated her, how stupid and naïve she'd been.

There was a spell of fine weather, though it was still cold, and she went for walks sometimes in the late afternoons or early evenings. She'd look up at the stars in the sky, which always seemed brighter on a clear frosty night, and it was a comfort to her to know that the same stars shone down on Lancashire. There was one particularly bright one to the north that she would watch out for and whisper to it to give her love to her family. Silly, that was, but a woman who worked as hard as she did, who had so little, was entitled to one act of silliness, surely? It comforted her, that northern star did.

★   ★   ★

Denby watched Hal Kidd's act, scowling. There was no justice in the world when a nondescript little fellow like that became so popular that a man of Denby's vocal talents had to jockey for position with him in theatres. He looked sideways at Elyssa. This was the second one he'd had since he lost Marjorie and she was much better than the first. Strangely enough, for all she acted out the smitten young woman on stage, this one hated men with a pure, single-minded passion and had made it very clear to him when she auditioned for the part of his assistant that he was not to lay one finger on her *in that way*. Which suited him just fine because if there was nothing between them, this one might last longer. The previous assistant had been a fool — and he'd been a fool too to bed her, so that it had been harder to get rid of her. He wouldn't make that mistake again.

But to his surprise, he still missed Marjorie sometimes. She'd been very restful and easy to live with, warm and loving in bed, and had kept his clothes in good order, too, something he now had to pay his landladies to do. If he'd married a woman like her originally, he might even have stayed with her. No, he wouldn't, because she was as disastrously fertile as Alice had been. Children were millstones that weighed you down and stopped you getting on in the world.

He tried to remember when the baby was due, but couldn't. She'd better not come to him for money afterwards, though. He had enough on his plate with his damned rapacious wife. It was a good thing he was earning more these days because that bitch had written yet again to demand extra money to buy the boys new clothes. They were forever growing out of them. And she'd sent one of those damned brothers of hers up to London to make sure he paid what she demanded, plus the brother's train fare. Did they think he was made of money?

Kidd came off stage to thunderous applause, walking right past him without even flicking his eyes sideways. Denby forgot the times he'd ignored the other man and glared after him. So ill-mannered not even to nod a greeting! What had he ever done to offend the fellow?

★ ★ ★

Hal walked slowly back to the men's dressing room, ignoring Sinclair because he couldn't bear to see that smug expression or talk to him after what the man had done to Marjorie. He sat down to take off his stage make-up, this being the last show of the night. It was so much easier when you had gas lights to work by, though their flames heated up the rooms to an uncomfortable degree when the weather was hot.

The manager poked his head round the door. 'I like that new sketch of yours, Mr Kidd. More importantly, the audience liked it too. I did wonder how they'd take to a bitter-sweet act, but they loved it. People are born sentimental, I sometimes think.'

'That's good.' Hal was tired, didn't really want to chat, but this manager was a talkative sort and you had to keep such men happy if you wanted to continue getting engagements with them. After a few more exchanges, however, the man was called away, so Hal gathered his things together and left quickly.

Next week he'd be playing at Melling's again, a place he enjoyed even if it didn't pay as well as the bigger places. But John Melling was friendly and the happy atmosphere he generated made playing there a sheer pleasure.

Athol looked at Renny. 'I want to go downstairs again today.'

'You ought to have a restful day. That stump is still a bit sore.'

'I had a restful day yesterday, damn you! I can cope with the discomfort, but if I have to stay in this room much longer, I'll go mad!'

'In the afternoon then. Shall I bring you the newspaper?'

'Is it time for the *Hedderby Post* again? What a treat! Why it seems like only yesterday I was reading about the fascinating activities of our little town.'

Renny turned and left the room, rolling his eyes at Wiv as he passed. He returned with the newspaper and they helped their master settle more uprightly in the bed. Renny lingered to suggest, as he'd suggested several times before, 'If we got a wheeled chair, we could take you out for a walk every morning and — '

'I'm *not* being wheeled around like a prize exhibit for people to gawp at.'

'Then maybe an outing in the carriage this afternoon?'

'No! What is there to see that I haven't seen a thousand times before?' He glared at both men. 'Get out!'

'Very well, sir.'

'No, just a minute!'

Renny turned round.

'Send Tait to me.'

The two brothers walked along the corridor,

not speaking till they were out of hearing and even then keeping their voices to the faintest of murmurs.

'What's he plotting with Tait?' Wiv asked. 'Don't tell me he's not up to something, because I won't believe you.'

'I've no idea. Tait won't speak about it. He comes and goes when Mr Stott tells him, and he's always got plenty of money to throw around these days.'

'He goes to that music hall every Friday. Paid for by *him*.'

'I think I'd like to go to the music hall myself. It'll make a change.'

'Perhaps we could both go?' Wiv looked at his brother, who seemed to be lost in his own thoughts. When the other didn't speak, he gave him a sharp nudge. 'I said, perhaps we could both go?'

Renny blinked then gave Wiv one of his sweet smiles. 'Yes. That'd be nice. Now, we'd better find Tait.'

★ ★ ★

Only when they were striding into the town centre on the Saturday did Wiv dare ask about something that had been puzzling him. 'Is he really getting better? That stump gets very red and swollen sometimes.'

'I think there are fragments of bone still in there, but he won't let the doctor touch him again. He must be in great pain every time he walks. He's a very brave man.'

'He's a sod. I wouldn't like to cross him, though.'

'No. But maybe I'll have to one day.'

Wiv blinked and his heart sank. He hadn't heard Renny talking in that strange distant way for a while, had been hoping his brother had settled down into a more normal life, stopped seeing the future as he did sometimes. He should have known better. 'Don't do anything to spoil this,' he begged urgently. 'We've never eaten so well or had such an easy life.'

Renny patted him on the shoulder. 'It'll all turn out well in the end, you'll see.' He stared into the distance and added, 'One way or the other.'

Wiv shivered at the look in his eyes, was relieved when they got to the Pride and Renny began to act normally again.

The show was a real treat. Wiv forgot his cares, forgot his master too and simply let himself enjoy the evening. He laughed till tears came into his eyes, sang along with the rest of the audience and marvelled at how clever the performing dogs were, nearly human it seemed.

In the interval he turned to Renny. 'I'd never have thought dogs could be so clever.'

'They're cleverer than most folk realise, given the chance. These have been given the chance to use their brains.'

'Migs is clever too. Didn't think she'd get so big, though.'

'Yes.'

'She doesn't like the master, does she?' Wiv shivered involuntarily as a sudden thought came

345

to him. 'You don't think he'll have her done away with if she upsets him, do you?'

Renny stared at him in surprise. 'Why should he? He hardly ever sees the creature.'

'He does some strange things in a whim and they say he never forgets anyone who's upset him and allus pays 'em back.'

'If he touches that dog he'll have me to reckon with.'

'Ha! What can *you* do against a man like him? For all his injuries he's still rich and powerful.'

Renny stared into the distance and for a moment or two it seemed to Wiv as if all the noise and bustle of the music room went away.

Then it came swooping back and as the Chairman walked out for the second half, he forgot the discussion and concentrated on enjoying himself.

It was a few moments before Renny settled into the show again. He was disappointed that nothing seemed to improve his master's temper and nasty attitude to the world. He'd felt drawn to come here, sure that some important task awaited him. Then he remembered the boys, especially Isaac, and knew that even if he failed with the master, he'd succeed in turning the son away from evil. He *knew* it deep in his bones, as he always did in such circumstances. He was proud of his special gifts — and felt honoured that he'd been given them to use for good.

★ ★ ★

When Marjorie saw the new posters and realised that Hal would be coming to Melling's, she felt so panic-stricken she even contemplated running away. Only she couldn't leave because she had nowhere else to go. What was she going to do? In the end, she went to Mr Melling again and asked if she could start work earlier in order to be out of the main room by the time the performers turned up to check out what the stage was like and rehearse with the small group of musicians.

He raised one eyebrow. 'Who is it you're avoiding this time?'

'Hal Kidd.'

'May I ask why? He's one of the nicest chaps on stage.'

'Because I'm ashamed of this,' she gestured to her belly. She hated the way it was starting to stick out, advertising to the world that she was expecting a child. Men no longer looked at her admiringly in the street when she slipped out to buy her food. Well, why would they? She was ugly, with reddened hands, worn clothes and hair a dull mess because it was hard to wash it in her little cupboard of a room with its tiny fireplace.

He sighed and shrugged. 'Well, you can start earlier if you want, but I think you're wrong. Hal Kidd wouldn't be scornful of anyone.'

Well she knew that, of course she did. But however kind Hal might be, she was still so desperately ashamed that she didn't want to see anyone who had known her when she was Elyssa, or even when she was simple Marjorie Preston of Hedderby.

The following Sunday John and his wife discussed Marjorie, about whom he was getting more and more worried. She still worked as hard as ever, but there was a hopeless look to her that went to his heart.

'She's paying the price for what she did,' Tilly said. 'It's always the women who suffer when men misbehave and there's nothing you can do about that, John Melling. At least you've given her a job and a place to live. Let that be enough. We have our own lives to lead and I'm tired of hearing you going on about *her.*'

'Hal Kidd is still looking for her and asking if anyone's seen her. We should tell him where she is.'

'It's none of our business. For goodness' sake, John! If she wishes to keep her condition secret, then you ought at least to respect her wishes. It's *her* life, after all, not yours. And if she goes I'll have to find a new cleaner and I have to admit she's shaped up better than I'd expected.'

He sighed and didn't press the point. When his Tilly got that look on her face you'd never change her mind and although his wife dealt fairly with those she employed, she expected them to work very hard and never got involved in their lives and troubles, if she could help it.

He went down to his office to work on his accounts, but couldn't settle and went to stare out of the window at the busy street below. It wasn't right, that girl suffering on her own, and if Mr Kidd was a friend of Marjorie's, surely he'd not scorn her or do anything to hurt her? No, of course he wouldn't. He wasn't that sort of man.

After a while, mind made up, John went back to work.

On the Monday morning he lingered in the foyer around the time the performers started coming in to prepare for the coming week's show. His wife was showing a new group the two dressing rooms at the rear and then said she had some shopping to do. Marjorie peeped out of the theatre, gave him a quick half-smile and slipped away upstairs to clean the office. She must have got up very early indeed to have finished cleaning the big room by now. His wife wouldn't have let her go if it hadn't been done properly. The poor lass was so pale and thin, apart from her stomach, she looked as if the slightest breeze would blow her away.

When Hal walked through the door into the foyer John stared at him for a moment, then strode forward to shake his hand. 'Mr Kidd. It's lovely to see you again. We do enjoy having you here.'

Hal was a little surprised at this effusive greeting, but smiled back at the owner. 'It's nice to be back. I always enjoy playing here.'

'I wonder . . . could I just have a word with you?' John glanced over his shoulder.

Hal was thoroughly puzzled now. 'Yes. Of course.'

'And could we go out into the street to talk? I'd rather what I said to you couldn't be overheard by anyone.'

Wondering what was wrong, Hal murmured

agreement and followed John outside. They walked briskly along to the end of the street and round the corner before the manager stopped.

'I don't know if I'm doing the right thing or not, but I'm so worried about that girl and I gather you're a friend of hers.'

Hal stopped walking to stare at him, hope stirring again. 'Marjorie? Are you talking about Marjorie who used to be Sinclair's assistant?'

John felt a surge of satisfaction at the eager expression on his companion's face. 'Yes.'

'You know where she is?'

'Yes.'

'Mr Melling, I've been looking for her for weeks — months — and not a sign. Please tell me where I can find her.'

'Before I do, may I ask why you're so concerned? After all, you're not a relative of hers, are you?'

Hal flushed. 'No, but I care about her. She vanished so suddenly what could I think but the worst? Sinclair is selfish to the core. He wouldn't tell me anything. I've searched everywhere, asked everyone I can think of, but no one's seen her. *He* has a new assistant, but Marjorie isn't appearing on stage any more that I can find.'

John sighed. Here was the difficult part. 'In her condition she can't do that.'

The younger man grew very still and watchful. 'Her condition?'

'She's expecting.'

'Sinclair's child?'

'Yes. She thought she was married to him, didn't know he already had a wife. I don't book

350

him any more, can't abide men who deceive women like that, then abandon them once they've got them into the family way.'

'Nor can I, Mr Melling. How is she living, then?'

'She's working for us — as a cleaner. It's hard work and dirty and lately she's been looking so tired.'

Hal took a hasty step in the direction of the little theatre. 'Is she there now? If not, do you know where she lives? I have to see her.'

'She knew you were coming here this week and got up early to do her work. She has a room at the back. I think she'll probably be hiding there by now.'

Hal turned and began walking towards the theatre, his face grimly determined.

John had to hurry to catch up to him. 'Mr Kidd, stop, wait! What are you going to do? I'm not having you upsetting that poor girl.'

Hal stopped, impatience in every line of his body. 'I'd not harm a hair on her head, Mr Melling. I love her, have done ever since the first moment I saw her. If she's in trouble, I'm hoping she'll let me look after her.' A smile creased his face briefly. 'And I'm sorry, but if I get my way you're going to need a new cleaner.' He began hurrying towards the theatre again.

John watched him go with a nod of satisfaction. He hadn't misjudged the man. Even Tilly would be touched by a love like that, whether she had to find a new cleaner or not.

19

Carrie sighed and went to peep into the music room, trying to distract herself by watching the new acts rehearse.

Eli saw her and came over to join her. 'Good, aren't they?' He gestured towards the stage where a man with three dogs was performing all sorts of tricks. 'They're as well trained as any dogs I've ever known, those. Cleverer than some humans, I reckon.'

She shrugged, not even seeing the animals.

He studied her downcast face. 'You're worrying again?'

'It's been more than three weeks since we've heard from Marjorie. I know something's wrong with her, know it here.' She pressed one hand against her chest. When a tear trickled down her face, she brushed it hastily away.

Eli put his arm round her and gave her a quick hug. 'I'm sure we'd have heard if anything had happened to her. She's with Sinclair, after all, so she's got someone to look after her.'

'She needs it. She always was a bit of a scatterbrain.' Carrie looked at him, her eyes brimming with tears, 'But I don't trust him.'

'No, nor do I really. Do you want me to go down to London and see if I can find out where exactly they are?'

She smiled at him, warmed by his willingness to set aside his busy life for this. 'No. Well, not yet, anyway. Joanna and Bram said Sinclair was appearing at the other side of town. When they went to his lodgings he wasn't in, neither was Marjorie, but the landlady told them Elyssa was well and seemed happy. I just don't understand why she hasn't written to us again or why she didn't get in touch with Joanna and Bram. They left a note, after all.'

He shrugged. 'She's a grown woman, has made her own life away from us. And I'd suspect Sinclair would be a demanding sort of husband.'

Carrie didn't say it again because Eli always looked at her cynically when she did, but she *knew* something was wrong with her next sister, she just did.

He looked down at her belly. 'How are you feeling? How's my little Charlie?'

She smiled. 'Kicking hard. I'm glad it's only a few weeks to go. I'm sick of this.' She patted her stomach. 'Anyway, it might be a daughter.'

'It'll be a son,' he said automatically, as he did whenever they discussed the baby.

She could tell when his attention wandered and left him watching the new acts. She was beginning to wonder if Eli would ever stand still for long. He'd got the Pride up and running, but he was losing interest a little now that the work here was becoming more routine. He was good at setting things up, she had to admit, and he thought of everything. There were even shutters on all the windows now to prevent anyone breaking in because none of them would ever forget Athol Stott's attempts to ruin their business.

But although he ran things efficiently enough, Eli already had his sights fixed on tearing down the present music room and building a proper theatre of varieties here. She'd seen the rough sketches, some of them crumpled and thrown in the wastepaper basket, others left on the back corner of the desk. But they needed more money behind them before they launched another venture.

She didn't think there were enough people in the town to fill a large theatre, but Eli said there would be by the time he'd built his new Pride. Hedderby was thriving and growing, with rows of houses being built wherever you looked and talk of a new cotton spinning mill.

She pulled a face as the baby kicked vigorously. There was no denying it was tiring carrying another life with you everywhere. Going into the small office she sat down and began looking through the bills that had come in this week. More and more she was taking over this side of affairs and enjoying it, too.

An hour later, as she was about to clear the desk up and make sure the Dragon was ready for the evening's trade, she noticed a piece of paper that had slipped off the desk into the wastepaper basket. She leaned down with a groan to pick it up. It was from their insurance company so she put it with the rest of the bills, ready to be paid the next day. She'd enjoy a stroll into town.

Mrs Latimer said there were things a woman could do to prevent herself from falling for child after child, and had explained about the special sponges you inserted. Carrie intended to get one after the baby was born. *She* didn't want ten children, as her mother had had, and she was sure Eli didn't either. In fact, she didn't want another yet awhile after this one.

★ ★ ★

When they got back to Melling's, John put one finger on his lips and led Kidd quietly through to the back, where a huddle of small rooms had been added on to the main building at various times. He pointed to a door, mouthed the words 'Good luck' and left Kidd to it.

As he went back into the foyer he bumped into his wife.

'I saw you taking Mr Kidd through to the back. You've not . . . '

'I've told him where Marjorie is.'

'What did you do that for?'

'Because he loves her.'

'A man like him can do better than her,' she said scornfully.

'Maybe he doesn't want anyone else. I didn't once I'd met you, for all your sharp tongue.'

Her expression softened, as it always did when he spoke of his love for her. She punched him lightly in the upper arm. 'Ah, get away with you.' Then she frowned. 'If he does take her away, you're to leave it to me to find a new cleaner. We're not running a charity here.'

'She's been a good worker.'

'I should think so, all she owes to you.'

He sighed and went back to work, wondering what was happening at the rear of the theatre.

He did hope Kidd would look after that poor girl.

★ ★ ★

Hal paused outside the door John had indicated, took a deep breath and pushed it open without knocking. He was giving her no chance to lock herself in and refuse to see him.

Marjorie looked up, saw who it was and cringed back, covering her face with her hands and saying in a muffled voice, 'Go away this minute! You've no right to burst into my room like this.'

He couldn't bear to see her like that, sitting huddled up in worn grey clothes in a poky little room. She should be on the stage, beautiful as a full-blown rose. 'Eh, lass, don't send me away. I've been looking all over for you.'

Taking a seat next to her on the bed he resisted the urge to pull her into his arms, afraid that might send her running away from him. Instead he took hold of her hand. Work-worn, it was now, and reddened, the skin puckered and chapped.

'Don't!'

But she didn't pull away as she said that, so the curl of hope inside him grew a little stronger.

'Don't what, Marjorie love?'

'Don't touch me.'

She pulled her hand away but when he took hold of it again, she sighed and let it lie in his.

'You haven't asked me why I've been looking for you.'

She stole a quick glance sideways. 'Why have you?'

'Because I knew Sinclair had hurt you and didn't believe the lies he was telling about you. I was worried you might be in trouble.'

'I'm managing.' That was the one source of pride she had left.

He gestured round the room. 'I think you can do better for yourself.'

For the first time she sat upright so that he could see her swollen stomach. 'With this?' she asked bitterly.

'Yes.'

She opened her mouth to contradict him, then closed it again and stared at him. 'I don't understand why you should be looking for me, let alone how I can do better than this.'

'I came looking for you because I'm fond of you, have been from the first time I saw you. Only why would a pretty girl like you look twice at a lumpy little fellow like me, who isn't even as tall as her, when a chap as good-looking as Sinclair was making eyes at you? I knew I hadn't a chance, but still I dreamed of you and thought of you.'

She stared at him in shock, her mouth half-open. It was the last thing she'd expected to hear.

'He told everyone you and he had just pretended to be wed, but I knew better. I've played at the Pride a couple of times since that first visit and I'm quite friendly with your family now. So I knew you'd had a proper wedding.'

'It wasn't a proper wedding because he was

married already. He didn't even use his real name. He's called Dennis Williams. Not as glamorous as Denby Sinclair, is it?'

Rage filled him at the thought of that man cheating her, but he controlled it, maintaining a calm, even tone. 'It doesn't surprise me.' He hesitated, not wanting to do anything that might frighten her away.

Words, held in for so long during the dreary weeks she'd been here, began pouring out of her and Hal let her talk, sensing that she needed this release.

'His wife came up to London with her brothers. When they beat him he just lay down and screamed, didn't try to defend himself. And he didn't even look at me or think about me. They could have killed me and he wouldn't have lifted a finger to save me.'

It burst out before he could stop it. 'Hanging's too good for men like him!'

'I knew how selfish he was by then, knew I'd made a bad mistake marrying him — but I didn't know how he'd cheated me until his wife came and told me.'

Her breast was heaving now with the emotion, and there was colour in her cheeks, put there by anger. He was relieved to see a shadow of the old Marjorie peeping out from behind the shabby young woman.

'Alice took me to her cottage in the country and kept me there till he'd found a new partner. I didn't try to get away because I didn't know where to go or what to do. Do you know, when he sent my things down to me, he stole my money? Can you believe that? He knew I was expecting his child and he still stole my money. When he did that, I knew I hated him.'

Hal had always thought of himself as a peaceful sort of fellow, but he suddenly understood what they meant by 'seeing red'. If Sinclair had been there at that moment, he'd have punched him in the face. But he had to think of her, not that sod, so he made a soothing sound and said, 'Go on.'

'His wife got my money back for me and then, after he'd found himself a new assistant, she told me I could leave. Only I didn't know where to go, so I came here because Mr Melling was always so kind and I thought he might help me find a job.'

'Aye, he is a kind fellow, Melling.'

'The only job he had was as a cleaner. *A cleaner!* Can you imagine how ashamed I feel, how degraded after being on the stage?'

'There's nothing to be ashamed of in earning an honest living, lass.'

She gave a tiny shrug and the passion died out of her. 'Well, it's all I've got now, isn't it? But I'm not going back to Hedderby like this.'

He watched her shrivel before him and couldn't bear it. 'Marjorie lass, there's something else you could do. I . . . ' he couldn't finish it because he was so afraid she'd laugh at him, but she didn't even look at him, she was so sunk in misery.

He took her hand and tried again. 'Look at me, Marjorie.' When she did, he took a deep breath and said all the things he'd been longing to for months. 'I love you, have done ever since I first saw you, and I want to marry you. Do you think you could ever care for an ordinary fellow like me? Do you think you could marry me?'

She pulled away. 'Don't mock me!'

'*Mock you?* I'm not mocking you, love. I meant every word I said.' She raised her head so slowly, he wondered if she'd even taken in what he'd asked, but she had, the surprise in her eyes showed it.

Swallowing hard, she looked down at her stomach then back at him. 'How can I with this?'

'Any child of yours is welcome in my life.'

She continued to stare at him for a few moments more then burst into tears, sobbing so loudly he couldn't help taking her into his arms. He let her weep against him, patting her back and making soft, soothing noises, waiting till the storm of tears had died down. Only then did he say, 'If you don't want to marry me, I won't say another word, but please let me help you, Marjorie, at least let me help you.'

'I didn't mean — you can't think — Hal, I can't do this to you. If I married you, I'd be taking advantage of your kindness.'

Relief that he had a chance with her made him unable to speak for a moment or two, then he laughed. 'I'd rather you did take advantage, if you don't mind, lass. I know this is the only way I'd ever get a wonderful girl like you to consider wedding me, but I promise you I'll do everything I can to make you happy — and I'll care for the child, too.'

Her words came out in a whisper, 'Oh, Hal.'

'What does that mean?'

'It means I can't think of anything I'd like more than to marry you — especially *you*, a man who's kind — everyone says how kind you are. I know I shouldn't do it but I c-can't help it, so if you really mean it, I'll be happy to marry you. I'm not strong like Carrie. I can't manage on my own, don't even want to.' She stopped and drew herself up looking earnestly at him. 'But I can promise you one thing. If you do marry me, I'll make you the best wife that's possible.' She waited for him to speak, but he didn't, just turned his head away. 'Hal?' She put her hand out and turned his face back towards her. 'Hal, you're crying.'

'Aye, that's the sort of chap I am. Soft as a lass sometimes. I'm crying because I'm happy. Eh, Marjorie, you really have made me the happiest man on earth.'

So they wept a little together, then he went to tell John Melling he'd be taking Marjorie away that very day while she started to pack her things, marvelling that a man could be so kind and generous. Hal made her feel warm and safe, and she'd do everything she could to make him happy, that she vowed.

But she didn't think it'd be all that hard with a man like him.

★　★　★

As the cab jolted along, Hal said thoughtfully, 'I think we should pretend the baby's mine. What do you think?'

361

'I'll do whatever you want.'

He smiled. 'No, thank you. I don't want to wed a doormat. I want a wife who has her own opinions and will tell me if she thinks I'm wrong.'

She gave him a wobbly smile. 'All right. Yes, let's pretend the baby's yours, not only because it'll make things easier, but because I don't want *him* to have anything to do with it.' She sighed.

'What's the matter?'

'Will you be shocked if I tell you I don't really want a baby, Hal? I've never wanted children. What I wanted was to go on the stage. That's what I love doing.'

At that moment the idea came to him.

'Hal? What's wrong. Why are you staring at me like that?'

'Because I suddenly realised . . . you could still do that, go on stage, I mean, if you don't mind doing comic sketches. I always end my act with a song, because that's what the audiences like, so you could sing with me, too.'

She stared at him for a moment, her mouth open in amazement. 'I could go on the stage again?'

'Didn't I just say so? But you'd have to do some comedy, help me make people laugh. It's a wonderful feeling to make people laugh and I think you could manage it just fine. I don't do knockabout comedy, that wouldn't suit you, but I act out little stories with misunderstandings where the audience can call out to us . . . well, I'm sure you could do it.'

'Oh, Hal.' She blinked furiously.

He held up one forefinger. 'No more crying. We're nearly there.'

So she mopped away the tears and even found herself smiling.

He left her sitting in the cab while he went into his lodging house to explain the situation to his landlady, pretending to be ashamed of getting Marjorie with child, saying he'd been searching for her everywhere. As he'd suspected, Mrs Berton's soft heart won over her stern morals.

'But you *are* going to marry her now?' she demanded.

'Of course I am, and as soon as I can. I'll buy a special licence and do it tomorrow if it's possible.'

'That's all right then. Eh, I do love a wedding.'

'Would you act as witness for us? I don't have any family here in London, you see.'

She beamed at him. 'Oh, Mr Kidd, I'd be delighted. And my Harry will be your other witness, if you need one.'

'That's so kind, but there's someone else who'd like to do that, I'm sure.' He gave her a hug. 'No wonder I always stay with you when I'm in London. You're the best, Mrs Berton, the very best landlady in England.'

'Get on with you! Now go and bring your young lady in to meet me.'

'She looks a mess, I'm afraid. She's been working as a cleaner to support herself and she's had some hard times. She's so thin and pale it worries me. But we'll start with a bath and a good meal, if that's all right with you. I'll happily pay extra for her.'

'There's nothing to be ashamed of in honest toil and of course she can have a bath. We'll feed her up too.' She coloured. 'There's just one thing! She'll be sleeping on her own until you're married. There'll be no hanky-panky going on under my roof.'

'I wouldn't dream of it, Mrs Berton.' Smiling, he went outside to bring Marjorie in.

His landlady took one look at the poor young woman and swept her off to have a bath and wash her hair, talking to cover her new guest's quietness and scolding gently till she won a smile or two.

It was over an hour before Marjorie came downstairs again to dry her hair by the fire, feeling very shy but like someone who'd set down a very heavy burden. Hal was waiting for her and the way his face lit up at the sight of her made hope flutter inside her, and something else lodge in her heart, something warm and happy.

'You look beautiful again!' He raised her hand to his lips and kissed it.

Behind them Mrs Berton sighed sentimentally before going back to her kitchen to make them a good hearty meal.

Hal led Marjorie to the couch and sat down, keeping hold of her hand. 'Do you have something to wear for the wedding tomorrow, or shall we go out shopping and buy you some clothes?'

She sat considering this, her head on one side. 'I'd like something new to mark a new start, I think.'

'Good. I'd like that too. And I'll be happy to

buy you whatever you want, so please don't skimp.'

But she shook her head. 'I've been saving my money — for after the baby's born, you know. I haven't got much but I've enough to buy my own clothes and I'd prefer to do that. I don't want to come to you with nothing.'

'You're bringing yourself and that's more than enough for me.'

There was a knock on the door and Mrs Berton bustled in with a loaded tray.

'Can you tell us where to buy a dress for my fiancée?' Hal asked. 'She wants something nice to get married in tomorrow, but I think it'll have to be second-hand because we can't wait for it to be made up.'

She considered this for a moment. 'Well, my sister runs a dressmaking establishment. She's very good at what she does and she has clothes that are partly finished and can be completed quickly, or sometimes there are things people have ordered and not been able to pay for. I could take you there, if you like, Miss Preston? If she hasn't anything suitable herself, she's bound to know where we can find something. I can spare an hour this afternoon in a good cause like this.'

Hal bounced to his feet and smacked a kiss on his landlady's cheek before she realised what he was doing.

She blushed rosily. 'Now, stop that!'

'If you can take Marjorie shopping, Mrs B, I'll go and find out about special licences.'

'Go to my church. It's just down the road. Tell

Reverend Bateson I sent you. He's a kind man and if it's possible to be married quickly he'll know how to do it.'

Marjorie went to stand by the window to watch Hal leave, deeply moved by his continuing kindness. As she turned she caught sight of herself in the mirror and smiled. She looked like herself again — well, except for the bump, which was now showing plainly. She frowned as she contemplated it. The thing that worried her most, apart from the actual birth, which she was dreading, was that she didn't see how she could possibly love Denby Sinclair's child, especially if it resembled its father.

The following afternoon Marjorie Annabelle Preston and Harold Benjamin Kidd were joined in holy matrimony by special licence, with Mrs Berton and Mr Melling as witnesses.

The bride had eyes only for her new husband. She smiled at him and took his hand proudly as they walked out of the church. Several times she surreptitiously caressed the gold ring he'd bought for her. It was a solid circlet and what it stood for was far more valuable to her than what it was, a visible sign of Hal's love, a love she didn't deserve but would strive to earn.

She'd sell the other ring that Denby had given her and give the money to Hal to add to their family savings, which he'd explained about. She loved the way he told her everything. The fact that he had savings made her realise he was a much cleverer man than people would think, a man in charge of his life and finances, rather like her sister Carrie. The sort of man she needed.

Then she smiled. She didn't only need him, she wanted him, liked him, enjoyed being with him.

Suddenly life was full of promise again and it was all because of him. He was a very special man, her Hal.

*   *   *

Essie played a counting game with little Sylvie's toes which had the baby gurgling and laughing, then swept her up in a hug, smiling when Nev came in and caught her doing this yet again.

He grinned. 'You're going to spoil her.'

'I can't help loving her. I wish she was my own.'

'She is in every way that matters.' He came across to join them, taking his daughter from Essie when she offered to get him something to eat.

'I met Carrie at the shops. There's good news about Marjorie.'

'Oh, thank heavens! How is she?'

He pulled a face. 'She's expecting and it's that Sinclair's baby, but it turns out she was never married to him because he already had a wife. Can you imagine that? He should be taken out and hanged. When she found out about it, she left him and got herself a job, but she said she was too ashamed to come home.'

'That was downright silly of her. As if we wouldn't have taken her in without a blink of hesitation! Her *and* the baby.'

'All's well that ends well. She's up and

married that nice Mr Kidd instead now.'

'No!'

'She has. And he doesn't mind about the child.'

'She's fallen lucky, then. Most men would.'

'Yes.'

'She should report that Sinclair to the law.'

'She says she doesn't want to because of his wife and children. If he can't earn money, they'll be the ones who suffer.'

'He doesn't deserve to be let off, though.'

'No. Well, people don't always get what they deserve, do they?'

'How's Carrie?'

'Looking bigger every time I see her. It can't be long now.'

'I'd better bake her a mother-to-be cake and take it over. She'll not want to be doing much cooking in her condition and it'll keep nice and moist for when she's laying up.'

He looked at her fondly.

She flushed a little but gave him a warm smile in return. No need to put it into words. They both knew they were well suited with one another.

*　*　*

Athol smiled as Renny let Dr Pipperday in. He had taken some laudanum and was feeling pleasantly hazy, the pain he lived with all the time at a distance for once. He wasn't going back to being dependent on the stuff, but the doctor was going to cut a couple more of the scars

368

today, the ones that restricted his arm movement, and he didn't want to jerk away at the wrong moment.

They came in accompanied by Wiv and the doctor laid out clean clothes and instruments on a little table, then turned to Renny. 'Are you going to mesmerise Mr Stott agan?'

'Yes. If you'd leave us for a moment or two, please?'

Even so the operation hurt. Athol tried not to move away from the pain of that bright little scalpel, but he could feel sweat gathering on his brow while the doctor worked on it and disgraced himself by groaning.

Dr Pipperday had to say it twice before it got through to him. 'It's over, Mr Stott.'

He let out a sigh. 'How did it go?'

'Quite well. I think we'll see further improvement.' He frowned. 'But you're too pale because of spending all your time indoors. The sun and fresh air are beneficial to the human body, Mr Stott. If you want to keep yourself in the best possible health and to heal properly, you'll have to start going outside.' He held up one hand. 'Yes, I know. You don't want to be seen in a wheeled chair, but if you'll just go out into the back garden when it's fine and sit in a sheltered spot in the sun, you'll find it helps, I promise you.'

Athol scowled at him.

Christy had been watching his patient more carefully than they realised. Lydia said he was a dreadful man and Christy was still worried by the look in his eyes. Only what to do about it?

369

You couldn't lock a man away in case he was a lunatic.

As he was walking home, he thought hard about the problem but could see nothing that anyone could do unless the man betrayed himself. The one Christy felt sorry for was Mrs Stott, whom he'd met two or three times now. She didn't bother to hide her dislike of her husband from him. And anyway, you could read it in every line of her body when they were in the same room if you knew what to look for. And Christy prided himself on reading those silent indications of what his patients were really thinking and feeling, just as Dr Grey had taught him.

He found himself walking more quickly as he got back home — and it really did feel like home to him now. And that was because of Lydia. He'd never thought to find friendship with a woman, but they shared the same passionate interest in helping the sick and often found themselves talking until after midnight without realising where the time had gone. He shared with her the information he read in *The Lancet*, and his own ideas about treating the sick, too.

And he didn't regard her in a motherly way, either. She was a fine figure of a woman, energetic and capable, as well as intelligent. It was that intelligence that made her so attractive, gave her eyes a sparkle. Ah, he was being a fool. She probably thought him just a boy.

20

As the weeks passed, Marjorie began to feel more like her old self, except that she was still being sick two or three times a day and couldn't eat some foods she had previously loved. She got tired easily, too.

Hal found her in tears one day and gathered her in his arms. 'Darling, what's wrong?'

'I'm just an expense for you. I can't help you with your act, can't do anything.'

'Rubbish. If you knew how lonely I'd been before, how I look forward to coming home to you each night, you'd not say that.'

She blinked at him through long lashes wet with tears. 'Really?'

'Really and truly.' He kissed her nose just to prove his point and the look she gave him was fond, definitely fond. Did he dare believe that would continue, grow into more? He hoped it would. He loved her so very much.

'How did the show go tonight?'

'It went well.' He stared thoughtfully into space. 'I really did trip when I was making my entrance and some of them must have remembered my old act and began laughing and calling out. So at the second house I tripped on purpose, then did the old being bewildered stuff, and they loved it. I think I'm going to start my act that way all the time from now on — though I'll find a variety of ways to trip, of course.' He smiled at her. 'And when you join me on stage, you can come on a short time after me and trip up, too.'

'I'd like to do that.' She looked resentfully down at her stomach. 'It'll be a while, though. I seem to have been like this for a million years. I feel so ugly.'

'You could never be ugly, my darling. Anyway, the time will soon pass. August isn't that far away.'

'And what then? Take the child with us wherever we go? Or put it out with a foster mother? I don't like either idea.'

'No, I don't. But I'm a big believer in things working out.' He pulled her to him for another hug and kiss, gazed into her eyes and said with all the assurance he could muster, 'They *will* work out, because we'll make them.'

She sighed and put her arms round him. 'You're a lovely man, Hal Kidd. I don't know what I'd do without you now.'

'Good, because I don't want you even trying.' He hesitated, then asked, 'I've been invited to play at the Pride again in June. Would you mind going back with me? There's bound to be talk about you and me, after you seeming to get wed to *him*, but we'll just have to brazen that out.'

'I'd love to go and see Carrie and the others. She'll have had her baby by then.'

'There's just one more thing. I wondered if I should leave you with your family to have the baby. You can't be racketing round the country with me for the final month.'

372

'I don't want us to be separated.'

'I don't either, but I think we'll have to.'

'We'll decide later.'

'I don't think we're going to have much choice, Marjorie love.' He knew she'd been feeling tired and run down, more than she'd admitted to him.

She looked at him with a sigh. 'I never want to be in this condition again as long as I live.' Then she flushed. 'Oh. You'll want children of your own. Sorry. I understand that. But — not many, Hal, please?'

'I suppose I might want children one day. I don't at the moment and there are ways to prevent it.'

'If you don't forget to withdraw,' she said bitterly.

'Is that what he did?'

She nodded.

'Well, I won't forget, love. I've more care for you — and for us — than that. But all I want at the moment is for you to have the baby safely and then for us to make a life together.'

★ ★ ★

Carrie woke suddenly in the night and lay for a moment or two wondering what had disturbed her sleep. Then her stomach clenched and stiffened. She waited, willing it to be just a passing thing, but in a few minutes it happened again and she realised she'd started to have the baby. For a moment panic set in, then she reminded herself of how her mother had given

373

birth with relative ease. Perhaps she'd be the same.

She tried to ease herself out of the bed without waking Eli, wanting to see how often the labour pains came before she roused him. But another pang caught her as she was standing up and she sat down suddenly on the bed, clutching her belly.

'Carrie?' Eli rolled over to put his arm round her and found the space empty beside him so sat up.

'I'm here, love. I've . . . started having the baby.'

He slid out of bed and grabbed his dressing gown from the chair, shivering in the chill night air. 'I'll get a light.'

He was back shortly with a lamp. 'Shall I fetch the midwife?'

'Yes. And can you wake Bonnie? I think it'd be better if I had someone with me. It's happening very fast, Eli.'

He gave her a quick kiss. 'I won't be long.' He went to rouse Bonnie, wishing they had someone else living here, then flung on some clothes haphazardly. Rushing out into the night, he ran up through the Lanes to the midwife's house, only to find that Granny Gates had been called out to someone else. He set off immediately to summon Dr Pipperday, determined that his wife was going to have someone experienced with her when she gave birth.

It took a minute or two to waken the new doctor and explain the situation. While Christy went upstairs to dress and fetch his things, Eli fidgeted from one foot to the other in the hall, muttering, 'Hurry up, damn you!' As footsteps sounded on the stairs he looked up in relief to see not only the doctor but also Mrs Latimer.

'She'll be all right, Mr Beckett,' Lydia said with a smile. 'First babies usually take their time.'

'She said it was happening fast.'

The three of them strode off through the streets, with Eli setting a brisk pace. When they went into the bedroom he stopped in shock because Carrie was already bearing down, groaning with the effort.

'Not the place for you now, Mr Beckett.' Lydia pushed him outside and looked at Bonnie, who was sitting holding Carrie's hand. 'Can you fetch me a bowl of hot water, please, Bonnie?'

'Yes.' Bram's aunt stood up, smiling down at the woman in the bed. 'I like babies,' she said softly. 'I'll help you look after it.'

Dr Pipperday quickly examined Carrie. 'Everything seems to be happening as it should. How are you feeling?'

'Relieved to get it over with and hoping I'm as quick at it as my mother usually was.'

'You seem to be doing all right,' Lydia said. 'That's lucky. It can be a long process the first time.'

Half an hour later the baby was born, a plump little girl with her mother's dark hair.

Carrie laughed when they told her it was a girl. 'Eli was so sure it'd be a boy.'

'She's lovely.' Lydia wrapped the infant in a piece of soft cloth and handed her to Bonnie to hold as she finished cleaning up the mother. 'I don't think we need you any more, Doctor. Perhaps you'd like to go and tell the father he has a daughter?'

Carrie let Mrs Latimer minister to her, glad to have the birthing over, loving the feeling of having her body to herself again. But when they put the baby in her arms she stared down at the small puckered face of her newborn daughter and intense love surged through her. Nothing prepared you for this feeling when you first held your child in your arms, she thought in wonder. Nothing!

There was a knock on the door and Lydia went to answer it to find Eli standing there.

'Can I see my daughter?'

'Come in!' Carrie called. 'Abigail wants to meet you, too.'

As she watched the two of them bend over their baby, their faces alight with joy, tears rose in Lydia's eyes. What wouldn't she have given for a child of her own body? She slipped out and went downstairs to the kitchen. Christy was sitting at the table, drinking a cup of tea and making laborious conversation with Bonnie. He looked up with relief as Lydia came in, starting to smile, then standing up in concern as he saw the expression on her face.

'What's wrong?'

She shook her head. 'Nothing, really. It just — always makes me wish Gerald and I had had children. I never fell for a baby, not once, so I suppose I must be barren. But I never lost the longing for a child.'

'Your husband could have been the one at fault, especially as he was so much older than you.'

'Well, we'll never know now, will we? It's not likely that I'll remarry.'

He looked at Bonnie. 'Why don't you go to bed now? There's no need for you to stay up.' Not until she'd left the room did he turn back to Lydia. 'How old are you?'

'Forty-two, nearly forty-three.'

'Young enough to remarry, surely? Are you still having your courses?'

She flushed at this personal question. 'I suppose so.'

'Then you should still be able to have a child. You should remarry quickly before you lose the chance to see if you can have a child.'

She drew herself up. 'What a stupid thing to say! How am I going to find a suitable husband? There isn't a queue of men waiting at my door and anyway, I have little to bring to a man.'

'Except your medical skills.'

'Most doctors would run a mile at the mere thought of a woman helping with their work in anything but the capacity of a nurse.'

'I'm not most doctors,' he said mildly. 'And actually, I've been thinking for a while how convenient it would be for us to marry.'

She gaped at him, then grew angry. 'I don't think that's funny.'

'It wasn't meant to be, but I'm sorry if I've upset you by saying it so bluntly. I never was famous for my tact.'

'You're surely not going to pretend you're in love with me?'

'No, but I do like you — very much indeed — and I feel comfortable with you. I'm a practical sort of fellow and I've been thinking for a while it might be a good idea for us to marry, given our circumstances.'

'Oh, yes, you'd really enjoy having a wife so much older than yourself!' She glared at him from across the room.

'If it was you, I would. And to tell the truth, I've never met anyone else I wanted to marry. Too interested in my doctoring, I suppose.' He held up one hand. 'Now don't say anything more at the moment. I can see I've taken you by surprise. Just give yourself some time to think about it. Are you staying here?'

'Yes, I'd better. Just in case Carrie needs something during the night.'

'Then if you don't need me any more tonight, I'll go home and get some sleep.'

Lydia was so lost in thought that it was a while before she went up to shoo Eli away and suggest they all try to get some sleep — if the newly arrived Miss Abigail Beckett would let them, that was.

But although the baby and its mother slept peacefully, Lydia didn't. Christy was a strange young man, seeming old beyond his years one minute, boyish the next. She did like him, but had never thought of him as a potential husband, had never even considered remarrying. It was a foolish idea of his, would make them the laughing stock of the town, given the age

378

difference. No, she couldn't possibly do it.

She tossed and turned on a makeshift bed in Carrie's room. Might she still be old enough to bear a child? Might it have been Gerald's fault?

No, Christy was just being silly. He'd have changed his mind by morning, be regretting his offer.

But what if he hadn't changed his mind? What if he really meant it?

She shivered, not ready yet to face what she might do then.

★ ★ ★

Maria was even more worried than usual. Athol seemed to be getting stronger by the day, was now able to get down the stairs unaided, and though Renny sometimes protested and said his master was pushing his body too fast, Athol had started to override his man's suggestions and do as he pleased.

She tried to keep the boys from annoying their father and tried to avoid him as much as she could herself, but it wasn't always possible because Athol had started going out into the back garden to sit and watch his sons playing. But their games became very simple when he was around, throwing and catching balls, hitting a shuttlecock to and fro, or sitting on the see-saw and swing that Renny had built them. When their father was around there were none of the games of imagination, where they sailed the seas in an old wooden tub or climbed a very small tree and perched in its branches like two stray exotic birds, shading their hands to look to the horizon and exchanging earnest remarks. And even the dog went quieter when he was there, hiding in the bushes or sitting with its eyes following Athol's every move, as if it mistrusted him.

Her husband continued to go out regularly in the carriage with Tait and though he never got out of it, he would come back looking pleased with himself, as if he'd done or seen something that pleased him. Tait continued to eat heartily and radiate smug satisfaction. Horrible man! He was the worst of the three, in her opinion, and several times she had to ask Renny to remind him to wash more often.

Wiv wasn't too bad once you got to know him and he had kept himself clean from the start. He always spoke very politely to Mrs Ibster, who agreed that he wasn't nearly as bad as she'd expected. As for Renny, both Maria and the housekeeper thought him a very pleasant young man, if a trifle strange, but Mrs Ibster said darkly that Tait was a nasty piece of work and she half-expected him to murder them all in their beds.

Benjamin and Isaac kept away from Tait, as did the dog, which acted as if it expected to be kicked by the fellow. If she caught him kicking poor Migs, she'd dismiss him on the spot. She sighed and admitted to herself that she wouldn't be able to do that. Her brief reign over her own home was over and Athol was in charge again. He wouldn't back her up against Tait, she was sure. He had found something useful to him in the man and she dreaded to think what it might be.

⋆ ⋆ ⋆

Christy didn't push Lydia to give him an answer and she let a few days go by before she raised the subject. It was as if she was outside herself watching what she was doing, watching how she got on with him. And she realised something she had taken for granted before: they dealt extremely well together.

But marriage? With a man twelve years her junior? No, she couldn't make such a laughing stock of herself.

Then a letter came from her sister. Amelia wanted to know whether she'd come to her senses or not. Was furious that she had taken a young man to live with her. It wasn't decent and if he didn't move out immediately, she, Amelia intended to take steps to deal with it, if she had to buy the house from the landlord to turn him out. Their parents must be turning in their graves.

Christy came in and caught her re-reading the letter with tears in her eyes. 'Is something wrong?'

Lydia shrugged. 'My sister. She can never write a pleasant letter, but must always be carping and complaining about something.'

He sat down beside her, his long thin legs stretched out in front of him, and she felt immediately comforted by his mere presence.

'What's she complaining about this time?' he

381

asked, his voice gentle.

On a sudden impulse she passed the letter to him. 'See for yourself.'

He read it through, then re-read it, before looking across at her again. 'Does your sister always treat you in this scornful way?'

She nodded. 'Amelia is quite well off. She didn't think Gerald worthy of me, made no secret about that, and wants me to go and live with her. I think I'd die first!'

'Is she that bad?'

'Worse.'

He put the letter on a small table and turned to her. 'Even more reason to give my proposal serious consideration. I didn't say half the things I intended to, but you should know that I've recently inherited a small annuity from an aunt, not enough for us to live in style, but enough so that if anything happened to me, you'd be able to live independently. We could buy this house, if you'd like, so that you felt secure here.'

'I wouldn't marry you for money, Christy.'

'What would you marry me for? Because the more I think about it, the more I believe it's an ideal solution.'

'I don't know.' She looked at him and saw such a warmth in his gaze that she admitted, 'I'm tempted, but — well, I'm so much *older* than you! What would people say?'

'Who cares? I'd not be marrying them. Do you really care so much for other people's opinions?'

'I — shouldn't do, I know, but I wouldn't want to look like an old fool.'

He took her hand and patted it absent-mindedly. 'You couldn't look like a fool. You work harder than two men and achieve so much. You're held in great respect in Hedderby, you know. Look at your mother and baby clinic, the group of ladies *you* organised who pay school fees for poorer children . . . people trust you.'

'Yes, but marriage is — well, between two people.' She could feel her face flaming.

There was a moment's silence while he thought this through. 'Would my touch be abhorrent to you?'

'No! Of course it wouldn't. It's me, my body's old, sagging. I'm not pretty, never have been.'

'And I'm an oddity, so tall and unlike the rest of my family that they disowned me.'

'You're a really good doctor.'

'And so are you in your own way. Oh, Lydia, it'd make things so pleasant and easy if we married.'

'And if I never managed to have a child?'

'Then we could adopt one or two. Heaven knows there are enough unwanted children in the world. They swarm the streets in London, stealing for a living. It used to hurt me to see them.'

The silence seemed to go on and on. She wanted to say yes, couldn't seem to say anything, looked at him pleadingly.

'I won't force you, but I will keep asking you. And if we do it, the sooner the better.'

She caught sight of the letter, such a horrible bullying letter, and suddenly she was tired of struggling on her own. She could feel her face going red again, but didn't let that stop her asking one final time, 'Are you *sure* it's what you want?'

His face lit up as he nodded. That gave her the courage to say in a breathless voice that sounded so unlike her usual capable tones, 'Well then, if you're sure you won't regret it . . . I accept.'

He pulled her to him and gave her a fumbling kiss, which made her guess that he wasn't experienced with women, then said very earnestly, 'No one can be sure of anything, Lydia. I'm sure it's what I want, but who knows what'll happen to us in the years to come? I won't pretend life with one another is guaranteed to be easy.'

'You're right. I'm being foolish. So yes, I will marry you.'

'We'll do it tomorrow, then. Why wait?'

'Tomorrow?' Her voice came out almost as a squeak.

'Yes.' He thrust himself to his feet. 'I'll go and see the parson this minute.'

He was gone before she could stop him and she sat there for a while, feeling frightened of what she'd done — but even more frightened of not carrying it through.

He was right. They worked and lived so easily together that it did make sense. But she didn't dare get up her hopes about a child. She'd done that all too often in the past and wept bitter tears when those hopes had not been fulfilled.

★　★　★

384

The new doctor's marriage was a nine-day wonder in the town. Even Essie had been a little shocked when Mrs Latimer came to see her and ask her to be a witness, but after some thought she decided it might work out all right. 'Though he's twelve years younger than she is. Twelve! It's a lot.'

'He has an old head on his shoulders, though,' Raife said consolingly. 'Give them a chance and they'll get on all right. They both of them love what they do, helping the sick.'

'She wants you to act as the other witness,' Essie said to her husband. 'I said you would. Is that all right?'

'I'd be honoured.'

'It's tomorrow.'

'They're not wasting any time, are they?'

'No. Well, why should they? Folk are already gossiping about them living together.' She smiled. 'That sister of hers will have a fit. I wish I could be the one to tell her.'

The following afternoon, they walked to the church to meet the bridal pair and found them dressed simply in their Sunday clothes, looking as incongruous a pair as you could meet, with him so tall and Lydia of barely medium height.

The wedding was quickly got over with, then Christy invited them back home to take a glass of wine to celebrate the wedding.

Essie enjoyed going in through the front door of the house where she had once worked. Bet winked at her, which meant her surprise had arrived safely. When they went into the little parlour there it was, standing on the small table with some plates beside it, a rich fruit cake covered in almond icing. It had been a rush to make it in time, but she'd done the topping the previous evening, with Ned and Edith helping her to pound the loaf sugar and sweet almonds, while she beat up the egg whites with a little rose water. The cake had turned out well, even if she did say so herself.

'I thought you should have a proper wedding cake,' she said diffidently.

Lydia stared from it to her, her eyes filled with happy tears. 'Oh, Essie! It looks wonderful. However did you make it in time?'

'The children helped me.'

'Then they must all have a piece tonight.' She turned a glowing face towards her new husband. 'I know it's silly, but this makes it feel special.'

'It always was special to me.'

Nev watched them indulgently, enjoying his participation in this event, which would, he was sure, set the town on its ears.

When the visitors had left, carrying a plate with some pieces of cake for the children, Lydia took another piece through to the kitchen to her maid, who had taken charge after Essie's departure, then returned to sit with her new husband.

After a few minutes they were both fidgeting. He gave her a wry smile. 'Shall we get back to work now? I'm not one to sit idly.'

'Nor me. Yes.'

When the busy day was over and they sought their bed together for the first time, it was he who was shy and confessed that he'd not had much experience, and Lydia was so busy soothing his fears that she forgot her own.

'That was wonderful!' he said blissfully afterwards. 'But it's even more wonderful not to be alone in the world.'

'Yes. Isn't it?'

They fell asleep hand in hand.

21

As the train drew into Hedderby Bridge station on a fine June day, Marjorie watched Hal summon a porter then hold out his hand to her. It was a huge effort to push herself to her feet and even with his help she had trouble getting down from the compartment. She clung to his arm, feeling exhausted as station noises swirled around her in a senseless babble, suddenly loud, suddenly distant.

Everything about her felt swollen, not only her stomach but her ankles and legs, even her fingers. And her head had been aching for days. Feeling dizzy, she concentrated on putting one foot in front of the other, but couldn't hold back a groan of relief as Hal eased her into the cab.

'Linney's,' he told the driver and watched impatiently as the bags and trunks were loaded.

When Essie came to answer the door to them, Hal cut off her exclamations. 'Marjorie's not at all well. She needs to go straight to bed, if you don't mind, and I think we should summon the doctor.'

After one shocked glance at her stepdaughter, Essie took charge, supporting Marjorie while Hal and the driver brought the luggage in. He paid the cab driver and as the horse clopped away down the hill, hurried to find his wife.

Marjorie was clinging to a chair back. 'I can't.'

'Can't what, darling?' Hal asked.

'Can't walk . . . up the stairs. Can't . . . '

He saw her eyes roll upwards and leaped forward just in time to catch her as she fainted.

Essie was by his side at once, helping hold Marjorie up.

He looked down at his wife's pale face. 'Could you help me carry her upstairs, do you think, Essie? If I were a story-book hero, I'd do it myself, but I'm not strong enough.'

'Not many men are.' She moved forward to take Marjorie's feet, worried that her step-daughter was still unconscious. As they laid her on the bed, Marjorie stirred and moved her head from side to side but didn't open her eyes. 'I'll send for Dr Pipperday then come back and help you undress her.'

Hal stared down at the woman he loved even more now than when he'd found her at Melling's. She was so easy to live with, kind, generous, fun. Their being together had become the most important thing in his whole life. He chafed her hand, relieved when she opened her eyes and looked at him as if she recognised him.

'Where am I?'

'Linney's.'

'Oh.'

'You fainted again, love.'

'So sorry — to be a nuisance, Hal.'

'I'm sorry you're ill, but you're never a nuisance to me. Now, let's get you more comfortable, shall we? Essie will be back soon.'

She gave a faint smile. 'I know I'm safe if she's in charge.'

By the time the older woman returned, Hal

had one of the bags open and a pretty nightgown spread out on the bed. Between them they got Marjorie undressed, by which time they could hear Raife letting Christy in. Footsteps sounded on the stairs and Essie went to let the doctor in.

Hal quickly explained what was wrong then Christy said, 'If you'll leave me with your wife, I'll examine her.'

'I want Hal to stay,' Marjorie said.

'I won't get in your way, doctor.' He went to stand at the back of the room while Christy finished his examination and questioned her about her health.

'I'll just have a word with your husband now, Mrs Kidd.'

Marjorie grabbed the doctor's arm. 'It's my body. I won't be left out.'

He sighed. He hated to tell young women this. 'It's something which occasionally happens to a woman in the later stages of pregnancy. We think it's a form of poisoning of the blood, but we don't know what causes it. The only thing to do is rest. That way, there's a chance of you having the baby safely. But I'm afraid it's risky for you both.'

They both stared at him, aghast.

'We're only supposed to be here for a week,' Hal said. 'We move around all the time because of my job.'

Christy gave him a very serious look. 'If you value your wife's life, you'll find a way to keep her somewhere safe where she can rest all the time until the baby's born.'

'She can stay with us and we'll look after her,'

Essie said at once. 'Her sister's only lately had her baby, so she can't have Marjorie. Though I'm sure Carrie will be round the minute she hears Marjorie's back.' She went to take hold of her stepdaughter's hand. 'You'll let us do that for you, love, won't you?'

Marjorie nodded, the ready tears starting to her eyes. 'Yes. I'm so grateful.' She looked beyond Essie to Hal. 'You'll come back — for the birth? Please. I need you.'

'I'll definitely come back. In fact, I'll see if my agent can find someone to take over my engagements for the whole of August. I *want* to be with you.'

Essie took Christy's arm and gestured towards the door. 'Perhaps you can tell me what to do, doctor?'

Marjorie looked at Hal. 'I've been nothing but trouble for you.'

His smile was so warm she could feel it wrapping her round with love. 'I'd rather have trouble with you than an easy life with anyone else.'

'I do love you, Hal. You're the dearest man.'

Her eyelids fluttered then closed and he watched her fall asleep. It was the first time she'd said she loved him and he knew she meant it. No mistaking that look on her face. He felt that same softening of his own expression when he looked at her. But she was so pale and weak that he felt helpless and afraid every time he looked at her.

Was he to gain what he wanted most in life only to lose it — and her?

* * *

Three weeks later, Hal came back to Hedderby to be with his wife as she gave birth to the child. She was sleeping when he arrived and he went only as far as the door to their bedroom, shocked that she looked worse, in spite of all Essie's care, with that mound of stomach pushing up beneath the bedclothes and her fingers so puffy she'd had to take off her wedding ring. As he had done so many times, he cursed Sinclair, who had put her in this position then abandoned her. Maybe if she hadn't had to work so hard when she was on her own she wouldn't be so ill.

He nodded to the girl sitting with her and went back down to talk to Essie. 'She doesn't look well.'

'No. We've cosseted her in every way we could, even hired help so she'd never be alone, but Dr Pipperday says it's her own body that's at fault. He comes to see her every day, you know, and he can always make her smile.'

'Has he been here yet today? I want to talk to him.'

'No, but he will be. We never know when he'll pop in.'

Hal walked restlessly to and fro, unable to settle. 'I see that your house changes are moving ahead.'

'Yes. Go and have a look.'

He opened the door leading to what had been the common lodging rooms and went to look round. Where there had been two big rooms, there was now a corridor with doors opening off it. Inside one of the rooms men were plastering the walls, their clothing covered with white dust and splatters. Hal stared at them for a moment or two, then walked back to the kitchen. 'It's going to look good.'

'Yes. We expect to have the rooms finished in a month or so. We're going to have a room specially for bathing in and doing the washing, with a boiler near the bath tub and a cold water tap to fill the boiler or to add to the bathwater if it's too hot. Nev is very clever about that sort of thing. There's even a drain to empty out the bathtub, so you don't have to lug buckets of water in and out. And he's going to make a covered walk outside to two necessaries. Two new ones he's having, one for the family and one for paying guests. We won't get wet going out there and ... ' She broke off, seeing that he wasn't really listening to her. 'I don't know why I'm beating your ears with this, when all you're concerned about is Marjorie.'

'Sorry. It all sounds splendid. Very modern.' He tried to smile at her, but couldn't. 'I can't thank you enough for your care of her. You must let me pay you for what you've spent.'

'You owe us nothing, Hal. She's family and so are you now.'

'But I can't expect you to keep her — and now me as well.'

'Well, how about you give me something towards the food? But that's all I'll take, and truth to tell, Marjorie's not been eating enough to count. The bedroom doesn't cost us anything, after all.'

'But you hired that girl to sit with her.'

'It was our pleasure and Jinny needed some easy work because she's been ill herself. Mrs Latimer, I mean Pipperday, looks out for some of the poorer lasses in town, and I try to help her.' Essie turned back to her work, speaking occasionally but mostly leaving him in peace.

Every few minutes Hal tiptoed up and down the stairs to see if Marjorie was awake. At last he was rewarded by the sight of Jinny helping her sit up in the bed. Her face was the same colour as the sheets, not a vestige of colour in her cheeks and her eyes had a shadowed, unwell look to them. She smiled at him and held out one hand, but when he took it, the hand lay limply in his as if she hadn't even the strength to hold on to him.

'I'm back to stay till you're over this,' he told her.

Her face lit up. 'You managed to arrange it, then?'

'Yes, of course.' He didn't say that his booking agent was angry with him, that withdrawing from two of the engagements had upset the managers, but Marjorie was more important than anything else in his life.

As the days passed she seemed to derive great comfort from his presence even more than from her sister Carrie's daily visits, but dozed a lot and let him do most of the talking. Every time she woke to see him sitting there by the bed, her eyes glowed with love, which warmed his heart. He tried to be polite to Essie, Nev, Raife and the rest of the young Prestons, hoped he had succeeded.

When Marjorie's labour pains at last began he was relieved, but after a few hours where nothing much happened, that relief turned to stark fear because she was so weak.

Mrs Pipperday came to be with her, sitting by the bed and encouraging her to look forward to a successful birth. Essie said the doctor's wife was the best midwife in town, and was doing more of that sort of work than she had with her first husband.

Hal wouldn't let them send him away, not yet, not till the actual birth happened, and sat in a corner of the bedroom, silent most of the time, feeling utterly useless and sick with worry.

The night seemed to go on for a very long time and as the false dawn brightened the sky a little, Lydia beckoned to Hal and took him outside the bedroom. 'I think we should fetch my husband. Things aren't going well and she's getting too weak to push properly.'

He nodded, unable to speak for a moment because of the fear clutching his heart, then he set off running through the empty streets, feeling outraged to see a beautiful dawn sky starting to shimmer in the east when his darling's life was in danger. He hammered on the doctor's door and Christy appeared almost immediately in rumpled clothes.

'Mrs Pipperday says to fetch you. It's not going well.'

Christy nodded. 'I didn't get undressed, had a feeling I'd be needed. Just let me get my things.'

Back at Linney's they found Essie sitting at the kitchen table with Nev and Raife.

'Couldn't sleep for worrying about that lass,' Nev muttered.

Essie half-stood. 'If you need anything, doctor . . . '

'I'll let you know. Keep some water hot.' Christy turned to Hal. 'It's better for everyone if you're not there from now on, believe me.'

So the four of them sat on in silence, then Essie bullied Hal into drinking a cup of tea. But he couldn't force down the food she provided, not a mouthful, not while Marjorie's life was in danger. Even Nev shook his head in response to his wife's offer of a piece of cake.

From upstairs came faint moans and footsteps walking to and fro.

Gradually, the rest of the Prestons woke up and came down to the kitchen. Dora and Edith had to leave for work almost immediately, so Essie made their breakfast and put their dinner together, glad of something to occupy her hands. They were soon out of the house, but each came to lay a hand on Hal's shoulder before they left and say, 'Tell our Marjorie we're thinking of her.'

That brought tears to his eyes, but he sniffed them away and nodded.

The younger children would be leaving for school a little later and usually had to be scolded out of bed, but today they were up betimes, sitting in the kitchen, needing the reassurance of the adult presence. Ted was in his last term of schooling now, usually a noisy creature, with all a healthy lad's boundless energy, but this morning he was very quiet as he ate the food Essie set before him, looking upwards occasionally as the footsteps passed and repassed. Grace and Lily, the youngest of the family, sat close together, staring from one adult to the other with wide, frightened eyes.

Hal didn't speak to any of them, wouldn't have known what to say, but he could feel their support as solidly as if they had their arms round him and as the younger ones left for school, they too came over, clutching his hand for a minute or two and whispering, 'Give Marjorie our love.' Carrie came round, stayed for a while, then reluctantly left to tend her own baby, promising to return in the afternoon, or if they sent for her.

As the morning wore on, the moans from upstairs grew very faint.

Lydia came down a couple of times to fetch clean water or ask for a cup of tea for herself and the doctor.

'How is she?' Hal asked in a hoarse plea each time.

'It's going slowly,' Lydia said. 'First babies sometimes do.'

'Can I come and see her?' he asked.

'Better not.'

In the early afternoon, Dr Pipperday came down, looking tired and sad. 'I shall need to use forceps to draw the child out, Mr Kidd, which can be a risky procedure.'

Hal's face went even whiter. 'It's Marjorie who matters. If there's any choice, save her.'

'It may comfort you to know that I have the latest obstetric forceps,' Christy said quietly, 'and that I trained to use them properly in London. Believe me, I know what I'm doing and I shall take the greatest of care of both Marjorie and the child.'

'Did she . . . send me any message?'

'She's not thinking clearly, is too exhausted.'

When the doctor had gone back upstairs, Essie burst into tears and buried her face in her apron. Nev went over to put his arms round her, hugging her close.

Raife came to sit next to Hal, his arm round the younger man's shoulders. 'We should mebbe pray.'

'Pray? What sort of god would make her suffer like this?' Hal demanded, his voice rising hysterically. 'I don't think I'll ever pray again.'

No one could answer him, but Raife patted the hand that lay clenched on the table and stayed very close to him.

It seemed a long time before they heard a miraculous sound, the faint wail of a newborn baby.

Hal started to his feet and was up the stairs before anyone could stop him. He hesitated outside the bedroom door, but he couldn't bear not knowing what had happened to Marjorie, not for a second longer, so he flung the door open.

She was lying so still and pale on the bed, his heart felt torn apart with terror. 'Is she . . . dead?'

Christy looked up from where he was stanching blood. 'No. But she's very weak. Close that door, please.'

He did so, leaning against it. 'I need to be with her. I don't care if men aren't allowed in at times like this, I'm staying.'

Lydia looked at Christy and he shrugged, then turned back to his patient. She looked down at the baby, a dark-haired girl with faint bruises where the forceps had gripped her but amazingly little damage, given the circumstances. Worried that she might be needed to help with Marjorie, she went quickly down the stairs with the infant. 'Can someone hold her while we attend to the mother?'

Essie stepped forward at once, arms held out.

'Is that poor lass dying?' Raife asked in a choked voice.

'It's in God's hands,' Lydia admitted. 'It could go either way. She's bleeding heavily.'

'Nay then, nay then,' Raife muttered and went to sit at the table again, head leaning on his hands.

Upstairs, Christy worked to stop the flow of blood and gradually it eased off. Lydia helped him clean Marjorie but they didn't move her, just watched — and waited.

His lovely young wife was so still and transparent Hal didn't dare take his eyes off her. He went to kneel by the bed, taking her hand, shocked by how cold it felt. He warmed it between his own, unaware that he was speaking his thoughts aloud. 'You have to get better, Marjorie love. I can't manage without you now. You've had the child, the pain's all over. You've only to rest and get better now, my love.'

When Lydia frowned and looked at Christy for guidance, he signalled to her to keep quiet. There was nothing else he could do to help

Marjorie, and he was sure it wouldn't hurt for her to hear her husband tell her he loved her.

'I've been planning our new act,' Hal went on. 'We'll get you a pretty dress, whatever colour you like. A new dress for a new act. We'll call ourselves Hal and Marjorie Kidd and we'll buy a special song of our own to sing together at the end of the act, one with a lilting chorus for the audience to join in. You'll enjoy seeing their happy faces. I'll have to teach you how to trip up, how to exaggerate what you do, but I'm sure you'll pick it up quickly. You're good on stage. We'll have such fun, my love. So all you have to do now is get better, then we can start rehearsing.'

He felt her hand squeeze his very weakly and stopped talking to study her face. 'So you're listening to me, are you? I hope you're liking what you're hearing.'

She squeezed his hand again and a very faint smile flickered on her face as her eyes half-opened then closed again.

Hal looked at the doctor in panic, terrified that she was dying, but Christy moved quietly to join him and feel for a pulse, nodding and smiling encouragingly as he found it. 'Stay and talk to her, Mr Kidd. It's clear she likes having you there.' He leaned closer to Marjorie, 'You're going to be all right now, Mrs Kidd. And so is the baby.'

With tears running down his cheeks Hal continued to murmur to his wife.

Christy moved back to join Lydia. 'I doubt she'll be able to feed the baby, will need all her strength to recover.'

'Do you think she will survive?'

'I think she stands a good chance with a husband as loving as Mr Kidd. Did you see her open her eyes for him when I couldn't get any response out of her? It's wonderful what the power of love can do.' He smiled down at her, because they shared their own secret.

She blushed and smiled at the father of the miraculous babe growing within her, then grew brisk again. 'I think I know just the woman to act as wet nurse. Kitty Giddings gave birth a few days ago and she always produces enough milk for six. She's a raucous type of woman, widowed a couple of years ago, and no one knows who's fathered the latest, but she keeps her house clean and looks after her children properly. I'm sure she'd help out and would be glad of the extra money.'

'You always seem to know someone. Come down and help me check the baby, then I'll come back here for a while to keep an eye on our patient. Nev can send someone round to Kitty's house.'

So for a few precious moments Hal was left with Marjorie, which was what he wanted more than anything. He kept on talking to her but now that they were alone, he was able to tell her how very much he loved her. Once she opened her eyes and gave him another faint smile, once she squeezed his hand — he knew it was a squeeze not an involuntary twitch — but mostly she drifted in and out of sleep and as he was never quite sure how much she'd heard, he told of his love over and over again.

22

Athol walked slowly and carefully along the hall towards the library, trying not to limp or move like one of those damned jerky clockwork figures he'd seen in an exhibition in Manchester a few years ago. He peered into his wife's small parlour, startling her so that she jumped and put one hand on her chest. 'What are you doing?'

'My household accounts.'

He stared round the room, pulling a face at the sight of that stupid embroidery of hers lying on one of the chairs, but acknowledging to himself that she'd had to have something to fill her time in the past year or so and at least this was harmless. 'I'll be in the library when Tait comes back.'

She nodded.

When he got there he eased himself into a chair, mindful of Renny's warning not to overdo it. This new leg was far better than the other one, but it still hurt, it always hurt, to put weight on the stump. Well, let it. He wasn't going back to lying in bed all the time or being pushed around in a wheeled chair like a baby.

He'd sent Renny on an errand, it was Wiv's day off and Tait, who was supposed to stay with him, was out making some special arrangements for him. It was bliss to be alone. He smiled, breathing deeply and with immense satisfaction. He could use his claw hand a little now, thanks to that lanky young doctor. He looked down at it and opened the fingers and thumb as much as he could, closing them again, then leaning his head back, still smiling.

Not long now, a few weeks at most, and he'd strike out at those who thought they'd got the better of him. Then people in Hedderby would see that no one — no one at all — did that and escaped retribution.

And after he'd taken over the management of the works again, his employees who had, from the sound of things, become extremely slack in their ways, would also learn to toe the line again. Trust Edmund to pamper them.

He'd set his cousin straight, too. Dear Edmund was rather vulnerable now that he had a wife and small son. Athol wasn't sure whether to get rid of young Preston, since the fellow was good with machinery and cheaper than an experienced engineer, but he'd certainly teach him to respect his employer, who was Athol not Edmund.

Once all that was sorted out the money would come in more quickly and he could deal with this urge for a woman, which had come upon him lately, proving once more that although his recovery had been slow, it was continuing.

★　★　★

Edmund stared at the note Tait had brought him, trying to hide his shock and dismay from Athol's henchman. So it had started. His cousin intended to take over the engineering works

403

again. Well, if he did, he'd be running it on his own because Edmund wouldn't work closely with him ever again and was only managing the works now because of Maria and the boys.

Robbie peered through the open door and Edmund shook his head. After a quick glance at the man standing there, Robbie turned and walked quietly away.

Tait scowled after him, then turned back to Mr Edmund.

'Do you know what's in this note?'

Tait nodded. 'It says Mr Stott is coming to visit the works.'

'Well, he can't come tomorrow,' Edmund said firmly. 'We're bringing in a new machine and the place will be in chaos, dangerous underfoot for him. I'll write him a quick note, but I'd appreciate it if you'd look through the door at the preparations so that you can explain to my cousin that I'm not making this up.'

Tait had already seen that the place was at sixes and sevens, but hadn't known why. He went to stand in the doorway, winking at a fellow he knew as he studied the new layout of the works carefully. Mr Stott would definitely want to know as much as possible.

When he turned round Mr Edmund was scratching away at a note, so he studied the office as well. This place was in a right old mess. Mr Stott had always kept things tidy, still did. You hadn't to leave anything out of place in his master's room or he roared at you.

Since Mr Edmund didn't look up, Tait went to stand by the door again, continuing to observe the inside of the works, scowling even more blackly at the sight of that Robbie Preston giving orders to everyone as if he knew more than they did. His friends had told him how that sod was lording it over folk as had been here when he was still wetting his breeches, and now Tait could see it for himself. Mr Stott wouldn't be pleased about that.

'Here's the note.'

Mr Edmund's voice just behind him startled Tait, but he turned quickly and took the proffered piece of paper. 'Busy here, isn't it?'

'We have plenty of orders coming in. And by the way, we keep a very close watch on the place at night.'

Tait looked at him, not in the least put out by what was hinted in that remark. 'Mr Stott will be glad to hear that.' As if his master would attack his own works, or risk damaging it again. He had another target in mind, one Tait approved of utterly.

He took the note, ambled outside and took his time walking back to the house. This was the life and could only get better with a clever master like his.

★ ★ ★

Kitty Giddings came to Linney's, a buxom woman with gigantic breasts and arms as muscular as most men's. She had her own baby with her and it was a rosy little thing, surprisingly clean for a woman from the Lanes and smelling of milk.

405

Lydia came downstairs to speak to her and they both studied Marjorie's newborn baby, which Raife was holding.

'Little, isn't she? Ah, the lovie, she's looking for the titty already.' She lowered her voice to ask, 'How's the mother?'

'Not well. Needs all her strength if she's to pull through, not producing much milk anyway. I'll go and fetch the father. Perhaps if Mr Linney held your baby, you could hold this one, get to know her.'

'What's she called?'

'They haven't named her yet.'

'Not right that.' Kitty smiled across at Raife, who was now holding her son. 'Mind if I sit down and nurse her? She looks hungry, poor mite.' She went to sit in the rocking chair, baring one enormous breast without any shame whatsoever.

Raife grinned and looked down at the little boy he was holding. A plump infant for one so young.

The silence in the room was broken only by the sound of Marjorie's daughter sucking contentedly at the woman's nipple and Kitty murmuring encouragements to her.

When Lydia and Hal came downstairs, the cosy scene that greeted them was enough to persuade both of them that Kitty Giddings would be a suitable wet nurse.

'How much should I pay her?' he whispered.

'Ten shillings a week, and perhaps Nev could give her some food as well. She's got small children as well as the new baby. He seems to

406

have ways of obtaining food cheaply and the better she feeds, the more milk she'll produce.'

He avoided looking directly at Kitty's bare breast. 'I'm happy for you to arrange it.' He turned to go upstairs again.

Lydia tugged at his sleeve. 'Just a minute. You haven't told me what you want to call the baby.'

'Ah. Well, we haven't really discussed it. Marjorie hasn't been well and it isn't my child, so I've left that side of things to her.'

'Well, she'll be in no condition to be choosing a name, so you'd better think of something. You can always use it as the child's second name if Marjorie doesn't like it.'

He thought frantically for a moment or two. 'Leah, then. It was my grandmother's name.'

'Old-fashioned but pretty.' She raised her voice. 'Did you hear that, Kitty. The baby's called Leah.'

The woman looked up and smiled. 'I like that. Mine's called Tam.' She grinned at the way Hal was avoiding looking at her. 'I'll have to take her home with me, Mr Kidd. I've two other little 'uns to look after and my mother living with me as well.'

'That's fine.' He fumbled in his pocket. 'Here. To start you off.'

The money vanished into the folds of Kitty's skirt and her smile grew even broader.

'I'll go and get Leah's things,' Lydia said.

'I'll go back to my wife.' Hal followed her.

Kitty looked at Raife. 'Doesn't he like babies? He hasn't come near his daughter.'

He hesitated, but didn't feel he could share the story with her.

She looked at him shrewdly. 'Or does it belong to the other fellow who pretended to marry her?'

He looked at her warily.

'The one she used to be on the stage with. I was passing the church when they came out, and when she came back, word went round about why she had a new husband. Eh, I used to watch her singing and dancing. Lovely she was. What happened to *him*, the first one, I mean?'

'Ah, well. It turns out he was married to someone else. She didn't know.'

A scowl marred Kitty's rather bovine features. 'I'd have snipped off his privates when he was asleep if he'd done that to me!'

'Don't talk about it to anyone, please.'

She smiled again. 'Not me. I've got me own secrets an' I wouldn't want them shouting round the town.'

Lydia came back with a bag of clothes and some bedding. 'I'll bring a drawer round for her to sleep in, and I'll come and see you for the next few days, just to make sure everything's all right. If you need anything, anything at all, send me word.'

Kitty nodded and heaved herself to her feet. 'Come in useful, the money will, I don't deny. But I'd not let this poor little creature starve, whatever. I'll look after Leah, don't worry, Mrs Pipperday. I like children. They're honest, children are, unlike some men.'

Raife picked up the bag and blankets. 'I'll carry these back for you, shall I, Mrs Giddings?'

Kitty nodded and went to take her son back from him. 'You'll have to. Two babies is enough for any woman.' She led the way out.

Lydia watched her go, looked down at herself and smiled to think she too would become a mother, then looked up to the bedroom where Marjorie lay and felt anxiety clutch her for a moment or two. Becoming a mother at her advanced age could be dangerous, but it was worth the risk, well worth it.

Humming under her breath, she went back up to keep watch over Marjorie so that Christy could go home and deal with his other patients.

She kept watch over Hal too, who was sitting in a corner of the room nodding off and then jerking awake. He hadn't wanted even to touch the baby, but had agreed to act as its father. She was beginning to worry about that. She was sure he wouldn't hurt little Leah, but children needed love and could sense when it wasn't offered.

* * *

Marjorie was very weak for the next few days, but Christy was satisfied with her progress, because she looked like a woman who wanted to live. He had still to talk to her and Hal, to tell them the other bad news, but he was putting it off until she was more able to cope with it, though some women never coped.

On the third day after the birth of the child Essie came up to give Marjorie a wash and as she was helping her into a clean nightdress, asked if she wanted to see her daughter now that she was feeling better. 'Kitty can easily bring her round. She only lives a few streets away.'

Marjorie shook her head. 'No, thank you.'

'Leah's a bonny little thing.'

She fiddled with the sheet, avoiding her stepmother's eyes. 'I don't want to see her at all, if you must know. I didn't want to have a child. And though I couldn't have got rid of her, now she's been born I don't want to raise her. I'm not . . . you know, feeling motherly.'

'You'll feel different when you hold her in your arms,' Essie said, trotting out the old saying, not taking her seriously.

Marjorie pressed her lips together and slid down beneath the covers. 'I'm tired. Tell Hal to go out for a walk. I'll have a bit of a nap.' She'd been sleeping a lot, but it felt to be what her body needed, and when she woke, Hal was usually sitting there smiling at her.

★ ★ ★

The following day Essie took matters into her own hands, sending a message to Kitty to bring the baby round to see its mother. Then she sat the wet nurse down with something to eat and carried the baby upstairs to where Hal was sitting with his wife.

They both stopped talking abruptly when she appeared in the doorway holding little Leah. Hal's face became expressionless and Marjorie actually scowled at her.

'I've brought your baby. You've not really seen her.' Essie approached the bed, sure that they

410

couldn't remain indifferent to such a bonny infant.

Marjorie shrank away, making no attempt to take the baby. Hal was watching his wife.

Essie set the baby gently on its mother's lap. 'Take her and give her a cuddle.' She stepped backwards, expecting to see the usual miracle of mother love.

Instead Marjorie burst into tears, covering her face with her hands. Hal picked up the baby, stared at it for a minute, then walked down to the foot of the bed. 'I know you mean this for the best, Essie, but Marjorie's not well.'

'She's well enough to hold a tiny baby.'

'She doesn't want to and I'm not going to force her.'

For a minute they stared at one another, each angry, then Essie took the baby from Hal and walked to the door, turning to say sharply, 'I'm disappointed in you, Marjorie Kidd. I thought you had a more loving heart than that.'

When she'd gone, Marjorie wept in Hal's arms, then subsided wearily on the pillows. 'I don't want her, Hal, don't want anything to do with her. I'm a terrible mother. You don't despise me for that, do you?'

'On the contrary. I don't really want her, either. It's you I care about, not that baby. I'll see she's well provided for, but if you don't want to raise her, we'll make other arrangements.'

Her eyes filled with tears. 'Oh, Hal, you're too kind to me. I do love you so.'

He bent to kiss her cheek. 'I'll have a word with Essie, make sure she doesn't do that again.'

411

Downstairs, Essie took the baby across to Kitty, but didn't hand her over. Instead she stood looking down at the child, her heart twisting with love. Poor little thing! To have a mother who didn't want you. How sad that was! And she had no children of her own body, had ached for them for years. Life was so unfair.

'Was she pleased with how I'm looking after her?' Kitty asked.

'She's . . . not interested in the baby.'

Kitty gaped at her. 'Her own child?'

Realising what she'd said, Essie looked at the other woman pleadingly. 'Don't tell anyone, please. I don't want little Leah to find out one day that her own mother didn't want her.'

'What's going to happen to her then?'

'I don't know.' She patted the younger woman's arm. 'In the meantime you're doing a splendid job of looking after her and I baked an extra cake this morning for you and your children.'

'They'll love that. We don't usually run to cake, though I can usually keep bread on the table, because unlike my stupid husband — an' I'm glad he's dead — I don't drink my money away and I'm not afraid of hard work.'

'I know. Everyone says how well you look after your children. But still, you've helped us out of a difficult spot and we're truly grateful to you, so if I make an extra cake or two, you'll not refuse them, I'm sure.'

Kitty grinned at her. 'No one ever said I was

stupid.' She took Leah back. 'Now, let me take this young lady home. My mother's looking after Tam, but he'll soon want feeding. Cheer up. Marjorie may feel differently once she's better. Women sometimes get a bit down after they've had a child.'

'Perhaps she will,' Essie said, forcing a smile. But she doubted it. That had been revulsion she'd seen in Marjorie's face.

And in Hal's.

★ ★ ★

A few days later, Christy came to check on his patient and found her sitting up in bed, looking pretty, if still pale, and laughing with Hal. He knew his task couldn't be put off any longer.

'I need to talk to you both,' he said, pulling a chair up to the other side of the bed from Hal, because he never liked to loom over people.

They were instantly alert, exchanging worried glances and then reaching out to hold one another's hands.

'During the birth, I'm afraid you were damaged internally, Mrs Kidd, badly scarred, and it's highly unlikely that you'll ever be able to bear another child.' He watched her carefully and to his surprise she stared at him as if he'd given her a gift, her eyes widening from wariness into an expression of relief and yes, joy. Then she looked at Hal as if trying to gauge his reaction.

He didn't hesitate. 'Thank goodness!'

Christy looked at him in surprise. 'Are you sure you don't mind that, Mr Kidd?'

Hal nodded. 'I'm quite sure. I don't want Marjorie ever to go through that again, don't want to go through it myself, either, to tell you the truth.' He looked at his wife. 'You're sure you're all right about it, love?'

'Yes. You know I've never wanted children.' She shot a shamefaced glance at Christy and explained, 'My sister Carrie and I had to bring the others up because our mother was always expecting and well, she wasn't a good mother. I've had enough of babies to last me a lifetime, more than enough.'

'How are you so sure she won't be able to have more children, doctor?' Hal asked.

'Well, your wife probably has a distorted or narrow pelvis because of malnutrition in childhood, which is why she had trouble delivering the child, and then the birth itself was difficult. She tore inside as she was being delivered and this will have left scars. You can feel them when you examine a woman who's been through that. For some reason that prevents a child being conceived, or if conceived, it's quickly lost. The womb is no longer — ' he hesitated, searching for a simple way to explain, ' — it's not a fit receptacle, cannot hold a child.'

'That's one problem solved then.'

'Is there another problem I can help with?'

'There is a problem, but not a medical one.' Hal smiled reassuringly at Marjorie and tried to make what they wanted seem more reasonable. 'My wife and I are entertainers. It's not a life suited for bringing up a baby, let alone the child isn't mine and to tell you the truth, I don't fancy

414

rearing another man's offspring, though I'd do it for Marjorie's sake if I had to.'

'I don't want to take the child with me, either,' Marjorie said. 'I'm going to ask Essie if she can help me find a foster mother, then keep an eye on things here. We'll pay for the child's keep of course. So if you hear of anyone . . . '

'I'll bear you in mind.' Christy stood up, relieved that there hadn't been a hysterical scene at his news but disappointed in her attitude. To him, a mother repudiating her own child was against nature. 'I'll leave you now. I shan't need to call in every day. You're clearly on your way to recovery, Mrs Kidd.'

★ ★ ★

Downstairs in the kitchen, Essie stood staring down into the fire at the heart of the big black kitchen stove. She'd not meant to eavesdrop, had been taking some clean linen upstairs, but she'd heard Marjorie's voice so clearly. The lass hadn't changed her mind, then. Eh, that poor baby!

Nev came in, saw her expression and asked at once, 'What's wrong?'

She explained. 'I don't like to think of our Marjorie's child being brought up by strangers. Nev, couldn't you and I — '

He guessed what was coming next and finished for her, ' — take the child?'

She looked at him anxiously. 'Well, couldn't we? We can afford it and if we keep Jinny on to help . . . '

'We've already got a child to bring up.'

'I wouldn't neglect your child, Nev, you know that, surely?'

'Aye, I do. But it's a lot to ask, us taking on someone else's baby. And this isn't just Marjorie's child, it's Sinclair's — or whatever he's really called. That sticks in my gullet, I must admit. I can't abide the fellow.'

'Oh.'

They stared at one another for a minute or two, then he said, 'I'll have to give it some thought, Essie lass, but I'll tell you frankly, I'm not inclined to do it. It's a lot of work and responsibility. *He* should be doing something, paying for his child.'

'Yes. Of course.' She went back to her cooking, bitterly disappointed by his reaction and trying to hide it.

He went out to look at how the workmen were progressing on the new rooms, pleased at how well the plastering had gone, then wandered out into the small back garden where he found Raife sitting on a bench in the sun.

'Dad? I — um — need to talk to someone.'

Raife looked at him in surprise. 'What's wrong, son?'

Nev explained.

Raife sat thinking. 'I don't like the idea of letting Marjorie's child go to strangers.'

'I'd make sure it was all right.'

'There's all right and *all right*.'

'What do you mean by that?'

'I mean *all right* as in loved, having family around you. You're a good father, Nev, whether you've bred the children yourself or not. Jane's

416

lads and lasses all turn to you for help and advice.'

Nev went pink with pleasure and tried to hide it by moving to stare out of the window, but his father's slow voice followed him.

'Leah is one of the family, really. And your Sylvie will benefit from having a sister near her own age. Only children can get spoiled.'

'There is that, Dad. But still, she's Sinclair's child . . . what if she grows up like him? I think I'll go for a walk, get a bit of sun on my face.' He got up and strolled off down the street, lost in thought, not knowing what to say to his wife's request.

A short time later Essie also went outside to see Raife, and like her husband before her, poured her worries into the kindly old man's ear.

Raife put his arm round her, not liking to see her so upset about anything. 'Nev was just telling me about it.'

'I can't believe he'd refuse, let strangers rear one of ours. I remember how upset Carrie was when her mother gave those twins away. Only it was Nev who arranged that, wasn't it? I'd forgotten. Maybe he only cares about his own daughter.'

'He cares about the Prestons, you know he does. He's changed since I came back to live with him, and for the better. He didn't understand what it meant when he and Jane gave those twins away, had never had a real family life before. And if you'd met my wife you'd see why. She doted on him, but didn't like other people much, so they kept themselves to themselves.

Nev's more like me, if he'll let himself be. What puts him off this baby is that it's Sinclair's. Let alone he can't stand him, what if the fellow tries to claim his child one day?'

'That's not likely, is it? A selfish brute like him wouldn't want to be lumbered with a child, especially if it cost him money. I hope Carrie and Eli stick to their decision never to have him play at the Pride again. *I* wouldn't go and see him, that's for sure. And anyway, how could he prove that the child was his? They've registered Hal as the father.' She sat there for a few minutes, then sighed. 'What do you think I should do about Nev?'

'Leave him be. Let him decide for himself. Better for that child to have a home with strangers who care for it than with someone who doesn't want it.'

But Essie shed some more tears as she was bringing in the washing, wiping them away on a crumpled handkerchief before she went into the house again. She supposed Raife was right, but oh, she couldn't bear to think of that child being brought up by someone else.

★　★　★

Two weeks after the birth of Leah, Marjorie went for her first walk, clinging to her husband's arm and turning up her face to the sunshine. Neither of them paid any attention to the carriage rumbling slowly past.

Inside it Athol stared out at the woman walking slowly down the street. Who was she? He knew most of the respectable people in town by sight. This one wasn't a poor woman from the way she was dressed, but not a lady, either. And who was the man? Probably her husband, he had that proprietorial air. As the carriage continued on its way Athol leaned back against the upholstery, not really taking in the scenery. To his surprise he couldn't get that pretty face out of his mind.

'Did you see that woman just turning on to High Street?' he asked Wiv.

'Dark hair, walking with a man smaller than her?'

'That's the one.'

'Mrs Hal Kidd, wife of the comedian who's appeared at the Pride a few times. She's Mrs Beckett's sister.'

'Is she now?'

'Just recovering from having a baby, nearly died she did. They're living with that Nev Linney.'

Athol nodded slowly. 'I see. You're sure of that information?'

'Yes. Heard it at the Pride last week.'

Athol closed his eyes, seeing again that fragile, beautiful face, smiling to think that Fate had suddenly handed him a way to get back at the Becketts — and please himself too. He felt a surge of desire and that filled him with fierce pride. What he'd gone through, the accident that still gave him pain-racked nightmares, would have killed most men, but he'd not only survived, he'd survived as a man. And would soon prove it again.

'Tell the driver to turn round and drive back along High Street,' he said suddenly. 'And he's to drive slowly once we get back into town.'

Wiv tugged on the string and leaned out of the window to shout his master's instructions to the coachman.

The couple soon came into sight again. They'd stopped now to talk to James Marker, who was standing outside his grocery emporium.

'Tell the coachman to stop. You can nip into Marker's and buy me some humbugs.'

Wiv kept his thoughts to himself and jumped out of the carriage so that Athol could sit there and continue to watch the woman without trying to hide his interest. She was lovely and the husband was clearly besotted with her. To his surprise, he felt sorry for them and wished his master's fancy had fallen elsewhere. Perhaps they'd leave town before Mr Stott could do anything. He hoped so.

Eh, he was getting soft in his old age, he was that!

The couple nodded farewell to the town's leading grocer and set off back the way they'd come. From the carriage Athol watched them until they turned the corner, then leaned back and smiled. Yes, he felt completely alive again.

23

Maria went out to stroll round the garden, enjoying the display of flowers at the front and then, still reluctant to go inside on such a lovely day, walking round to the back. The gardener and his lad were working on the rear flower beds, so she nodded a greeting and went past them into the walled vegetable garden. Renny had planted a lot more herbs this year and their clumps of different greens marched along the side wall.

He was working in the far corner, hidden by the gooseberry bushes till she was further along the path. Hearing her steps he turned and smiled up at her, not at all subservient.

'Everything is looking very healthy,' she said.

He nodded. 'This garden was well designed by whoever built the house. It's sheltered from the wind and yet catches the sun.'

'I thought you'd have gone out with my husband.'

His smile faded and he shook his head. 'Mr Stott doesn't seem to need me as much these days.'

'He owes a lot to you — though I don't know how you stand him. He's not an easy man to serve.'

'I'd hoped to help him, but I've failed.'

She frowned. 'I don't understand what you mean. You've helped him greatly.'

'He's turning to evil again. I had hoped to prevent that.'

She didn't try to deny it, wasn't surprised he could sense it too. 'He's plotting something.'

'Yes. I'll try to prevent him hurting people but he's a strong man, strong in purpose even if not in body now. I'm worried he'll dismiss me.'

'Why should he?'

Renny looked into the distance for a moment. 'Because I see the truth. He doesn't like that.'

'I hope he doesn't. You've done wonders for the boys.'

His expression brightened. 'Yes. I think I've succeeded there. Isaac won't tread lightly through life, but I think he'll tread honestly.'

It was a strange conversation to hold with a servant, but then Renny Blaydon was more than a servant. Everyone knew that, even Athol.

When she left the vegetable garden, the dog came running up to her, followed by the boys, rosy cheeked and laughing, so she dismissed the governess, suggesting Miss Cavett go and get a cup of tea in the kitchen, and enjoyed a few minutes of her sons' company.

Eventually she knew they'd better go inside before Athol came back.

Isaac walked next to her. 'Father doesn't like Migs,' he said abruptly. 'You won't let him send her away, will you?'

'I'll try not to, but he's the master of the house, head of the family, and I can't stop him.'

'If he tries to kill her, I'll kick him.'

She stopped walking, amazed. 'Why should he do that?'

'He said he would if she growled at him again.'

'I don't think Renny will let him hurt her.'

'Renny's a servant. He has to do as he's told.'

'Well, *I* won't let your father hurt Migs, either.'

He smiled at her then ran off, yelling at the top of his voice, with the dog following him, barking and grinning, as only dogs can.

Maria continued on her way, thoughtful now. It was a rash promise to make, but she meant it. Somehow the thought of him hurting the children's dog and what that would do to them filled her with quiet determination. Mostly she just endured his ways, but sometimes . . . ah, sometimes you had to act, to stand up for what was right.

As she reached the front of the house, the carriage clopped round the side and she knew that Athol had returned. She hurried up to her bedroom to check from the window how he was looking and saw him limping towards the house. His expression was so smug she was sure something had happened while they were out.

Renny also watched his master return from the gateway of the walled garden. He slipped into the house and washed his hands, then changed out of his old gardening clothes into the garments he wore to attend Athol.

He was waiting in the bedroom to help take off the artificial leg, but Athol waved him away.

'It's not hurting.'

'I can see the pain in your face, sir.'

'Well, it's not hurting much and I prefer to

423

wear it, so that I look more normal.'

Renny saw the stubbornness on the other's face, the resentment too, and knew he couldn't prevail. 'Can I get you anything, sir? Something to eat?'

'You can tell Mrs Ibster to set a place for me at table. I shall be having lunch with my wife.' He waved dismissal.

Everyone in the house had turned watchful lately, Renny could sense it as he ran lightly down the back stairs to the kitchen. Just as well, really. It didn't do to offend the master.

But it wasn't good for children to be brought up like this.

★ ★ ★

That night as they were getting ready for bed, leaving Tait on duty in Mr Stott's dressing room, Renny asked his brother what had happened during the outing.

Wiv had been worrying about it all day and told him about seeing Mrs Kidd and the master ordering the carriage turned round. 'He didn't say why, but you could see it was to watch *her*. He used to be a devil for the women, Tait says. Used to have them whether they wanted it or not. I hope he's not starting all that again.' He gave Renny a wry smile. 'I don't mind stealing, or bashing someone in a fight, but I do draw the line at murder and forcing women.'

'So I should think. And it's about time you drew the line at stealing, too. Our Mam would be turning in her grave if she knew what you'd become.'

Wiv scowled at him. 'We can't all be as perfect as you.'

'Far from perfect.' Renny stood with his nightshirt in his hands, staring into space. When he spoke, his voice had that eerie tone to it that always made Wiv shiver. 'Something bad is going to happen soon and I don't know how to prevent it.'

He jerked into action again and finished getting ready for bed, but just as Wiv was falling asleep, he said suddenly, 'You must tell me what he gets up to, Wiv. He's not taking me out with him these days. That's because he's hiding something from me. If he didn't need my herbal potions and my help with that artificial leg, he'd have dismissed me weeks ago.'

Wiv sighed. 'Nothing good lasts for long, does it?'

'This isn't a good job, brother.'

'It's the easiest one I've ever had. And all right, I'll tell you everything he does. Now let a fellow get some sleep, will you?'

But Renny didn't get to sleep for a long time. Sometimes he could sense what lay ahead, but this time the darkness around Athol Stott seemed impenetrable. All he knew was that evil was ruling the man again.

If he was following women that meant he was feeling a man's desires again. That could drive a man to do all sorts of things.

* * *

425

Hal had to return to work the following week, couldn't put it off any longer. He didn't think Marjorie was strong enough to travel with him yet and they wound up having an argument about that, because she disagreed.

'I want to be with you,' she insisted, tears in her eyes. 'I don't want us to be separated ever again. And you did say I could be part of your act. You — you did mean it, didn't you, Hal? You weren't just saying it to distract me?'

'Of course I meant it. I'd not lie to you, love.'

His smile was so warm and loving it made her curl up inside every time he turned it on her.

'I think we could work up an act that'd be very popular. I'll see if I can buy us a new song, but in the meantime we could start practising, if you feel strong enough, then when I leave you could keep on practising till you join me.'

They tried going over some moves in the kitchen, which was the largest room in the house now, but there were people coming and going all the time, as well as Essie cooking and Jinny helping her look after Sylvie, not to mention Kitty bringing little Leah round to see her 'Auntie Essie' and her mother. Marjorie was used to holding her baby daughter now, because everyone expected her to do it, but she still felt no warmth towards the infant, who only reminded her of a very bleak period in her life and a man she'd rather forget.

She and Hal soon abandoned rehearsing at Linney's. They tried the Pride instead, but there were cleaners working in the early morning and artistes coming in to rehearse in the afternoons, not to mention Raife and his musicians going through new pieces.

It was Jinny who suggested the Methodist church hall, a new building which was much used in the evenings but mainly empty in the daytime. The minister was happy to let them use it in return for a small donation to his organ fund, so they went along there.

First Hal taught Marjorie to trip properly, which caused a great deal of laughter.

'You're a natural,' he told her. 'You're sure you won't mind making a fool of yourself in public?'

'I won't mind at all. It's good to make people laugh. There's too much sadness in the world. I've seen people come into the Pride looking downcast and go home at the end of the evening chatting happily to friends. And I've been thinking of the costume. I think I should exaggerate everything: bows too big, hair too fluffy, colours too bright — everything too much.'

He pictured her dressed like this and a smile quirked the corner of his mouth. 'Yes. What fun it'll be working it all out.' He hadn't seen her looking so animated since well before the baby was born, loved to see her glowing like this.

When Marjorie showed signs of tiredness they went back to their bedroom at Linney's and after a lie-down, experimented with her clothes. This necessitated her going out later for some ribbon to trim up her stage costume with bows and loops, but he wouldn't let her go out on her own.

'A man will look silly in a ribbon shop,' she protested. 'The draper's is only at the bottom of the hill. I'm quite well enough to get there and back on my own two feet.'

'I'm used to looking silly and you, madam, have to get used to a husband who can hardly bear to let you out of his sight.'

Her expression softened. 'I don't mind that at all.'

As they were strolling back with their purchases, the dark carriage they'd seen several times came trundling along High Street, slowing down as it drew level with them.

Hal looked at it with a frown. It seemed too much of a coincidence that whenever they were out, this particular carriage would appear. Not only that, but it seemed to linger nearby as if someone was watching them from the windows which had drawn semi-transparent blinds so that you couldn't see who was riding in it, only the dark shape of a head. 'Who does that carriage belong to?' he asked Marjorie suddenly.

She followed his pointing finger and shuddered. 'Mr Stott. He's a horrible man.' She explained what had happened, how he had kidnapped her sister, nearly got Carrie killed and been cruelly injured himself.

'But he's recovered now?'

'So people say. He's got three men working for him, not the sort who usually serve the gentry. They come into the Pride, but not many people will sit next to them. One of them's a nasty fellow who used to work with my brother Robbie. Tait, he's called. He's a friend of the overlooker at the mill, too. Benting was sitting with Tait at the Pride on Saturday. Look, there's

Tait getting out of the carriage now. Let's go up this side street and take another route home. I don't want to go anywhere near him.'

Hal humoured her but when he glanced back, he was surprised to see the man following them. There was no other explanation because there were no shops in this narrow lane, so why else would he have taken this particular turning? 'Could you walk more quickly, love?'

'Why?' She turned, following his gaze and shuddering when she saw Tait. 'Yes.'

She was out of breath by the time they got back and stood panting in the hall as Hal went to peer out of the parlour window and watch the man stroll past the house then return. He stopped to study the house, eyes narrowed against the sun.

'He *was* following us, wasn't he?' Marjorie said from behind him.

'I think so. I wonder why.'

'He wouldn't do that without his master's permission, would he?'

'I doubt it.'

'And Mr Stott, his master, used to be known as a womaniser.' She swallowed hard. 'Hal, can't I come with you next week? *Please!* I don't want to be left on my own in the town, not if Mr Stott is taking an interest in me.' She still had nightmares occasionally about the overlooker at the mill who leered at her when he saw her. That was silly, when the incident was long past, but you couldn't control your dreams, could you? She'd never told Hal about those times but she did now.

He studied her, worried about how agitated she'd become. 'I think you'd better come with me then. So we'll need to make arrangements for fostering the baby.'

She closed her eyes in sheer relief, then opened them and put her head on one side, an endearing habit she had when thinking. 'Kitty can look after her for a while yet, surely? After all, Leah will still need a wet nurse for some months, won't she? And I like Kitty. She's a good sort and cheerful. Essie likes her too.'

He nodded, making up his mind to have a word with Nev and ask his advice.

He felt as if it had been a sunny day, then clouds had covered the sun suddenly and now there were shadows everywhere, with a chill wind blowing.

★　★　★

Jinny was walking back to Linney's with the shopping when Tait Arner stopped her. She tried to sidestep him, but he grabbed her arm. When she squeaked, he shook her. 'Be quiet. I'm not going to hurt you, you silly bitch, I just want to know something.'

She stilled, staring at him, terrified because he had a reputation for violence in the Lanes.

He forced a smile to his face, trying to talk more softly. 'I thought you'd know, because you live at Linney's now, don't you?'

'Yes.'

He could see that she was still suspicious. 'That comedian, Kidd, is he going to be playing

430

at the Pride next week? Only someone said he was leaving, but I've a cousin coming to stay and I know he'd enjoy the show.'

She felt relief run through her. 'No, he won't be here next week. He and Mrs Kidd are leaving on Sunday. He's got an engagement in London.'

Tait stepped back, touching his cap. 'Pity. That fellow makes you laugh fit to bust.'

'I've never seen the show,' she said wistfully.

'Not even on your night off?'

'No. My mam needs all my wages for food. But I will be going soon. They're making some changes and when that's finished, Mr Eli says he'll let me in for nothing.'

'Changes?'

'Building a better room where the performers can sit round the back. They've been working on it all week, Mr Kidd says.'

'Nice place, the Pride.' He forced another smile. 'Thanks for that. I'll make sure to go and see the show this week then.'

She walked off home, feeling jealous of the way everyone but her had been to the Pride. Then she thought of how hungry her brothers and sisters would be without her money and told herself not to be silly. She was lucky to be eating properly, to be helping her mam and the others. When she went inside, Essie smiled at her. 'There you are, love. Let's put the shopping away then we'll have a nice cup of tea.'

As they sat together, Essie asked suddenly, 'Do you like working here?'

Jinny looked at her, wondering what had prompted the question. 'Oh, yes, Mrs Linney. I

431

love it here and Mam's ever so grateful for the money.'

'Would you like to stay on, work here all the time?'

Relief flooded through Jinny. 'Yes, please.'

'That's settled, then. I'll have a word with your mother.' She broke off to stare at the girl. 'What's wrong? Why are you crying?'

Jinny sniffed and tried hard to stop. 'Because I'm so happy, Mrs Linney.' And joined the other woman in laughing at that, even though her cheeks were still wet.

★   ★   ★

Carrie stood in the side doorway of the Pride and watched the customers settle down ready to enjoy themselves. Was it her imagination or was a rougher element coming these days, men she recognised vaguely from the back alleys of the Lanes? And there weren't as many women in the cheaper seats. Indeed, a few of the women who'd been regulars on Saturdays seemed to have started coming on Fridays instead, though that wasn't nearly as convenient for them. She couldn't understand why they'd changed but was beginning to wonder if it was because of these men.

She mentioned it to Eli at the interval, but he only shrugged.

'As long as they behave themselves, their money's as good as anyone else's, and there's been no trouble with them, none at all, love.'

She looked across at Marjorie, who had come

432

to the show for the first time tonight, flanked by Dora, Essie and Ned. Her sister was thinner than before the baby but more beautiful, somehow, with extra character in her face, put there, Carrie suspected by the long months of struggling alone. Well, life taught most folk some hard lessons, didn't it?

★ ★ ★

In the audience, Tait set his chair slightly sideways so that he could watch Mrs bloody Kidd. She looked better now and was smiling at something Beckett was saying to her.

His friend Jack Benting followed his gaze and nudged him. 'Pretty, isn't she? I was the first to have her, you know.'

Tait looked at him scornfully. 'Everyone knows you didn't. Don't know why you keep pretending that.'

'Because it's true.'

'Give over! All the lasses say she didn't let anyone near her till she wed that singer chap.'

'I'm telling you — '

Tait grabbed a fistful of shirt and pulled Jack closer. 'Even if it were true, you'd be better keeping it to yourself. Mr Stott doesn't like to share with anyone.'

His friend pulled away, straightening his shirt and throwing a dirty look in Marjorie's direction, but saying nothing else.

After a minute or two Tait smiled and clapped him on the back. 'What do you say to another pot of beer, courtesy of Mr Stott?'

'I say yes please.' He lowered his voice. 'Is he really well enough to chase the lasses again?'

'Well, he's showing an interest, that's for sure.'

'They say he looks like the devil come to earth.'

'They'd be right, but you get used to his face. And he's a good master, pays well, feeds you well. You can't ask much more, can you?'

'No.' Jack took a sup of beer and said casually, 'It seems Forrett's going to sell the mill.'

'Is he? I hadn't heard owt.'

Benting tapped his nose. 'Keep it to yourself. Now his wife's dead he wants to have some fun afore he cocks up his toes. He's going to live by the sea somewhere. St Anne's, was it? I can't remember.'

'All right for some. You an' me will have to work till we drop.'

Benting shrugged. 'At least I'm the overlooker. It's a better life than most and there are some very accommodating lasses at the mill.'

★ ★ ★

When Tait got back he went to see his master, as he always did after he'd visited the Pride.

'You're late.'

'I had to wait till everyone had gone home to have a look round the back. Good thing it was a full moon.'

'Well, what's the news?'

'Mrs Kidd was there tonight, watching from the side near the Chairman's table.'

'How did she look?'

'Pretty. Nearly her old self again.'

Stott smiled, feeling desire rising in him at the memory of the young woman's pretty face and softly curved body. He'd have her before too long, had to, needed to prove himself. 'Any other news?'

'Well, they're building that new room on at the back, like I told you, and it's all open. I had a quick look round and any fool could get into the place that way, as long as he didn't break his neck tripping over the piles of rubbish. Right old mess, the back yard is.'

'Mmm. Go on.'

'Forrett's selling the mill. Going to live at the seaside, Benting says.' He squinted at the fire as he tried to remember anything else. 'I think that's all, sir.'

Athol nodded and handed over a coin. 'You did well. Keep your eyes and ears open. And those fellows you told me about, the ones who'd like to earn some extra money — make sure they're available next Saturday. If the Kidds are intending to leave next week, I want her caught and brought to me that day.'

'Here?' Tait was startled.

'Where else, you fool.'

'But won't someone hear her?'

'Not if the gag is tightly in her pretty mouth till I've taught her to keep quiet.'

'What about the husband?'

'He'll need killing. You're on duty that night. You'll see to it for me.'

Tait nodded and kept his face straight but he didn't like the sound of that, hadn't bargained

435

for murder. Murder had a way of coming out these days, because these new police forces didn't like it in their territory.

As he settled down in the little room next door to his master's, he began to wonder — and not for the first time — if Mr Stott wasn't a bit mad, no, more than that, raving mad. Maybe it was time to leave. Thanks to Mr Stott's largesse, he had some money saved for the first time in his life, enough to get away from Hedderby *and* his fool of a wife. Maybe he should do just that. There was a late train left the town . . .

He couldn't settle, because suddenly what had been like play-acting to humour his master was beginning to seem all too real. Kidnapping a woman with a husband and lots of brothers and sisters was stupid enough, but to bring her back here? That was senseless. It'd be the first place people would look, because some people were bound to have noticed his master's carriage driving up and down the main street every time Kidd's wife went out for a walk.

The worst thought hit him just as he was sinking towards sleep and made him sit bolt upright in the bed.

What if Renny found out what was being planned? You could never be sure what the fellow would do or say next. But of one thing Tait was certain: Renny wouldn't agree to be part of such plans. And Wiv wouldn't let anyone hurt his brother.

In fact, the fellow gave Tait the creeps sometimes, the way he talked and looked at you.

Mr Stott wasn't the only one touched in the attic in this house. Renny had a few slates loose as well.

All in all, the future here didn't look good.

24

Hal consulted Nev about little Leah. 'I'll make sure she's looked after all right, but I'm not going to pretend about this: neither Marjorie nor I want her.'

Nev looked at him resentfully. 'She's Marjorie's daughter, not mine, why are you telling me about it?'

'I'm not asking *you* to have her just — you know — keep an eye on her. Kitty can continue to look after her for the time being. She's a decent soul, if a bit rough, and we can't take Leah away from her till the child is weaned.'

'I know.'

'So will you do it, keep an eye on her for me?'

Nev sighed. 'I suppose so.'

'You don't want to? Why?'

Nev shrugged. 'Because I didn't like that fellow who fathered her and I think bad blood will out, so I'd as soon me and mine had nothing to do with her.'

'Oh.' Hal stood up. 'I'm sorry to have troubled you then.'

Nev stretched out one hand, then let it drop. 'It's not just because of that; it's Essie. She wants us to look after Leah ourselves, and I've already said no to that.'

'We'll find someone else then. Down in London, perhaps. If you'll just keep an eye on her until she's weaned, I won't trouble you further.'

'What do you mean, 'down in London'?'

Both men turned to see that Essie had just come in.

'Don't pretend you weren't talking about Leah, because I know very well you were.'

Her voice was sharper than Nev had ever heard it and his heart sank. 'Just discussing their arrangements, love.'

Essie dumped her string bag of shopping on the table and went to check that the kettle was full and push it on to the hottest part of the stove. She was trying to control herself, but it made her blood boil to hear these two talking as if Leah was a parcel to be passed around. Maybe she shouldn't have eavesdropped but if she hadn't, who knows what they'd have arranged?

She turned round and folded her arms across her chest. 'You're not sending that child away.'

Nev scowled at her.

'You're not!' she repeated.

'Which child?' Marjorie appeared in the doorway.

'Yours,' Essie snapped. 'The one *you* want to throw away like a piece of rubbish.' She was pleased to see Marjorie take a step backwards and turn pale. But of course Hal was across the room in seconds, his arm round his wife's shoulders.

Essie turned to her own husband, who was scowling down at the table now, avoiding her eyes. 'The years I've hungered for a child. *Years!*' Her voice broke and she had to swallow hard

439

before she could continue. 'I can never have one of my own now, but I can bring up yours, Nev, yes and love her like my own. And if you don't want yours, Marjorie Kidd, I'll take her too!' A sob escaped her and she dashed away a tear. 'If you won't let me have Leah here, Nev, I'm sorry but I'll go somewhere else, because I know your Sylvie will be cared for properly, but I don't know that Leah will.'

She startled everyone by bursting into tears.

Nev couldn't bear her pain any longer. Though it went against the grain to give in, he pulled Essie into his arms, rocking her to and fro, saying over and over again, 'You can keep her. Essie, listen to me: you can keep her.'

It was a while before his words penetrated, even longer before she could stop crying.

'I didn't realise,' he said softly, 'how very much you'd hungered for a child.'

'No one did. What was the point? But I used to weep for one many a time. And now — now I can have two and I'll *make* them mine. You'll see.' She glared across the room at Marjorie. 'If you don't know what matters in life, that's your loss.'

Marjorie had stopped weeping, but was still in the shelter of Hal's arm. 'I can't help what I am, Essie. I've never wanted children, but most of all, I don't want *his* child. If I could, I'd have her adopted, like Mam did with the twins, so that I need never see her again.'

'Good! Because I'm making it a condition that me and Nev adopt her properly, then she'll be our responsibility in every way and you can never take her away from us.'

'Stop berating Marjorie, Mrs Linney,' Hal said quietly. 'You've got what you want. Let her live her own life now.'

The silence was so fraught with emotion, he led his wife out and up to their bedroom, where she wept incoherently against his chest.

When they were on their own, Essie mopped her eyes again and raised Nev's hand to her cheek. 'Thank you, love. You don't know how much this means to me.'

'I'm beginning to see that. And I'll do my best to be a good father.' He'd never heard such raw anguish as there had been in her voice. What a pity she could never have a child of her own body!

But he worried, somewhere inside him, that Leah would one day realise she was a cuckoo in the nest, that her mother hadn't wanted her. Or — worst of all — find out who her father was. What would she do then?

⋆ ⋆ ⋆

Upstairs, Hal coaxed Marjorie into stopping weeping. 'Come on, now. It doesn't matter what anyone else says. I love you.'

'But she's right. I *am* a bad mother.'

'There are some things you can't do in life, love, and this is one of them. You were meant to shine on the stage, not wipe babies' backsides.'

'Oh, Hal, I'm so lucky to have you.'

'We're lucky to have found each other.'

They sat there for a while, just being together,

then she stood up. 'We'd better think about packing.'

'Shouldn't you have a rest?'

'No. I'm feeling much better now and I can't wait to get away from Hedderby. I nearly died here. It may sound superstitious, but I don't feel comfortable here any more. Especially if Mr Stott is . . . you know, taking an interest.'

'I won't leave you alone for a minute till we leave. You'll come to the theatre with me every evening and you won't even go outside to the necessary on your own. We'll hire a man to walk back with us after the show, too, because I'm not good in a fight, never was. Eli will know someone, I'm sure.' He decided to give her thoughts a new direction. 'Now, let's discuss our new act . . . '

* * *

The dog found the door open and rushed outside, panting for freedom. A man's furious yell echoed through the whole house, so loud that people stopped what they were doing. It was followed by the sound of someone falling and a walking stick clattering on the paving stones outside the library, though that second set of noises only reached the ears of the people in the rear of the house.

Isaac left his desk to stare out of the barred window, then rush towards the door. As his governess tried to hold him back, he pushed past her and ran down the stairs, his boots drumming on the thin carpet of the second-floor stairs, then

442

muffled by the thick carpet on the main stairs.

His mother was just coming out of her bedroom as he passed and called, 'What's wrong?'

He didn't stop, just yelled, 'Migs tripped Father up. Didn't you hear him yell?'

She'd been so lost in her thoughts that though she had heard something she hadn't realised what it was. 'Dear God, no!' For a moment she stood still as the implications of such an accident sank in then ran after her son, who had already disappeared into the servants' quarters.

Renny also heard the yell from where he was compounding some of a new herbal mixture in the back scullery. He too understood the implications and groaned softly before he dipped his hands in the bowl of clean water and ran into the kitchen.

Mrs Ibster was at the kitchen window. 'Migs has tripped up the master. He'll have it killed now for sure. He's threatened to often enough.'

Isaac arrived in time to hear this. 'No! I won't let him! I won't!' He was outside before anyone could stop him, stopping dead at the sight of his father lying on the ground.

Renny ran out, closely followed by Tait and Maria.

'I'll have that dog killed before the day is over!' Athol shouted. 'Somebody catch it and tie it up.'

Tait dashed towards Migs, who wriggled out of his reach under the bushes.

Renny went to help his master sit up, sensing from the jerks and shudders how badly the fall had hurt him.

'Get me to that bench,' Athol ordered. 'Then help Tait catch the dog.'

Maria tried to hold Isaac back but before she could get a firm hold on him, he went to stand in front of his father, his face red with anger. The resemblance between the two of them was very marked for a moment.

'*I won't let you hurt Migs!*' the boy declared.

'If you try to stop me,' Athol said, his voice as harsh as his expression, 'I'll have you thrashed to within an inch of your life. What are you playing at, Tait? Catch the creature and tie it up, then fetch me a sharp knife so that I can cut its throat. And you, Isaac, will watch me do it.'

Maria stepped forward, feeling calm now the moment had arrived. 'Stay where you are, Tait!'

For a moment surprise kept everyone silent.

Athol was the first to recover. 'Do as I told you, Tait.'

Renny stepped forward. 'No! There's no need.'

The dog was whining in its throat now, crouching under the bushes as it usually did when Athol was out in the garden.

'I've given my orders. If you can't obey them, then you can get out of my house,' Athol said, his voice quiet but with acid in every syllable.

'I can take the dog away, sir, and find it a new home. There's no need to kill the poor creature. It didn't mean to trip you.'

'There's every need, because when I give orders I expect them to be obeyed.'

'I won't let you kill it, Athol,' Maria said. 'And in such a barbaric way, too. If you force Isaac to see that, it'll give him nightmares for years.'

444

'He's too soft and it'll do him good to learn how harsh life really is.'

Tait had been edging towards the bushes, ready to obey his master, but when his mistress moved suddenly to stand between him and the dog, he stopped, not wanting to hurt her, looking at his master for instructions.

'Get out of the way, Maria, damn you!' Athol shouted suddenly.

Isaac was sobbing now, but as he moved towards his mother, Mrs Ibster appeared behind him and dragged him back into the kitchen. 'Leave your parents to settle this,' she whispered.

He cast himself into her arms, sobbing loudly, and she hugged him to her, murmuring, 'There, there!' as he wept bitterly. 'He's gone too far today,' she muttered to her head maid. When the sobs died and the boy tried to get away from her, she shook him lightly. 'Listen, Master Isaac, you'll make it worse if you go out there. If anyone can stop the master, it's your mother and Renny. You'll only make matters worse, because your father won't back down in front of you.' She was doubtful if Mr Stott would back down at all, had shuddered to see the evil so clearly written on his face. If it weren't for her poor mistress she'd have left this place years ago.

'I hate him!' Isaac said. 'He's wicked and I won't call him Father ever again. I won't!'

She drew him into her own sitting room, where she sat him down, staying between him and the door, worried sick about her mistress, but not daring to intervene.

Outside Maria looked at Renny. 'Take the dog

and leave. You've done your best, but it's over now.'

'You'll not disobey the master,' Tait said at once, more sure of his ground here. As Renny nodded to Maria and moved towards the dog, he stepped forward confidently to intercept him.

There was a brief struggle, then Tait fell to the ground, stunned.

Renny looked at Athol. 'Remember this: 'All they that take the sword shall perish with the sword' *Matthew 26:52.*'

'Religious claptrap!' Athol scoffed, wincing as he moved injudiciously. But the other man's voice had had an echoing sound and Athol's tone lacked conviction.

Maria watched Renny as he bent towards the dog and snapped his fingers. It crept towards him, keeping a watch in Athol's direction, still shivering.

Without a backward glance Renny walked from the garden, the dog following, pressed close against his heels.

Athol turned the full heat of his fury on his wife. 'Go to your room or by hell you'll be thrown out of the house as well.'

Without a word she turned and went indoors, wondering how he would punish her. For she was very certain that he would. He always made someone suffer when he had been upset.

He looked down at Tait, who was still only half-conscious, then shouted, 'Someone get the coachman to help me to my room.'

It was several minutes before Tait stirred and no one went out to help him.

In her room Mrs Ibster talked gently to Isaac till he had calmed down.

He blew his nose a final time then looked at her sadly. 'I know *he* will have me beaten, but I'm not sorry we saved the dog, however much he hurts me. I'll miss Renny and Migs, though. I wish I could go with them. When I grow up, I'm definitely leaving Hedderby and I'm never coming back. I won't stay with *him* a minute longer than I have to.'

She could only pat his shoulder and send a maid to check that the master had gone back into his bedroom, then, when the coast was clear, she took the lad back up to his governess, knowing Miss Cavett would have seen what happened from the windows of the schoolroom which overlooked the back garden.

The governess was sitting at the table, but her face was pale and the knuckles of the hand clenching the ruler were white.

'Sit down and get on with your work, Isaac. I suggest you two boys keep very quiet indeed for the rest of the day.'

Isaac sank into his seat, reaction setting his limbs trembling, his whole body weak with fear of the coming beating. He got no work done and for once this brought him no scolding.

★　★　★

Renny walked out of the house and stopped at the corner of the street, bending to caress the dog until it had calmed down. He didn't have any regret about what he'd done today. It would have been horrific if Isaac had seen his father kill the dog like that, and anyway, he could do no more for Athol Stott, who had now turned completely to the doing of evil.

He straightened up and breathed the sweet morning air deeply. Where should he go? What should he do next? Something told him he should stay in the district. Well, he was worried about Mrs Stott and the boy and maybe he'd be able to help them. Then he saw the chimney of the engineering works and it came to him that there was only one person who might have some influence on Athol Stott, or ability to resist him. But he didn't want to be seen talking to Mr Edmund.

That was easy. He'd go to Out Rawby and wait for the man to come home. He'd seen a signpost to it on his rambles around the countryside but had never been there.

When he arrived in the small hamlet he smiled at the feeling of peace and sanity. Taking the dog across to the horse trough, he let it drink, then drank himself from the clear water that gurgled out of the little spout set above the trough then overflowed and ran away towards a stream he'd just crossed. There was a bench nearby so he sat there, waiting for someone to come past. When a woman walked along the only street of the hamlet, he stood up and made to touch his cap, then remembered he no longer had one, so nodded politely before asking her where Mr Edmund Stott lived.

She pointed out a house to him. 'He's not at home, though. He works in Hedderby. His wife and the maid will be there, if you want to leave a message.'

'Thank you.' He went to knock on the door and when a woman answered, asked if he could speak to Mrs Stott.

She looked at him suspiciously.

'I have a message for her husband,' he explained, 'and I was wondering if Migs here and I could earn ourselves something to eat while we wait for him to come home from work.'

'You'd be quicker going to see him at the engineering works.'

'The message is about Mr Athol Stott and I'd rather not be seen at the works. There are still men there who pass on information about what happens to their former master.'

Grania hesitated, then said, 'You'd better come in and I'll see if the mistress is free.' She led him through to the kitchen at the rear and indicated a wooden chair, then hurried to find her mistress.

Faith looked at her in dismay. 'I don't like the sound of this.'

'Nor do I.'

'What's the man like?'

Grania thought for a moment, then shrugged. 'I'd say he was an honest soul. He has a nice smile. He's got a dog with him, a big, lop-eared thing. It looks like the sort which would like to play with children and it's clearly fond of him, which says something.'

'I'd better see what he wants.'

'He asked if he could earn some food for himself and the dog while he waited.'

'We'll see about that after I've heard what he wants. Don't leave me alone with him.' She went down to the kitchen and as she entered, Renny stood up and the dog stood with him. She stared at it. 'Isn't that Isaac and Benjamin's dog?' She'd seen the boys taking it for walks, she was sure, when she'd been shopping in Hedderby.

'Yes, ma'am. Or at least it was.' He explained what had happened.

The two women listened to his tale, making soft exclamations of shock and disgust at what Athol had threatened.

'But why do you want to see my husband?' Faith asked.

'Because I'm worried about what Mr Stott will do to his wife and sons. I thought maybe Mr Edmund could keep an eye on them.'

'I don't think anyone can stop *that man*.'

'They may need somewhere to escape to. I believe he's completely insane now.'

'So does Edmund.' She sighed. If her husband clashed with his cousin there might be violence and she didn't want Edmund getting hurt, or their little son. If there was trouble, they might have to leave Out Rawby, which she'd hate to do. She felt safer here in a village where everyone lived close together and cared for one another than she had ever done in Hedderby, because she knew how strongly Athol Stott disapproved of a common person like her marrying into the family. 'You'd better stay and tell him yourself what's happened. And if you'd care to do some weeding while you wait, I'll pay you for your work and feed you. Our gardener is old and he's

450

not well, and I'm in no condition to be bending down at the moment.' Without realising what she was doing she laid one hand on her belly, which was just starting to swell with her second child.

Renny smiled at her. 'Another fine son for you and your husband.'

She couldn't help returning his smile. 'We hope so.'

★ ★ ★

'Lock my wife in her room,' Athol ordered Tait. 'And send Wiv to me as soon as he returns.'

'Are you going to sack him?'

'None of your business.' Athol lay back on the pillows, waiting till the laudanum had taken effect, furious that he'd needed it, but he'd hurt the stump badly when he fell.

So Tait went along to Mrs Stott's bedroom and hesitated before knocking on the door. 'The master says to lock you in your bedroom. Sorry, missus.'

'Can you ask Mrs Ibster to bring me up some food, then?'

He frowned, looked back towards his master's bedroom along the corridor, then nodded. 'Yes, missus.'

'Did he say anything about the boys?'

Tait shook his head. 'He's took some of that laudanum an' he isn't talking much. The fall must have shook him up or he'd not have took it. He's lying on his bed.' He shut the door and locked it, then went down to the kitchen to relay her orders and explain that the master wanted his wife locked in.

Mrs Ibster listened tight-lipped. 'I'll take her up a tray.' She looked at the clock. 'If *he* doesn't need you, do you want to get your dinner while you can? Wiv should be back soon and he's always hungry. There's some of my lamb hotpot today and a roly-poly pudding.'

'Thank you.' He licked his lips at the thought of the food. She was the best cook he'd ever come across and gave you generous helpings, so he made sure he did nothing to offend her.

* * *

Once Tait had closed the door, Maria began to pace up and down the bedroom. She was worried sick about what Athol would do to Isaac, wished she could spirit the boys away from here. If Athol beat her, she didn't care. She had helped prevent a heinous act today and saved her son from seeing something which would have given him nightmares for years, she was sure.

When there was a knock on the door and the key turned in the lock, she stood up, worried it might be Athol. But it was Mrs Ibster with a tray.

The housekeeper set the tray down on the dressing table and came across to press a key into her hand. 'The spare one. In case you need to get out. We've a few minutes before Tait comes up to check on you because I gave him a big plate of hotpot. He'll do anything for food, that greedy guts will.'

The two women looked at one another.

'It's Isaac I'm worried about,' Maria confessed.

Mrs Ibster sighed. 'I daren't go against the master openly.'

'I know.'

'I've brought an extra plate for you to hide some food in the wardrobe. I wouldn't put it past him to keep you on bread and water.'

'I'm not hungry.'

'Always well to be prepared.' She took the extra plate, put food on it and put it inside the wardrobe, then left, locking the door and leaving the key in the lock.

She was sure they were in for difficult times, not sure if she'd still be here next week. A woman could only take so much.

*   *   *

Wiv walked into the kitchen some time later, whistling cheerfully and carrying the parcel of books he'd picked up for his master at the railway station. But the whistle died on his lips when he saw the tearful faces of the maids and the anxious expression on Mrs Ibster's face. 'What's happened?'

They explained.

He sat down on a kitchen chair, feeling as if the world had slipped sideways under him. But the first thing was, of course, his brother. 'Where did Renny go?'

'We don't know.'

'Hell!'

'Language!'

453

'Sorry, Mrs Ibster. I'm a bit shocked.'

'We all are. And there's the poor mistress locked in her room and me dreading hearing Tait go up to the schoolroom to fetch poor Master Isaac down for a beating.'

'Did Renny take his clothes with him?'

'No. Master said to get out and he just walked away with that dratted dog.'

'How am I to get his things to him then?'

'That's the least of my worries,' the house-keeper snapped.

'Yes. Sorry.' He stood up. 'I'd better go and see if *he* wants these, then.' He picked up the parcel of books and set off up the back stairs.

Outside his master's bedroom he hesitated, took a deep breath and knocked.

'Come!'

The voice was so irritable his heart quailed, but he had to find out if he'd been dismissed as well. 'It's only me, sir. I've got those books you wanted. The train was a little late, so I had to wait.'

Tait peered through the half-open dressing room door, lifted a hand in greeting and vanished again.

Athol's voice sounded slurred. 'Did they tell you what happened today?'

'Mrs Ibster did mention it, yes.'

'Your damned brother has been dismissed.'

'Yes, sir.'

'The point is, are you loyal to me or to him?'

'You're the one who's paying me, sir, and I do like the job.'

'Ha! Well, if you stay, you're not to contact

454

your brother again, not under any circumstances.'

'Yes, sir. I mean, no sir.'

'Now, open that package and leave it by the bed. I've had to take some laudanum and I'll need a nap, but I'll look at the books later. I'll take my meal up here tonight. Mrs Stott is to be served nothing but bread and water, and no one is to speak to her. She's to stay locked in her bedroom until I say she can leave it.'

'Yes, sir.'

'Go and make sure Mrs Ibster understands that.'

Athol watched his servant leave. He'd rather have dismissed the fellow, but that would have left him at Tait's mercy and Tait could be rather clumsy. He'd have to find another man to help him. Things worked better with three than two. He tried to decide how to do that but the drug was making his brain function slowly and in the end he gave in to it and let himself slide into sleep.

Wiv went downstairs and relayed the instructions to Mrs Ibster, who nodded.

When the two maids left the kitchen to go back to their duties, he hesitated, looked over his shoulder to make sure Tait hadn't followed him down and whispered, 'If you should hear anything about Renny, you'll let me know? Master says I'm not to speak to him, but he'll need his clothes and such.'

She nodded. 'And if you should hear voices coming from your mistress's bedroom or see decent food on her tray, you'll not say anything either?' She stared hard at him.

He winked at her. 'You can trust me, Mrs Ibster. Now, is there anything for a hungry man to eat?'

'Indeed there is, especially a hungry man who can keep his mouth shut.' As she was setting a platter of hotpot in front of him, she asked idly, 'Where do you think your brother went?'

'Beats me. But Renny's like a cat. He has this ability to land on his feet, so I'm sure he'll have found somewhere for himself and the dog.'

'I hope so. It was a nice animal, that, very friendly towards those who were kind to it.'

'Didn't like the master, did it, though, not from the very start? I knew it'd not be allowed to stay.'

They looked at one another and didn't say anything else, but both knew they had found an ally and both were certain there were more troubles ahead.

Nasty bugger, Mr Stott, Wiv thought as he chewed blissfully at a piece of lamb. Well, I draw the line at what I'll do for him. Not putting my head in the hangman's noose for anyone. Renny's right about that. A quiet life is what I want now, and no trouble with the law.

★ ★ ★

Marjorie and Hal went into the church hall to rehearse every afternoon.

'This time we'll do it right from the start,' he said. 'As if we were on the stage. The only thing missing will be the music.'

With much laughter and several false starts,

they went through the little scene he'd worked on for Marjorie's debut, and by the time the afternoon ended, they were both perfect.

'Do you want to try it out on Saturday?' Hal asked suddenly. 'Or would you rather do it somewhere you're not known?'

She put her head on one side, then smiled. 'I'd like to try it.'

'You're sure?'

'Yes. I've ached to go on stage again. You've no idea.'

'Well, the dress is ready.' He chuckled at the mere thought of the ridiculous concoction she'd been working on for days. 'We'll bring it along tomorrow and ask Raife to come too and play the piano here for us. I'm sure he won't mind.'

'And maybe Essie as well?'

'Essie?'

She put up her chin. 'Yes. I want to *show* her why I like going on stage. I want to make her laugh.'

The following afternoon they carried out their plans, with Essie sitting in the church hall, cuddling Leah and Jinny beside her cuddling little Sylvie. Hal had been dubious about bringing the babies along, but Marjorie had insisted. She wanted an audience, knew Jinny would love to be involved, and above all she wanted Essie there.

Hal came on stage, with his famous trip and bewilderment. Then Marjorie followed him, tripping as well, carrying out a courtship that had them falling over each other, even as they danced and sang.

And Essie, determined not to be impressed could see for herself how Marjorie blossomed when performing, how confident she suddenly became. Beside her Jinny was the first to laugh, but Essie's hearty chuckle was soon sounding regularly.

Raife supplied the calls usually made by members of the audience, to watch out, or mind your step and Jinny soon began to join in.

When it was over, Essie and Jinny clapped and laughed heartily, and a third person joined in. The minister stepped out of a half-open door at one side of the hall, a smile on his face, clapping loudly.

'She's good, isn't she?' Essie said, thinking aloud. 'Really good.'

'She's wonderful. I laugh just to see that dress. Did you ever see anything as silly?'

'No, I never did.' Essie stood up and walked forward. 'You were good, Marjorie. More than good. You seem like a different person on the stage.'

Marjorie nodded. 'I feel different, freer somehow, and I'm going to enjoy making people laugh.'

'So . . . ?' Hal looked at his wife, one eyebrow raised in an unspoken question.

'I'm coming on stage with you on Saturday night.'

They all walked home together and though that closed-in carriage followed them, Marjorie didn't let on she'd noticed it. But it made her shiver every time she saw it and it took some of the brightness from the day.

25

The following morning, Mr Stott's stump was inflamed and he winced as Wiv started to strap on the wooden leg.

'Perhaps you should leave it for a day or two, sir?' he suggested. 'Give your leg a chance to heal. It's a bit swollen today.'

'I'll wear the leg and walk like a man,' Athol said harshly. 'Finish helping me dress, then send Tait in to me and don't come back till I ring for you.'

Which meant, Wiv reckoned, that his master was up to something and Tait was helping him out. After he had found Tait and sent him clumping up the stairs, Wiv hesitated then looked at Mrs Ibster, jerking his head in the direction of the maid.

She nodded and sent the girl to clean out the parlour.

Wiv took a risk. 'I'll feel better if I know what's going on between the master and Tait, Mrs Ibster. Could you set out some food to look partly eaten and I'll just nip upstairs and see if I can hear anything? Then I'll hurry down and it'll look as if I've been here eating all the time.'

'You'll tell me what you hear?'

He nodded, accepting that a bargain had been made.

Upstairs he slipped into the dressing room, relieved to see that the door into the bedroom was slightly ajar. He tiptoed across to listen . . .

'You've got the men ready for action after the show on Saturday?'

'Yes, sir. Pleased to earn a bit, they are.'

'They'll hold their tongues?'

'Old friends of mine, they are. Won't say a word to anyone.'

'You'll go to the show as usual, then come back for me. I'll give Wiv something to make him sleep. You'll have to wheel me to the Pride in that damned chair, but once I'm there, I'll walk.' He touched his ruined face briefly. 'This shouldn't show too much at night. Oh, and set someone to watch whether *she* leaves. I'm guessing she'll stay on after the show to say goodbye to her dear family, since it's her last night in Hedderby for a while.'

'Yes, sir.'

'Make sure you and your friends have got a lighted lantern or two. When we set the place on fire we want it to catch quickly, so that the others can't escape.'

Wiv listened in horror. How did the man think he'd get away with this? He'd thought for a while that his master was seeing the world as he wanted it to be, not as it really was, but this went beyond reason.

He realised suddenly why Mr Stott wanted to set a fire. His master had been horribly burned himself, so wanted to inflict that on others. Well, Wiv didn't share his warped desire to hurt others and was sick of working in an atmosphere of hatred and fear. All he wanted at his age was to make enough money to feed himself and have a

460

roof over his head. Was that too much to ask?

There were people at the Pride to protect Mrs Kidd and her sister, but in a fire things could go wrong, dreadfully wrong. How the hell was he to warn them?

He decided he'd heard enough, didn't want to risk his own life, so tiptoed back downstairs.

Mrs Ibster took one look at him and poured a dash of her cooking brandy into the half-full cup of tea standing by the place she'd set at the table. She pushed it towards him and stayed close, not wanting anyone to hear what they were saying. 'What did you find out? You look dreadful.'

'He's planning to burn down the Pride — and it sounds like he wants the people who live there to die in the fire.'

Mrs Ibster couldn't move for a minute, so shocked was she, then she fumbled for the nearest chair and collapsed into it. 'You've got to warn them.'

'How can I? Who's going to believe me? He's not done anything yet and by the time he has it'll be too late.'

They stared at one another then, as they heard heavy footsteps on the stairs, Wiv picked up the cup and drained it while the housekeeper reached for the teapot. 'Another cup of tea, Mr Blaydon?'

Wiv nodded and picked up the half piece of cake, taking a bite. It might have been made of sawdust for all he tasted, but he chewed stolidly.

'The master's having a little rest, so I thought I'd see if there was a spare cup of tea,' Tait said. 'Got any more of that cake going, Mrs Ibster?

461

He licked his lips at the thought.

'Yes, of course.' She cut him a thick slice of the fruit cake.

'You don't look your usual self today,' he commented.

'No. I didn't sleep very well.'

When she took up a tray for Mrs Stott later, Tait came out of the dressing room at the same time. He looked down at the tray and lifted the cover off the plate to reveal a good deal more than the dry bread the master had ordered. She mouthed the word, 'Please.'

He grinned and waved her past.

She breathed a sigh of relief but knew he'd be pestering her for extra food all the time from now on in return for keeping quiet about what she was feeding her mistress.

Unlocking the door she went into the bedroom, not commenting on the way her mistress's eyes betrayed that she'd been weeping. Closing the door she set down the tray and whispered, 'Mr Stott said you should have only bread and water. Tait saw me bringing this up but he'll keep quiet — well he will if he wants extra pieces of cake.'

'Don't take risks, Mrs Ibster. I can manage perfectly well on bread. I'm not really hungry, too worried about the boys. How are they?'

'Quiet. He's ordered them to stay in the schoolroom until he sends for them to be beaten.'

Maria closed her eyes and prayed for guidance to protect her sons. When she opened them, she repeated, 'Don't take risks. I don't know what

I'd do without you.'

'You leave that to me. There's something else you should know.' She told her mistress what Wiv had overheard and the two women looked at one another in dismay.

'What am I going to do?' Maria murmured. 'He's worse than I thought.' She stood thinking for a moment or two then said in a low voice, 'If you find out anything else, let me know. And if you can, let Renny know too.'

'We haven't heard from him, don't know where he is.'

'Surely he'll send word to Wiv? They are brothers, after all.'

'Mr Stott told him not to speak to his brother.'

'I can't see Wiv taking any notice of that. He's very protective about Renny.' She looked towards the door, hearing the handle turning.

Tait came in. 'No more talking. Who knows what you're plotting?' He laughed heartily at his own joke and shepherded Mrs Ibster out, groping her breast on the way.

She slapped his hand away and snapped, 'Stop that. I'd rather leave here than put up with that sort of thing, then who'll give you extra cake?' She saw the doubt in his eyes and added, 'I mean that. I don't like being mauled around. I was glad when Mr Ibster died. Mushrooms, it was. Must have been a toadstool among them.' Which was a lie, because she'd never been married, but the hint was enough to make Tait take a quick step backwards.

'No offence meant. It's just that you're a fine figure of a woman.'

'Don't do it again, that's all. And if you get tempted, think of the good food you'll lose.' She marched off, head held high, inwardly shaking. But he didn't follow her.

When she got back to the kitchen she closed the door and leaned against it, putting her head in her hands and fighting against tears. You could only take so much.

★ ★ ★

Edmund got home from the works earlier than usual, because it was his wife's birthday. He greeted her with his usual lingering kiss, then held her at arm's length. 'What's wrong?'

With a sigh she explained about the man waiting patiently in the kitchen.

'I'd better see him at once.'

Edmund took Renny outside and as they strolled round the garden listened to a description of what had happened. 'Dear Lord, what next?' he murmured.

'Something worse, I believe, but I don't know exactly what,' Renny said. 'He's been planning something for a while.'

'I'd better call in and see him tomorrow. I can take the books to show him. We've had a couple of big new orders.' He studied Renny. He'd met him once or twice, seen him with the boys and been surprised that a man who seemed kind and gentle would choose to serve Athol Stott. 'Do you have anywhere to go?'

'Not yet. But something will turn up.' He looked down at the dog, which had followed him

464

closely round the garden. 'I'll have to find a home for Migs, then let the boys know she's all right. They'll be worried.'

'You can stay here for a day or two. There's an unused room at one end of the garden shed where you can sleep. If you take over the gardening, that'll pay for your keep.'

Renny gave him a singularly sweet smile. 'I'd be happy to do that, sir, and we both thank you.' He bent to pat the dog as he spoke. 'I'm afraid I didn't have time to get my clothes and other possessions.'

'I'll see if Mrs Ibster can get them out for you.'

'If I could trespass further on your goodwill, perhaps you'd send word to my brother where I am?'

'I'll try. Can he read?'

'Yes, sir. We both can.'

'If you'll come up to the house, you can pen him a note.'

'Thank you, sir.'

'And I'll get Grania to find you some bedding and a towel, then send Robbie out with them.'

Renny nodded. He stared down the long narrow garden. 'It's a good place this. You and your family will have some very happy years here.'

Edmund blinked in surprise at the certainty of his tone, then decided not to question the statement. Renny had a childish simplicity about him that was very appealing and the fellow was probably just wishing them well. He hoped the wish would come true. He and Faith both loved the house and enjoyed living in Out Rawby, where the neighbours were friendly and cared about you. He wanted to bring up his children here, his son and the new one, others if they were so blessed. Some might say he'd married beneath him when he wed his pregnant mistress, but he loved Faith dearly and was happy with her. Unless Athol started interfering again, he'd be happy to go on running the engineering works for his cousin, happy to keep everything just as it was.

★ ★ ★

The following morning Edmund left the works just before ten o'clock and walked round to Athol's house, which sat brooding in its immaculate gardens. Why did the place always look so hostile and closed to the world these days? It hadn't always been like that. Could one man really change the feel of a whole house?

He found his cousin sitting in the library, looking paler than usual and with a faint sheen of perspiration on his brow.

'Are you well? You look — a bit tired.'

Athol shrugged. 'As well as can be expected. Sit down. What brings you round here on a working day?'

'I thought you'd like to look at the order book. Things are picking up, as I foretold, and the new machine is already starting to pay for itself.'

Athol studied the figures and nodded. 'Good, but surely not a reason for you to come round in the middle of the day.'

'I heard you'd had a fall.'

'How did you hear that?'

'One of the men at the works told me.'

Athol narrowed his eyes. 'I doubt that. There hasn't been time for word to get round.' He stared at Edmund for a moment, then said, 'That fellow came to you, didn't he? Renny. I dismissed him for disobeying me. I hope you haven't been fool enough to give him a job.'

'He passed through Out Rawby, stopped at my house to say he was worried about your wife and the boys. I didn't think you'd hurt them, but I couldn't get what he said out of my mind, so I came round to see you.'

A sneer curled one corner of Athol's lip. 'I hope Renny Blaydon walks a very long way before he stops, because if I hear he's still in the district I'll make sure he pays for his defiance of me.'

'How did he defy you?'

'He stopped me killing the dog, which had become unruly. My wife helped him, which is why she's locked in her bedroom and will stay there until I can bear the sight of her again. As for your older nephew, I intend to beat him soundly for answering me back. He won't do it again, I promise you.'

'He's only a child!' Edmund protested involuntarily and wished the words unsaid the minute they left his lips.

'And like all children, needs teaching obedience. Would you like to watch me beat him?'

'Heavens, no!'

Athol laughed, a thin sound with no real mirth in it, then reached out for a handkerchief and

467

mopped his brow. 'It's unseasonably warm today, don't you think?'

Edmund didn't think it was warm, but avoided a direct answer. 'I enjoy this late sunshine.'

'Stay and have a cup of tea with me. We'll need to start making plans for the works. There's still a lot of ground to catch up financially.'

'If we continue to get orders as we have the past month, we'll have more than caught up by the end of next year. We have a reputation for top quality products and I'm working on a new way of assembling some of the small machinery we're making now, a way that will make them more profitable to us.'

'Clever, aren't you?'

Edmund could hear from the sharp edge to his cousin's voice that this wasn't really a compliment. Well, Athol never had known how to give praise where it was due. Yet another of the reasons the men were happier now. He let his cousin lead the conversation, surprised at how rambling it was, how Athol jumped from one subject to another and hardly let him get a word in edgeways. If it were anyone else, he'd think the man was lonely, but Athol had never tried to make friends, didn't seem to need them.

When he'd finished his tea, Edmund took his leave. In the hall Mrs Ibster herself brought his hat and saw him out.

'You don't know where Renny is?' she asked. 'Only his things are still here.'

'He's staying with me, doing some gardening,'

he whispered. 'If you put his things down by the rear garden gate, I'll send someone to pick them up later. And he's written a note for his brother.' He passed it to her. 'How's Maria?'

'Worried sick about what the master will do to the boys. He visited her this morning to gloat on how hard he intended to beat Isaac for defying him.'

'There's nothing I can do to stop him or I would, believe me. But a man has the legal right to chastise his own children.'

But he hated to think of Athol beating little Isaac merely for defending his dog.

★　★　★

The beating took place that afternoon. Tait went up to the schoolroom and entered without knocking. 'The master wants to see the boys now. You're to bring them down and stay with them, Miss Cavett.'

All three occupants of the room looked at him in terror.

'I'm not going,' Isaac shouted. 'I'm not!'

Tait smiled and went across to pick up the lad, who began kicking and struggling. 'He said to carry this one down if I had to. You'll bring the other one, won't you, miss?'

Miss Cavett nodded.

Maria heard her son yelling and crying as he was carried past her bedroom door and pressed against it, tears running down her face. The sound faded as Isaac was carried downstairs, then she heard more footsteps and little

469

Benjamin weeping as he too was led down to his father.

When the key turned in the lock of her bedroom, she jerked back.

Wiv stood there. 'Sorry, ma'am, but the master wants you there as well.'

Without a word she followed him down the stairs into the library.

Athol was sitting with a cane in his hand. He smiled as she was led in and pointed with it to a hard wooden chair. 'If you'll sit down, my dear?'

She did as ordered, suspecting any protests on her part would increase his pleasure in this.

He nodded to Tait, who dragged Isaac before him. 'Take off his shirt then hold him still.'

When the child's thin little back was bare, Athol swished the cane in the air a couple of times then brought it down. Scream followed scream as he beat his son mercilessly and the back was soon striped with red welts.

By now Miss Cavett was sobbing uncontrollably.

Maria could bear it no longer and flung herself between the cane and her son, catching the blow on her arm and wincing at the viciousness behind it. She waited for another blow to descend, but it didn't.

'Take him back to the schoolroom, Tait.' He looked at Benjamin. 'I'll beat *you* tomorrow, just to reinforce this lesson to obey your father. Take him away, Miss Cavett. Wiv, wait outside.'

When Maria was alone with her husband, Athol smiled. 'Down on your knees and beg forgiveness of me for interfering.'

She did as he asked, forced words to her lips and waited. Suddenly, without warning the cane whistled down and cut her across the cheek, making her cry out in shock and pain. She cowered away, couldn't help it, even though she hated her own cowardice. The cane whistled down several times before he laughed and rang his handbell.

Wiv came in.

'Take your mistress back to her room and lock her in.'

Wiv did as he was told, but was shocked to the core by the sight of her face, with the red welts striped across it.

She said nothing as they walked up the stairs, passing Tait on the landing. He stared at her in open surprise.

Wiv waited for her to go into her bedroom, then locked the door.

Tait was waiting for him. 'There are better things to do to a woman than that,' he muttered. 'It was only a dog, after all.'

Wiv didn't say anything. They both went down to find out what their master wanted.

In her room, Maria walked across to her dressing table and stared at her face in the mirror. Mechanically she found a clean handkerchief, wetted it and bathed the cuts, wincing.

She was beginning to wonder whether the only solution to the present dilemma was for her to kill Athol. They'd hang her for it, but at least her boys would be safe and she was sure Edmund would bring them up if they were orphaned. Only, could she do it?

She stared at her battered face and knew that if he continued to hurt her boys, she could do anything to save them.

★　★　★

That evening after work Robbie went to pick up Renny's things but before he returned home, he decided to pop in at the Pride to see his sister Carrie. He found her and Marjorie with their heads together in the kitchen talking earnestly.

'You look very solemn,' Carrie greeted him. 'Is something wrong?'

'Trouble at Mr Stott's house. He's sacked one of his men, that Renny. He's staying with Mr Edmund for the moment. I don't want to talk about that now, though. I came to see my sisters and it seems to me you've forgotten how to hug a fellow, Marjorie.'

With a laugh she came across to give him a hug.

'We're just planning a little celebration after the show on Saturday,' Carrie said. 'Marjorie and Hal are leaving on Sunday, so the whole family is coming to watch the show, then we'll have some cake and wine as a sort of farewell. Can you join us?'

'I'd love to.' He turned to his second sister. 'You're looking well again, Marjorie love.'

'I'm feeling well. I'm appearing on stage on Saturday, with Hal.'

'Singing?'

'Sort of. I'm going to see if I can make people laugh. Hal's been teaching me.'

'I don't know how you do it. I'd be terrified if I had to get up on that stage.'

'I love it. I get a bit nervous beforehand, or I used to with Denby, not so much with Hal, but once I'm on the stage, I'm fine.'

'What about the baby?'

Marjorie's happy expression faded. 'Essie and Nev are going to look after her for me. I can't take to her, Robbie, I just can't. She reminds me of *him*.'

There was an awkward silence, then he shrugged. 'Essie will make a marvellous mother. Pity she never had children of her own.'

'Yes. And the doctor says I can't have any more children, which suits me just fine.'

'What about Hal? Doesn't he want children?'

'No. What he wants, what we both want, is to appear on stage and make people laugh, just as *you* want to spend your life fiddling with machines.'

They were both silent for a moment or two, contemplating this, then Marjorie stood up. 'I must go and have a rest. I still get a bit tired.' She grimaced. 'One of Bram's cousins is escorting me because Mr Stott is being a nuisance.'

When she'd left, Carrie looked at Robbie. 'I can't imagine any mother giving up her child, but then our mother did the same thing, only she gave up two of them. Do you ever wonder where the twins are, what they're doing . . . whether someone loves them?'

'Not really. They're gone now. And at least Marjorie will see little Leah from time to time.

Beside, she's doing what she wants. That's her choice. You can't have everything you want in life, can you? So you take the best of what's possible.' A sudden image of Gwynna slipped into his mind, as it did occasionally, but he couldn't have her and become an engineer, so he too had made a choice. 'I'd better get back home. I'll see you on Saturday.'

26

Maria felt she would go mad if she had to spend much longer shut in her room. There were no books to read, no sewing, nothing but her own thoughts and worries chasing themselves round and round her brain. And the sight of her damaged face in the mirror. She spent hours standing by her bedroom window, watching the clouds pass across the sky and the wind ruffling the treetops, but saw no signs of her sons playing outside.

She looked forward to her whispered exchanges with Mrs Ibster, which were the only human contact she had to break up the monotony. But even then Tait often appeared and jerked his head towards the door. When he did, Mrs Ibster would breathe deeply, set her lips firmly together and walk out, her narrow back stiff with disapproval.

On the Friday morning the door opened to show Athol standing in the doorway and Maria's heart began to beat faster from fear.

'Come here!'

She went towards the door and he studied her face with its red stripes where the cane had hit it, smiling as if pleased by what he saw.

'Whenever you look in that mirror of yours, I hope that you'll remember your duty as a wife. Because if you don't, I'll give you a more permanent reminder. You did, after all, promise to love, honour and *obey* me, did you not?'

She felt it prudent to nod, hoped the fear and hatred of him warring inside her hadn't shown on her face.

He moved backwards and said to someone next to him, 'Lock the door again.'

Wiv came forward, avoiding her eyes as he closed the door.

She'd hoped that Athol had come to let her out again but clearly this was not to be. Why, she couldn't understand. What was the use of keeping her locked up like this? She began pacing up and down the room again, restless for lack of exercise, still terrified for her boys. He'd said he was going to cane Benjamin to reinforce the lesson of obedience, but she was sure it was more to hurt her. He'd no doubt summon her downstairs to watch that and she didn't think she could hold back from intervening, even with the weals on her face to remind her. Bad enough to see Isaac caned, who at seven was a sturdy little boy, but Benjamin was only five and small for his age like her side of the family, his skin so baby soft and tender. He cried when he fell down, snuggled against her for a cuddle, sometimes put his thumb in his mouth. How would he cope with a caning? It hurt so much. She fingered her face.

After pacing for a while she went to stand by the window again. A grey day this, threatening rain though none had fallen yet. The wind was blowing strongly from the west. Perhaps that was what was keeping the rain from falling?

As she stood there, arms wrapped around

herself, she suddenly remembered Athol's face. He had been paler than yesterday with hectic fever spots on his cheekbones. Was he sickening for something? She hoped so. And he'd winced as he turned away. Presumably the stump was still hurting him after the fall. Good. If anyone deserved to be hurt, he did.

Ah, dear heaven, how long was he going to leave her in here? And when she got out, how would she endure years of being married to a man like him?

To what would he drive her if he continued to hurt her sons?

★ ★ ★

Marjorie smiled at Hal as they finished rehearsing their act yet again in the church hall. 'I did better that time, didn't I?'

'You did really well. You seem to have a feel for the timing, even without an audience to prompt you. You'll enjoy it more with an audience, I think.' He held out his arms to help her down from the small stage, then whirled her round and round in a crazy waltz up and down the room, humming a tune. When they'd finished, he kissed her, a kiss like no other that he'd offered her, a kiss that set her whole body tingling.

'I want you, my darling,' he whispered. 'Do you want me? Are you able to love me now?'

'I want you very much, have done for a while. And yes, I'm well enough again.'

'Then we'll go back and have a little rest in our room, shall we?' He grinned wickedly, waggling one eyebrow at her.

She gave an elaborate yawn. 'I'm sooo tired.'

He offered her his arm and led her out into the street, thinking that life couldn't get much better than to be married to the woman you loved, especially when she wanted you as much as you wanted her.

But the dark carriage was waiting outside the hall again. He stopped involuntarily at the sight of it.

'Don't look at it,' she said quietly. 'I always ignore it completely.'

'I can do better than that.' He leaned towards her and gave her a long kiss, the sort of thing he normally wouldn't do in public.

When he drew away, she smiled. 'See, the carriage has vanished.'

It hadn't, of course, but he could only see her as he led her back to Linney's.

Inside the carriage, Athol watched them kiss and gripped the head of the walking stick, which was all he'd allow himself to make movement easier. He had to concentrate to keep back the red rage that threatened to overflow. That man might be married to her but he wasn't going to enjoy her for much longer. 'Not yet,' he murmured to himself, 'not — quite — yet.'

When he had control of himself he turned to Wiv, who was looking out of the other carriage window. 'Tell them to drive me home. I'm feeling a little tired today.'

At the house he went to the library and sank down in his big armchair in relief. The stump was hurting more today, damn it! And there were phantom pains, as if he still had a right leg. But he didn't intend to give in to any of that. He saw the decanter and decided to have a drink of port. He didn't feel like getting up for it so rang his hand bell and when Wiv came, ordered him to set the decanter on the small table next to him and fetch a glass.

The rich ruby liquid slid down his throat so easily the glass was soon empty, but he refilled it, spilling a little because he was so tired, and sipped more slowly this time.

Wiv peered in later and saw that his master was sleeping. From then on, he and Tait took turns to peep in, but Mr Stott slept away the afternoon.

Which was a relief to the whole household. Wiv hadn't been looking forward to seeing his master cane the younger lad. The older one had woken in the night, crying out in pain. He'd heard it from his bedroom, which he had to himself now because Tait was sleeping permanently in the master's dressing room. Miss Cavett had got up to Isaac and she'd sat with the boy for some time, murmuring as he sobbed. A poor mousy creature she was, but she loved those lads and did her best to protect them.

As if anyone could protect them against a father like that!

Wiv's father had beaten them when they were lads. A heavy hand he'd had too. When Renny got big enough, he'd started fighting back, trying to protect Wiv as well as himself, and as soon as he was strong enough to win, the beatings had stopped. But it'd be a long time before little

Isaac was big enough to fight back.

Wondering how Renny was doing, Wiv turned over again and tried in vain to get comfortable. Had his brother got his clothes and stuff? They'd been removed from the back of the garden, Mrs Ibster said.

Eh, Wiv even missed that stupid fool of a dog. He'd enjoyed watching the lads play with it and it'd come up to him a few times to be made a fuss of. Strange that. He'd never wanted to pet dogs before, but Renny had showed him how Migs liked to be tickled. He'd also shown him the pleasure of helping little lads learn how to do things.

If Wiv had as much money as Mr Stott, he wouldn't waste his time on revenge, but would enjoy himself. Mr Stott was mad, ought to be locked up in a bedlam, he reckoned. But rich people could do anything they liked and get away with it, it seemed. Even mad ones.

★ ★ ★

By the middle of Saturday afternoon Marjorie had most of their things packed and was feeling excited about going on the road again. She was quite sure it'd be different with Hal. Everyone liked her husband and landladies would probably do as he wished without grumbling. And he wouldn't expect his wife to wait on him like a servant, well, he didn't now. It was lovely the way he tried to spoil her, helping her with anything and everything, while she in turn tried to spoil him now that she was so much better.

She looked up as he came into the bedroom.

'Nervous?' he asked, with one of those lop-sided smiles she loved to see.

'A bit. I always am beforehand but I forget about that once I'm on stage.'

'Nearly time to go to the Pride. Do you want something to eat first?'

'Just a piece of bread and butter. I don't know why, but I always like that before I go on stage.'

In the kitchen Essie was cooking tea for everyone and Dora was sitting mending her skirt and complaining about the overlooker.

'Don't let him start on you,' Marjorie advised. 'Tell Nev if you're having trouble with that horrible man. Nev will sort it out.'

'I can sort it out myself,' Dora said with a toss of her head.

Her sister was so confident, Marjorie thought with a sigh as she ate her bread and butter. She wondered if it was bravado or if Dora really was clever enough to stop Benting from pestering her. Well, that wasn't her business now.

There was a knock on the back door and Kitty came in with little Leah. Marjorie saw the expression on her stepmother's face and held back a sigh of exasperation. She knew who'd arranged this.

'Sit down, Kitty love,' Essie said. 'Let our Marjorie hold her baby.'

'No, thanks. I'm dressed to go out and I don't want her being sick on me like last time.' She went across to stand closer to the baby, surprised as always to think that this little creature had grown inside her. She tried hard to feel

481

something for Leah, as she'd tried so many times before, but she felt nothing. 'She's looking well. You're a good mother, Kitty.'

'I like babies.' Kitty dandled Leah, making noises at her and the baby gurgled and smiled.

'How's your little son?' Marjorie asked to fill the silence.

'Well. He never ails a day, that one. Be a big fellow one day just like his father, but I hope he'll have more sense in his head.'

Hal came in, took in the situation at a glance and went to put his arm round his wife. 'Finished, love? Only I want to get there a bit early tonight.'

'Yes.' Marjorie threw him a grateful glance. 'I'll just nip up and get the rest of my things.'

He watched her go with a smile. Essie cleared her throat and he turned towards her.

'I'll have the adoption papers ready for you to sign next time you come back.'

'Of course. We can sign them whenever you want.'

She looked at him in exasperation and he grinned at her, daring to say, 'Let it go, Essie. Marjorie's different from you. She'd not make a good mother. It'd sour her.'

'I just need to be sure she won't change her mind.'

Dora looked from one to the other. 'I don't want to have children, either,' she announced. 'I got sick and tired of babies when Mam was alive.'

'What did that mother of yours do to you all?' Essie asked, throwing her arms wide and rolling her eyes at the ceiling. 'It's not natural, young women not wanting babies.'

Dora laughed. 'Well, natural or not, that's how we are. And any road, we had babies one after the other all the time we were growing up. Even when I was a little lass, I had to help look after them.'

Marjorie came down the stairs, smiling at Hal. 'Will I do?' She had the silly dress on, but was carrying a dark cloak over one arm.

He looked at her with his heart in his eyes. 'You look beautiful whatever you wear.' Taking the cloak he put it round her shoulders, giving her a quick kiss on the cheek as he did so.

When the two of them had left for the Pride, Dora sighed. 'I hope I meet a man one day who loves me like Hal loves our Marjorie. It makes my toes curl to see the way he looks at her. She glanced at the clock. 'I'm looking forward to going out tonight, aren't you, Essie?'

'Yes, I am.'

Leah began to whimper and Kitty heaved herself to her feet. 'Better get home and give those other youngsters of mine their tea. And this little lady is due for a nap.'

'Is your mother looking after the others for you?'

'Yes. I don't know what I'd do without her. She's better than a husband any day.' She laughed loudly at her own joke.

'Give her to me for a quick cuddle.' Essie held the baby close, feeling a surge of love at the perfection of the little hands that were waving in the air, the rosebud mouth that was capable of

483

making such loud noises. 'Eh, she's a bonny child, isn't she?'

Kitty nodded. 'They're all bonny at that age, I reckon.'

'Take the rest of that cake with you. You know where I keep my clean rags to wrap it in. Just bring the rag back next time you come. I need it for wrapping up their dinners for work.'

Once Kitty had taken the child and left, Essie glanced at the clock and went back to check her cooking. 'It's ready now. Get that table set, Dora, then call everyone in. I want to wash the dishes before we leave.' She glanced out of the window and added, 'It's been a funny old day, hasn't it? I thought it was going to rain this morning and it didn't, but the sky still seems overcast. I reckon there's a storm brewing. I hope it holds off till we've got back from the theatre.'

★ ★ ★

On the Saturday when Mrs Ibster took up her mistress's food at midday, she whispered that it was to happen tonight, from what she'd overheard. The two women stared at one another in consternation, then Tait appeared in the doorway and Mrs Ibster had to leave.

'I'll come with you when you bring her next meal,' he said. 'And make sure it's only bread and maybe a bit of cheese. Don't want the master getting mad at us, do we?'

She didn't answer but when he followed her downstairs she watched him surreptitiously. He seemed on edge, standing for a time in the

484

kitchen, biting one corner of his lip and staring into space, then leaving without a word.

When Wiv came down she risked asking him what they should do but he shook his head. 'I don't know. I can't let him burn the Pride down, but how can I stop him? Dare I even try?'

She didn't know what to think, but got more and more worried as the day passed and she wasn't able to speak to her mistress again.

After the evening meal, Tait brought Wiv a glass of wine. 'You're to drink that if you want to keep your job.'

Wiv stared at him in shock. 'What's in it?'

'Nothing that'll hurt you. Come on. Drink it up.'

Wiv picked up the glass, sniffed at it and realised that it was laudanum. He looked at Tait and shook his head. 'No.'

'Then you're fired and you're to leave the house this minute.'

'You can't mean that?'

'I do. He's not having a servant who won't do as he's told, whatever it is.'

'I want to see *him*. I'm not taking your word for that.'

'You can't see him. He's having a little rest. I'm just carrying out his instructions, which you should do too.' His voice became coaxing. 'Think again. You'll lose the easiest job you've ever had if you don't obey him.'

'Then I'll have to lose it, won't I?'

'Go and pack your things, then.'

Mrs Ibster, who had been standing with her ear pressed to the scullery door while the two men talked, felt fear run through her. If it wasn't for her mistress, she'd leave here like Wiv, and what's more, she'd go this very minute. But she couldn't leave that poor woman on her own.

She heard footsteps come down the front stairs and went to peep through the baize-covered door that closed off the servants' quarters. To her surprise, it was Wiv. He ran lightly across the hall and out through the front door, shutting it gently behind him.

He hadn't even taken his things! And he'd used the front door. What was he afraid of?

She went about her duties as normally as she could though she felt sick with dread inside. She'd not let on that she'd heard or seen anything, that'd be best.

★ ★ ★

Tait came into the house carrying a cudgel and went upstairs, ready to knock Wiv unconscious. The master didn't want him on the loose, ready to tell what he'd seen, and nor did he.

But the attic was empty and Wiv's possessions were still in his room. One drawer was open, its contents scattered on the floor. With a growl of anger, Tait spun round then searched the attics and the rest of the house hastily. But the other man had gone. He must have slipped down the front stairs and got out because Tait would have seen him if he'd gone out the back way.

Damnation! The thought of what Wiv might do, who he might talk to made Tait even more worried. His master might be confident about tonight's activities, but he wasn't nearly as sure. If life had taught him one lesson, it was that things never went as you planned them. On a sudden thought he ran upstairs again and looked for his money belt which contained his savings from working here. He'd wear it tonight and if the worst came to the worst, he'd run away.

Only it wasn't there.

'I'll kill that Wiv when I find him,' he growled and went off to tell his master that he'd knocked Wiv unconscious and tied him up, as ordered.

★   ★   ★

As dusk fell Tait kept an eye on the clock and just before ten he went into the kitchen. 'You're all to get to bed now, the master says.'

Mrs Ibster and the two maids gaped at him.

'We don't usually go to bed until after our employers, in case they want something,' she said icily.

'Well, today the master's tired and he wants the house quiet. You disturb him, coming and going. So do as he says and get to bed. I'll lock up down here.'

Mrs Ibster looked at his determined expression and decided not to argue. 'Come along, girls.'

They filed up the stairs, carrying a lighted candle each. As they passed close to Mrs Stott's room, Mrs Ibster said in as loud a voice as she dared. 'I don't know why you want us in bed so early. Who's to stoke up the kitchen fire tonight if I'm not there?'

'I'll do it. Now shut up and get to bed.' Tait gave her a shove towards the attic stairs.

When they turned into the short corridor which housed the women servants' quarters, he grinned at them and took the key out of the main door, waving it at them. 'Just to make sure you don't disturb Mr Stott . . .'

Mrs Ibster watched in dismay as he turned it in the lock. Since Tait and Wiv came to work here, she and the girls had been locking themselves in so that no one could creep into their bedrooms during the night. None of them trusted Mr Stott's new menservants.

There were spare keys in a box on the pantry wall. She'd make sure she had one of her own up here from now on, but for the moment there was nothing she could do but go to bed.

'It's to be hoped the house doesn't catch fire or we'll be trapped,' one maid said, with an exaggerated shiver.

The other burst into tears. 'This settles it. I'm giving notice tomorrow.'

Mrs Ibster left them to get ready for bed and went to sit in her own room and worry. She worried even more when she heard the carriage being driven out from the side of the house. Though she couldn't see anything from her window, there was no mistaking the sound of horses' hooves, harness jingling and wheels rattling over the bumpy drive. The master was going out and heaven help the people at the Pride.

This was the final straw. If she got through this night alive, she'd leave and never come back.

And like Wiv, she'd go without saying anything. Not even for her poor mistress could she bear to stay here any longer. Mr Stott was getting stranger by the day and Tait was getting more impudent. He was a strong man and the way he looked at her sometimes gave her the shivers.

★　★　★

As the show came to the last act of the night, Carrie made sure everything was all right in the pub and went next door into the Pride. She wanted to see Marjorie on stage in her new role. She smiled across at her husband, admiring how healthy and handsome he looked. Goodness, he had a loud voice!

Bonnie had taken her baby daughter round to spend the evening at Nev's house, to keep Jinny company and leave Carrie free to enjoy the family party. They would be staying there overnight, so she was hoping for an undisturbed night's sleep, a rare gift for a mother of a young baby.

The act on stage, a minstrel troupe with blacked-up faces, finished their final song. Very popular with the Hedderby audiences, minstrels were, and their songs were so catchy she even found herself humming them, though only when no one was around. She knew she hadn't got a good voice.

Eli's voice boomed out again. 'And now, ladies and gentlemen, the moment you've been waiting for, the star act of the evening, Hal Kidd, the Prince of Laughter.'

Hal came on stage and did two of his sketches, then struck a pose and called, 'See you in a minute' to the audience, then gestured to the Chairman to take over and walked off.

Eli banged his hammer again. 'And now we have a delightful surprise for you. The Prince of Laughter has a princess waiting to join him on stage. His wife Marjorie will be appearing with him for the very first time tonight. Let's give her some encouragement, eh? She's a Hedderby lass, after all.' He started clapping and the audience joined in enthusiastically. He ran his eyes over them. None of the rough types here yet. They usually came to the second house.

Raife and the musicians struck up Hal's new tune, a funny little melody that had a skipping feel to it. When he tripped up a couple of yards after coming on stage, enough of the audience had seen him do this before to roar out, 'Watch your step, lad!' entering into the spirit of things, as usual.

Hal walked round the imaginary obstacle, shaking his head, stretching one foot out to feel the ground and nearly overbalancing as he did so.

One of the lads who sometimes walked on for sixpence marched across the stage, not tripping, and Hal mimed amazement before rushing across to examine the ground again.

He was marvellous, Eli thought, smiling himself. It wasn't that what Hal did was so funny, it was the man himself who made anything he did seem comical. He only had to look at the audience sometimes and waggle his eyebrows and they would begin to laugh.

Suddenly Hal stopped dead and looked off stage, sighing and clasping his hands at his chest. 'She's coming,' he confided to the audience, and gave another loud sigh. As he moved to one side Marjorie came walking on, clad in the silly dress with too many bows, and pretending not to see him. Just as he had, in exactly the same spot, she tripped, and the audience roared with laughter as she too examined the ground.

For the next five minutes, the two of them played out a shy courtship on the stage, half the time falling over their own feet or one another, with Hal confiding in the audience and trying to get up his courage to ask her out walking. 'Shall I?' he asked. The audience started shouting to him to do it. With their encouragement he made an effort to ask her and lost his courage at the crucial moment, turning and running away. More people called out.

'Go on, lad!'

'Don't be shy!'

When he eventually asked her and she accepted they came to the front of the stage and sang a song together.

Eli nodded approval. Marjorie's voice was good and this was a distinct improvement on Hal's solo singing. The audience was soon singing the chorus with them.

You're my little darling, my bonny little
darling,
You're the one I'll marry in the spring.

When the song ended, the applause was enormous. After taking a bow and doing an encore of one verse and the chorus, they walked off arm-in-arm, tripping at the exact same place and leaving the audience laughing all over again.

'And that, ladies and gentlemen, is the end of your evening of pleasure. We have to clear the room for the second house now. Do come again to the Pride.'

Carrie walked across to join him as the audience filed out. 'She was good, wasn't she?'

'More than good. I don't know why I laughed. I've seen him perform that sketch before. It's just . . . '

She finished for him, 'Hal makes you laugh, whatever he does. And now Marjorie is doing it too. Are you coming to get something to eat and drink before the second house?'

'I'll just see them all out first.'

★ ★ ★

The second house saw the music room filled to bursting point. The rough fellows were there in even greater numbers and Eli stood by the entrance, arms folded, watching them come in with a deliberately stern expression on his face. He usually found you could stare them down, but there was something about some of these fellows tonight that made him feel uneasy. The smug looks of a few of them seemed to say they knew something he didn't. Well, he wasn't standing any nonsense or rowdy behaviour from them.

He glanced across at Bram's brother Michael, a sturdy fellow who worked full-time at the Pride now as doorman, and saw that he too was watching the audience more carefully than usual.

But apart from the laughter being over-loud nothing untoward happened.

Hal and Marjorie ended the show to the same thunderous applause, then the big room gradually cleared.

As soon as the place was empty, Michael and his assistant doorkeeper went outside to pull the night shutters across the outside windows and lock them into place, while Eli checked all the outer doors and gates. Then all the staff left and the Prestons gathered in the snug to say goodbye to Marjorie and Hal. Gas lights sputtered on the walls, but the warmth they provided was very welcome because it had turned quite chilly.

'You did really well tonight, lass,' Raife told Marjorie. 'Never seen a better comedy act. It makes you laugh but leaves you feeling warm and happy, too.'

Her face was alight with joy. 'It felt so good to be on stage again.'

Hal, never far away from his wife, came to join them. 'I knew you could do it. We'll have to work out some other sketches for the two of us now.'

Essie came across and Marjorie looked at her warily. 'I only wanted to tell you how well you did,' she said. 'I've never seen you look as happy.'

'Thank you. It's where I belong. But I wouldn't have left Leah if I hadn't been sure she'd be well looked after, you surely know that.' She gave the older woman a quick hug. 'And you'll make a wonderful mother.'

'Shall you really not mind?'

'Mind what?'

'Her calling me mother.'

'No.'

So they hugged again for good measure.

'I forgot to go out to the necessary,' Marjorie said.

'You'll not go on your own,' Hal said at once.

'I'll go with her,' Essie said. 'I'm a bit that way myself. It's my age.'

'Here, take the key!' Eli unhooked it from behind the bar. 'And don't forget to lock the door again when you come back inside. Can't be too careful.'

The others gathered around the bar counter where Carrie had set out some things to eat, knowing everyone would be hungry. As usual when the Prestons were assembled, people were laughing and talking. Hal was complimented on his new assistant so many times that he never stopped smiling.

Then he caught sight of the clock and frowned. 'Marjorie and Essie have been gone a long time. I'll just go and check that they're all right.'

'I'll come with you,' Nev said.

27

Since she'd been refused any more candles and had only a stub left, which she was keeping for emergencies, Maria usually went to bed early. But tonight she couldn't settle, kept worrying about Mrs Ibster's warning. She didn't get undressed and went to sit in her rocking chair from where she could watch out of the window.

When footsteps came up the stairs some time later, she went across to the bedroom door pressing her ear against the crack between it and the frame. She heard Mrs Ibster say, 'I don't know why you want us in bed so early. Who's to stoke up the fire tonight?'

Then she heard nothing for a minute or two till one set of heavy footsteps came down the attic stairs and went along into her husband's room.

'It's time, sir.'

Tait's voice. Time for what, she wondered? She couldn't hear what they were saying from then onwards, only that they were talking, but she did hear her husband slowly negotiate the stairs. His artificial leg had a way of thumping down that couldn't be mistaken.

After that there was silence and she went back to her vantage point by the window. Clouds were scudding across the sky, covering the moon, uncovering it for a few minutes, then plunging the world into darkness again.

The back door opened below her bedroom window and she leaned out, trying to see what was happening. The moon was kind enough to give her a brief glimpse of two dark figures making their way towards the stables. One moved slowly and jerkily, so she knew it was her husband. The other must be Tait.

She heard the sound of horses' hooves and carriage wheels. The horses sounded restless, as if impatient to leave. Sounds carried so clearly at night. Where was her husband going and what mischief was he planning now?

Finally the carriage was driven out along the drive and then there was only the rustle of leaves or the shed door rattling in the rising wind to break the silence of the night.

Now was the time to act, while Athol was away. She went to feel under the mattress for the spare key Mrs Ibster had given her, panicking for a moment when she couldn't find it. Then her fingers touched something hard and with a low groan of relief she pulled the key out. Still she hesitated for a moment then put the key in the lock ready, before taking off her slippers and putting on her outdoor shoes. She wasn't going to sit here like a coward while her husband hurt someone else.

She had no doubt who would be his target: those who'd been there when he was injured in the boiler explosion. In his ravings and delirium during the first few weeks of incapacity he'd sworn vengeance time and time again, though the accident had been his own fault not theirs. Why had a man so evil survived those injuries?

She fumbled for the box of congreves she kept in the top drawer next to her bed and struck one, lighting the stub of candle. Making sure it was firmly jammed in the candlestick she went outside on to the landing and listened. No sound of anyone moving about below. Should she go downstairs first or up to the attics? It was a desperate need for human company and support that sent her up to the attics.

The door to the women servants' quarters was locked as usual, but tonight the key was in the outside instead of on its hook inside where it was usually placed after the three women locked themselves in and went to bed. Why did Athol want them all locked in tonight?

Maria took the key and inserted it into the lock, calling out, 'It's me, Mrs Ibster.'

On the other side she found her housekeeper fully dressed and staring at her by the flickering light of the candle stub. 'What's happening, Mrs Stott?'

'I'm not sure, but Athol's gone out in the carriage and Tait with him.' She looked over her shoulder. 'Where's Wiv?'

'He left the house earlier. Dismissed, but he ran away without packing his things. I think Tait was going to knock him unconscious, though I can't understand why.'

'What is going on?'

'Nothing good, ma'am. Where do you think the master's gone?'

'I'd guess he's intending to get his revenge on the people at the Pride. He's never forgiven them for refusing to sell him the land and he blames them for his accident.'

'Hah!'

'I think we should go for the police. I can't see what else to do.' And if they didn't catch her husband in some nefarious act and lock him away, she'd have to seek refuge with Edmund and Faith, because Athol would kill her for this, she was sure.

She looked at the maids. 'I think you two will be safest staying here, but I hope *you* will come with me, Mrs Ibster.'

'I'm not staying. I'm packing my things and leaving this very minute,' one of the maids said at once.

'I'm leaving too,' the other agreed. 'Sorry, Mrs Stott, but I can't be doing with this. I'm a respectable woman and this house is full of villains and thieves now.'

'I'll come with you, ma'am,' Mrs Ibster said quietly.

'Thank you.' Maria squeezed the housekeeper's hand and they left the maids to their packing.

'I want to check on the boys before we leave.'

They went along to the area where the governess and boys slept. Again she found the door to that short corridor locked from the outside. She unlocked it and went inside, knocking on Miss Cavett's bedroom door.

The governess peered out. 'Oh, it's you, Mrs Stott. What's happening? Tait came and locked us in.'

'I don't know, but I didn't want to leave you and the boys trapped here. I'm going after my husband and I may have to call in the police. I'll just peep in on the boys.'

The sight of her sons, fast asleep and huddled up together in the big bed brought tears to her eyes. It made her feel braver just to see them, but she tore herself resolutely away.

When they got down to the kitchen Mrs Stott flung a cloak round her mistress's shoulders and got one herself from the hooks near the back door. 'They're only the old things we use to go outside to the necessary when it's raining, but — ' She broke off to grab her mistress's arm with a muffled cry.

The back door handle turned with its usual squeak and the door began to open . . .

$\star$ $\star$ $\star$

As Marjorie pushed open the big outside door that led into the yard behind the pub, it swung back so quickly she thought at first it was the wind. But someone grabbed her and pulled her out, so she screamed loudly, kicking out at her assailant.

By then it was too late for Essie to run back and she was grabbed and hauled outside as well. As she too struggled and screamed, one man hit her over the head with a cudgel and she crumpled to the ground.

By now the man holding Marjorie had his hand over her mouth and another was tying a rope round her ankles to stop her kicking. Then he tied her hands together, fondling her breasts roughly as he did so. Laughing at her desperate struggles, he stuffed a gag into her mouth and the two of them carried her down the yard to the side gate.

Terror filled her and she tried to buck against the men but in vain. A carriage was waiting in the alley, shown briefly as the racing clouds uncovered the moon. She knew then who had captured her and that terrified her even more.

The men bundled her inside the carriage anyhow and shut the door. She could only see the outline of the man waiting for her because he had a walking lantern with its single pane of light trained on her.

'They tell me you did well on stage tonight,' he said as calmly as if this were a normal social occasion.

She could only shrink back and stare at him in horror. It *was* him. Oh, dear heaven this was a nightmare come to life. They said he was horribly maimed, had only one leg, had a grotesque face because of the burns, and mothers used his name to frighten little children into behaving themselves. 'You be good or Mr Stott will come and get you,' they said.

'You'll be safe here,' he said in a light, conversational tone, reaching forward to run one finger lightly down her cheek. 'You'll be able to watch as the music room burns to the ground — and your husband with it.'

He laughed at the expression on her face but didn't touch her again. She knew he was looking at her, though, could feel his eyes running over her face and body. If he attempted to ravish her she thought she might die of revulsion and terror.

Someone knocked on the carriage door. 'We haven't got much time, sir.'

'Till later, Marjorie,' he said softly, then raised his voice to order, 'Help me out and leave the carriage door open so that she can see what happens.'

'Do you think that's wise, sir? She might fall out.'

'Tie her to the handhold, then.'

So the door was left open and she was propped up to watch helplessly as *he* limped through the open gate and across the back yard. The horses snorted softly and the carriage moved to and fro a little, but someone was up on the driving seat and murmured to them, so they settled down again.

Hal, she kept thinking inside her head. *Hal, don't let them catch you. I love you. I need you.*

★ ★ ★

For some reason the lamp that usually lit the way to the necessary had gone out. Fear for his wife's safety made Hal move outside but Nev paused in the doorway because he wasn't good at seeing in the dark.

Hal had hardly gone one step when someone tried to hit him on the head. But they managed only a glancing blow and he was able to yell, 'Get help, quick!' before they struck again and his voice cut off short.

Already nervous enough to have taken a couple of steps backwards and never a fighting

501

man, Nev ran for the snug as fast as he could.

'Bugger it,' said a voice behind him. 'He got away.'

'The others will be in place by now,' another voice said.

Nev burst into the snug yelling, 'Help! Someone's attacked Hal!'

Even as he spoke the door behind him slammed shut and when Eli pushed his way to it, he found it locked from the other side. 'What the hell's going on?' he demanded, shaking the door, but not finding it give at all. The key was missing from the lock. He headed for the door at the other side of the room, which led into the pub, closely followed by Robbie, while Nev stayed next to his father, panting.

The door into the pub was also locked. The two men exchanged puzzled glances and tugged at it, but it was solid wood, designed to keep intruders out.

'Come on, girls.' Carrie lost no time in arming herself with a bottle and her sisters Dora and Edith followed her example.

Raife looked at his son. 'We can't let the women be more brave than we are.' He went and selected his own bottle and Nev, feeling a bit foolish, not sure he could hit anyone, did the same.

'We'll have to batter that door down,' Robbie said. 'If we both throw ourselves against it — '

'It opens inwards and it's solid wood. There must be an easier way.' Eli turned towards the one window looking out on to the street, but the night shutters were locked in place on the outside and he'd had them made of metal for safety, so knew he'd never manage to break out from the inside.

'I don't understand. Why would anyone want to lock us in?' Eli asked.

Robbie shook his head.

Carrie came across to stand beside him. 'What are we going to do?'

'We'll have to break the window and batter down the shutters somehow.' He glanced round. 'We'll use one of the small tables. You girls stand by the doors with your bottles and hit anyone who tries to get in.'

'Do you think it'd be easier to break through the back of the store cupboard?' she asked suddenly. 'Isn't that the wall made of plaster and wood from when you did the alterations?'

Eli threw her a quick glance of approval, because she always seemed to see the patterns in buildings more easily than others did. He ran to the store cupboard, which was behind the bar at one side, clearing the contents off one shelf with a quick swipe of the arm, heedless that the bottles and glasses shattered around his feet. He knocked on the back of the cupboard with his clenched fist and it rang hollow. 'It *is* only plaster,' he said. 'Well done, Carrie love. We'll see if we can get out this way. But first we'll have to knock out these shelves.'

Even as he spoke there was a smell of smoke and a few curls of white smoke drifted under the door.

Edith screamed and pointed, but the others had already seen it.

'The place is on fire!' For a moment shock held Eli still, then he said grimly, 'Find something to stuff under the door, Carrie love, to prevent the smoke from coming in and choking us. Come on, Robbie. It seems we have very little time to do this.'

But it was slow work because the shelves had been well built and they were lacking tools of any description.

★　★　★

Tait helped his master from the carriage into the rear of the music room. 'There's no need for you to come any further inside, sir. It's caught light nicely, as you can see.' He pointed to the corner of the room. 'It'll be dangerous to stay here much longer.'

'I want to see their faces when I tell them why they're going to roast alive. Have you got that pistol I gave you?' Athol pulled one out of his own pocket as he spoke, a pistol he'd loaded carefully earlier. Tait followed suit wishing Wiv hadn't stolen his money, or he'd not be here.

The noise of the fire roared in their ears and there was no gas lit out here, so the men didn't notice or hear the hole that was being made in the cupboard.

The pain in his stump seemed to have gone completely as Athol walked to the door to the snug. In fact, his whole body felt full of energy, as it used to be before his accident. 'Open that door, but keep them back,' he ordered. 'Shoot if they try to rush you.'

Tait held his ground beside his master reluctantly. This wasn't in the plan and it was a bloody stupid thing to do.

Inside the snug, Carrie called suddenly, 'Someone's unlocked the door. The handle's turning.'

Eli and Robbie moved to join her as it opened slowly to reveal a group of men with mufflers round their lower faces and in their centre the most horrendous sight they had ever seen. Like a creature of nightmares, Athol Stott had a face that was burned and twisted down one side, and in the flickering glow of the flames he seemed like the devil incarnate.

'Stay where you are!' he snapped, pointing the pistol. 'I'll kill the women first if you move.'

Eli pushed his wife behind him. 'What's going on?'

Athol laughed, a harsh sound. 'I'm burning this place down, but I wanted you to know *why* you were burning, Beckett. You really should have sold it to me. And although no one will be able to prove anything, people in the town will guess that I arranged this. It doesn't do to cross me, you know. I *always* get my revenge.'

Eli was so amazed by what he was hearing that for a moment he couldn't speak. 'Have you run mad?' he managed at last. 'You surely don't believe you'll get away with this?'

'Oh, I think I shall. The evidence will, after all, have been burnt, and you with it.' He signalled with one hand.

As he pointed the pistol steadily at them, one of the masked men stepped forward and pulled the door shut, locking it again.

'Let's get you away from here now, sir,' Tait suggested.

'Only as far as the back yard. I want to watch this place burn to the ground.'

'Sir, you really should get right away. People will be coming to fight the fire soon.'

'Let them come. In fact, I'm here for the same reason, aren't I? I was out for a drive and came to offer my help.' He threw back his head and laughed. 'In fact, I *will* try to save them once we're sure they're dead. I'll enjoy being a hero.'

More laughter followed. He seemed to have forgotten the girl waiting in the carriage, but was speaking so loudly she surely must have heard him.

The men Tait had hired shifted uneasily, suddenly nervous of him.

Tait wondered whether to drag his master away by force or even to run away himself, money or no money. It was one thing to plan an attack like this, then slip away, quite another to linger and be noticed on the scene of the crime. He didn't like that, definitely not. In fact, even as he watched one man did slip off into the darkness.

'Did you bring that comic fellow inside?' Athol asked.

'Yes, sir.'

'Then he'll burn too. I hope you tied the rope very tightly round him. I don't want him to escape.'

Tait nodded, but he'd suddenly realised that he hadn't ordered anyone to tie Kidd up. Still, the fellow had been unconscious. The smoke and fire would get him quite quickly and he wouldn't be able to get out because they were here.

★ ★ ★

Inside the snug, the small group locked in were coughing as smoke forced its way in through any crack or crevice it could find. Eli and Robbie were bashing away at the back of the cupboard, choking as thicker smoke coiled in through the gap making it hard to breathe.

The gas lights suddenly went out, leaving them in darkness lit only by the flickering flames beyond the hole the two men were making. It was very hot in the room now and the writhing smoke made the figures seem like ghosts.

'Here, put these round your faces.'

The two men turned to find Carrie standing there with two of the damp cloths that had been covering the food. She helped them tie these across their noses and mouths, then left them to it while she did the same for herself and checked that the others were similarly protected.

'We're not going to get out,' Dora said suddenly. 'We're going to burn to death. Look!'

Flames were licking through one corner of the door on the music room side.

'We can slow down the fire, pour beer over it.' Carrie went to the bar and drew a pint, then threw it over the bottom of the door. The liquid sizzled and began to evaporate as it trickled down in a dirty stream on to the cloth that was plugging the big gap at the bottom of the door, but by that time Edith had arrived with another glass of beer.

'What do you think happened to Marjorie and Essie and Hal?' Edith asked.

Carrie shook her head. 'I don't know. This whole thing is madness. Surely he won't get away with it?'

'Who's to know he did it if we all die in here?' Edith shivered as Dora threw another pot of beer on the door.

'We're through!' Eli called, his voice booming eerily through the smoke-filled darkness. 'Come on, everyone!'

They felt their way across the room.

★   ★   ★

Hal choked and spluttered, then groaned as his head throbbed. He opened his eyes to see flames nearby and another bout of coughing doubled him up. Where was he? What was happening? The last thing he remembered was . . . fear lent him the strength to sit upright, though dizziness kept him from further movement for a few seconds.

Then he realised that the place was on fire and jerked to his feet. Even as he became aware that he was in the music room, a flaming beam crashed down on the stage. He staggered away from it, towards the back.

Marjorie! Where was she? What was happening?

He tripped over something soft and looked down to see a figure lying on the ground,

508

motionless. Essie! Her hands were tied behind her and she was only semi-conscious. He began to drag her away from the worst of the flames.

A man emerged from the doorway leading to the pub and Hal stopped, terrified one of them had come back to finish him off. Then he realised with a great throb of relief that it was Eli.

'Hal? Is that you?' He looked down at Essie. 'She isn't dead?'

'No, but she's not fully conscious. Have you seen Marjorie?'

'No. Not since she went out.'

'Where is she? Someone hit me on the head as soon as I got out into the yard and next thing I knew I was back in here.'

Dishevelled figures peered through the doorway and Eli called Robbie across to help him pick up Essie. 'We'd better go out through the pub.'

But Hal had seen no sign of Marjorie inside so slipped away towards the back door, one arm raised to cover his mouth against the choking smoke. She'd gone out that way, so he would too. He had to find her.

Eli led the others into the house place, where there was less smoke. He told Raife to take the key to the pub's main doors from the hook on the wall and then they all went out into the big public room of the Dragon.

Setting down Essie, Eli unlocked the front door and saw the others outside. Only as they stood gulping in great breaths of fresh air did he realise that two people were missing, and one was his wife! But even as he turned to go back inside and look for her, Carrie came stumbling out of the doors of the pub with something wrapped in her skirt.

'Where the hell were you?'

'Getting tonight's takings and our money. We'll need it more than ever now.' They stared at one another in mute despair, then went out into the street.

People were gathering and suddenly buckets appeared at the end of a chain of volunteers.

'They'll never put it out now,' Raife whispered to his son.

'That mad sod has a lot to answer for,' Nev agreed, 'but we're here to testify it was him.'

'They've gone for the fire engine,' a man shouted.

'Good,' Raife said automatically, but he didn't think that would do much good. The fire engine was kept at the back of the livery stables with its tank full of water, but it had to be hitched up to some horses. It would be a while before they got it here.

'They'll never put it out now,' Eli said dully, putting his arm round Carrie's shoulders. Suddenly he felt boneless, as if he had used up every last shred of energy. She was sobbing, making no attempt to hide her distress and as he pulled her closer he realised his own cheeks were wet.

Dora and Edith were bending over Essie, who had recovered enough to sit up with her back against the wall.

All they could do was stand and watch as their

hopes and dreams went up in smoke.

Then he suddenly realised what had been nudging his mind. 'Hal's missing.'

'He went out the back way to try to find Marjorie,' Carrie said.

Eli removed his arm from her shoulders. 'We have to find him.' Shouting at Robbie to follow him, he pushed through the onlookers towards the lane that led up the hill to the rear of the Pride.

★ ★ ★

Hal's throat felt raw by the time he got to the back door. It was open, banging in the wind that was fanning the flames into an inferno. In spite of the heat he took the time to peer outside to make sure no one was waiting for him. At the other side of the yard he saw the black carriage and beside it, Athol Stott, who seemed to be paying some rough-looking men. They nodded, pocketed the money and slipped away one by one.

Two of the men were talking to one another, glancing towards Stott and shaking their heads.

Where the hell was Marjorie?

Even as Hal watched the carriage rocked and she stepped down from it behind Stott's back, a rope dangling from one wrist. She pressed herself against the coach, trying to edge along it. But before she could get away, Stott turned round and saw her, grabbing the trailing end of the rope and pulling her towards him.

Hal bent to pick up a piece of wood and began

to run towards them.

She was struggling against Stott and the fellow was rocking about as if finding it difficult to keep his balance. With a mighty heave, she shook him off and he fell back against the coach. As she tried to run away one of the two men who'd been talking barred her way.

She obviously hadn't realised the man running towards her was Hal, so he yelled out, 'Marjorie, it's me!'

Sobbing, she ran right into his arms but he shoved her behind him and threatened the two men with the stick.

Stott threw back his head and laughed, a dreadful sound and the sight of his demonic face made Hal hesitate to tackle him. That twisted face was made worse by the light flickering over it, sending shadows jumping from one crater of skin and bone to the next. Behind Hal, Marjorie whimpered.

'You can't escape!' Stott roared.

The man who'd barred Marjorie's way seemed to be trying to pull Stott back to the carriage, but he shook him off and came staggering down the yard towards them with that uneven, rocking gait.

Hal braced himself for the two to attack him, but the other man didn't follow Stott and instead, ran off up the lane. So there was only Stott to be dealt with. Maybe there was some hope.

Marjorie screamed in his ear, 'I'm going to find something to hit him with.'

Then Stott was upon him, lurching forward.

He was not only much bigger than Hal, but was also fuelled by his madness. He shook Hal off like an annoying insect and jerked round to find Marjorie confronting him with the coal shovel in her hand.

He laughed, a wild sound that carried even above the roaring and crackling of the fire. 'Come here and I'll let your little man go.'

'I'm not going with you,' she yelled at him.

As he moved towards her, laughing, he stumbled and she seized the opportunity to swing the shovel with all her might, catching him an almighty blow on the undamaged side of his head. He staggered back and Hal, who'd picked up the piece of wood and crawled along the ground, hit out at Stott's good leg so that it went from under him and he fell backwards through the doorway. As he struggled to right himself, Hal leaped to his feet, seized Marjorie's hand and dragged her down the yard towards the waiting coach, which no longer had a driver.

Figures appeared at the gate and for a minute Hal slowed down, terrified it was more of Stott's men. When he saw Renny and Wiv, he brandished his piece of wood panting, 'Help is coming. Don't touch us!'

Renny's voice seemed to echo loudly and his expression was serene and kindly. 'We're here to save you not harm you. Help them down to the street, brother, and leave Stott to me.'

He walked past Hal and Marjorie towards the open doorway from which flames were shooting outwards in great gouts. Stott was lying with one arm protecting his face, struggling to get up.

Even as Renny stood there, he heard a cracking sound and looked up to see the building starting to crumble at that corner. Then he knew that fate was taking a hand and he wouldn't have to kill the man.

'Help me!' Stott croaked, holding out one hand.

But Renny turned and walked away. Behind him he heard a scream as the beams collapsed. Then there was only the roaring of the fire and the cracking of other beams as they gave way.

He was glad he hadn't had to do the deed, but he would have killed Stott if there had been no other alternative. You'd put down a mad dog without a second's hesitation and this man had been far more dangerous. The world was a better place without him.

And Renny might not have saved Stott's soul, but he had saved his brother and helped two little lads, would go on helping them too, if Mrs Stott would allow it.

★　★　★

Hal and Marjorie stumbled down the hill to Market Street, so closely enlaced Wiv thought they seemed more like one person than two. He was tired and worried as he followed them. Mr Edmund, to whom he'd fled, had said he wouldn't be in trouble for this, but you never knew what the law would do. And he *had* stolen Tait's money, though no one knew that.

When they got to the street he hesitated,

wondering whether now would be the time to run away, but Hal swayed suddenly and he had to step forward to help Marjorie support her husband.

'Sorry,' Hal mumbled. 'Feeling a bit dizzy now. They hit me on the head.'

Suddenly people surrounded them, all talking at once it seemed, and Wiv knew it was too late to escape.

Out of the darkness two policemen came striding, their top hats showing above the heads of the crowd and marking them out as some of the new law enforcement officers.

Trust the police to turn up once all the trouble was over, Wiv thought sourly. Then someone said, 'That's one of Mr Stott's men. Grab him!' and men stepped forward to secure his arms. He couldn't summon up the energy to struggle, but stood quietly in their grasp. Then Renny was beside him, with Mr Edmund.

'Let that man go! He came to warn me, refused to get involved in these crimes.' As the men beside Wiv hesitated, Edmund repeated that Wiv was innocent.

'Don't even try to leave,' Renny said softly as if he could read his brother's mind. 'I'd follow you and bring you back.'

'I wasn't.'

'You were, you know.' Renny grinned at him then turned to Mr Edmund. 'Your cousin stumbled back into the Pride and before I could get him out, the roof caved in on him.'

'Pray God he won't have survived this time,' Edmund muttered. 'Show me.' He went round

515

the back with Renny, followed by the two police officers. The rain had dampened down the flames a little though the fire was still burning, but they were able to get close enough to the rear door, to see the charred figure of a man lying there.

'You're sure this was Mr Stott?' one of the policemen said to Renny.

'I saw him fall into the doorway myself. He was very unsteady on his feet. There was nothing I could do to help him. I was lucky to escape with my own life.'

'He's definitely dead this time.' Edmund breathed a sigh of relief. 'I'll go and inform his wife.'

'She's down in the street, standing in the doorway of Marker's Emporium,' one of the policemen said.

So Edmund went to find her.

She stepped forward to meet him when she saw him walking down the street, heedless of the rain which was now pouring down. 'Athol?'

'I'm afraid he's dead.'

For a moment she stood very still, saying nothing just staring at him with huge shadowed eyes, then she began to shudder with relief so strong it nearly took her senses away, holding on to Mrs Ibster's arm as tears streamed down her cheeks. 'He's really, truly dead?' she asked.

Renny came to join them. 'He is.'

She began to weep in loud, gusting sobs.

Edmund felt sorry for her but there was too much to sort out, so he turned to the two men. 'Wiv and Renny, would you take Mrs Stott and

Mrs Ibster home, please? They can do nothing here.'

Renny went to put an arm round the sobbing woman and she leaned against him.

Wiv looked at Mrs Ibster. 'Want to take hold of my arm? You look done in.'

She nodded.

He could feel her trembling. Well, he felt more than a bit shaky himself. He didn't know what was to happen, but Mr Edmund had spoken up for him and they'd listen to a gentleman like him, surely? 'How are the lads? Did *he* hurt little Benjamin?'

'They're fine. And no, he didn't cane Benjamin, but Isaac will be marked for life by the beating, poor lad.'

'Well, at least one of them escaped.' As they neared the house, he asked, 'You haven't got anything to eat have you? Only I've not eaten for hours.'

'Is this a time to be thinking of food?' she demanded then relented. 'I dare say I can find you something, if it's only bread and cheese. But I'll have to see to Mrs Stott first.' She watched her mistress leaning against Mr Edmund, walking slowly and heavily. Life would be different now, for them all. She was glad she wouldn't have to find herself a new position.

When they got back, the kitchen fire was out. 'You can make yourself useful, Wiv Blaydon,' Mrs Ibster said. 'Get that fire lit.'

Upstairs there was a sound and Miss Cavett crept down towards them.

'Mr Stott's dead,' Mrs Ibster said briskly. 'So

517

we can all breathe easy. You bring them lads down to see their mother. It'll comfort them all.' Then she surprised them all by bursting into tears and having to lean on Wiv to be comforted.

* * *

Eli didn't realise it was raining until someone tugged his arm and said, 'You ought to get under shelter now.' But he shook his head. He couldn't leave, could only watch in mute misery as the flames licked from the roof of the Pride to the roof of the pub.

'If only it'd rained sooner,' Carrie said from next to him, then she let out a cry and pushed through the crowd. 'Marjorie! Are you all right? They didn't hurt you, did they?'

The sisters hugged and Eli went to stand next to his brother-in-law. 'Who hit you?'

'Stott.'

'I hope you hit him back.'

'I did. But it was Marjorie who struck the best blow. She knocked him through the doorway of the Pride with the coal shovel and the roof caved in on him.'

'So he's dead?'

'Very.'

'That's the only good thing about tonight.' He looked back at his dream, burning still, hoping the rain would hide the tears running down his cheeks.

'Let's get the ladies under cover,' Hal said. 'Nothing we can do will make a difference now.

We'll go back to Linney's. We saw the others and they've gone ahead.'

Eli put his arm round Carrie and they followed Hal and Marjorie along the street and up the hill to Linney's. In the kitchen there he found a bedraggled, smoke-stained group with Raife making the tea while Jinny bathed Essie's head.

They'd be talking about the fire and its consequences, Eli was sure . . . and he'd have to confess that because of his foolish parsimony he and Joanna were both ruined — because he'd not insured the place. He hadn't said anything, just decided that with the shutters to prevent break-ins and all the fire buckets scattered about the building, they'd be all right. He'd been extra careful when locking up, making sure every gas light was safely out.

And he'd been a fool!

Now that the music room and pub had burned down, they owned nothing more than the land the Pride had once stood on. How would he ever make that up to Carrie?

He'd said his music room would be the Pride of Lancashire, but now it was no more than rubble and charred beams, and as for him, he was the fool of Lancashire.

It was Nev who asked the question he dreaded.

'You'll be all right, won't you, Eli? You'll have the insurance money to rebuild with.'

He took a deep breath. 'No, I'm afraid I won't. I didn't insure it. I thought if we were very careful we could save the money — No, Carrie love, let me finish. They have to know how stupid I've been. It's all my fault, no one else's.'

'Shh.' She put one finger on his lips. 'I thought the letter from the insurance company had fallen into the wastepaper basket, so I went ahead and renewed the insurance the next time I went into town. In fact, I increased it because of the improvements we'd made.'

The room spun round him and he had to clutch his wife. 'Are you telling the truth?' he asked, his voice hoarse. 'You're not just trying to comfort me?'

'No, love. I'm telling the truth. We're well insured.'

So he had to bury his face in her shoulder and hide there until he could regain control over his emotions.

At the other side of the room, Marjorie and Hal were sitting together.

'I think you'd better wait a week before you join me,' he said. 'You've only just recovered and after tonight — '

Like her sister, she put one finger on her husband's lips and made a soft, shushing noise. 'I did well on stage, didn't I?'

'More than well. You're a natural.'

'And I'm probably in a better state than you. You were knocked out and you're going to have a black eye tomorrow.'

His hand went up involuntarily to his face and he winced.

'I'm coming with you,' she said. 'I'll have to get another costume, though.' She grimaced down at the filthy rags she was wearing, some of the bows charred, some of them ripped off as she'd struggled with Stott and his men.

'But I — '

'I'm coming, Hal, and that's that.'

At the other side of the room Raife banged on the table. 'I just wanted to say something.'

They all looked towards him.

'It's been a terrible night, terrible. But look at us. We're all alive and only slightly battered. Don't you think we should be thankful for that, whatever other troubles we have to face?'

'Aye, we should,' Nev said. 'Though I hope I never have to live through another night like it.'

'There are two little babies upstairs who give me hope for the future,' Essie said. 'And another one a few streets away, who'll be coming to live here in a few weeks. They're more important than any pile of bricks and stones.'

Nev looked at her proudly. She was right. Suddenly it didn't matter that little Leah was Sinclair's daughter, didn't matter at all. Life was what mattered, and loving one another. He went to whisper that to his wife, who rewarded him with a glowing smile.

Marjorie stood up. 'Hal and I will still have to leave in the morning, but we'll be back as soon as we can.'

'You'll be back to top the bill at my new theatre of varieties,' Eli said. 'I'm going to build it on the same site and it'll be as much the Pride of Lancashire as the old place was.'

'And my wife will be the star of it,' Hal said. 'If we had wine, I'd make a toast to her.'

521

'There's nothing wrong with a good cup of tea,' Raife said mildly.

So they raised their cups and drank first to the new theatre, then to the new northern star, their very own Marjorie.

CALICO ROAD

Anna Jacobs

Calico Road runs through a Lancashire hamlet up on the moors. And in 1827 its folk are a thorn in the side of the vicious mill owner in the valley below . . . Toby Fletcher's father ignored his bastard son while alive. Now Toby is the owner of the old inn, with all its secrets. Then Meg Staley comes to Calico and Toby finds her wandering the moors, cold and starving, and brings her back to the inn . . . Working there, Meg rebuilds her life, but then the secrets of Calico Road come crashing down on her and those she has grown to love . . . Will they find a way to defeat an evil man, or will he again wreak destruction?

OUR EVA

Anna Jacobs

Eva Kershaw is happy living with her dear friend Alice, who has been like a mother to her. Their house in the Lancashire village of Heyshaw has been an oasis of peace. But now, three years after the end of the Great War, Alice is dying. Eva is further upset by the unexpected arrival of Gus Blake, Alice's nephew. Alice's main regret is that she never had children, and she's determined Eva shall not make the same mistake. She sees in Gus — young, handsome and confident — the answer to her prayers. Eva is torn between her desire to make her friend happy and her instinctive mistrust of Gus. Then Alice's will presents Eva with a difficult — and dangerous — decision . . .

OUR POLLY

Anna Jacobs

It's for her little son Billy's sake that Polly puts up with an unkind mother-in-law and an isolated farm. Then Billy is knocked down by a car, his father is killed attempting to save his life, and Polly is left with a child who may never walk or talk again. The malicious Dr Browning-Baker is determined to have Billy taken away from his mother, depriving him of the exercises and stimulation that are his only hope. Forced to flee to the Fylde coast, Polly and Billy find that their future may lie with another damaged family. But danger threatens their fragile happiness . . .

OUR LIZZIE

Anna Jacobs

Lizzie Kershaw is an independent spirit. At twelve she loses her father, and her happy family life ends as her mother grows to resent her. Then circumstances push Lizzie into an early marriage, where she finds her mother's petty cruelties replaced by her husband's frequent beatings. But she is a survivor. When World War I breaks out, Lizzie's husband is forced to join up and she seizes the opportunity to run away. She finds independence and friendship in a munitions factory — plus the promise of a new love. But as war ends, the shadow of her husband looms again. Can she break free of him and find happiness?